THE PORTAL

ONLY AN OCEAN APART

DEAN HAMILTON

ISBN: 978-1-64704-674-3 (paperback
ISBN: 978-1-64704-675-0 (eBook)

Library of Congress Control Number: 2020932279

*To my mother, Kathryn, who devotedly
read stories to me as a young boy.*

Acknowledgments

Thank you to the song writers, artists, and music companies who allowed me to reprint their lyrics in this book: David Bowie and TRO-Essex Music International, Inc., for "Space Oddity"; Elton John, Bernie Taupin, and Hal Leonard for "Rocket Man"; Sarah Brightman and Alfred Music for "Only an Ocean Away;" and John Kay, Rushton Moreve, and Hal Leonard for "Magic Carpet Ride."

To my wife, Jayne, to family members, and to great friends, who supported me and encouraged me to write. This book would not have been possible without you.

1

Cole Hollingsworth tossed a hundred-dollar bill onto the polished mahogany bar. A generous tip by any standard, considering he had just signed the check for four glasses of fifty-year-old Laphroaig single malt scotch, which already included the house gratuity.

"Thank you very much, Mr. Hollingsworth," the bartender responded appreciatively.

Cole nodded but said nothing, making his way toward the front exit and out to the darkened parking lot of Gull's Point Golf Club, located on the southern tip of Newport, Rhode Island. Over the past few months, how many times had he been the last member to leave the men's grill? What did it matter, really? Taking a deep breath, he inhaled the salt-tinged breeze gusting off of the neighboring Atlantic Ocean, attempting to clear his head. As the horizon continued to darken, the sea took on an angry look. Less than a year ago the ocean had been Cole's friend, but that was then.

Exactly one week from tonight, Cole would be back at Gull's Point, one of the most elite country clubs in America, to attend a gala celebration in honor of his thirtieth birthday. This event would also mark his coming into his inheritance, in the form of a vast trust fund courtesy of his iconic billionaire father, former head of Hollingsworth Enterprises. The following Monday, Cole would ascend to the presidency of the publishing empire his father had built. He had never felt so unprepared for anything—and yet it was all about to come true.

Glancing out toward the shoreline, Cole tapped his electronic key fob and heard a sharp chirp in the distance. The outside lights of his Maserati Gran Turismo GTX-S flashed briefly, revealing its location in the darkened lot. The car resembled a stealth fighter more than an automobile, two-toned black paint with more curves and fins than a mermaid. He recalled the day he had purchased it during a birthday trip to Italy one year ago. Mario Marinello himself, the CEO of Maserati, had presided over the transaction. Cole had spent a full day training with one of Italy's top Formula One race drivers getting acclimated to the super sports car.

He placed his hand, palm-side down, against a scanner above the door handle and spoke into a voice-recognition system located on the top of the car. A mechanical voice responded.

Cole Hollingsworth confirmed. Please enter.

A soft click followed, and the driver's-side door sprang open about three inches. Cole pulled the door open the rest of the way and eased himself onto the plush leather seat. A year later the upholstery still smelled of new leather. Buckling up the seat belt system, he pushed the starter button and the engine roared to life, rumbling angrily through the four-pipe exhaust system. As he pushed down quickly on the accelerator, the engine revved to a feverish pitch, scattering a flock of birds nesting in a nearby white oak tree. Cole smiled.

When he pushed a second button, the car lit up like a Christmas tree, instrument panels flashing instantly to life, the navigation system engaging, while the radar-tracking module performed self- adjusting tests. Cole pressed down on the accelerator a second time, just for the fun of it. A woman's voice suddenly sounded through the cab forward speaker system.

That won't be necessary, Cole. The car is sufficiently warmed up and ready for driving. By the way, are you still mad at me? The voice was sexy, alluring.

"You know I can't stay mad at you for long, Serena, even though you piss me off sometimes," Cole replied mockingly. At the Italian auto factory, Cole had been given a choice of voices and gender to act as the voice-interactive system. He had chosen the tone of a sexy Italian actress and named her Serena, after a movie of the same name that had been a family favorite. In addition, he chose a license plate with the same name, adding the numeral 1 after it, as if it were a space shuttle or something.

I'm glad you're not still mad. It was really just a big misunderstanding. Now, where would you like to go tonight? Serena cooed.

Cole continued to be amazed by the technology of his car. Serena had been created by a joint collaboration between Italy and Switzerland and a company called Intel-Swis, an artificial intelligence software development firm. It was as if the car could think for itself—respond independently to its driver. React to his concerns and literally think its way out of a situation. The more it interfaced with its owner, the more the computer system got to know the driver.

"I'm headed home, Serena. No plans this evening."

But, Cole, it's Friday night. Don't be such a stick in the mud. It's time to have fun. I'm in the mood for some clubbing tonight. Why don't we go home and you can freshen up, then we'll head over to Club Echo.

"It's been a long week, and I'm tired. Besides, I don't need another hangover tomorrow. I've got a tennis match and then dinner with old family friends, or don't you remember?"

Of course I remember. I just thought we should start celebrating early, that's all. Serena sounded disappointed.

"I appreciate the sentiment, but home it is." Cole engaged the clutch and eased the gearshift into first, guiding the car slowly out of the lot and onto Ocean Avenue. He stepped down hard on the accelerator and the eighteen-inch Pirelli P-7 tires gripped the asphalt like the claws of a cat clinging to the side of a tree.

We've been drinking again, haven't we? Bad day on the links? Serena questioned.

Cole ignored the voice and headed home. Without warning, the car's navigation system took control, limiting its speed, apparently based on Serena's assessment of Cole's blood alcohol content.

Three-point-seven miles until reaching desired destination, a second mechanical voice noted.

"You take all the fun out of owning a car like this," Cole complained, apparently addressing both voices.

It's only because we care, Serena replied. *What did you expect when you paid over two and a half million for us?*

"Less attitude!" Cole groused.

Baby, I've got enough attitude for the both of us! Serena laughed fetchingly, which only served to infuriate Cole further. He went quiet, fuming.

Reaching a gated entryway to the right of the road, Cole guided the car onto his property and the half-mile drive along the wall of cliffs to his home, located near the famous Cliff Walk area in Newport. He sat back in his seat and closed his eyes, as the Maserati's navigation system took full control. Guided in part by Google and Microsoft, the car drove itself up the steep incline of Coral Canyon Drive, around hairpin corners until reaching the well-lit driveway and the looming five-car garage. The garage door farthest to the right rose automatically, and the Maserati slipped into its spot like a private jet into its hangar.

Safely home, Serena said. *Enjoy your evening, Col—*

Cole pushed the ignition button and all systems went dead, cutting Serena off in midsentence. "Good riddance," he muttered. At least he'd had the last word. That counted for something. He exited the sports car and made a mental note to leave the Maserati in the garage tomorrow. He would drive one of his other cars.

The five-car garage was spotless: a collection of polyurethane-lined floors, polished aluminum walls, and soft lighting. Two other sports cars and an SUV shimmered under the overhead lights, meticulously clean. Next to the cars stood a Ducati 1199 Panigale R, a top-performing racing motorcycle. It was scary fast, dangerous, tempting. Cole had stopped riding it six months ago, after the tragedy, although he couldn't quite give it up altogether, so it sat like a silent sentry—a ubiquitous reminder of what could happen at the drop of a hat.

Cole headed up the stairway to the first-floor landing of his three-tiered architectural wonder. Designed by world-renowned architect, Vettorio Barsant, the home had been featured in a dozen magazines and had won numerous design awards. His house contrasted starkly with the stately mansions nearby, perched atop priceless lots overlooking the ocean. Mansions once owned by the Vanderbilt family, the Astor family, and other shapers of American history, along with the summer homes to Presidents John F. Kennedy and Dwight D. Eisenhower.

Sitting atop a jagged, windswept cliff overlooking the Atlantic, Cole's house was a beacon of shimmering light amid a sea of darkness. The structure had been unofficially nicknamed *The Lighthouse,* a term that appealed to Cole, although he couldn't say exactly why. He liked to think that in a tumultuous world, there existed the light of truth somewhere, if only in his mind's eye. It was within the confines of this structure that Cole did his deepest thinking. Always in private.

Cole ran an electronic card over the biometric lock, entering a service area adjacent to the kitchen. He walked through twin glass doors into the living room, one of several sitting areas located throughout the house. When he issued a voice command, a fire sprang to life in the grate of a two-sided fireplace—one side facing the living room, and the other side facing a formal dining area. A large oil portrait of his parents hung above the fireplace.

A row of blinds began to open, exposing a long wall of solid glass, overlooking the nine-hundred-foot drop to the rocky shoreline below. The windows were akin to a painter's canvas, revealing pinpricks of diffused lights in an inky sky. A full moon hung obliquely in the backdrop, illuminating the passing clouds, like wraiths floating on the breeze. Miles away, a rotating beacon revolved across the inlet, from one of the few functional lighthouses remaining in the area. The dull sound of a foghorn echoed in the distance.

Cole reached for a glass, filling it first with ice cubes and then with the amber liquid of Glendronach, his favorite Scotch. He headed for a white leather chair next to a top-of-the-line Meade Max 20 telescope, parking his body squarely facing the ocean view. At six-foot-three and 190 pounds, it took more than a few drinks to render Cole intoxicated, although he had begun to lose track of how much he was consuming lately.

The only thing separating him from a horrific fall to his death was the two-inch-thick glass that formed this side of his house, perched precariously over the crag's edge. Someday, many years in the future, nature would wear away the cliff that supported the house and it would all come crashing down—the bluffs washed clean of man's arrogance. Oddly enough, this thought did not bother the heir-to-be. To Cole, it was just the natural evolution of things. *It would make a good story*, he thought. He envisioned the headlines: *"Drunken Billionaire, Cole Hollingsworth, Crashes to His Death as His Mansion Collapses into the Atlantic."* A fitting end.

Gazing out of the window at the bottomless ocean of water, thoughts of his soft-spoken mother and his overbearing father came flooding back. Had it only been eight months since the terrible accident at sea? The day their luxury wooden yacht, *The Headline Scoop,* had been ripped apart by hurricane-force winds and torrential rain in the middle of a South Atlantic squall. It seemed like yesterday—or it could have been years—the cutting knife of regret having managed to distort even the passage of time itself. After months of relentless searching by the Coast Guard, the Navy, and the best private maritime investigators money could buy, only a life preserver from the yacht had been found. No bodies, no concrete evidence of what had actually happened—just another mysterious incident of lives lost at sea. There had been storm warnings, but for a former America's Cup skipper like his father, they were ignored, as if they didn't apply to him. In the end, it was his father's own arrogance that got him.

Cole continued to sit pensively, sipping Scotch and reflecting on his life. A member of Newport's social elite, an infamous womanizer—an only son born with the proverbial silver spoon in his mouth. His life at Gull's Point, socializing with politicians, captains of industry, and powerful lobbyists—those people who would fast track faulty drugs onto the market before it was discovered they caused birth defects in 15 percent of the babies born to the women using them. Perhaps that's why women were not allowed to become members. Influential businessmen, who would buy companies, sell them off in pieces, and shutter entire towns, leaving unemployed Americans without benefits and struggling to make ends meet. The movers and the shakers of the world. Was Cole becoming one of them? He hadn't thought so, and he pondered how it would be possible to avoid it.

The fog continued to roll in, and everything became blurred, including Cole's vision. As he had failed to eat dinner, the Scotch silently took control. Soon he was lost in deep slumber, adrift in an endless ocean in the middle of nowhere. A ship suddenly materialized in front of him, ghostlike. Specters of his parents called out, beckoning him to come aboard. He struggled valiantly to join them, but just as he was stepping onto their yacht, it splintered into a thousand pieces, crushed by a seventy-foot wave. All he could hear were the screams of his mother, pleading with her son to save them. Then all went calm, and Cole was again drifting aimlessly in a void of liquid space, alone.

The recurring nightmare stalked him like a lioness.

2

A gaseous orb rose gradually out of the sea, casting its brilliant light through the wall of glass on the edge of the cliff. Cole opened his eyes to the full strength of the sun's intensity. The shock momentarily blinded him. Covering his eyes, he looked away. He had forgotten to close the blinds during the night. His head throbbed, and his throat felt like sandpaper. The gas fire was still burning silently on the grate, casting a surreal light on his parents' portrait. He felt like he was going to throw up, but there was nothing in his stomach other than excess bile. Walking shakily to the kitchen, he opened the Sub-Zero twin-door refrigerator and retrieved a bottle of orange juice, then stuck his head inside the freezer. A blast of frigid air shocked his senses. Taking a long draught of the juice, he simultaneously pushed the button of his Keurig coffeemaker. The French roast was ready in a minute. He didn't bother adding the usual cream and sugar; he just wanted something strong. For a moment he considered adding a shot of brandy—a little hair of the dog. He refrained, though, thinking that wouldn't help his tennis match. Grabbing the steaming mug of coffee, he headed over to the elevator and the top floor master suite. He needed a shower. He checked his watch. Nine-ten a.m. He had exactly fifty minutes to shower, shave, sober up, and be at the East Shore Racket Club, a twenty-minute drive south.

Hot jets of water rained down on Cole's neck and back, relieving the cramps he had developed sleeping in the leather chair. *Why did I allow myself to get drunk again?* He cursed. Another night spent drinking alone and brooding.

Half an hour later, he walked through the kitchen, grabbed two overly ripe bananas and a fresh refill of coffee, and headed downstairs to the garage. Following a quick glance across the space, his eyes landed on the Ducati. It was fast and agile, and the thought of fresh air whipping across his face sounded good. His gaze momentarily focused on the Maserati. He was not in the mood for another of Serena's lectures. Then he quickly decided on the Audi R8 Spyder convertible. It was fast, too, and it didn't talk back.

Opening the door, he tossed his tennis gear onto the passenger's seat and entered. The Audi was mostly engine, visible through the rear glass shield. He maneuvered the car down the snakelike driveway and onto Ocean Avenue. The fog of the previous evening had long since disappeared, and the day was a glorious one, with sunlight shimmering off of the metallic silver hood of the R8. Although it only cost a fraction of the price he had paid for the Maserati, the Audi was remarkably nimble and quick, and he weaved his way along the coastal highway, passing cars whenever sufficient straightaway sections presented themselves. He honked and waved good-naturedly as he zipped by, not wanting to offend neighbors, but not wanting to be late. The few people who recognized him already knew about his reputation for fast cars, and they shook their heads as he passed.

Cole arrived with one minute to spare. His best friend and attorney, Art Barkley, was abnormally anal when it came to punctuality. Art was sitting impatiently on the veranda off of the main clubhouse when Cole arrived. Art was flanked on either side by the stunning Swanson sisters, identical twins decked out in the latest designer tennis outfits. The scene reminded Cole of a Ralph Lauren photo shoot. Sidney and Shelby Swanson were athletic, gorgeous, and well-educated socialites whose singular mission was snagging the most eligible bachelors on the East Coast. Of course, royalty would do, but Europe seemed so bourgeois and stiff. A sexual scandal could lead to ruin. Neither sister could stomach that prospect.

Cole was prime bait, Art not so much. But that didn't stop Art from making a move. He had secretly admitted his fantasy to Cole—the fantasy of having both sisters in his bed at one time. Slender and tall, Art possessed neither the looks nor the charisma that defined Cole. With angular features, shortly cropped brown hair, and a pale complexion, Art appeared more like a male mannequin behind finely tailored clothing, always impeccably dressed. The attorney had saved Cole from more than one scrape with the law, and Cole owed him. Cole knew that, so he agreed to go along with Art's plan.

Everything was scripted down to the last detail. A leisurely lunch, a couple of sets of hard-fought tennis, a shower at the club to freshen up, cocktails, and then a home-prepared meal at Art's condo. Art was an accomplished gourmet, and few women could resist a great meal prepared by the opposite sex. And then…then a romp in the sack. *Not a bad day,* Art mused. Cole's role in this scheme was critical, and the two friends had gone over it in detail. Art left nothing to chance.

The sisters lit up like neon with Cole's arrival. He took a seat opposite Art after embracing both women.

"Art, good to see you, ol' chum," Cole said, unable to resist overplaying his role. Art frowned.

"Nice to see you, too, Cole. While we were *waiting* for you to show up, we were discussing your upcoming birthday. How are the plans for the party coming along at Gull's Point? I hear it's going to be quite the event." Art paused, pretending to wait for an answer. "I don't suppose there's room for a couple more guests?" he added slyly. "I know two great women who would love to attend."

The sisters gazed expectantly in Cole's direction.

"Well, I think we could accommodate the two of you. For the life of me, I don't know why you weren't on the original invitation list. Please accept my apologies. I'll send an e-mail to my executive assistant *tomorrow* to correct this oversight. We'd love to have you as our guests," Cole replied, emphasizing the word *tomorrow*, as though the invitation was contingent on what would happen between now and then.

"We'd love to attend!" Sidney gushed.

"I have the perfect dress to wear," replied Shelby, and the sisters giggled like schoolgirls being asked to the prom. Art smiled inwardly.

A moment later, the waiter appeared to take their lunch orders. The racket club specialized in haute cuisine prepared with reduced caloric content, with an emphasis on fresh seafood. Lunch was exceptional, and soon the foursome was on the center court hitting warmup shots back and forth. For a moment there was indecision on who would be partners with whom, but in the end mixed doubles prevailed. Although he was the far better player, Cole's role today was to be the loser, making Art appear to be the tennis stud.

All went according to plan. Two sets later, after a 6-4, 7-6 tiebreaker, Sidney and Art slapped high fives, then ran to the net to shake hands and gloat.

Cole apologized profusely to Shelby for blowing the match. Shelby remained gracious in defeat. She wrapped her arms around Cole and hugged him for his valiant efforts—a hug that lasted a bit too long.

Whispering in his ear, Shelby added, "We may have come up a little short on the score today, but that doesn't mean you won't score big tonight." She drew away, gazing alluringly into his eyes, while running her perfectly manicured nails down his chest to the top of his tennis shorts. Her forefinger slipped below his beltline and she tugged gently on it. Cole felt a slight jolt of adrenaline surge through his body, imagining Shelby's ridiculously long legs wrapped around him in the heat of passion. For a moment he considered abandoning the plan, until his gaze met Art's scowl—his friend silently instructing Cole that Shelby was off-limits. Cole sighed, smiling back at Shelby as if to say, *I couldn't have wished for more.*

"Why don't we hit the showers and meet back inside at the main bar around five o'clock? They're expecting you two in the women's locker room, and I've arranged for massages. I hope you don't mind?" Art offered, then quickly added, "Enjoy!"

Cole rolled his eyes. He could just picture the male masseuses lubing up the girls and preparing them for more physical activity later in the evening—physical activity he himself would have no part of.

Two hours later, the twins appeared in the well-appointed lounge, dressed in skintight black slacks and blouses that were similar in style yet different enough to maintain their individuality. Their long strawberry-blonde hair had been transformed from ponytails into flowing, windswept-looking curls, with fresh makeup expertly applied. What a pair!

Heads turned as they made their way to a table on the far side of the room, overlooking center court. Cole and Art stood to greet them, and the foursome sat in unison just as a cocktail waitress appeared out of nowhere. Designer martinis were ordered, and everyone took a collective sigh, relaxing.

"Looks like the massages did you good," Art said, eager to get the evening kicked into high gear.

Cole could almost sense his friend beginning to salivate.

"We had no idea the club had such wonderful services. Everyone was so attentive and pleasant. We could have spent an entire day there." Sidney spoke for the both of them, while Shelby nodded her appreciation. "That was very nice of you, Art."

"It was my pleasure. The spa is available to you anytime," Art replied, beginning to separate himself from Cole, emphasizing his personal contribution toward their entertainment. Although Art was not nearly as wealthy as Cole, he was a top attorney and well off in his own right. Art turned toward his friend.

"Good game, ol' chum! I believe we owe you a rematch, that is if you're up to it." Art chuckled good-naturedly.

"You're on, Art," Cole responded. He'd love nothing better than to get Art out in a game of singles and trounce him, 6-love, 6-love in front of the girls, but that wasn't going to happen anytime soon. Cole refrained from commenting further. The drinks arrived, and not a minute too soon.

"Art, I had no idea you were such a good tennis player," Sidney said.

"Nonsense, we're just a great team. You played really well. And Shelby, you played great, too. You just needed a little more support, that's all." Art winked in Cole's direction.

Cole clenched his teeth. What an arrogant son of a bitch. Art would pay for this, Cole thought, when the time was right.

"So, what are you two gentlemen making us for dinner tonight?" Shelby said. "I'm starving after that workout."

Cole couldn't help but wonder if she was referring to the tennis match or the massage behind closed doors. He couldn't linger on that thought too long, though. The time had come to set the stage— to bait the hook—and Shelby had teed it up nicely.

"I'm sorry, ladies, but I have a previously scheduled dinner engagement tonight, with very old, very close family friends. I tried to get out of it, but they've come from out of town…and I promised." Shelby's eyes flashed with disappointment. "But you're in good hands with Art. He's a great cook. I know he won't let you down. I'll do my best to get away as early as possible and join you for an after-dinner drink…" Cole hesitated, "and dessert." He smiled in Shelby's direction.

"We'll miss you, buddy. Give me a call when you're on your way. I'll try to keep these gorgeous women entertained until you rejoin us," Art said, endeavoring to sound sincere.

Cole downed the last of his martini, rising abruptly.

"Thanks for the game, ladies. We will definitely do it again. Oh, and thanks for the drink, Art. I really must be going."

Without waiting for a response, Cole swept away, vanishing through the main entrance doors to the great disappointment of the Swanson sisters. An awkward silence lingered. Art motioned quickly to the waitress to bring a fresh round of drinks.

"He has another date, doesn't he?" Shelby said accusatorily, knowing full well Cole's reputation as a playboy. "Old family friends? That sounded a bit contrived."

"No, honestly, it's true. He really wanted to have dinner with us. But it's the Featherstones, two of his parents' closest friends and business partners. He's known them all his life. He couldn't refuse. But if I know Cole, he'll find a way to get over later. Now, let's enjoy another drink and then the limo will take us back to my place and I'll cook you the best dinner you've had in a long time," Art said confidently. Both women nodded, realizing they couldn't do much else about it.

3

It was true, Cole did have a dinner engagement with the Featherstones, but he had no intention of returning to Art's condo. That was the deal. Art would feed the sisters full of gourmet food, expensive wine, cognac, and whatever else he could find, and then let nature take its course. The bastard!

A couple of hours later, Cole dressed in black slacks, a button-down collared white shirt, and a charcoal-gray herringbone sports coat. He went to the tie rack and pondered which one to select. Cole despised wearing ties, but they were a necessary evil in his world. To him, ties seemed like a totally useless garment—good for nothing other than catching spilled bits of food or drink. After scanning the rack several times, he defiantly decided not to wear one after all. The decision felt good. He was tie-free. He sprayed on a bit of cologne and ran his fingers through his thick black hair. It was time to go.

On the way down the stairs, he wondered how things were progressing at Art's place. Checking his watch, Cole smiled ruefully, envisioning the two or three empty bottles of expensive cabernet standing like sentries to the evening's upcoming events. By now, dinner would most likely be coming to its conclusion—Art wouldn't waste too much time on that—and he would be putting the finishing touches on some decadent dessert and pouring strong after-dinner drinks. It was still too early for Cole to arrive and Art had them all to himself. A gentle coaxing into the living room, a burning fire, and some music, while he maneuvered the twins closer to the bedroom. Art was a master at leading witnesses to a predetermined outcome in a courtroom, but could he close the deal in the bedroom? Attorneys that commanded $650 an hour were usually damn good closers. Cole anticipated receiving Art's text sometime around midnight bragging about his conquest. He considered leaving his iPhone at home, just to spite him.

Cole entered the Audi again, casting another disdainful glance over at the Maserati, as if to say, *you're being punished again, Serena.* After making his way onto Ocean Avenue, he again headed south toward Newport to meet the Featherstones and their daughter, Lindsay. He hadn't seen Lindsay since high school, with the exception of a passing hello at his parents' memorial service. He couldn't even remember what she looked like. Everything had been a blur during the weeks that followed his parents' disappearance and subsequently confirmed deaths. As he drove along the coastline parallel to the setting sun, he hoped this wasn't going to turn into a fixup, another blind date. Why was everyone trying so hard to set him up? The last thing he wanted was to be tied down. Although Cole liked and respected women for more than just their physical attributes, he wasn't ready to get serious. He wasn't ready to fall in love.

Handing his keys to the parking attendant, Cole sauntered toward the front glass doors of Breeder's Steakhouse, one of the finest restaurants in the area. Breeder's took the same approach to preparing beef as did the folks who raised thoroughbreds for racing. It was serious business eating beef. Their steaks literally melted in your mouth. It had been a long time since he had eaten here. It was his father's favorite restaurant, too, and Cole was well- known inside the exclusive dining establishment. As Cole entered the spacious, marble-lined foyer, covered with exotic flower arrangements and caged birds, the Breeder's manager approached with extended hands, smiling.

"Mr. Hollingsworth, it is wonderful to see you. Welcome… welcome." He grasped Cole's hands, shaking them vigorously.

"Paul, please call me Cole. Mr. Hollingsworth is…was my father." Cole hesitated, appearing momentarily struck with an immutable sense of loss, but he recovered quickly. "And it's good to see you, too."

"Of course…Cole," Paul replied, but the words sounded forced. "The Featherstones are anxiously awaiting your arrival. Please follow me."

The manager led Cole to a corner table next to a large glass window. Cole stopped abruptly, a pained expression crossing his face. This had been his father's table. The rounded corner booth sat eight, and the family had celebrated many birthdays and holidays here over the years. And now, here were his father's close friends sitting there waiting for him, having obviously chosen this table for a reason. It couldn't have been a coincidence. It was one of the two or three best tables in the restaurant and was normally reserved for only the most influential people, and there was a roomful of influential people waiting for tables behind him.

Jacob Featherstone edged out of his seat and rose to shake Cole's hand. Looking in his direction, the two women remained seated, hidden partially by shadows, the low-hanging lights making it difficult to see them clearly.

"Thanks so much for coming, Cole. We know it was short notice, and with a busy social calendar like you must have, we're flattered you would take the time away from your demanding schedule to dine with us," Jacob said in a tone that sounded too sincere.

"Nonsense, Mr. Featherstone, how could I say no to you? I'm so glad you called. This is an unexpected treat. Mrs. Featherstone, Lindsay, great to see you, too." Cole performed a slight bow of his head in their direction.

"Cole, please call me Jacob, you're an equal now. Don't ever forget that." Jacob extended his hand in the direction of the empty space next to his daughter, and the two men took their seats.

"Oh, Cole, we are so thrilled you could come tonight," said Mrs. Featherstone. "And as luck would have it, our Lindsay is in town this weekend, too, and she insisted on joining us tonight. Lindsay, you remember Cole, don't you?" Her voice sounded slightly slurred.

"Yes, Mother. We went to school together. Or don't you remember?"

Cole immediately felt the tension lacing between Lindsay and her mother as a handsome waiter approached, nattily dressed in a black tuxedo and crisp white shirt.

"May I bring you another round of drinks?" he inquired politely. Margaret pushed her empty glass forward expectantly. It was apparent she had already consumed more than one; her cheeks were turning rosy and not from too much makeup. Mr. Featherstone was nursing what appeared to be a half-full vodka Gibson still sitting in front of him, and Lindsay was drinking mineral water.

"Cole, what's your pleasure?" Jacob said.

"Scotch on the rocks, please." He turned toward the waiter. "Whatever you're pouring will be fine, I'm sure." The young man nodded and turned his gaze toward Lindsay.

"And for you, miss, what's your pleasure?" The slightest hint of a smile appeared on the waiter's face, as though he was referring to something other than a drink.

"Molson on draft, if you have it?" Lindsay replied stiffly, still glaring at her mother.

"Coming right up." The waiter moved efficiently through the crowded room toward the main bar. Now at eye level and bathed in the soft glow of diffused lighting, Lindsay turned to face Cole.

Cole did an immediate double take. No longer sporting thick

glasses and braces—as he remembered her wearing in high school— she had blossomed into an incredibly beautiful woman, smooth-faced with plump red lips that naturally parted. She reminded him of a cross between a young Meg Ryan, with an understated beauty, and yet she possessed the sophistication of a Sophia Loren, a woman who was to be taken seriously. He couldn't help but stare. Her long, luxurious auburn-colored hair fell about her shoulders, flirting with the paper-thin straps of her low-cut black gown.

"Lindsay?" Cole stammered, as he continued to gaze into her slate-colored eyes.

Jacob and Margaret looked on hopefully. So much depended on tonight. Lindsay's expression remained implacable.

"What? Is something wrong, Cole? Why are you staring at me like that?" Lindsay replied with a hint of sarcasm.

"No…no, of course not, nothing's wrong. It's just that I, um… you've changed!"

"We've all changed…" Lindsay hesitated briefly, "well, all of us except you, that is. You still seem the same to me. I saw the way people looked at you when you came over to our table. Like you're the conquering hero or something."

"Lindsay, that was uncalled for. Where are your manners?" Mr. Featherstone exclaimed. "It's not Cole's fault he was born into an influential family. And by the way, he's handled himself in an exemplary manner, if I do say so myself. His parents would be proud," her father said, ignoring Cole's bad-boy, womanizing reputation, well-documented in the society magazines.

Lindsay looked as if she was about to issue a strong rebuttal, but the image of Cole's parents' memorial service flashed in her mind. The empty caskets. It seemed cruel to continue to challenge him, even if he deserved it, so she remained tight-lipped, biting her tongue. Still, she had no intention of letting him off the hook. This was a test—a contentious one, perhaps—but she needed to know whether Cole was still the cocky, self-absorbed, rich boy she had grown up with.

"It's alright, Mr. Featherstone—I mean, Jacob. I admit, I was pretty arrogant growing up. And I didn't exactly treat Lindsay like she was part of the group. She has every right to think of me that way."

"See, honey, Cole *is* a gentleman. I told you. Please be cordial. We're celebrating tonight," Mrs. Featherstone said, reaching for the Old-Fashioned the waiter had just brought to the table, spilling some of its contents on the white linen tablecloth.

"What exactly are we celebrating, Mother?" Lindsay replied.

Her mother hesitated as though she couldn't remember.

"Just being back together again. It's been over six months, after all. You remember how close we were with Cole's parents? They were instrumental in helping your father finance his business in the beginning. We'll never forget their generosity." Margaret looked over at her husband wistfully, as if those days of extravagance were little more than a fleeting memory. Jacob frowned back, silently instructing his wife to choose her words carefully.

"Yes, Mother, I remember how close you were to Cole's parents, how you sucked up to them. And now it's Cole's turn to be sucked up to, isn't it?" Lindsay looked away, ashamed. Ashamed for her part in the grand charade her parents had cooked up. She didn't know all of the details, but she believed nothing good could come of it.

"That's enough, young lady!" Jacob said. "It wasn't like that. We considered them to be among our closest and most treasured friends. It nearly killed us when—" Jacob stopped, becoming emotional. "When they were lost at sea. We miss them terribly."

You mean, you miss their money, Lindsay thought. Sensing the conversation was about to turn ugly, Cole raised his glass in a toast in an attempt to intervene.

"To old friends and to great memories," Cole said.

"To old friends," Jacob echoed. They all raised their glasses, clinked them together, then downed their drinks as if they were the last ones they'd ever have.

The waiter approached to take their dinner orders. The men ordered rib eye steaks, one of the house specialties, Margaret went with the lobster Thermidor and another Old-Fashioned, while Lindsay selected the Gulf prawn salad with a balsamic vinaigrette.

"Would you care for wine with dinner?" the waiter asked.

Jacob scrutinized the wine list, which looked more like a book, for expensive reds. "The 'eighty-nine Chateau Margaux, I think."

"Excellent choice, sir. Would you like that decanted?"

"Yes, of course." Jacob turned to Cole. "The 'eighty-nine was one of your father's favorites. He had excellent taste in wine."

"He did enjoy his wine. As a kid, I used to hide out in his wine cellar when I got in trouble. I remember it being large and dark and filled with alcoves to hide out. It was the last place my parents would look for me. I remember all those old dusty bottles. I thought they must be bad, since no one ever drank them." The Featherstones laughed, although Lindsay remained subdued. "I never really paid that much attention to his collection until after his death, when Sotheby's approached me about auctioning it all off. It raised nearly two million dollars. I was shocked."

"And that's what you used to pay for your Maserati?" Lindsay interjected. "I saw the article about it in *People* magazine. One of a kind, I think the journalist said." Lindsay glared into Cole's eyes, as if such extravagance was reprehensible.

"Actually, I donated the proceeds from the auction to charity. Half of it went to the Ronald McDonald House and the other half to help fund substance abuse programs in Rhode Island schools."

Lindsay blushed pink, but refused to abdicate her position. No matter how Cole had paid for the car, it was still way over the top. "Nice write-off," she replied hastily. Cole ignored Lindsay's comment.

"I know your father would have loved that. He was quite the philanthropist himself," Jacob said, attempting to lighten the conversation. "He continues to be sorely missed by all who knew him." A hush fell over the table, like a moment of silent respect had just been called for.

"Do you miss your father, Cole?" Lindsay said with such indifference it took a moment to register.

"Lindsay!" Margaret exclaimed. "Of course he misses his father. How could you ask such a thing!"

"It's okay, Mrs. Featherstone. Everyone knows my father and I didn't always see eye to eye. I realize he was just trying to prepare me to take over for him someday, but that day seemed so far off, and now…" Cole hesitated, turning morose. "In many ways he was a generous man, but to me…well, it was just different, that's all." Cole turned to Lindsay. "I do miss him."

Lindsay spotted the emotion forming in Cole's eyes, but it disappeared quickly. She didn't bother mentioning Cole's mother; she didn't want to remind Cole of the real pain of losing her. She knew they had been very close but that Mr. Hollingsworth had ruled the household—and just about everything else he came in contact with.

"So now that you're turning thirty, the empire falls to you?" Lindsay said, but her query was much more a statement than a question. Another hush fell about the table as all three Featherstone's waited for Cole's response, although for different reasons.

"Yes, I suppose it does. But there is still a board of directors and an acting CEO. I will become the president of the company and in time, the CEO. That is, if I don't manage to screw everything up." Instead of laughing, the thought of failure seemed to add an intolerable weight to Cole's demeanor. The look in his eyes did not escape Lindsay. Still, she said nothing.

"Will you be in charge of mergers and acquisitions?" Jacob said. "I'm sure you're eager to move in other directions with the digital age upon us. There are many new opportunities for a company like yours. Your father, God bless him, wasn't convinced that digital technology and the Internet would replace traditional publishing as fast as it has. We had many conversations about that," Jacob said, pausing, allowing Cole to consider the statement before continuing.

"You're right, of course," Cole replied. "We're already allocating more resources in that area. We've ramped up our e-publishing division and will be coming out with a remarkable smart device to compete with the Kindle and the Nook, and even the iPad, although this hasn't been officially announced. This information is not for public disclosure yet, I'm sure you understand." Cole hesitated. "It wouldn't be a bad time to invest, if you get my drift?"

Mr. Featherstone smiled knowingly. "I'll call my broker Monday morning."

"Nothing like a little insider trading to start off the evening," Lindsay said. "No wonder everyone distrusts the people on Wall Street so much. The rich just get richer." She turned to Cole. "Anything else you can tell us that will help fatten our wallets?"

Cole appeared wounded by her accusation, but he kept his cool. He continued staring at Lindsay, thinking she was more than a little interesting—and feisty as hell. Not at all like he remembered her, as a timid, awkward schoolkid. Where had she been and what had she done to reinvent herself? What had caused such a dramatic change?

Lindsay looked away, Cole's penetrating gaze unnerving her.

"You know, Cole, I have a small group of tech investors with great marketing ideas and we're…uh, *they're* looking for some venture capital, in the neighborhood of fifty million. We're having a little get-together tomorrow afternoon on my yacht. We'd love for you to join us. I think you'd like these guys," Jacob said.

Lindsay rolled her eyes. *You mean on your rented yacht, don't you, Dad?*

"Thank you, Jacob. It sounds interesting, but unfortunately, I can't make it tomorrow. How long are you in town? Perhaps we could get together for lunch."

"We'll be here through Wednesday. Got to get back to business. Lots going on." Jacob pulled out his cell phone to check his upcoming schedule, as if struggling to find a slot in his busy calendar to fit Cole in. "Lunch sounds great. Would it be alright to call your office on Monday to schedule?"

"Sure, I'll let my executive assistant know you'll be calling. Her name is Grace Foster," Cole said.

"Wonderful. I look forward to it."

"So, Lindsay, are you leaving on Wednesday, as well?" Cole said.

"Lindsay will be staying on. She's on some special assignment. She won't tell us what it is, though. Top secret, I imagine," Jacob said, smirking.

Lindsay glowered at her father for answering the question himself.

"That sounds intriguing. If you're in town next weekend, I'd love to have you to my birthday dinner. It's being held at Gull's Point. I bet there'll be quite a few people you'd know. It'll be fun. Besides, we need someone like you to shake up the place. It's a bit on the stuffy side."

"Sounds delightful. I didn't know women were allowed on the grounds now, other than strippers and high-priced escorts. You've come a long way, Cole," Lindsay retorted.

"It's not that bad, Lindsay, really."

"Yeah, right! I think I'm busy Saturday. But thanks for the invite."

"Honey, you're free. You told us earlier you were wondering what you were going to do next weekend. Don't you remember?" Margaret replied, glassy-eyed.

"Come on, Lindsay. I promise no pole dancers will show up. And I'm sure people will be roasting me pretty badly. You should enjoy *that*, at least."

Lindsay struggled to suppress a grin. Now, that was something she would enjoy…and besides, she had just received the invitation without even having to ask for one.

"Okay, okay, I'll come, but don't cancel the pole dancers on my account. How do you think I paid for graduate school?"

Margaret gasped, dropping her Old-Fashioned. Jacob looked like he was about to implode, his beefy face turning scarlet.

"Just kidding…just kidding!" Lindsay exclaimed, although Cole wasn't totally convinced.

There was something about tonight that was beginning to feel uncomfortable. He couldn't put his finger on it, but it felt like the evening had been orchestrated somehow. Like he was a pawn on a chessboard, being maneuvered in a complicated game of cat and mouse. He flashed back to Art and their contrived plan for the Swanson sisters. Was everybody this conniving? Right then and there, he decided to see it out. This new Lindsay was unlike anyone he had ever met. She was no longer the awkward schoolgirl he had grown up with. She intrigued him more and more with each passing minute.

Dinner arrived, wine was poured, and the conversation turned less edgy. The food had been prepared with precision, every ingredient of impeccable quality. The aged steaks cut like butter, and the seafood tasted as if it had just been caught and brought up from the ocean. The wine was exquisite, velvety smooth with hints of dense blackberry and warm spice. The restaurant certainly lived up to its reputation. Even Lindsay savored her meal without a single demeaning comment.

As the dinner plates were cleared, Cole glanced at his watch. Ten thirty. It was time for the call. Art would be waiting impatiently after convincing the Swanson sisters that Cole would be arriving any minute.

"Excuse me, but I need to make a quick phone call. I'll be right back," Cole said as he rose from the table.

"Of course, take your time," replied Jacob.

Lindsay watched as Cole made his way quickly through the main dining room and out of sight. *What could be so important that he needed to excuse himself this late?* she wondered. Another woman, no doubt.

4

The phone rang two times before Art answered. He had been anticipating the call, his iPhone at his side.

"Cole, it's about time. Where are you?" Art said, with a well- rehearsed sense of urgency.

"I'm still at the restaurant. I'm not coming over. I know how terribly this must disappoint you. Can you find a way to forgive me?" Cole responded mockingly.

"I can't believe you're not coming over!" Art exclaimed, looking over at the twins, shrugging his shoulders in disbelief. "You promised, and besides I've got a great dessert and a terrific bottle of cognac waiting." Art's expression turned to one of aggravation, as if his best friend had just abandoned him forever. "What am I supposed to tell the girls?"

"Tell them I'm sorry. Feed them some more liquor and have fun, you son of a bitch!" Before Art could reply, the line went dead. Cole was gone and Art was on his own. He turned to the sisters and began to explain, calculating his next move carefully. Moments later, Cole returned to the booth and sat down next to Lindsay.

"I'm terribly sorry about that, but it was important and I didn't want to bore you with the details. Now, where were we?" Cole said nonchalantly.

"Oh, it wouldn't be a bore. Why don't you share the details with us? We've got nothing better to talk about," Lindsay said.

Cole considered Lindsay's request for a moment.

"Okay, if you really want to know," Cole replied, fed up with Lindsay's sarcasm. He began to recount exactly what had transpired during the day, the plan he and Art had concocted, and the need for him to call at precisely the right time. He didn't leave out a single detail. The Featherstone's sat in rapt silence until Cole finished his story. You could have literally heard the proverbial pin drop; it was that quiet. No one knew what to say. The awkwardness of the situation suddenly became unbearable. Then Cole laughed out loud.

"Gotcha, didn't I?" It was as if a gigantic helium balloon had just been punctured, releasing all of its pressure in one great *swoosh*. Margaret choked, slapping her hand down on the table, as though she had never heard anything quite so funny. Jacob broke out in a fit of laughter, telling Cole that he was a master storyteller just like his father. Lindsay gazed at Cole through squinted eyes, unsure whether what Cole had just told them was the truth or not. He had been so convincing, the details so well-articulated, it seemed impossible that anyone could have made up such a story in the blink of an eye. All the while the young waiter was standing nearby, waiting and listening, loving the story. He approached.

"Dessert, anyone? Perhaps a glass of cognac to go along with that?" The server addressed Cole, then looked quizzically at Lindsay with a sleazy expression, as if to say, *Hey, this guy is kind of kinky—are you into that sort of thing?*

Lindsay averted her gaze, understanding perfectly what he was implying.

Cole cleared his throat. The Featherstone parents considered the waiter's offer, thinking that dessert sounded good and that a snifter of cognac would hit the spot, too. After all, the evening was moving along as well as they could have hoped.

Breeder's was mostly deserted by the time they finished dessert and their after-dinner drinks. Mrs. Featherstone was in the tank and barely able to keep her eyes open. Jacob did his utmost to keep Cole's attention away from his wife's inebriated condition by telling tired old stories of past vacations the families had spent together over the years. Lindsay was growing restless, irritated by her parents' behavior. The waiter brought over the check. Unsure who would be paying the $1,570 dinner tab, he placed it squarely between the two men and then took a step back.

Cole reached over first but was beaten to the punch by Mr. Featherstone, who swiped it quickly away. But when Jacob picked up the check, he nearly choked when he saw the figure. With tip it would come to over $1,800. Cole noticed the consternation on Jacob's face.

"Jacob, please let me get that. You're in my town now, and I insist."

"Nonsense, we invited you." Jacob fidgeted with his wallet, praying that the MasterCard he selected would have sufficient credit left on it to cover the tab. Grimacing, he handed the waiter his card. When the young man returned with the receipt to be signed, Lindsay broke the nervous silence.

"So, Cole, do you have any plans after dinner?"

Surprised, Cole met her gaze, wondering if she meant it or if he was just being tested. "No plans. What did you have in mind?"

"Maybe a little dancing? It's been years since I've spent time in Newport. You can show me the hot spots. I'm sure you know where they all are."

Cole smiled. This was familiar territory, and he definitely held the advantage. Maybe now he could find out what Lindsay was really up to. "Okay, but I warn you, I'm a lousy dancer."

"I doubt that," Lindsay replied, smiling alluringly.

"No, really, I am."

"Then I'll just have to teach you," Lindsay said confidently.

The foursome rose and headed out the double glass doors. The parking attendant hailed a cab for the Featherstone's and handed Cole his car keys. The Audi was parked next to the entrance.

"Where's the Maserati, Cole? What—you're slumming in the Audi tonight?" Lindsay scoffed. "And I was looking forward to a ride in it."

"I bet you were. Your parents are gone now, Lindsay, you can cut the BS. How do you really feel about it?" Cole replied tersely. He had taken about all he could stand. *Why was she being so confrontational?* He wondered.

"How do I feel about it? Like you're a spoiled rotten rich kid who has no idea how the rest of the world lives." Lindsay glared at him, stiffening as he opened the car door for her. "I can open my own door, thank you."

Cole said nothing. He slid into the driver's seat, started the car, and headed downtown toward the nightclubs. After a few minutes of silent driving, Cole finally turned toward Lindsay.

"Why did you invite me out if I infuriate you so much?"

Lindsay sighed. "Because my parents wanted me to."

"That's a great reason! I can take you to your hotel or wherever you're staying if you'd prefer." Cole's voice had an edge to it, like he'd had about enough of Lindsay's sarcasm.

Lindsay remained silent, recalling the promise she'd made to her parents—a promise she was finding increasingly difficult to keep. Her parents were in desperate shape financially, barely able to keep a few steps ahead of the bill collectors. How they had managed to come up with the money to rent the yacht or pay for dinner tonight was anybody's guess. She supposed her father had borrowed it from his questionable investor pals. But her parents had been good to her, paying for her many years of higher education. Sending her on trips. She owed them. But this would be the last time. Besides, Cole could afford it. What was a few million bucks to a family like his?

"Keep driving. I need a drink," Lindsay said, unable to look at

Cole. What a mess she had gotten herself into. This wasn't like her. She desperately wanted to tell Cole the truth, but she instinctively knew that if she did, she would lose him. He would never believe the real reason she was here—and it had nothing to do with her parents' scam.

"Call Club Echo," Cole instructed his hands-free phone system. After three rings, a voice answered.

"Club Echo, Bart speaking."

"Hey, Bart, it's Cole. I'll be there in ten minutes. Can you save me a table for two?"

"You got it, buddy. See you in a few."

Lindsay made a sound resembling a muffled snort.

Cole pulled into the entrance of Club Echo, stopping abruptly. Exiting his car, he tossed the keys to a nearby parking attendant. Without waiting for Lindsay to open her own door this time, he pushed past the long line of people waiting to get inside, slapped a C-note into one of the bouncer's hands, and entered. He stopped just inside the front doors, looking back as Lindsay was trying in vain to explain why she should be let inside ahead of all the other people in line.

"Craig, she's with me," Cole shouted to the doorman. The muscular guy moved aside, allowing Lindsay to pass by, amid a murmuring of unappreciative comments from the crowd.

Inside, the place was utter chaos. Lights flashing, music blaring, sexy girls wearing next to nothing and dancing in gilded cages hanging from the ceiling. A human mosh pit gyrating to the latest rap song being spun by the DJ, who looked more like an alien than a human being. The bass speakers were oppressive, pounding out the bottom beat. Cole headed straight to the bar while Lindsay scrambled to catch up.

"Hey, Cole, haven't seen you in a while. What ya been up to?" the tall, blonde bartender said. She looked like she belonged in *Playboy* magazine, with legs up to her shoulders and large, firm breasts protruding out of her blouse, leaving little to the imagination.

"Hey, Kari, how about a Scotch on the rocks." He pointed to Lindsay. "She'll have a Molson Light." He didn't wait for Lindsay to respond.

"Sure thing, baby. Anything for you. I've missed you," the bartender replied. Lindsay rolled her eyes. The drinks appeared on the polished aluminum bar a moment later. Lindsay grabbed the Scotch before Cole could retrieve it. She chugged it down, then grabbed the beer.

"Order some more drinks, lightweight!" Lindsay growled.

"Lightweight? Are you suggesting I can't handle my liquor?"

"I'm not suggesting anything, *baby*! I've just missed you, and I want to get this party started," Lindsay exclaimed, doing her best imitation of the sexy bartender.

Cole turned back to the bar. "Kari, two more, please."

Kari looked up. "That was quick…but then, you always were pretty fast at the draw," Kari said, allowing an alluring look to linger between them. Again, Lindsay grabbed the Scotch first, leaving the light beer for Cole. Then she quickly disappeared into the crowd, dancing.

"What's up with her?" Kari said.

"You don't want to know, believe me. Can I exchange this for a Scotch?" Cole pushed the bottle forward. Kari poured a double and slid it back in his direction, as if to say, *you're going to need this with that girl.*

Cole headed into the crowd to find Lindsay before she could cause any trouble. He found her in the center of the main dance floor moving rhythmically to the music, her hands up in the air, her eyes closed. The glass of Scotch was gone. She wasn't dancing with anyone in particular, or maybe she was. The floor was so crowded, Cole couldn't tell. He pushed his way closer.

"Lindsay!" Cole shouted above the din. "Why don't we find a table?"

Lindsay briefly opened her eyes, spotting the nearly full glass of liquor in Cole's hand. She danced closer. Before Cole could react, she scooped the drink away.

"Thanks, I was getting thirsty." She retreated again into the belly of the crowd, as Cole stood stiffly, surrounded by spinning, sweaty bodies and looking totally out of place.

Having put sufficient space between her and Cole, she handed the drink to a stranger standing nearby, who appeared like he might enjoy a Scotch. He looked preppy, just like Cole.

It took a while, but Cole finally tracked Lindsay down, standing in a corner talking to a well-built black man who looked like a heavyweight boxer or maybe a Navy Seal from the nearby Naval base. Cole stood for a moment scrutinizing the scene before stepping forward.

"Oh, Cole, there you are. Where have you been?" She stumbled forward, wrapping her arms around Cole's neck, hanging on to him. The black man moved closer, protectively.

"It's okay, man. She's just had too much to drink." Cole turned away before there was any trouble, practically dragging her across the floor.

"Hey, where do you think you're going? I want another drink," Lindsay demanded.

"I think you've had enough for one night. I'm taking you home."

"The hell you are. I wanna have some fun!" Lindsay turned and pressed her backside close to Cole, dancing to the raucous music, moving her slender form up and down against his body. Her scent was intoxicating. In less than an hour, she had transformed into a wild woman, sexy. It took a fair amount of restraint on his part not to wrap his own arms around her, burying his face into her luxurious mane of hair. He stood for a while, allowing her to brush up against him, before grabbing her shoulders and spinning her around.

"Listen, Lindsay, I get it. You want to dance. I'll get a table and you can go dance as much as you want. Just don't drink any more. You'll thank me in the morning. When you're done come and get me. I'll be right over there." He pointed to an empty table near the entrance. "Really, go on, have fun."

Cole moved away, taking a seat at the empty high-top table—the only empty table in the entire place. He started talking to one of the bouncers who had obviously been holding it for him. Lindsay glanced over at the crowd and then back at Cole. Her plan wasn't exactly working like she'd intended it to. Cole was supposed to be *the* party boy, so why was he being so standoffish? She was doing everything she could to get his attention, having spent five hundred dollars on the sexiest dress she could find and practically throwing herself at him. She danced seductively for a while longer, pretending to have fun, occasionally glancing in his direction to see if he was even watching. Disappointed, she eventually returned to his table slightly out of breath.

"Are you always this boring, Cole?" she said playfully. She ran her finger down the side of his cheek and onto his neck; her long, painted nail tickling him. His head jerked back. Her pale, slate- colored eyes bore into his. "Or maybe I'm just not good enough for you. You'd like that blonde bartender, wouldn't you? Hey, I've got an idea. What about a threesome? The bar should be closing soon."

"Stop it, Lindsay. You've obviously got me mixed up with my friend Art. Besides, you've had way too much to drink."

Lindsay moved closer to Cole, rubbing up against him, playfully biting his ear, the tip of her tongue exploring its curvatures. He started to move away, but she reached her left hand around his neck and drew his head closer, startling Cole with her strength.

"Cole, take me to your house. I want to make love on top of a cliff," she whispered into his ear. "Come on, baby, I've haven't been laid in months."

Cole stared at her for a long moment.

"Okay, if that's what you really want," Cole agreed, thinking this was the only way he'd be able to get her out of the club and to stop drinking. He had no intention of taking her to his home, but she didn't need to know that just yet. He handed the bouncer another large-denomination bill and ushered Lindsay outside. Craig handed Cole his keys and walked the couple to the car. A final tip and they sped away, disappearing into the darkness, the blaring music fading in the distance.

Lindsay stroked the back of Cole's neck as he guided the Audi agilely through curved city streets, heading away from the downtown area. Instead of turning left onto Ocean Avenue, though, he swerved right down a long, narrow alleyway, past shuttered designer shops and over a section of cobblestone-lined streets.

"Hey, where are we going? This isn't the way to your house," Lindsay said suspiciously.

"No, we're not going to my house. We're going somewhere a lot better." They exited the alley and drove into a sparsely filled single-level parking lot. At the end of the lot stood a dilapidated- looking building with a large neon sign, pulsating with the words *Grinder's Beat* in fluorescent orange.

"Is this your idea of a joke?" Lindsay exclaimed, appearing to have sobered up quickly. No longer slurring her words, she sat up rigidly, looking annoyed.

"Don't you remember this place? It's been around forever."

"What is it, some sort of strip joint?" Lindsay replied.

"It's only the most famous coffeehouse and used bookstore in Rhode Island. I can't believe you don't remember it."

Lindsay thought for a moment. The name did sound vaguely familiar, but it had been many years since she'd lived in Newport.

And in those days, she'd had no interest in drinking coffee or perusing used books.

"So, what are we going to do, drink coffee and read?" she replied sarcastically. "Tell me they at least serve alcohol."

"Occasionally, but only during special events. Besides, they've got the best coffee on the East Coast. I think you've had enough to drink tonight." Cole eased his car into a parking slot, killing the engine. Lindsay frowned, remaining seated while Cole opened her car door.

"Come on. I know you'll like this place. It's totally you," Cole said, unable to suppress a grin, adding to her frustration. Reluctantly, she exited the Audi, refusing to look at her companion, then walked briskly in the direction of the front door.

Inside, the place felt like a time machine had suddenly transported them back to the 1960s. The walls were littered with photos of rock legends, famous authors and poets, a smattering of politicians, and photos of other people Lindsay did not recognize. A few classic guitars were hung near a small corner stage at the far end. A microphone stood at the front of the stage near a single wooden chair, silent, as though the ghosts of Muddy Waters or Allen Ginsberg might suddenly appear.

But no one came; no one shared a blues riff or recited beat poetry. Near the back of the stage, two small Fender amplifiers lined the wall. Above the amps hung a tattered-looking poster emblazoned with skeletons and red roses, announcing an upcoming Grateful Dead concert at Fillmore East, circa 1968. The stage stood eerily silent, a requiem to days long gone. Neither she nor Cole had been "children of the flowers"; she only knew what she had heard or studied in history books about the turbulent decade that spawned a social revolution that eventually failed. Soft jazz played in the background.

Between the entrance and the stage stood a long, wooden coffee bar. To one side of the bar a doorway led to a room housing shelves of books. It, too, appeared to have seen better days. The rest of the open space was filled with tables and an assortment of mismatched chairs, some with worn-looking cushions and others without. The room was mostly dark paneling, with wood- framed windows spaced across three walls that faced out toward the parking area and the alley beyond. Nothing harmonized, but there existed a feeling of comfort somehow. The large room was quiet and smoky. Apparently, the ownership hadn't taken notice of the no smoking in public places law passed years ago. Among the few smokers who inhabited the place, most were puffing on pipes, the smoke from the aromatic tobacco spiraling upward, trapped by the low-hanging asbestos ceiling. Lindsay was sure she smelled the scent of marijuana coming from the back room, mixed with the distinctive aroma of freshly brewed coffee.

There was no blaring music or scantily clad coeds dancing in cages. No *Playboy* bartenders, just an old, distinguished-looking man with long white hair tied back in a ponytail, and a couple of college students making and transporting coffee to the various tables. No one seemed intent on impressing each other. People were huddled in small groups drinking coffee and talking, or sitting alone reading a newspaper or a book. Nobody noticed as they moved across the room and took seats near the stage. As far as Lindsay could tell, no one recognized Cole, or if they did, they paid him no attention. Lindsay felt the stress instantly drain from her body. This was a long way from Breeder's or Club Echo. *Why did he bring me here?* she wondered.

Cole motioned to one of the waiters, and a young man who looked to be in his late teens ambled over, dropping a faded menu on the center of the table. He gazed at the couple curiously, as if surprised to see someone like them in his establishment, but he refrained from saying anything that might offend. Instead he smiled genuinely. "I'll be back in a moment to take your order." He shuffled away.

"Why did you bring me here, Cole?" Lindsay said, unable to

keep silent any longer. Cole looked up from the menu and started to speak, then hesitated.

She saw in his eyes that he wanted to ask her something but he seemed reluctant to reveal just what. Following an awkward silence, he finally spoke.

"I brought you here for the truth. It's hard to be truthful, let alone to hear anyone speak, in a place like Club Echo. You were too uptight with your parents at Breeder's, and I felt like you were hiding something from me. There's nothing for you to hide behind here. Just the ghosts of a bygone era, and I don't see you as the type of person who particularly cares for charades. Just be honest with me, okay?"

Lindsay was taken aback. Cole had cut right to the chase and somehow had seen inside her, sensed what she was feeling. She hadn't expected this from him. She leaned back in her chair, sighing and debating just how much to tell him. He was right. There was no escaping him now. The only other thing she could do would be to leave. Just as she was about to speak, the waiter reappeared, bringing a welcome reprieve.

"What would you like?" the waiter inquired. Cole ordered a nonfat latte, Lindsay a pot of green tea. She had the sudden feeling this was going to be either a long night or a short one, depending on what she said next. The waiter returned shortly with their order. Cole took a sip and placed the cup back on the table, fixing his gaze intently on Lindsay's face. Lindsay took a deep breath.

"Okay, Cole, let's have it your way. How about a truth for a truth? You tell me exactly who you called at dinner and why, and I'll tell you what I can about my parents."

Cole considered for a moment before answering, until a smile spread across his face. He checked his watch, a vintage 1945 Tourbillon by Girard-Perregaux. Although the watch cost six figures, it was understated and elegant, not gaudy like the typical Rolexes worn by scores of wannabes.

The sight of the watch momentarily took Lindsay's breath away. She had only seen one before, in the Louvre Museum. She averted her gaze, trying hard not to think about the wealth and privilege Cole's position represented. A surge of anger shot through her, but she somehow remained poised.

"I can do better than that. I can show you firsthand," Cole said, retrieving his phone from his coat pocket, and began dialing.

"Hey, Art, it's me. How's it going, bro?" Cole paused, while he listened to Art's reply. "Hey, buddy, can you hang on for a sec? I need to pay the check, then I want to hear all about it. Don't leave out a single detail." He paused for a moment, then raised the phone back up to his face. "Okay, I'm back." Cole lowered the phone again, and to Lindsay's surprise, handed it to her. She took hold of it reluctantly, confusion etched on her face.

"Go on," Cole whispered. Lindsay pressed the phone to her cheek listening, while Art began to describe in vivid detail the events of the evening. It was one thirty in the morning, and apparently the Swanson sisters were both passed out in his bed. His plan had worked flawlessly. Once the sisters had gotten over their disappointment that Cole would not be coming over, things fell smoothly into place. He thanked Cole again for playing his role to perfection. With each detail of the conquest that Art described, Lindsay's face contorted, until she could barely stifle her laughter. She put her hand against her mouth, struggling to remain quiet, until she couldn't take any more. She handed the phone back to Cole and burst into a laughing fit, excusing herself from the table.

Cole, of course, hadn't heard the details, but it didn't take much imagination to understand what Art had been saying. The variety of expressions on Lindsay's face had said it all.

"Good job, Art. That's one for the record books. I've gotta go. I'll talk to you tomorrow."

Cole placed the phone back in his pocket just as Lindsay returned to the table. She sat down shaking her head. "Men!" she exclaimed. It was hard to stay mad at Cole after that, He hadn't been lying after all. Still grinning, she met Cole's gaze.

"You really ought to think about getting some new friends. That was disgusting."

"Tell me about it. Art's a piece of work. If he wasn't such a damn good lawyer, I'd…" Cole's voice trailed off as he thought about all Art had done for him over the years and how supportive he had been after his parents had gone missing.

"The way you told the story at dinner, I just couldn't believe it, and yet, I did sort of believe it. I didn't think anyone could come up with a story like that on the spur of the moment. Now I know you were telling the truth." Lindsay hesitated. "But that doesn't excuse your behavior in the whole scheme. Those poor sisters, they never stood a chance, did they?" Lindsay broke out in laughter again.

"No, I don't suppose they did." Cole laughed, too, as he envisioned Art sitting in bed between the pair of passed-out twins, smoking a cigar and gloating.

"Well?" Cole said. "Now it's your turn."

Lindsay's face suddenly went pale. She had momentarily forgotten about her end of the deal. This had been her idea, and now she needed to own up to the bargain, but the words stuck in her throat. Even though her parents deserved it, this was a betrayal.

Cole saw the consternation in her eyes as she struggled with what to tell him. Cole suspected he knew what was going on. He had seen the anxiety in her father's face when he examined the dinner check, practically choking when he saw the amount. The fact that Mrs. Featherstone had developed a drinking problem also hinted that there were problems. The tension between the three family members had been unmistakable, and it pointed to only one thing. Money was involved. And then there was Lindsay's transparent attempt at seduction. Pretending to be drunk and wanting to make love on top of the cliff. She just didn't seem to be the type of woman to throw herself at a man for casual sex. And yet, here she sat, one of the most beautiful women he had ever met—a mixture of intelligence, physical beauty, and intrigue.

Cole decided not to push too hard. He could feel Lindsay's anguish…and besides, she had been a pretty good sport when it had finally come out that Cole was really a player in Art's hedonistic plan of sexual conquest. That couldn't have been easy for another woman to hear.

"Look, Lindsay, I think I may know what's going on. It has to do with your father's investor friends, doesn't it?"

Lindsay nodded but said nothing. A look of shame crossed her face.

"I got the impression that your parents might have experienced some sort of financial setback and were reluctant to ask me for help. Hey, it happens to everyone. My father went through it a half-dozen times before he was finally secure enough in his own business ventures. You probably didn't know that. All entrepreneurs experience their share of failures before they get it right. I'll listen to their proposal, and if it sounds plausible, I'll be happy to help."

Lindsay couldn't believe what she was hearing. Cole had somehow figured it out on his own and was willing to help. This wasn't the Cole she had known. This was someone totally different. Her eyes moistened with appreciation. He reached over, covering her hands with his.

"I said not to worry about it. Now, relax and tell me all about yourself."

Lindsay's mouth dropped open in bewilderment. She didn't have a clue where to start. Was this soon-to-be-billionaire actually interested in what she had experienced after graduation from high school—after they went their separate ways? Or was he simply placating her until he could say a respectable good- bye, deal swift-ly with her conniving parents, and be done with the whole mess? She had seen Cole only once during the past thirteen years, and that was only briefly at his parents' memorial service. She had been dressed in all black, her hair pulled up under a hat. They'd shared a fleeting glance as he passed by during the funeral procession. They had bumped into each other during the luncheon that followed, ex-changing a quick *hello* and *how are you.*

She had followed him in the society pages, had read about the Maserati, and had seen pictures of his house in *Architectural Digest.* But there had been no meaningful contact, indeed no contact at all. She assumed he had forgotten all about her—just one of the nerdy friends he had put up with during his early school days. Cole was the most popular, self-assured boy she had ever met. He stood out in sports and in academics, and he always got the prettiest girls. And now…now she was sitting across from him in some iconic hip-pie hangout in the middle of the night—where cutting-edge poets had poured out their souls and legendary rock stars had jammed for free—and he was holding her hands, offering comfort and not judg-ing her scheming parents.

Instinctively, she pulled back her hands, releasing herself from his spell. While they touched, she was far too vulnerable to him. She needed separation. She needed fresh air. Her head was spinning, wrapped up in a delusion. She was acting like a schoolgirl again, mesmerized in his presence.

"Excuse me, Cole. I'll be back shortly." She rose, but instead of heading to the restrooms, she strode out the front door. She stood for a long moment in the cool night air, collecting her thoughts. It all seemed like a dream. She reminded herself of the real reason she had come back to Newport. Helping her parents in their scam to get money was only part of it. There was something far more important that concerned Cole's parents directly—and it had nothing to do with money.

Lindsay returned a few minutes later, spotting the white- haired man she had seen upon their arrival sitting with Cole and talking. Their conversation seemed to be a serious one. Lindsay approached.

"Excuse me, am I interrupting?" Lindsay said.

"No, not at all. Please have a seat. This is Bill Banks, the owner of Grinder's. We were just talking about a plan to revive the place. You know, bring back some of the great legends of rock and blues, mixed in with some newer Indie musicians. Maybe some hip comedians, too. Try and modernize the place. Bill's got some great ideas, he just needs financing. The banks these days focus on only those investments that are iron-clad. They lack such imagination, it's ridiculous." Cole turned toward Bill. "Bill, this is Lindsay Featherstone. We grew up together. She's back in town for a few days with her parents and we were just catching up."

"Lindsay, it's a pleasure to meet you. Any friend of Cole's is a friend of the Beat." He took her hand in both of his, shaking it warmly. "Well, I'll leave you two alone to reminisce. We do a lot of that around here," Bill chuckled, winking at Cole. "Thanks again, Cole. And don't be a stranger." The owner ambled away, disappearing into the kitchen like a memory from the past.

"You are certainly full of surprises, Cole Hollingsworth. If I didn't know better, I'd swear someone had hired an actor to impersonate you tonight. I don't get it."

"Hey, there's more to life than just business." Cole paused, gazing deeply into Lindsay's eyes. "There are expensive sports cars, one-of-a-kind watches, mansions, you know, that sort of thing. I'm a multi-dimensional guy, after all."

Lindsay was about to start in on him again, when the smirk on his face stopped her cold. "You're kidding, I hope."

"Almost had you, didn't I? Now, you were about to tell me all about yourself?"

5

Lindsay gazed at Cole in silence, contemplating where to begin. So much had happened. How do you tell someone you've had a crush on for most of your life that you're no longer the same person? She supposed she should just start at the beginning.

"After high school graduation, I decided to leave. I needed to get away and start fresh. I guess what I really needed was to reinvent myself. I didn't like who I was or where I was going. I spent two years at a junior college before being admitted to Princeton. I earned my undergraduate degree in biology, with a minor in photojournalism. From there I spent one year working as a research assistant. I took night classes and earned my master's in photojournalism, but my real passion was marine biology. For the next four years I worked and attended MIT, earning a PhD in oceanography. I—"

Cole waved his hands, stopping Lindsay in midsentence. "Whoa, hold on a second. You're telling me you're a doctor? You've spent your entire life in school?"

"Yeah, I guess. I do have a 'Dr.' attached to my name, but I try to ignore it unless I'm in a situation where I need to establish credibility. People look at you differently when you have a title." She smiled, with a hint of sadness, as if she had lost something along the way—missed out on life somehow while immersed in study and research. Cole was momentarily lost in her allure.

"So, do you have a job now? Where do you work?"

"Actually, I don't work for a company, if that's what you mean. I was awarded a research grant after my doctoral thesis was published. I'm kind of freelancing now, doing research…" Lindsay paused pensively. "You know, that sort of thing."

"No, I don't know. What are you researching?" Cole replied, looking mildly impressed.

"This and that. I'm basically studying the ocean. I won't bore you with the details, you wouldn't be interested."

"Who says?"

"I do. Cole, you're a businessman…among other things." Lindsay smirked at his well-earned playboy image. "I can't imagine you'd be interested in marine biology. Come on, be honest!"

Cole leaned back in his chair. "No, I don't suppose I would be. Not that I don't admire what you've accomplished." He hesitated, seeming to stumble over his words. "I guess I—I just don't know much about what you do, that's all. So, where are you going from here?"

"I'm just here for a little R and R. And I'm going to your birthday party, of course. I wouldn't want to miss *that* event. Then it will be time for me to get back in the saddle, or should I say boat, and cruise on out of here. There's work to be done," Lindsay said, almost wistfully. The pair stared at one another, her statement seeming to draw the conversation to an end. Cole checked his watch and did a double take. It was five fifteen in the morning. They had passed the night away talking. Soon the sun would be up. It was too late now to think about sleep.

"How about some breakfast, and then I'll take you to your parents'," Cole said. Yet there was a hint of melancholy in his voice.

"That sounds good. My parents will love the fact that we're returning in the morning having failed to change clothes. They'll read all kinds of lasciviousness into that!"

Cole dropped a generous amount of cash on the table and the pair left Grinder's, passing by their young server fast asleep behind the coffee bar. The place was open all night, but only Cole and Lindsay remained. As they stepped outside, the first signs of dawn emerged, casting a glorious light and highlighting the sparkling waves of crimson-colored water beyond.

"This is my favorite time of day," Lindsay said, as she stretched cramped muscles. "It's beautiful, isn't it?"

"Yes, it certainly is," but Cole wasn't looking at the sunrise. Their eyes met for an instant, and Lindsay blushed.

"There's a little French bistro a couple of blocks away. They serve a mean omelet," Cole said. Lindsay nodded, but said nothing, closing her eyes and taking in a deep breath of the salt-flavored air. They walked in silence toward the bistro, which was already bustling with activity. Lindsay glowed in the early morning light, as if she was lit from within.

The aroma of freshly baked pastries and espresso replaced the saltiness of the gentle sea breeze. Cole suddenly found himself ravenous, and at the same time, he wondered if food alone could satisfy his hunger.

After a delicious and much needed breakfast, they headed back to the parking lot to pick up Cole's car. They climbed into the Audi and headed toward Newport Harbor, where the Featherstone's yacht was moored. Cole eased the sports car into a slot near the long, wooden pier. The clubhouse was serving breakfast, feeding the fortunate few who would be spending the day on the water. Cole opened Lindsay's door and waited while she exited the passenger's seat.

"I think this is as far as I go. It's probably best if your parents don't see me right now," Cole said.

"Are you kidding? This is exactly what they've been waiting for. You're not getting off this easily, buddy." She tugged at his arm, leading him to the front entrance of the clubhouse to face the music. The large maritime clock on the portico above showed the time as seven fifteen.

Upon entering, they spotted Lindsay's parents immediately, sitting at a nearby table and nursing cups of coffee. The line of adjacent tables faced the open side of the clubhouse with a spectacular view of the colorful sailboats, extravagant yachts, and the harbor beyond. Jacob was reading yesterday's *Wall Street Journal,* while Margaret sat glumly hiding behind a large pair of very dark sunglasses, obviously suffering from a hangover.

"Good morning, parents," Lindsay remarked with more than a hint of sarcasm. Jacob looked up, smiling broadly. Margaret attempted a smile but appeared to be in pain. Her face looked puffy and pallid.

"What a pleasant surprise. Won't you join us, Cole?" Jacob offered good-naturedly.

"I'd love to, Jacob, but I really must be going. As I mentioned at dinner last night, I have another commitment today. I just wanted to make sure Lindsay made it, um, safely home," Cole replied awkwardly.

Jacob scrutinized the couple's appearance. Cole was unshaven. Lindsay had the same sexy dress on, which now looked completely out of place at the marina in the early morning hours.

"You two light up the town last night?" Jacob asked.

"Yeah, we closed down just about every club we could find. Cole really knows how to show a girl a good time," Lindsay answered. She turned, kissing Cole lightly on the mouth and thanking him. "I'll talk to you soon, Cole." She smiled fetchingly up at him, suggesting that they were hiding a dirty little secret. It was Cole's turn to blush. He excused himself and walked briskly away, leaving Lindsay to face the inevitable questions that were sure to follow.

6

Cole guided his car up the steep driveway to his house, wondering what the hell had happened last night. Lack of sleep had made his brain fuzzy. He could still faintly smell Lindsay's perfume on his coat. He wondered what she was telling her parents about their night together. He rather doubted it would include spending the night in a coffee joint, talking. As he pulled into the driveway, he spotted Art's Range Rover parked near the front entrance. The driver's door was open, and Art was lounging in the front seat reading the morning newspaper. Cole's newspaper. Cole cursed. This was all he needed now—a rehash of the Swanson sisters' conquest. He shut off the ignition, groaned, and exited the Audi.

Art stepped out of the SUV, dressed in a casual outfit that probably cost over a thousand dollars. The more relaxed the look, the more it cost, Cole knew. Art's deck shoes alone were worth more than five hundred dollars, if they were worth a penny. Art strolled over to greet Cole and stopped short as he noticed his friend's appearance.

"Cole, it looks like I'm not the only one with a story to tell. You pulled another all-nighter, you dog? And here I thought you were just returning from the gym?" Art let out a belly laugh.

"What are you doing here, Art? I need some sleep."

"*Au Contraire,* old buddy. There's no time for sleep now. You've got exactly thirty minutes to freshen up before we pick up the

Swanson sisters—"

"What! No way, Art. That wasn't part of the deal."

"Well, it is now, if we ever want to speak to them again. I had to promise that we'd take a cruise on your yacht today and have a picnic lunch. It was the only way I could close the deal last night. I've already taken care of the food. You just have to show up and pretend to have a good time, that's all. Then it'll be over, I promise. You can sleep later."

"It's never over with you, Art, you son of a bitch."

"Dude, this is important or I wouldn't be asking." Art paused. "Hey, you got a hangover again? You don't look so good."

"No, I don't have a hangover. I'm just tired."

"Who were you with last night? Old family friends? Yeah, right. Come on, 'fess up."

"The Featherstone's brought their daughter to dinner. We went to grade school together. I hadn't seen her in years. We spent some time together reminiscing. That's all."

"That must have been some kind of reminiscing. It's eight in the morning, Cole. I like your action, though. The Featherstone's buy you an expensive dinner at Breeder's and then you screw their daughter? And I thought I was the sick one!" Art exclaimed, laughing.

"Fuck you. And I didn't screw their daughter," Cole replied, glaring at his friend. Art saw that Cole was becoming highly agitated, and since he didn't want to blow the deal on future action with the twins, he backed off.

"Okay, okay, if you say so. Now, please hurry up and get ready. I'll be waiting in the car."

Cole acquiesced, entering his house and taking a quick shower. He dressed in wrinkled khaki shorts and a worn T-shirt, a pair of sandals, and a Boston Red Sox hat. He didn't bother to shave. Donning a pair of Ray-Ban aviator sunglasses, he returned to Art's car twenty minutes later.

"Dude, you look like shit! The sisters will be decked out in designer wear up to their asses. They're expecting a classy time— and to be seen. You know how they are," Art complained. "Please go back inside and change. We've got time."

Cole glared over at his attorney, his expression implacable. "I'm going, aren't I? That should be enough. I'm not changing, so make up your mind."

Art reluctantly agreed, although the expression on his face turned ugly. He jammed the gearshift into drive and sped away, fuming. He had envisioned a dream relationship with at least one of the sisters, if not both, but Cole was about to blow all of that. As they drove in silence toward the Newport Yacht Club, Art pondered how he could use this to his advantage. He just needed an explanation for Cole's shabby appearance that the girls would believe, and then things would settle down. He had spent a small fortune on the picnic lunch; it consisted of an assortment of caviar, gourmet cheeses from northern California, chilled Maine lobster, bottles of French champagne, and the finest chardonnay he could find from the Napa Valley. The alcohol had worked last night, and there was no reason to think it wouldn't work today—that is, if the sisters stayed around long enough. He just had to get them onto Cole's yacht and then everything would be fine.

The parking lot at the yacht club was nearly full when the foursome arrived. It was one of those perfect days for sailing: sunny with a strong breeze blowing off the coast. The water shimmered with an iridescent quality in myriad hues of aquamarine. The Bay was already littered with graceful sailboats sporting brightly colored flags and over-the-top yachts, as the social elite of Newport enjoyed a day of leisure.

The Swanson sisters were, as Art had predicted, dressed to the nines, in casual elegance that screamed with sexual innuendo. Even Cole could not ignore them. Ordinarily, he would have jumped at an opportunity like this—crazy sex aboard his yacht with two of the most gorgeous women in Rhode Island—but there was something gnawing at him, something he couldn't quite put his finger on. *Was it something that Lindsay had said? Or perhaps had left unsaid?* Cole wondered. Maybe it was the way she had said it, pensively—as if there was something much deeper to the research she was doing. The feeling continued to grate on Cole's nerves as they walked past the open veranda of the clubhouse toward Cole's slip, one of two his family permanently owned. Most were leased, but the club had graciously agreed to sell the precious spaces to the Hollingsworth's after Cole's father had donated the money to upgrade the clubhouse and the pier.

Cole suddenly stopped in his tracks, as they passed the table still occupied by the Featherstone's. He was shocked to see them still sitting there; they should have been gone long ago. Facing him sat Lindsay, engaged in a heated conversation with her father, while Margaret quietly sipped a Bloody Mary. Art bumped into Cole's backside, dropping one of the ice chests containing the wine. The impact echoed loudly off of the wooden planks, and the disturbance caught Lindsay's attention. She looked up, her slate- colored eyes seeming to flash and change color all at the same time, as she spotted Cole flanked on either side by the stunning Swanson sisters.

Instinctively, Cole pulled down his baseball cap, as if the action would somehow make him seem less conspicuous. But he was caught—like a deer in Lindsay's headlights—only her eyes seemed far more ominous than mere car lights racing toward an impending collision.

For a moment the scene froze, everything moving in slow motion. Jacob looked over, his eyes widening. Hadn't his daughter just spent the night with Cole, and now here he was with what looked like a pair of high-priced escorts heading toward his yacht? This seemed too much, even for Jacob. Margaret looked on with disdain, motioning to the waiter to bring her another drink. But the expression on Lindsay's face cut deepest, a look of shock that quickly turned to contempt. Cole was busted, in a big way. He had no defense, determining that anything he might say would do little good. So he simply shrugged his shoulders, smiling apologetically in Lindsay's direction, then strode away in silence with his companions following behind, wondering what had just taken place.

"Cole, what was up with that?" Art whispered after the girls had stepped onto the Horizon E70, a gorgeous sixty-nine-foot yacht of Italian design.

"It was nothing. Don't worry about it," Cole grumbled. The look on his face convinced Art not to inquire further.

Art knew when it was appropriate to push his friend and when it was not. He suspected it had something to do with the Featherstone's, although he had only met them briefly. But their daughter, that was something else altogether. She was breathtaking in a different sort of way—mysterious, beautiful, with an alluring sense of power. Art couldn't find the right words to describe her, and for one of the top attorneys on the Eastern Seaboard, that was saying something. No wonder Cole was being mute about her; he obviously wanted her all to himself. *Now, this is interesting*, Art mused. That just meant more Swanson's for him. Art smiled to himself, eager for a repeat performance of last night, all tangled up in legs that never seemed to end.

For the rest of the afternoon Art was on his best behavior, attending to the sisters' every need, describing the nuances of the food and wine he had chosen while they motored their way between the other vessels to the outer limits of Newport Bay. The sisters relished in the attention and bright sunshine, and soon they were topless, sunning themselves in the buff. The thongs they wore, substituting as bikini bottoms, left little to the imagination, either. Art offered to apply sunblock and the sisters giggled, acting like schoolgirls again.

Cole worked the navigation controls to steer them farther out in the Bay as the girls waved to onlookers, who were mostly gawking in their direction.

"What's wrong with Cole today? He seems so distant," Shelby said.

"He's not feeling well. I think he had too much to drink again. You know how he can be," Art said with a sympathetic glance in Cole's direction. "I know he really wanted to be here today, but a hangover and the ocean don't go together very well. Just give him some space, okay? He'll feel better once he gets his sea legs under him."

Shelby agreed, while Art refilled her glass with more champagne, staring longingly at her exposed breasts. The patterned white flesh of a plunging neckline, combined with the deep golden tan of the rest of her body was almost too much for Art to take.

Sidney had just taken a position next to Cole and appeared to be asking him about the yacht's controls. She brushed her nearly naked body close to Cole, hoping to entice him to pay her some attention. *Perfect timing*, Art thought.

"Shelby, why don't we take our champagne below deck and let Cole and Sidney be alone for a while?" Art strongly suspected that at some point, Cole would reject Sidney's advances while he and Shelby were doing their thing below. Then, out of frustration, Sidney would probably make her way down to the sleeping cabins below and be welcomed with open arms.

As the day wore on, Cole retreated further and further inside himself, frustrating Sidney all the more. She was practically throwing herself at him, but to Cole, it was like she didn't exist. The alcohol was beginning to take its effects, and after a concerted effort to get Cole to come on to her, she left him to his brooding. She grabbed a bottle of chardonnay and headed toward the cabins below. The sun was beginning to disappear to the west, and the waters of Newport

Harbor were changing hues, reflecting darker shades of indigo. The wind began to die down, and many of the sailboats limped back to their respective moorings, whether at the Newport Yacht Club or elsewhere. Cole maneuvered the *Horizon* closer to shore, then killed the engines. He faintly heard the sound of laughter coming up from below. At least someone was having a good time. All Cole could think about was the astonished look that had crossed Lindsay's face. But what did she expect? It wasn't like they were dating. She came here with a purpose—to help her parents help themselves to his inheritance. And now *she* was judging *him*? Still, he knew there was more.

Cole unlocked the small lifeboat hanging from the starboard side of the yacht, lowering it into the water below. He activated the switch to drop the anchor and watched as yards of heavy rope quickly unwound. Donning a life preserver, he climbed down the metal ladder and into the lifeboat, placing a duffel bag with the sisters' clothes beside him. The craft was equipped with twin outboard motors and a set of oars and oarlocks. Not wanting to disturb Art and hoping to slip away unnoticed, Cole placed the wooden oars into their locks and rowed away in silence. Having spent time on the rowing team at Harvard, Cole was an expert with small boats.

A wry smile crossed his face at the thought of Art discovering he had been abandoned and left alone to commandeer the vessel. As smart as Art was, he was practically helpless when it came to mechanical issues. He could always call the harbormaster and someone would be out to help him get back to shore. But this would deal a blow to Art's pride, appearing incompetent to the Swanson sisters while they scrambled to find their clothes. *That's the least Art deserves,* Cole thought.

Cole guided the lifeboat into an empty slip, tied it off, and ascended the steps to the upper level of the pier. He walked along the long, wooden dock, inspecting some of the smaller yachts moored in temporary slips nearby, wondering which one belonged to the Featherstone's. The larger vessels, costing millions of dollars, were positioned out in the Bay. He knew it wasn't one of those. As he casually strolled by the clubhouse, he knew it was too much to hope that Lindsay would still be there. The table was empty. Turning right, he headed toward the docking office to ask about Jacob's location. Once the information was secured, he walked down to the end of the dock to a modest-looking vessel, but nice enough. It was somewhere between a large motorboat and a small yacht, not as pretentious as he might have imagined. It seemed to fit the situation. Cole stepped onto the deck.

"Jacob…Margaret, are you aboard? It's Cole." He waited for a response while gazing out into the Bay to check on his own boat, which hadn't moved. Jacob emerged from the front cabin, looking weary.

"What can I do for you, Cole?" Jacob asked, his voice controlled, yet sounding strained.

"Is Lindsay here? I'd like to talk to her. To explain."

"Lindsay's resting. Apparently, she didn't get any sleep last night. She's exhausted. I really don't want to wake her. Why don't you try calling her tomorrow?"

"Yes, of course…tomorrow. Look, Jacob, it's not what it appeared to be. I was just doing a favor for a friend. Art Barkley is my attorney, and he promised the Swanson sisters a day out on the water. Since he doesn't own a boat of his own, he asked me to oblige. They're still out there." Cole pointed in the direction of his yacht.

"Cole, it's really none of my business what happens between you and Lindsay. She's a grown woman, and it's been a long time since she's listened to my advice. She puts on a game face like she's tough, not vulnerable. But deep down she has a heart…and I suspect a fragile one at that. I just wanted you to know, that's all." Jacob went silent. This was all he was going to share with Cole about his daughter's state of mind.

Is this part of Jacob's act, or is he actually being a father? Cole wondered.

"I'll remember that. Speaking of tomorrow, are you still planning to call me?" Cole asked, all business now.

"Yes, if it's still okay?"

"Of course, it's okay. I look forward to meeting your team. I'm available after eleven." Cole extended a hand, and the two men shook. Then he turned away and quickly disappeared down the pier, while Jacob watched anxiously. He would only have one shot at this, and it needed to be perfect. He returned to the cabin and continued to work on his sales pitch. Cole might not be the most experienced businessman he had ever dealt with, but he was smart and, Jacob thought, not one to be easily fooled.

7

"**M**r. Hollingsworth, I have a Jacob Featherstone holding for you on line two. Will you take his call?" Cole's executive secretary's voice sounded through the intercom.

"Yes, Grace, please put him through. Good morning, Jacob. Everybody rested up?"

"Yes, thanks. There's nothing quite like spending the night on the water. It sort of lulls you to sleep and rejuvenates you, all at the same time."

"It does seem to have that effect on people." Cole smiled inwardly at the six messages sitting on his desk that Art had left, not a single one complimentary. He only hoped his boat was still in one piece.

"So, what do you say to lunch at my office around one o'clock? "I'll have food brought in. How many will be attending?"

"Are you sure we can't take you out? I have one of the private rooms reserved at the yacht club," Jacob replied.

"I think I've seen enough of the yacht club for a while. Please cancel the reservation and just come to my office, if you don't mind the drive."

"Okay, if you insist. That's very generous of you, Cole. There'll be three of us, along with however many of your staff will be attending. See you at one." A hint of relief was in Jacob's voice.

Cole hit the button on his intercom. "Grace, please order lunch for four from Le'toille and have it brought to my private conference room at one thirty. No alcohol, just iced tea and coffee."

"No problem. Will there be anything else?"

"Please hold all of my calls while I'm meeting with Mr. Featherstone. I'll let you know when we're done. Thanks."

Cole's thoughts turned to Lindsay. He wondered what she was thinking, knowing her father and his investor pals would soon be here with their pitch. Was it legitimate, or was it just another scam, like so many he had seen before? His family's wealth drew would- be investment proposals like bears to honey. It was all part of the game. The trick was to determine which ones had legs. Speaking of legs, he decided it was time to return Art's call. He couldn't procrastinate much longer. He prepared himself for an earful as he dialed Art's cell.

Sure enough, Art started in on him before Cole could get a word out. The Swanson sisters had been humiliated. How dare Cole take their clothes? Luckily, they'd found a couple of towels to partially cover up with. The rescue team was still laughing when they docked the yacht into Cole's slip and escorted the trio to their car. After he'd dropped the twins off, they'd slammed the doors to Art's car and stomped away, but not after screaming at him not to bother calling them again.

Cole pulled the receiver away from his ear, trying very hard to stifle a laugh. Turnabout was fair play. Maybe Art would think a little more before launching his next scheme. He pulled out the guest list for his upcoming birthday party from a desk drawer, scratching Sidney and Shelby's names off. It felt good.

Cole was waiting in his conference room when Jacob and his two guests arrived. Grace showed them in, offering them a nonalcoholic beverage. All three guests chose iced tea, while Cole stuck to bottled water.

"Cole, please shake hands with Gerald and Robert Cunningham. These are the men I spoke to you about, who are going to help revolutionize the transfer of information over the Internet. Gerald … Robert, this is Cole Hollingsworth. His reputation precedes him, as you already know." Jacob was careful not to mention Cole's father, ensuring that the spotlight for the company's future success rested solely on Cole's shoulders.

"Welcome, gentlemen. Please have a seat and make yourselves comfortable. Lunch will be served in half an hour, so we can get started right away. I'm eager to hear your proposal. It's not every day that I get a recommendation from someone like Jacob." He turned with a slight bow in Jacob's direction, as if to say thank you and to show the older man respect. Cole paused briefly, as a hint of intuition flashed briefly in his head. These guys really didn't look like a Gerald and Robert Cunningham, but what's in a name anyway? They were impeccably dressed and oozed confidence. He didn't suppose Jacob would bring amateurs with him, and brushed off what was probably just a silly thought. A case of nerves at his first big deal.

Gerald placed a dark leather Cartier briefcase on the conference room table, but refrained from unlocking the six-digit combination lock on top. That would come later. Robert took bound copies of various documents from his briefcase and laid them out before him, but oddly, did not choose to distribute them just yet. Gerald began, obviously the spokesperson for the group and the older brother. Both men were dressed in Armani suits and appeared self-assured, which initially impressed Cole. These were not amateurs, Cole thought again.

"Cole…" Gerald hesitated. "May I call you Cole?" Cole nodded. "Jacob mentioned to us that you are considering changing the direction of Hollingsworth Enterprises from a more traditional daily newspaper and publishing company to a digital one. I hear you are about to launch a smart pad that rivals Apple's, that you plan to offer entertainment, as well as news, to all of your customers, in only a way that someone with your vast network can. It seems you are well-positioned to do just that." Gerald paused. "However, there are others who are doing the same thing, and quite frankly, they may have an advantage over Hollingsworth Enterprises, since they are—how should I say it—more technologically advanced. This is where we come in." Gerald unlocked the briefcase, but stopped short of opening it. He continued.

"For the past four years, my brother and I, along with a small group of tech investors, have been developing a different way of transferring data and entertainment over the Net. We call it *Windowpanes on the World*. That's the brand name for now. We wanted to call it *Windows on the World*, but couldn't get past Microsoft's trademark on the term *Windows*. We have successfully completed prototypes for eyeglasses that are linked into the Internet and transfer anything you can get over a smartphone directly to the wearer of the glasses on a special screen. There is audio, also. Everything is wireless."

"Excuse me, Gerald," Cole interjected. "But if I'm not mistaken, Google has already developed that technology and is test-marketing it now. They're calling it *Google Glass*. My understanding is that it will come out to the mass market in the next year."

"You are absolutely correct, Cole. We've not only seen the reports and preliminary marketing strategies, but we have one of their prototypes already back at our offices. The test-market model they are offering now is being upgraded and that's why it isn't fully available to the public yet. It's very cool. We couldn't be happier that Google is pioneering the way for us. Their advertising and promotional budgets are off the charts..." Gerald's voice trailed off at the expression on Cole's face.

"Help me understand, Gerald. Why would you want Google to introduce their product before yours? Google has tremendous user loyalty, similar to Apple's. Once they corner the market, only companies like Apple and Samsung would have the resources to penetrate that market effectively. How do *you* intend to accomplish that?"

Gerald smiled. The hook was baited. "First of all, have you seen Apple's stock lately? It's falling faster than Lindsay Lohan's credibility. They're too tied up in legal disputes with Samsung over their smartphone patents. This will keep them occupied for years as they fight each other over market shares, not to mention smart pads—a market that neither company can abandon. They're too heavily invested. Meanwhile, Google will step in and make a big splash, but we predict after the initial rush to own a pair of their glasses, sales will be sluggish. And the reason why..." Gerald paused for effect. "The reason is simply price. The price point announced for introduction is somewhere between sixteen hundred and two thousand dollars per pair. Mr. and Mrs. Average Consumer can't afford that. Most people who would be interested have already invested in a smartphone and a smart pad, and the idea of coughing up another sixteen hundred dollars or more will be a tough pill to swallow. The price of *Google Glass* will not be coming down significantly for at least four years since it will take that long for Google to recoup their initial developmental costs."

"So what does that mean for us?" Cole said. Gerald secretly relished the fact that Cole had just switched his vernacular from *you* to *us*. That meant he was interested.

"What it means for us is that we have developed a very similar product that competes nicely from a feature's perspective, but is approximately half the price. We can initially offer our glasses for eight hundred ninety-nine dollars per pair, complete with the required software."

"How can you offer a similar product for that much less?" Cole replied, unconvinced.

"It's all in the development. Our product has been engineered in

China. We had the good fortune to hire a disgruntled employee from Google, who was instrumental in developing the technology. He wanted a piece of the action for his contribution, but Google blew him off, reminding him that all product development undertaken as an employee of the company was Google's property, exclusively."

"If you copy Google's design, they have every right to sue your employee and you, if there has been a breach of ethics or any stolen company technology. You could be done before you even get started. Google will find out about your product quickly, if they are not already aware of its development. There aren't too many secrets in the tech world anymore, especially with our dependence on China."

"That's the beautiful part of it, Cole. We already hold patents on our product. We've brought along copies for your review. Our employee was able to redesign the glasses so that we are not copying Google's technical patents. No one has a hold on the Internet—or eyeglasses, for that matter. You can patent certain aspects of eyeglasses, but not the concept of glasses themselves, just like you can't stop another company from introducing smart pads. Ours will not only access the Internet but will be available in both prescription and nonprescription models. With our prior knowledge of the technology, we were able to avoid the hundreds of millions of dollars in development capital required. Therefore, our prices can be significantly lower and still maintain the necessary profit margins." Gerald went quiet to allow Cole a moment to reflect on everything he had just explained. Following a lengthy silence, Cole leaned forward in his chair.

"So, what is it you want from me?"

This time Robert responded. "We need fifty million dollars in venture capital to initially launch our product in the States. Once we have attained the prerequisite sales volume to generate sufficient profit, we will launch globally."

"I thought your brother just stated that you had successfully avoided the need for a high amount of development capital. I'm confused."

"Yes, Gerald was correct in his statement. We are asking for the money primarily for advertising and promotion, along with ten million to produce the required inventory of glasses to service the initial demand. The tech companies we're working with in China require a significant amount of upfront money before they'll start production. It's just the way they do business over there." Robert picked up the stack of documents and distributed them around the table.

"I've prepared a pro forma P&L, along with a five-year sales forecast for your review. The third document outlines the costs of production and distribution. The final document contains copies of the patents. I'm confident you'll find all the documents in order. A great deal of time and effort have gone into preparing these reports. If anything, we have erred on the conservative side, so as not to over-promise results. Should you decide to invest with us, we want you to be assured that your money is in capable hands and that the return to you will be more than equitable."

Cole took a few minutes to glance through the P&L and then the sales forecast. He didn't bother to look at the production reports. That could wait. Jacob edged forward in his chair.

"Any questions, Cole?" Jacob said. Cole met Jacob's gaze.

"Only one. Why me?"

"Two reasons, really. First, I consider you to be an up-and-coming star in the communications industry. We want to work only with the best. The second reason has to do with your father. You remember how he helped me financially to build my dream company. I couldn't have done it without his assistance. I'll never forget that kindness. I want to repay the favor. I'm just sorry he didn't live to see this, but somehow, I believe he'll know. You are more like your father than you know, Cole. And I say that purely as a compliment," Jacob stated convincingly.

"And now for the pièce de résistance." Gerald opened his briefcase and carefully extracted a beautifully printed carton with full commercial graphics applied—a high-quality digital mockup of the retail package. The *Windowpanes to the World* logotype had been artfully embossed with silver foil on a backdrop of endless blue sky, containing a few scattered clouds. "Here, you open it." Gerald handed the package to Cole and the room went silent.

Cole opened the box, revealing a pair of glasses unlike any he had seen before. Gingerly, he took them out and carefully examined them. Excellent craftsmanship. He suddenly felt like he was holding the future in his hands. Something powerful. And he was getting the chance to get in on the ground floor. This was the opportunity he had been looking for, to propel the family- controlled business into the future. Maybe he wouldn't be a failure after all. It was difficult to contain his excitement, but he knew his reaction was critical. There were still many details to be negotiated before any money could change hands.

"Cole, we only have this one prototype with us today. But I would like to get you a working model in the next week or so. Our firm in China is manufacturing additional models as we speak. I'll have one delivered to you by courier with complete instructions for its operation. I'd like you and the members of your board to test it out. Then we think you will be as convinced as we are that this is a great opportunity for all of us." Gerald leaned back in his chair, confident that the pitch had been well-received. It was just a matter of time. He could see the enthusiasm in Cole's eyes.

A moment later they heard a knock on the door. Grace entered the room pushing a cart containing lunch. The aroma of fresh herbs and lemon suddenly filled the room. Warm plates of Sole Meunière set in a delicate lemon-butter sauce were placed in front of each guest, accompanied by slender strips of white asparagus and crisp, fingerling potatoes. Fresh iced tea was poured. A chocolate mousse and a pot of coffee remained on the cart.

"Just ring me when you've finished your entrées and I'll serve dessert. Enjoy!"

"Thank you, Grace. You've outdone yourself," Cole said. The guests thanked Grace in unison. Lunch was beautifully prepared, and the four men chatted about sports for a while, relieving some of the intensity of the meeting. Dessert was served, and the topic returned to the proposal.

"So, gentlemen, what does Hollingsworth Enterprises get in return for our fifty million, should we decide to invest?" Cole said. Gerald cleared his throat.

"A fifteen-percent stake in the new company and a six-percent annualized return on your initial investment. That's three million in cash per year, along with a cut of the profits and eventually stock and dividends, when we take the company public," Gerald replied confidently, as if this was a deal that could not be turned down.

"Fifteen percent seems a little scant for fifty million in capital. Let's be honest, if the new venture goes bust, we're out one hell of a lot of money. There's a fair amount of risk associated with this venture, especially with Google about to become a major player in the market. I think twenty-five percent would be more in line, which would make us all equal partners. I think I can sell that to the board." Cole went silent, as did the rest of the men in the room.

"Cole, may we have a moment alone to discuss your counteroffer?" Gerald said respectfully.

"Of course. I'll be in my office next door. Just come and get me when you've arrived at your decision." Cole excused himself.

There was really no need for a discussion, but the investors needed Cole to think there was. At this point, they would have pretty much agreed to anything to get the fifty million dollars.

What Cole did not understand was that they didn't own any patents, nor did they intend to produce mass quantities of the glasses or set up global distribution networks. The three men planned to split forty million between themselves, and deposit the money in untraceable, offshore accounts. They would invest some, or all, of the remaining ten million to produce a small number of glasses—a direct rip-off of *Google Glass*—run some promotions and advertising, just enough to get Google's attention, and then wait for the lawsuits to pile up. By then it would be too late. They wouldn't bother to defend the lawsuits; they'd simply stop production, without admitting guilt, take their product off the market, then quietly disappear onto foreign soil. Google would be delighted not to be forced to spend millions on lawyers' fees, and that would probably be the end of it. If anything, it would bring more attention to Google's products. Free publicity was never a bad thing. There would be no criminal action taken. Just another Asian knockoff that everybody was used to by now. Hollingsworth Enterprises would not be able to recoup their investment and would eventually write it off as a bad debt. Cole had simply made a bad investment and had not done the due diligence he'd needed to do upfront. It was simply a lack of experience. It would be an expensive lesson, but in the long run, it would make Cole a better businessman. For the most part, the plan was flawless—but only if they could obtain a quick agreement.

Jacob appeared in Cole's office twenty minutes later, smiling. "You drive a hard bargain, Cole, but we're in agreement. Equal partners it will be." Jacob gestured for Cole to rejoin them and then waited until Cole had exited his office before following him back into the conference room.

"It sounds like we may have a deal, at least in principle. I'll call a board meeting tomorrow," Cole said.

"Fortunately, the requisite board members are in town this week. Jacob, did you say you were leaving this Wednesday?"

"Actually, we're leaving early Thursday morning. I need to be back in Florida and attend to other business matters," Jacob replied.

The real reason, of course, was that the threesome had basically run out of money and couldn't afford the $9500.00 per day rental on the yacht, the crew, and the slip at the yacht club.

"Excellent. I hope to have an answer for you before you leave." Cole paused, as though he wanted to say something else, but refrained. "Is there anything else, gentlemen?"

"No, that should do it for now. Here's my card with my cell number and e-mail, if you should have any further questions before your board meets." Gerald handed Cole his card. "My brother and I are staying at the Newport Hyatt until Thursday, as well. We look forward to hearing from you and your team. Thanks again for your time, Cole. It was a true pleasure meeting you." Gerald reached out to shake hands. "And please call me Gerry."

Cole escorted the three men out into the main lobby, walking them to the elevator. One could almost imagine the men entering a speakeasy. The dark mahogany paneling and plush auburn- colored carpet reeked of a bygone era. Most modern corporations were housed behind metal and glass façades these days, with works of modern art hanging on walls, overlooking polished tiled floors.

"Jacob, can I have a word?" Cole said as the three men entered the elevator. Jacob turned to his business partners.

"I'll meet you downstairs in a few. Yes, Cole, what's on your mind?"

"It's Lindsay. Have you spoken to her today?"

"Only briefly, this morning. She was headed out to do some shopping, I think. We're supposed to have dinner this evening."

"Do you have her cell number? I'd like to call her and apologize for yesterday. I don't want her to get the wrong impression."

"Of course, Cole. I'm sure she'll understand once you explain." Jacob scribbled a number on his business card, then handed it to Cole. Jacob then turned, pressed the elevator button, and said nothing further. A sudden jolt of guilt shot through him. When Lindsay discovered the truth of what he and his associates were planning, he knew he could kiss any relationship with his daughter good-bye. But then, they hadn't been close for a long time. Fifty million dollars would help ease that pain, though. He entered the elevator, failing to turn and face Cole, remaining still as the door swished shut. Cole watched with a puzzled expression before turning and heading back to his office to send an e-mail to the members of the board.

After Cole pushed the send button on his computer notifying the board members of the need for a meeting tomorrow morning, Cole lingered in his office, pondering what to say to Lindsay, if she even bothered to answer his call. What had she said on Saturday night? *A truth for a truth?* Perhaps that was the best way. He now knew what her father was after—a shitload of money. But the deal seemed solid, and the group certainly had supplied ample documentation that their plan was legitimate, including certified patents, a profit-and-loss statement prepared by a reputable accounting firm, and all the facts and figures the board would want to enter into a venture like this. All incredible forgeries, which Cole couldn't see through. There was really no reason *not* to believe. Besides, he had seen the product himself. It was impressive. It was about time Hollingsworth Enterprises entered the twenty-first century.

The phone rang five times before Lindsay answered. "Hello, this is Lindsay."

"Lindsay, I'm glad I caught you. It's Cole. Is this a good time to talk?"

"What…you taking a break from the Swanson sisters? Oh, that's right, you were going to meet with my father and his investor friends today. Your little *sexcapades* will have to wait until tonight, I suppose."

"Lindsay, it didn't happen like that, honestly. I was just doing Art a favor. It was the only—"

"Cole, don't bother. I happened to see the half-naked girls take off with Art after you brought that little love boat of yours back to dock. It appears there was more to your plan than you told me, but I guess that part wasn't up for discussion Saturday night, right?" Lindsay's tone of voice was seething. Cole could feel it all the way up to his office.

"I wasn't there. I left before—"

Again, Lindsay cut him off before he could complete the sentence. "Yeah, right! And the yacht moored itself on its own. Or is your boat like your Maserati, and drives itself?" Lindsay paused. "Cole, why did you call me?"

"If you'd give me half a second, I'll tell you. Christ, you're a stubborn woman!"

Lindsay rolled her eyes sighing heavily, but refrained from interrupting again. "Okay, but please make it quick. I've got something important to do."

"You know what, it's not important after all. I called to apologize, but all of a sudden I can't remember why. Have a nice life, Lindsay." Cole slammed down the receiver, cursing.

Lindsay hit the redial icon on her phone, but it went straight to voice mail. Cole had obviously recognized her callback number and was refusing to answer. Lindsay stalked off, ill-tempered, realizing again she had been too harsh with him. She couldn't afford to alienate him further.

8

Tuesday morning at ten, six of the board members entered the main conference room to find Cole sitting at the end of the long black table. He had seven sets of documents spread around and a serious look on his face. While he basically had good relationships with the other board members, he was the prodigal's son, born with a silver spoon in his mouth. Everyone was well aware of his lifestyle, the expensive sports cars, *and* the women. Still, he had made it through Harvard Business School and had excelled in his master's program at Yale—and had captained the Harvard men's rowing team. It was hard to fake that. But Cole was not his father, and there existed an undercurrent of concern about how the soon-to-be thirty-year-old would lead the company into the future. William Gaines, the chairman of the board and acting CEO, who would normally have sat at the head of the table, acquiesced and took a seat on the side, intrigued to hear why a sudden unscheduled board meeting was necessary.

Coffee was served and idle chatter came to a halt as Cole stood, facing the group.

"Gentlemen, thank you for coming on such short notice. I know you all have busy schedules, and I wouldn't have called you here if it wasn't important." Cole glanced around the table, making direct eye contact with each member before continuing on.

"I believe you all remember Jacob Featherstone, one of my father's oldest friends and business partners." All six heads nodded. "Well, he's in town with his family and I met with him and two of his investment partners yesterday to listen to a very interesting proposal. I'll cut to the chase." Cole had often heard his father use that phrase and he decided it was appropriate now.

"His group is seeking fifty million in venture capital to introduce a visionary product to the market. A product very similar to what Google is working on. Eyeglasses that connect to the Internet."

Murmurs spread across the room at the mere mention of the Google company name. Was Cole serious? The looks of concern did not escape Cole.

"I know, I know, I was skeptical at first, too. But the more I listened, the more interesting their proposal became. They have developed a first-rate product and they hold patents of their own. Sitting before you are copies of the documents they gave me. You'll find a full accounting in their pro forma P&L, a five- year sales forecast, a detailed accounting of all production and distribution costs, and a marketing plan. Before you take the time to review everything, understand this one very important fact. Thanks to Google's extensive and costly development process, they are able to offer the product to the market at nearly half of what Google will be charging. It's really a very clever plan. They are counting on Google to market their product first, advertise the hell out of it, and after the initial rush to buy the glasses at a cost of sixteen hundred dollars or more, come out with a product that does everything Google's product does. Their price? Eight hundred ninety-nine dollars, including the software to operate the eyeglasses. Oh yeah, I almost forgot, their glasses will be offered in both prescription and nonprescription models. The prescription glasses will be priced two-hundred dollars higher."

The room suddenly went quiet. Cole sensed a remarkable change in attitude, as most of the board members began shuffling through the documents.

"Have you actually seen their product, Cole?" Mr. Gaines asked.

"Yes, they showed me a pair, along with the packaging they are considering using. It is an impressive product."

"*Windowpanes on the World?*" another board member said. "Yes, they wanted to call it *Windows on the World*, but couldn't get past Microsoft's trademarks on the word *Windows*. I still think it works, though," Cole said confidently.

"Do you have a pair of glasses you can show us?" Gaines said.

"Not yet. They couldn't leave the sample with me, but they are sending me one next week from China via courier. As soon as it arrives, I'll let everyone know."

"What do we get in return for our fifty million?" Gaines asked, and the expressions of the board members' faces hardened. This was the real issue, great product or not. Cole proceeded to fill the group in on the negotiations. The serious expressions eased substantially when they heard the terms. Cole had managed to negotiate a very favorable return on their investment, if it was successful. Cole stressed the need to "get in the game," as he phrased it. To enter the twenty-first century and become a player in the new age of information transfer. Most heads nodded as he took them through his personal vision—a vision that was shared by more than a few people at Hollingsworth Enterprises. All in all, Cole did a credible job of presenting the proposal and the opportunity before them. Gaines was impressed. Maybe this kid was more like his father than he had originally thought.

"If there are no further questions, I'll leave you to analyze the documents. Jacob and his group depart early Thursday morning. I was hoping to give him at least a handshake agreement before then. I believe the reason they couldn't leave the prototype with me is that they have another meeting scheduled to pitch their product. They know they have a winner and want to move forward as soon as possible. They simply need the money to get mass production rolling." Cole's final comments were intended to create a sense of urgency with the board. He knew from previous experience that they had a propensity to procrastinate. He also knew that, to a man, they were motivated by a singular principle: greed.

When no one presented further questions or objections, Cole thanked them for their time and walked purposely out of the conference room, wishing more than anything that he could be the proverbial fly on the wall. The conversation that would follow would be an interesting one.

9

"Jacob, it's Cole. I have good news. Are you available to meet later today?"

Jacob nearly dropped the phone and felt a sudden urge to do a jig. He knew what this meant. They were going to get the money. Not wanting to sound too relieved, he composed himself.

"What time were you thinking, Cole? I have a conference call at three o'clock, but that shouldn't take more than forty-five minutes. I'm available after that. Should I include Gerald and Robert?"

"Yes, they should definitely be present. Why don't we meet on your yacht? We'll have the privacy we need there. Say about four thirty."

"Looking forward to it. We'll see you then." Jacob hung up and immediately called the Cunningham brothers with the news. The sale had been far easier than Jacob could have hoped for. He was amazed the board was able to make such a quick decision. But then, Cole's father had always been impulsive when he wanted something. Cole must be the salesman his father was. Taking nothing for chance, the brothers would be coming over posthaste to prepare for any unforeseen details or curveballs Cole might throw at them. There were normally numerous rounds of negotiations on a deal this big.

Cole sat back in his chair, considering all that had happened during the past five days. He was about to make a mark on his father's company. If this venture was successful, it would be a coup, something not even his father had achieved at such a young age. He might even become tech's new golden boy. Everyone in the Silicon Valley would soon know his name. He was reveling in his own self-aggrandizing when his musings were cut short by the sound of his cell phone. He glanced at the number. Lindsay Featherstone. Lindsay? This was the last person he expected would be calling him. What did *she* want? Surely not to apologize. For a split second he considered not answering. But after the sixth ring, just before it went into voice mail, he pressed the button to answer.

"Hello?" An awkward silence followed.

"Cole...it's Lindsay. Do you have a minute?" Her voice sounded strained, like she hadn't slept in a while.

"Yeah, I have a minute. What's on your mind *now*?"

Lindsay ignored the obvious sarcasm. She guessed she had earned it. "I just..." She paused, struggling to get the words out. "I—I just wanted to thank you. My father told me that you're meeting with him later today and that it appeared Hollingsworth Enterprises is going to finance the deal. He also told me he believed you were responsible for convincing the board of directors to move forward. He was very impressed and..." She hesitated again. "He was *thankful*." Her final words were filled with emotion as she pulled her phone away, her eyes welling with tears. She didn't understand the details of the deal, had no idea how much money was at stake, but she knew enough to know that Cole had been taken advantage of, big-time. And that she was an accomplice to it, even though she had only played a minor role. At least her father and mother wouldn't have to worry about the bill collectors much longer. The expression on her father's face had said it all. Maybe her mother would stop drinking. Maybe...she wouldn't have to see her parents again.

"You're welcome," Cole replied in a flat tone. "It's as good a deal for us as it is for them. It's just business, that's all." Cole waited for a response, but there was only silence. "Was there something else, Lindsay?"

"No, not really." Another extended pause. "Am I still invited to your birthday party?"

Cole's mouth dropped open. "Yeah, I mean, you were never really uninvited. I'm glad you're coming. I'll add you back on the list."

"You scratched me off the list already?" Lindsay said, but there was a hint of humor back in her voice.

"Yes, along with two others. The Swanson sisters. I hear they're pretty mad at me for stealing their clothes when I left the yacht early. By the way, I never got to finish my explanation of what *really* happened. I seem to recall you wouldn't let me get a word in edgewise."

"You stole their clothes? I can't believe it. Why?"

"To teach Art a little lesson. Anyway, enough of that. I look forward to seeing you Saturday night. Until then…"

"I look forward to seeing you, too. Until then." Lindsay slowly lowered her cell phone back into her purse, emptying her glass of pinot grigio. She had needed the wine to summon the nerve to call Cole. Her father's plan having been successfully completed, it was now time to initiate her own plan—a plan that could have a far more profound and lasting effect on Cole Hollingsworth than the loss of fifty million dollars.

10

The following two days passed in relative harmony. The deal had been consummated and the money would soon be transferred to the investment group to start production of the smart glasses and begin the marketing program. The board hadn't even waited for the prototype to arrive. The offices were abuzz in anticipation of their new groundbreaking venture. No one could stop talking about it. No one could stop talking about Cole, as if he were the next Steve Jobs.

Saturday night arrived, and the birthday celebration that had weighed so heavily on Cole the previous week seemed far less threatening now. In fact, he was looking forward to it. He had decided to drive the Maserati. He figured Serena had earned "time back on" for good behavior. She hadn't talked back to him in a week. That alone was newsworthy. No matter what, it was still a thrill to drive the one-of-a-kind super car. He might even give Lindsay a little test drive, that is, if she could hold her emotional outbursts in check. He had brought a little surprise for his birthday party just for her. He smiled as he anticipated her reaction.

Cole selected a black Armani tux, with thin charcoal-gray pinstripes, from the many hanging in his closet, along with a full-length black silk tie. He always felt like a geek wearing a bow tie. He didn't much care for regular ties, either, but tonight was different. He took additional care grooming himself. By the time he reached the garage, he looked like a male model on the front cover of a fashion magazine. After going through the voice- recognition protocol that allowed entry to the Maserati, he sat in the luxurious leather driver's seat. He pushed the buttons that brought his technological wonder to life. The garage door swung open, and he eased the car outside.

Oh, Cole, you look wonderful tonight, Serena responded, with a hint of a gasp. He suddenly felt like Batman, like he was on a mission to save the world. He only wished he had a pair of the smart glasses to don when entering the Gull's Point ballroom. He cursed himself for not insisting that Featherstone send him a pair sooner. Cole revved the engine, and the angry-sounding exhaust echoed through the still night air.

Happy birthday, Cole. I'm so glad you invited me to the party, Serena quietly cooed.

"You are my favorite girl, after all. But I expect you to be on your best behavior tonight."

Of course. Aren't I always?

Cole let loose a loud snort, but said nothing in return.

The iron gates to Gull's Point Golf Club were open, guarded by three security officers. The driveway to the clubhouse was ablaze with freestanding lights that had been brought in just for the event. The parking lot was nearly full with row after row of luxury sedans and sports cars, but nothing was as impressive as Cole's Maserati. The single parking space next to the clubhouse entrance, normally reserved for the club president, had been left unoccupied tonight in honor of Cole's special day. He guided the car into the slot, and the driver's-side door automatically opened. He said good-bye to Serena, and she wished him well in return. He strode up the red carpet that led the way inside, anticipating the flood of guests that would soon be greeting him. He could do without that part. It still made him uncomfortable. He could count on one hand his true friends, and if Art was at the top of the list, he wasn't in the best shape, friend-wise.

He entered the spacious ballroom fashionably late, to an explosion of lights and burning candles. The place looked like it was on fire, the party already in full swing. Servers, decked out in designer tuxedos, balanced sterling-silver platters of sparkling champagne and elegant hors d'oeuvres. A mass of people dressed as though this were a king's coronation strolled throughout the room, smiles glued to their faces like plaster. Cole was immediately recognized, and a hush fell over the spacious entryway. Time seemed to stand still for a moment, and he felt like he was moving in slow motion. Then suddenly the room burst into applause, like he had just won an Oscar. Forcing a smile, Cole braced himself for the onslaught of well-wishers, many of whom were already scheming how they could participate in the vast inheritance that was about to change hands, as well-wishers often do.

It might have been twenty minutes, or it might have been an hour, Cole couldn't tell, as he stood shaking hands and exchanging greetings with everyone. All the members of the board of directors were on hand, accompanied by an assortment of spouses and partners. They ranged from dowdy society type wives filling in for conspicuously absent mistresses, to trophy wives, who seemed to get younger with each passing year. All facets of society, all levels of wealth and power, were well-represented tonight. Some of the guests he knew fairly well, others looked vaguely familiar, and some appeared like complete strangers. Cole suddenly wondered how he would get through the night. His jaw muscles were already beginning to ache from smiling. He popped another breath mint into his mouth.

Cole weaved his way through the lobby into the grand ballroom, a supersized version of the entryway. Tables of elegantly prepared food were situated along one side of the room, surrounded by temporary bars lined with people waiting for drinks. All refreshments and entertainment had been paid for by Hollingsworth Enterprises. On the opposite side, a stage was set up for a small orchestra, who had yet to show up. By the time the music started, Cole planned to be nowhere near the dance floor.

Outside, the swimming pool was lit with floating candles and adorned with strings of glittering lights above. More tables laden with food and an outside bar were visible through the large glass windows overlooking the manicured grounds. *That area looks safer*, Cole thought. At least he would be away from the dance floor. Just as he was about to make his move, however, the musicians begin to file into the room and take their seats. Cole continued to be besieged by guests as he edged his way outside. There was no way he'd be dancing tonight; the thought horrified him. Giving a speech was child's play; dancing was something altogether different. Waltzes and two-steps were for old people and professionals, not him. He'd stepped on enough feet already in his lifetime, and he refused to make a fool of himself again. He was far too cool for that.

Cole felt a tap on his shoulder, followed by high-pitched laughter that sounded familiar. He turned to face Art, dressed in an expensive designer tux—with a Swanson sister firmly attached to each arm. Cole's mouth dropped open. The twins were dressed in sparkling gowns of matching lime green that shimmered under the lights. Art was all smiles. His bow tie matched the color of the sisters' gowns perfectly, obviously a planned move. It suddenly occurred to Cole that the color of Art's tie was akin to a lion's urine, marking out his territory where trespassing would not be allowed.

"It's great to see you Shelby—Sidney. I'm so glad you decided to come. I thought after my little prank, well… Please accept my apologies. I don't know what came over me."

"Not to worry, buddy. It's been the talk of the town for the past week. Local TV has even been hounding the girls for the story." The twins giggled as if they were embarrassed. "A little notoriety never hurt anyone. All is forgiven," Art added and high- fived his friend, and the sisters each gave Cole a kiss on both cheeks and wished him the happiest of birthdays. Following a few minutes of polite conversation, the threesome melted into the crowd, leaving Cole standing alone, surrounded by the cream of Newport society who had suddenly appeared to have forgotten all about him.

The sound of instruments warming up filled the room. Out of the corner of his eye, Cole spotted a lone figure near the bandstand, silhouetted against the darkened windowpanes directly behind. Dressed in a simple, yet elegant gown of deep forest green that hugged her slender body, Lindsay stood staring directly back at him. Her thick auburn hair fell to her bare shoulders like a waterfall reflecting the sunset. A necklace of shimmering bronze metal adorned her slender neck. She stood in silence, gazing at Cole, as if her eyes possessed the power of a zoom lens, drawing him closer and closer into focus. Before he realized it, he found himself walking in her direction, as though propelled by an invisible force.

A moment later he was standing a few feet in front of her, their eyes locked in an intense gaze. She smiled then suddenly turned, pointing to the silver stripper's pole stationed at the left of the bandstand.

"I see you were expecting me." She laughed fetchingly.

"I thought it might come in handy, so I had it specially ordered for you…just in case," Cole teased.

"Is that what you want for your birthday, Cole?" Lindsay replied seductively.

Her question momentarily stunned him. She was actually being serious. He saw the conviction in her slate-colored eyes. Cole choked, covering up his inability to respond. Normally when a beautiful woman said something like this, he had a hundred comebacks, but tonight was different. The rest of the room seemed to fade away, dissolving into a faint haze. All that remained was Lindsay— mesmerizing, intoxicating. For an instant he became confused. There was something else in her eyes; a beckoning, a hidden truth? He couldn't tell exactly what, but he couldn't look away. At that moment all he wanted was Lindsay. But for what reason? Was it for sex, or was it something else? The answer eluded him.

"I think we'll leave the pole-dancing to the Swanson sisters. By the way, have you seen them tonight?" Cole said.

"How could I miss them? Art certainly looked full of himself. I assume you're all on speaking terms again?" Lindsay asked matter-of-factly, as if the answer to her question meant nothing to her.

"More or less. At least until the next disaster happens. It's only a matter of time. If you stay around long enough, you'll see."

"I don't plan on staying that long, Cole." Lindsay's tone turned solemn. They eyed each other in silence. *What is it she wants?* Cole wondered. *Why is she being so mysterious?*

"What is it you're not telling me? I feel like you're hiding something again. Like you want to tell me but you're afraid," Cole said.

Lindsay's eyes darkened. "Listen, Cole, I know you have obligations to fulfill tonight, which *will* include dancing, by the way." She paused at Cole's startled expression. "I saw the way you were looking at the band and the dance floor. Remember, you admitted to me last Saturday night that you're a lousy dancer. I'd be willing to bet my last dollar that you're afraid to be embarrassed. But that's not the point. When all the toasts have been made and the party is winding down, meet me outside by the fountain. Then we can talk."

Before Cole could respond, Lindsay was striding away out the back door, disappearing into the darkness. Cole stood for a long moment, perplexed. It was only after the chairman of the board tapped him on the shoulder that Cole came back to reality.

"Good evening, Cole," Bill Gaines said. "You remember my wife, Sonya?" Cole squinted at the statuesque blonde. It had been some time, at least some time since he'd seen the CEO with *this* particular woman.

"Yes, of course. Sonya, it's wonderful to see you. It *has* been a long time. Thank you for making the trip."

Sonya smiled, flashing perfect teeth that somehow seemed to fit her perfect body—neither of which had been a stranger to the medical miracles of reconstructive surgery. Sonya lived in Beverly Hills most of the year and could have been a poster child for the area, only she wasn't exactly a *child* any longer. Bill had divorced his first wife after a tumultuous affair with the aspiring actress- model. Sonya had never really made it in Hollywood, at least not on the silver screen, but she had hit the jackpot with Gaines, an independently wealthy businessman who had a propensity for travel. She had the perfect life. She lived and played where she wanted, surrounded by admiring friends. Yes, she was forced to overlook the occasional dalliance of her husband. But then, all powerful men had dalliances. Bill visited their mansion four or five times a year, when he grew tired of the East Coast or Europe.

"Well, Cole, we have more than your thirtieth birthday to celebrate tonight. I was just telling Sonya about the new smart glasses we're about to launch. This couldn't have come at a better time. We needed to hit a homerun and you've done it. Your father would be very proud. By the way, when are we going to get some samples? People have been hounding me to get their hands on one."

Cole grimaced, again silently cursing Jacob for not sending him a pair straightaway. "We should be getting samples in the next week. I sent an e-mail to Jacob this morning asking him to expedite the shipment."

"Good. I look forward to receiving a pair. I'm surprised they didn't have more available when you met. Didn't you find that a bit odd?"

"Yes, and no. They had no idea whether we would be interested or not. They did have other meetings scheduled to pitch the technology. They only had the one prototype with them and probably didn't feel comfortable leaving it with us, or with anyone else for that matter, until all the details of a deal had been inked," Cole replied, yet something in Bill's question unnerved him. Now that he thought about it, it did seem unusual.

"If you say so. Enjoy the evening, Cole. You deserve it." That said, Mr. and Mrs. Gaines turned to face a small group of friends. Sonya gave Cole a quick hug and the pair disappeared into the crowd, again leaving Cole to stand by himself, wondering.

The rest of the evening was a series of instant replays: an assortment of people coming up, smiling, offering congratulations, and then abruptly leaving to spend time with others. Cole realized he had little in common with the majority of these people. He rarely socialized or ever spent quality time with them. It was mostly business or a polite exchange at one of the various functions he was obligated to attend. He had his golfing buddies, a couple of people at the office he'd occasionally grab a beer with after work, and Art. The long line of women he had shared nights with were mostly a fleeting memory, made hazy by excessive alcohol consumption. Here he was, surrounded by a crowd of glamorous and successful people, and yet he had never felt quite so alone.

The obligatory toasts and roasts were made—all predictable—a few old stories shared about his father, and then the music began in earnest. As the dance floor filled, Cole made his move. Grabbing a Scotch, he navigated his way through the crowd, past the band, and out the side doors. A scattering of people was still outside talking, but the night had grown chilly and most were headed back inside. Glancing around, Cole noticed a single figure standing at the highest point of the outside deck, gazing out to the darkened ocean beyond. A pale light from a waning moon filtered through the clouds, casting an eerie glow. Lindsay looked more like a statue, or a water feature, or some sort of mythical sea goddess, than a real-life person. Her slender form remained motionless, her long hair blown about by the stiffening breeze coming off the ocean. If he didn't know better, he might have thought she was emitting her own faint form of light.

Before Cole could call out to her, she turned and reached out both of her hands, beckoning him to join her. He was drawn to her in a way he had never been drawn to a woman before. It was as if she commanded an invisible power over him, and still, he could not identify its source. It felt like a combination of sexual desire, mystery, and a strange sense of respect for who she was, what she had become—how she had managed to change herself into a seemingly new person. In that moment, Cole realized he didn't know her at all. She had become an enigma to him.

Cole approached Lindsay's still-outstretched hands. He took hold of them as she smiled ruefully up into his face. He felt a cold shiver shoot up his back, like a spike of electricity had suddenly shocked him. And for the first time in a very long time, he felt cold fear.

11

Cole and Lindsay stood gazing at each other in silence, as the surf pounded against the shoreline in loud, angry bursts. It sounded like thunder booming, followed by the hissing of a thousand giant vipers as the white foam subsided, snaking its way back to oblivion and hiding the secrets that lay beneath. Secrets that Cole had no idea existed.

Lindsay remained silent, turning to look out toward the ocean again, her expression unremitting. Then it hit Cole like a tidal wave. Lindsay and the ocean were somehow connected. This had been the missing piece of the puzzle that made her seem so mysterious. How he knew this, he could not say, only that he knew it to be true. He had sensed the same connection in the early morning hours after their night together at Grinder's Beat. The salt-tinged breeze had seemed to renew her somehow.

Her hands suddenly felt like quicksilver in his, like she might slip away any second, liquefying and returning to the sea. He grasped her hands more securely, terrified he might lose her. Her palms felt wet, the faint smell of salt water emanating from her body. Lindsay's gaze returned to Cole, her slate-colored eyes turning black, matching the color of the water beyond. She smiled again but differently this time, as if to say, *your beginning to understand, aren't you?*

The silence passing between them spoke volumes. Cole saw

in those eyes an unfathomable depth of knowledge, of dark secrets untold—like portals to another dimension of understanding.
Mesmerized, Cole found himself unable to speak, unable to express
what he was feeling. All he could see were her eyes, drawing him
closer and closer until they scorched his own. For an instant everything went blank and he was temporarily blind, as an image began to
materialize out of deep shadows. Breathless, Cole stood spellbound,
as the images in the recurring nightmare of his parents' death appeared like an apparition before him. They stood facing Cole, pleading with their son to save them as the herculean waves crashed down,
splintering their wooden yacht into fragments.

"No!" Cole screamed. "This can't be happening!" He knew he was
awake and yet, somehow reliving his tortuous dream. How could
Lindsay know? How could she have conjured the terrifying images
that haunted his dreams? His heart raced at breakneck speed, his
breathing becoming irregular. He felt like he would pass out any
second if he didn't escape this place. He tried to run, but stood para-
lyzed, unable to move, imprisoned in a living nightmare. Rapidly
losing all sensation of connection to his body, all that remained was a
nebulous state of consciousness—a single thought of how he should
have been there to save his parents. They had begged him to come
on the trip, to get away from the countless one-night stands and
drunken escapades that had become his life. They told him family
time was what he needed— time to discuss his inheritance, time
to talk about the future. They wanted so badly to help, but he had
refused their offer, caught up in himself and the never-ending party
that only his family's wealth could sustain. And now...now they
were dead and Lindsay was forcing him to relive the tragedy. Would
he ever escape it?

Cole struggled to break free of her grasp, desperately wanting
to escape her clutches—to run back to his house on the cliffs and
drink himself into obscurity. He wanted nothing of his inheritance;

he wanted nothing more to do with Hollingsworth Enterprises. He wanted only to forget, to pray that the pain would vanish. He was shaking, sobbing uncontrollably as he felt Lindsay's grip loosening. She wrapped her long arms around his neck, drawing him close. She held him until his shaking subsided, and for a moment his pain was gone.

"There's still a chance to save them, Cole," she whispered in his ear. It sounded at first like an echo from a far-off voice, dreamlike. She hadn't really said that, he was just imagining it, a fleeting moment of hopefulness. Then she said it again.

He pushed away from her, wondering what sort of evil game she was playing. Had she finally found a way to get back at him for all of the taunts and mean-spirited pranks Cole and his friends had played on her during their school days? Was this just another method of torturing him before she left his life forever? He stared at Lindsay in utter disbelief, slowly regaining his composure and preparing to confront her. His face flushed with anger; his body back in his own control.

"Did you just say what I thought you said?" Cole replied incredulously. "You think my parents can be resurrected somehow?" He scoffed at the mere suggestion of it. "How can you be so cruel?"

"Yes, Cole, you heard me correctly. There's still a chance." Lindsay's ethereal appearance abruptly vanished. She now appeared dead-serious. "But there's precious little time left. We should leave at once. In fact, we must leave this morning. I've made all the arrangements."

Cole's mouth gaped. This was madness! Leave for where? He couldn't possibly leave in a couple of hours, or any other time for that matter. He was on the brink of one of the biggest product launches in the history of the company, and he wasn't about to defect and go on a wild goose chase to search for his dead parents. *Yes, they are dead. You can't bring people back to life*, Cole pondered.

"Lindsay, this is ridiculous. You can't be serious." Cole paused.

"Why are you doing this to me? You know I just invested fifty million with your father and his business partners. We'll be starting production in a matter of weeks. We have to start our marketing campaign on Monday morning, and this business deal will take all of my time for the next year, at least."

Lindsay turned away, unable to face him. The sudden change in her demeanor startled Cole. What was she thinking now? Her mood swings seemed endemic. One moment she was Lindsay Featherstone, and in the blink of an eye, she was someone—or something— totally different. Perhaps she was schizophrenic—a psychopath. That would explain a lot. Only a mentally ill person could believe they could actually bring his parents back to life.

"Cole, there is nothing left for you here. I mean, yes, you'll soon have a tremendous amount of money of your own, but…" Her voice trailed off. She just couldn't tell him. She couldn't shatter his world, especially tonight, when he was in the spotlight, his apparent success with the new venture a shining example of his coming of age. But it was an example built on a house of cards that would all come crashing down around him. She turned away again.

"What do you mean, there's nothing left for me here? There's everything left, can't you see that? And I was hoping that maybe you'd like to be a part of it, too."

Tears welling in her eyes, she turned back to face him. "I can't, Cole. You don't understand and…and I just can't tell you everything right now. I gave my solemn promise. All I can ask is for you to trust me, about your parents, I mean." She wiped her eyes, overcome with emotion. How could she tell him that her father had blatantly stolen fifty million dollars from him? Had lied and connived and unabashedly taken a fortune from the family who had supported him all of his adult life. She suddenly felt sick to her stomach.

"What is it you're not telling me, Lindsay?" Cole's tone was softer now at the look of anguish on her face. He had always been a sucker for women in distress, although he did his best to hide that side of himself. It was bad for his playboy image—a sign of weakness.

"Please, Cole, don't tell me anymore about your business or your future in it. I came here for one reason and one reason only. To convince you that mysteries exist, well beyond your current understanding. There is life after death. My doctoral thesis postulated it, and recent experiences have confirmed it. And now…now I can prove it. Come with me, Cole, and allow me to show you things you could never have imagined."

"You *are* crazy, Lindsay! I was beginning to really like you. But you've gone too far. I'm sorry, but I can't help you prove your theory. You'll just have to find another way." Cole turned and was about to head back inside when he felt a strong grip on his shoulder.

"You're the only one who can." Lindsay's voice was weak but determined. "Please, Cole, help me."

Cole stopped dead in his tracks at the sound of the helplessness—or was it desperation in her voice, but he refused to turn to face her.

"Why me?"

"I need money to continue my research, and you're the only person I know who has enough. I also know what your parents' disappearance is doing to you." She stopped short of using the word *death*. "I can see it in your eyes. I felt it at dinner last weekend. It's constantly with you. It stalks you. The feeling is so pervasive that at times it practically immobilizes you. That's the reason I was able to summon those images in your mind only moments ago. I want, as much as anything, to purge you of your guilt."

Stunned by Lindsay's brutal honesty and insightfulness into his soul—whatever that *soul* was, he had little understanding of it— Cole struggled with a reply. He stood for a moment, mystified. How could this woman he hadn't seen in thirteen years know him so well?

"Guilt? Why should I feel guilt?" Cole said.

"I think you know why, Cole. Do I really need to say it out loud?"

"How did you make me see those images?" Cole said, accusation in his voice.

"I hypnotized you, without you knowing it. It's a little trick I learned back at school. I then mentioned your parents and told you to remember. That's all it took. I'm not sure exactly what you saw, but the look of terror on your face was undeniable."

"So, it's money you need. This really isn't about my parents, is it? At least you could be honest about it," Cole replied. It really wasn't what he had wanted to say, but he couldn't allow himself to become that vulnerable to her. He could not confide that he would give up every dollar of his inheritance to see his parents one more time, if only to explain his arrogant behavior. To say good-bye. To find peace.

"Yes, Cole, it is about money, at least to some degree. I'm at a crossroads. While there are people who believe in my theory, there are many who think like you do. That it's preposterous, so they will no longer help financially. But I won't let the naysayers distract me. I know I'm right." Lindsay hesitated. "But I'm doing this for another reason, too. I'm doing this for you and for your parents. I feel…um, I feel that I owe it to you. You will understand in time."

"How can I think your theory is preposterous or not, when I don't even understand what you're talking about? You've left one little thing out. What is it, exactly, that your theory postulates?"

It was now or never. They had arrived at a point of no return, to an impasse that must be successfully traversed. She knew she'd only have one chance to convince him.

"Are you familiar with the theory of abiogenesis? That life was formed in the primordial soup at the bottom of the earth's oceans and spread onto land through the evolutionary process?"

Cole nodded. "I read something about it in one of my science classes at school. But I never paid much attention to it. Where life began has never really interested me that much. There are so many convoluted opinions and theories and they all get mixed up in eso-teric religious beliefs. I prefer to think about how to live one's life now rather than how it all began."

Lindsay suppressed a serious urge to lash out at Cole for his shallowness, but bit her tongue. She needed to remain cool and in charge of this conversation.

"Okay, I get that. Most people feel the same way. The concepts of the creation of life, and life after death are so abstruse that it can be difficult to get your head around them. If we can separate religious ideology from scientific fact, the evidence of such a theory is quite overwhelming. When we finally see through the veneer, there is a beautiful logic to it. And to a large degree, science and religion do go hand in hand, that is, once we free ourselves from the hypocrisy of it all." Lindsay began to describe abiogenesis in more detail, while Cole listened patiently—until he had finally heard enough.

"Lindsay, slow down. I get it, okay? Yes, the theories you just de-scribed make sense, at least on some level, but I still don't understand how this affects me, or relates to my parents' deaths?"

"I was getting to that. Your parents' yacht sank near the Caribbean, right? In an area historically referred to as the Bermuda Triangle..."

Cole raised his hands, cutting Lindsay off in midsentence. "I've heard enough. You're not going to tell me my parents' yacht was swallowed up by the Bermuda Triangle, are you? Come on, that's only a myth, some kind of legend made up to scare people. It's a rough part of the ocean with strong currents, that's all."

"I'm not trying to tell you that. There *is* no actual Bermuda Triangle, at least not as it's been described in the media or in novels. I just told you that the underlying premise of abiogenesis is based on a combination of ammonia, methane, and hydrogen, exposed to highly charged energy in a reducing atmosphere that existed in pri-mordial earth. This process transformed those basic elements into more complex amino acids, the building blocks of life, and thus living matter was created from inert materials. It's kind of like a big kettle of soup that's been exposed to extreme heat. It changes the various ingredients into something else, something that is much more complex than a single ingredient. You could say it is not unlike cooking."

"Yes, I basically understood that part of your explanation, but I still don't see—"

"Cole, if you would just be quiet for a moment and listen, you might better understand!" Lindsay said determinedly. Cole went quiet, looking wounded. He had had about enough, but he didn't want to appear ignorant. He gestured with his hand for Lindsay to continue.

"The area known as the Bermuda Triangle was very different in prehistoric times. That part of the ocean was a perfect melting pot for the various elements I just described. It also contains thermal vents deep under the ocean. As the earth was forming, approximately three and a half billion years ago, the sun's energy was much more directly focused on our planet. The earth's full atmosphere had not yet been formed. In essence, the first forms of life were created deep in the ocean. That's what has been referred to as the primordial soup. And to this day, that part of the ocean contains the same elements that created life in the first place, only they exist in a more dormant state now."

"Okay, Lindsay, you've convinced me. I'm a believer in abiogenesis. So what?"

"You're missing the point..." Lindsay hesitated for a long moment. "Maybe I'm going about this the wrong way. You asked me about my thesis. It uses the theory of abiogenesis as its foundation. What I'm postulating is that life *after* death, whatever is left when our bodies die, returns to the sea. Our souls don't go to heaven or hell. Neither exists. It's kind of like purgatory, but in a nonreligious sense. The afterlife force of each of us spends time there until we are absorbed back into the fabric of life itself. Into the living earth, we return from where we originated. This force sustains all life on this planet. It contains the knowledge base driving the human race to advance. It is the sum total of all of our experiences ..." Lindsay stopped at the look of disbelief on Cole's face.

"What I'm trying to tell you, Cole, is that your parents are there. And I believe there is a way to save them. I know this sounds like science fiction, but it's real. I've spent the past two years doing extensive research in that area in deep-sea submersibles, including a forty-million-dollar bathyscaphe, named the *Deepsea Challenger*. You may have heard of it when the movie director James Cameron set the record for the deepest manned dive to the bottom of the Mariana Trench in March 2012. Well, I've been deeper than that. I unofficially hold the record. But I prefer that not to be public knowledge, at least at this point. I've seen things—" Lindsay abruptly stopped, realizing that if she wasn't careful, anything else she might say would likely persuade Cole to turn and run. She couldn't afford to let him escape now.

The lights inside the ballroom had gone dark. Suddenly, a mourning dove landed on the adjacent fountain, bobbing its head up and down and staring directly at Cole.

"Look!" Lindsay gasped. "A mourning dove. It's a sign. They represent truth, you know. Isn't it beautiful?" She moved closer, stroking its neck. The dove cooed, remaining stationary as if mesmerized by Lindsay, too.

Cole glanced over, startled to see the first rays of sunlight emerging over the horizon, like the fire of lava flow from atop a distant volcano. Twice in one week they had spent the night talking until sunrise. Lindsay looked even more beautiful in the pale glow of morning light. The dove fluttered away. Cole gazed at her in amazement, then remembered that he hadn't even bothered to say good night or thank his guests. What must they be thinking?

"It's too late," Lindsay uttered. "I'm sure your guests will understand. They know what a flake you can be." She laughed, and for maybe the first time since they had reconnected, the sound of her laughter was as warm and real as the rising sun.

Shocked that Lindsay could apparently read his mind, Cole was about to rebuke her comment, when he was drawn to the smile on her face. He melted just a little. How could he remain mad at her? She had been as honest as anyone had ever been with him, with the possible exception of his mother. She seemed sincere in wanting to help him resolve the death of his parents, even if she really couldn't do anything about it. What the hell—he needed to get away. During the course of the evening, against his better judgment, he had decided to play along. A trip to the Caribbean sounded like a nice reprieve. The staff at the office could handle the initial details of the new product launch—that's what he paid them good money to do. There was always e-mail to help keep in touch for the short time he'd be away. Besides, the thought of sand, sun, tropical drinks, and Lindsay in a bikini sounded a whole lot better than sales forecasts and financial documents. He'd have the rest of his life to deal with those.

"When do we leave?" Cole said.

"We leave in four hours. Now, let's get out of here before you change your mind!"

12

Cole placed Lindsay's overnight bag in the cramped trunk of the Maserati and set off for his house. The couple was immediately greeted by Serena, who sounded sleepy. Maybe she was programmed to sound that way at five thirty in the morning.

Did you enjoy your party, Cole? Serena sounded as if she were yawning. *You must have, considering the time of morning it is. I see you've brought along a companion. I hope you'll introduce me.*

Lindsay let loose a squeak, or was it a gasp? Cole wasn't sure. "This car talks to you?" Lindsay said, astounded.

"Yes, and sometimes she talks too much!"

Just being sociable, Cole, Serena replied.

"Okay, you win. This is Lindsay Featherstone. She's the daughter of my father's friend, Jacob Featherstone. We had dinner last weekend at Breeder's."

Oh, so that's where you went after you grounded me. Hello, Lindsay, it's nice to meet you. I've heard all about you.

"How, when…what did you hear?" Lindsay replied, casting an astonished look at the dashboard.

Cole likes to talk while he's driving. You know, organize his thoughts, practice speeches, talk about women.

"So, what did he say about me?"

He said you infuriate him, just like I do. Serena paused. *I think we're going to be fast friends, you and I.*

"That's enough, Serena. You promised me last night you were going to be on your best behavior. Or don't you remember?"

That was last night, Cole. Today is a new day. Serena laughed.

Cole cursed under his breath, while Lindsay did her best to suppress her laughter. This was some kind of car after all. Cole hit Ocean Avenue and stepped down hard on the accelerator. The road was basically deserted this early in the morning. The car took off like a rocket, and in less than three seconds they were cruising at eighty miles an hour.

"What's your hurry, Parnelli? Slow down," Lindsay instructed.

This is how Cole acts when he's grouchy. Spoiled little boy. You'll see, Serena declared, as if she knew Cole better than anyone else.

"That's enough!" Cole admonished. "Lindsay, I thought you said we only had a couple of hours until we leave. I'm assuming we're taking a flight out of Green Airport near Providence. That's about an hour's drive from here, so that doesn't give us much time. I need to shower and pack and send out some e-mails so people know I'm not showing up for work tomorrow morning."

"You won't need to take that much with you. Just a few changes of clothes. Make sure to include shorts and swim trunks. We can rent everything else we'll need when we get there. I forgot to mention, we won't be taking a commercial flight. We'll be flying on your corporate jet. It's already on standby at Newport State Airport, so we're close," Lindsay replied.

"What? How did you accomplish that little feat? Our pilots only take their orders from a few designated people within the company."

"Oh, you'd be surprised at what a little flirting can do. It goes a long way. Men are so naïve," Lindsay said.

Serena laughed again. Cole wanted to punch Serena, then realized it would only cause damage to the car and probably to his hand, as well.

"Women!" Cole bellowed, unable to come up with anything appropriate, and both women burst out laughing.

So, where are we off to, Cole? Serena asked.

"*We* are off to nowhere. You're grounded again. Lindsay and I are going to the Caribbean for a little R-and-R."

"That's not very nice of you, Cole. Serena was just kidding. Lighten up," Lindsay said.

That's what I keep telling him. But you know how he is, Serena replied, sounding the least bit disgusted.

"Alright, you're not grounded. But no unmanned trips while I'm gone. I heard about the last time I left town. You were spotted driving alone on Shoreline Boulevard with the windows down and the radio blaring. Fortunately, I knew the cop that spotted you and he knew enough about the car to leave you alone. He did make sure you made it home safely, then sent an e-mail to my office."

That son of a bit—

"Serena!"

Lindsay couldn't believe what she was hearing. What a car! She could spend all day in it. This was the best form of entertainment she'd had in some time.

"I wish we could take Serena with us," Lindsay said. "Can she swim?"

"No, she can't *swim,*" Cole replied mockingly. "But I'm thinking about giving her a chance. Would you like that, Serena? How about a little dive off the cliff? I bet you'd do a great impression of a swan dive."

Serena remained mute. Fortunately, they had arrived at the driveway to Cole's house. Cole guided the car up the winding road and into the garage. Exiting the car, Cole turned back.

"I'll talk to you later, Serena."

Serena said nothing.

"It was lovely to meet you, Serena. I hope I'll see you again," Lindsay said.

It was lovely to meet you, too. When you get bored with the old grump, contact Bill Herndon. He's chief of security for this house. Bill's cell phone number flashed on the dashboard video screen. *He'll get word to me and I'll come pick you up at the airport, and then we'll have some real fun.*

Cole slammed the door. Lindsay couldn't contain her laughter, which only added to Cole's frustration. She patted the Maserati on the hood and walked silently behind its owner into the house on the cliff. This car was worth every penny Cole had spent on it. He had finally met his match in wits…and then some.

While Cole cleaned up and changed, Lindsay gazed out the thick plate-glass window hanging on the edge of the cliff, watching the restless sea churning below. It would only be a matter of hours until she could join with it again. This she would need to do in private. She wondered if she would ever stand here again, in this famous *Lighthouse* that Cole had built. At least she'd had the opportunity to see it. And she had taken a ride in the Maserati—a once-in-a-lifetime experience for people like her. She smiled as she recalled everything Serena had said. Perhaps Serena was in love with Cole, too. How ironic. It was always the men who loved their cars, not the other way around. Lindsay couldn't allow herself to become distracted, though. The idyllic life that all of this portended was only a fairy tale. She was a scientist, a researcher, a seeker of deeper truths. She didn't have the luxury of falling in love and settling down. This could not possibly be the life for her.

She noticed an unusual-looking book lying on a glass table to the right of a white leather chair. It looked to be very old, with a cracked binding, the edges of the pages lined in gold filigree. She approached for a closer look and was stunned to see the author's name: Dante Alighieri. This had to be one of a handful of fourteenth-century original copies of Dante's *The Divine Comedy: Inferno*, an epic poem describing the nine levels of hell. She couldn't imagine Cole owning a book like this, let alone having it on display in his house.

She turned around, only to see Cole standing there, silently watching her from the far end of the living room. *How long has he been there, watching me?* she wondered. For a fleeting moment, he looked like a boy again, his eyes full of wonder, of hope. And yet there existed an enduring sadness in those eyes. What was he thinking? Did he believe her theory, or was he just going along to placate her? Was he hoping to ultimately get her in bed? Was this just another vacation for him—an extended one-night stand? Who was Cole Hollingsworth, really?

"Interesting choice of book," Lindsay finally said. "Why this one?"

"It keeps me grounded, you know, so I won't fall off the cliff into total debauchery."

Lindsay smirked, a distinct hint of sarcasm in her next words. "So, what level are you on?"

Instead of answering her question directly, he looked over at the portrait of his parents hanging above the fireplace, the glow of soft firelight illuminating their faces. His mother would have passed quickly through the levels to paradise. She was a saint. His father— well, that was another story. Cole hadn't read the translation of the poem for many years, but wasn't there something about avarice and pride, something to do with the seven deadly sins? If so, his father would be mired deep within the confines of suffocating darkness, anguishing. Cole turned back to Lindsay.

"I suppose I'm somewhere in the middle. And here you stand on the threshold to save all of us," Cole replied surreptitiously. "It must be something to bear that sort of responsibility." At the look in Lindsay's eyes, Cole immediately wished he could take that statement back.

"It's time to go, I think," Lindsay said, breaking the intense connection between them. Lindsay wondered what Cole was thinking about her. He was most likely thinking she was some whacked-out smart girl who had nothing better to do than traipse around the globe on other people's money. How would Cole react when he found out that her father had fleeced his company for a fortune? What would he think of her then? She shuddered at the thought.

"What's wrong, Lindsay?"

"Nothing. I'm just a little nervous, I guess. This is a really big step. I don't want to disappoint you."

"You won't disappoint me, Lindsay. I'm actually intrigued by your theories. And I have a fondness for the tropics. Everything seems more intense down there. The moon and stars appear closer, the colors brighter. The food tastes better. And then there's the rum. The best I've ever had."

"You've spent a lot of time in that region of the world?"

"Yeah, I guess you could say that. It relaxes me. I've often thought about building a home down there, but my responsibilities won't allow me to live there permanently, even with all of the technology that exists today. The virtual workplace doesn't apply to me." Cole almost sounded sincere.

Lindsay attempted to squelch the sudden image of her and Cole lying on a secluded beach together, drinking rum and making love. An uncomfortable silence lingered. It was as if they both knew that once they took a step outside of Cole's house there would be no turning back.

13

A sleek, black limousine was waiting outside ready to whisk them away to Newport State Airport. Both of the Hollingsworth private jets shared a hangar there. Newport State was a smaller airport with less traffic and home to aviation enthusiasts and private jets. Half an hour later they arrived, and the driver helped them carry their luggage over to the Dassault Falcon 7X, the smaller of the two company jets. The Boeing Business Jet 2 had been Cole's father's personal aircraft and contained a master bedroom, a boardroom, and an executive suite. Somehow Cole felt uneasy traveling in it, the tragedy of his parents' death was still too fresh in his mind. The plane reminded him of the many trips they'd taken together, the arguments they'd had while onboard, the tension that laced between them ever-present.

Frank Martin was standing alongside the Falcon, dressed in a formal pilot's uniform. His copilot and attendant were at his side, ready to take the couple's carry-on bags aboard. Their smiles appeared well-rehearsed as they greeted their boss. Cole introduced Lindsay to the crew. Lindsay shook hands with everyone while winking at Frank, as if their little secret would remain a secret.

Once they were aboard and seated, the jet's three turbofans fired to life—their high-pitched roar dampened from intruding too harshly into the main cabin. The jet taxied onto the runway as Frank communicated with the tower. With only one plane ahead of them, their wait would be minimal. Inside the dimly lit cabin, portholes on each side filtered in outside light like laser beams. The attendant was seated in a separate chair near the door to the cockpit, where the two pilots sat. Soft New Age music drifted in from invisible speakers. Every detail of the interior spoke of luxury, down to the brass handles and polished mahogany paneling. Frank's voice crackled over the loudspeakers, drowning out the music.

"Please prepare for takeoff. Our flight time will be approximately five hours and thirty minutes."

A sudden surge, like the beginning of a roller coaster ride, sent a wave of butterflies through Lindsay's stomach. Although she had been on her share of flights over the years, she much preferred traveling by boat; it felt more grounded to her. She could stand outside and smell the salty air and feel the breeze in her face. On a plane, the sky was her ocean and there was nothing between her and a thirty-five-thousand-foot drop to the ground below. Cole noticed the knuckles of her hands turn white as she gripped the armrests tightly. The jet gained altitude quickly. Lindsay remained quiet, gazing straight ahead until the craft had leveled off and the *Remove Seat Belt* sign flashed on. The attendant unbuckled and approached the couple.

"Would either of you like a beverage?" he asked politely. "Food service will begin in forty-five minutes."

Lindsay didn't require persuading. Her frazzled nerves needed calming.

"I'll have a vodka and tonic," Lindsay replied. "Heavy on the vodka, please."

"How boring," Cole interrupted, as though Lindsay was incapable of ordering for herself. "This is supposed to be a vacation, remember? We're headed to the tropics," Cole said, attempting to camouflage the truth behind their trip. "Rodney, please bring us a couple of Mai Tai's."

"Coming right up, Mr. Hollingsworth." Rodney departed into the service area.

"This is not a vacation, Cole. You know that," Lindsay exclaimed in a hushed tone. She didn't want Cole to get the wrong idea.

"I know that, but the crew doesn't. I don't think it would be a particularly good idea for them to know what we're really up to, do you?"

Lindsay shook her head and sat back in her seat. Cole was right, of course. No one would believe them, and if the truth got out, it would start an avalanche of rumors. Anything to do with the death of Cole's parents, and the reporters appeared out of the woodwork, anxious for one more tidbit they could speculate on about what the young heir might be up to with his newfound billions. The media would like nothing better than to hear that Cole and a mysterious female oceanographer were off diving to the depths of the ocean floor searching for the victims of Cole's family tragedy. Hell, Cole didn't even know that yet. It was up to her to lead him along one step at a time.

"By the way, Lindsay, how did you really get this whole thing set up and convince Frank to be at the ready? What if I hadn't agreed to come?"

Lindsay hesitated; she'd been hoping this question wouldn't resurface. "I told your pilot that this was a surprise birthday gift for you. You were about to take over the presidency of the company and needed one more getaway before all of that responsibility came crashing down on top of you. I think he understood that." Again, Lindsay wavered. "I also promised him there would be a nice personal bonus for him if everything went as planned."

"I assume the *personal* bonus would be coming from my checkbook? Never mind, don't answer that. If we hadn't shown up and the crew had been coerced into working on their day off without receiving any bonus pay, don't you think Frank would have been the tiniest bit upset?"

"I suppose so, but…" Lindsay's voice trailed off.

"But what?"

"I had it covered. And here we are. I think we've discussed this topic sufficiently, don't you?" Lindsay smiled apologetically.

"Not quite. I'd like to know how you had it *covered…*"

"Okay…alright. I told Frank that if you were a no-show, then he could collect, um, another form of payment. He jumped at the suggestion. I think he was actually hoping you wouldn't come." Lindsay smirked. Cole's eyebrows rose and his face flushed.

"You *little* tramp! How dare you try to seduce my pilot."

"Oh, that's rich! Listen to you, the king of seduction." Just as their exchange was growing heated, Rodney returned with the drinks, balanced on a silver platter and accompanied by a bowl of Macadamia nuts. He handed the bowl-shaped crystal glasses to the pair with a linen napkin for each, then placed the bowl of tropical nuts on a center table between the two seats. The drinks were adorned with fresh chunks of ripe pineapple and miniature umbrellas on top.

Lindsay extended her glass as if to make a toast. "Truce?" she said.

"Truce," he said, but didn't look altogether convinced. While sipping his drink, Cole wondered whether Lindsay would have made good on her promise of payment to the pilot if he had refused to make the trip. The odds had been against him coming, she must have known that. That would have made great watercooler gossip back at the office. He could just hear it: *Cole's personal pilot hustles away Cole's mysterious and beautiful companion, after he fails to show up for a scheduled flight. No doubt drunk again.*

Cole pulled the tiny umbrella from his glass and placed it on the table, determined to get her back for that little dig. He had seen in her expression a fair amount of pleasure at his poorly disguised jealousy over the thought of her and Frank frolicking in bed together.

"Lindsay, since you've spent a lot of time in the tropics, you probably know the legend about miniature umbrellas in tropical drinks?" He picked up the toy and twirled it between two fingers, allowing their gazes to linger. Lindsay looked surprised.

"No, I can't say I'm familiar with that legend. I, unlike you, spent most of my time there doing scientific research, not lying on the beach drinking and ogling all the coeds strolling by. Oh, excuse me, I suppose you consider your activity to be *research*, too. Determining which poor, unsuspecting girl would be your conquest later that evening."

Cole remained unusually calm, although it took some effort on his part. Then he smiled.

"There's a method to that research. You know, deciding whether it should be a brunette or a blonde, and whether the blonde is *really* a blonde. You may be surprised at how often they're not." Cole paused. "And that can be a big disappointment if you have your heart set on a *natural* blonde." Cole took a long drink from his glass.

Lindsay's blood pressure skyrocketed, but she wasn't about to let him get the best of her, either.

"What about redheads, don't we count? Or are we only the dregs left over when everything else fails?"

"No, not at all. Redheads are great, too. You can always tell a true redhead by her skin tone and the color of her eyes. I have no doubt that you are a natural redhead, Lindsay."

Lindsay was about to stand and throw her drink in Cole's face, when his hand rested on her forearm, stopping her.

"No reason to get violent. I'm a lover, not a fighter. Now…where were we? Oh yes, I was about to tell you about the umbrella legend."

If Lindsay had been on any vehicle other than a plane, she would have stomped out and never returned. But where could she run to at the moment? She'd simply have to grin and bear it until they landed. This promised to be a torturous flight, trapped alone with this self-absorbed billionaire asshole! He was finally showing his true colors. It hadn't taken long. And to think she'd almost bought into all that bullshit he had fed her at Grinder's Beat or during the previous evening—like he cared about anything else but himself. Suddenly, she didn't feel so guilty about her father's scam.

Cole cleared his throat.

"As I was saying, the indigenous peoples of the tropics have long held the belief that food and drink were gifts from the gods, as sustenance for their lives. They feared the god of storms the most. They believed the tropical storms that wreaked havoc on their islands and took so many lives were actually retribution for their sins, and polluted the water that they depended on for almost everything. To help protect themselves from the torrential rains, they invented the modern umbrella. These umbrellas were originally fashioned from bamboo and dried banana leaves and were considered sacred. So, when guests were served any beverage, a miniature umbrella was placed on top of the drink as protection against the deadly waters and the storm god. And to this day, the legend has continued, although the beautifully hand-crafted miniatures that the natives made have been replaced by cheap imitations mass-produced in Asia. When you think about it, it really is a beautiful legend, isn't it?" Cole handed his umbrella to Lindsay reverently. "Maybe this one will protect us on our journey."

Lindsay stared at Cole in disbelief. How could he go from a complete jerk one minute to sharing such a heartfelt story with her the next? It really was a beautiful legend—a legend that she was actually familiar with, but for a different reason. Stunned that Cole knew about it, even though he had the particulars mixed up, she'd feigned ignorance so she could hear his version. Cole would discover that later. There was no need to tell him now. And wasn't it just like the soft-spoken people of the tropics to come up with such an interesting custom? For it to endure to this day was quite remarkable. She held the tiny replica in her hands thoughtfully.

"It is a beautiful legend, Cole. Thank you for sharing it with me. I wonder why I've never heard it before, having spent so much time in the area and with the local people," Lindsay fibbed.

"That's probably because it *isn't* true. I made it all up!" Cole choked down a laugh. "Gotcha, didn't I? That will teach you to offer bonus money or sex to one of my employees. You could have just come to me, you know. I would have taken care of everything."

Lindsay looked wounded, but at the same time she realized she had little comeback for Cole's accusations. They were true, after all. She never would have gone through with it, at least the sex part, but Cole didn't know that. She looked away. Remaining silent for a long time, she gazed out one of the side portholes into an ocean of blue sky, subtly changing hues as the Falcon rocketed toward their destination.

14

Lindsay was snoozing when the pilot's voice jolted her back to full consciousness.

"We're approaching the airport and should be on the ground in approximately twenty minutes. I'm waiting for confirmation from the tower. Please take your seats and prepare for landing. It may be a little rough."

The unfamiliar voice had an ominous tone to it. This wasn't Frank's voice. The inside of the cabin had grown dark while Lindsay slept. She suddenly felt disoriented. The jet twisted and dropped in the sky, buffeted by a sudden surge of wind. The porthole windows were being pelted by heavy raindrops. They had entered some kind of storm system, and the turbulence only grew more violent as they approached the island of San Salvador. The contents of Lindsay's lunch seemed determined to escape, while fine beads of perspiration formed on her brow. She glanced over to Cole for an explanation, but he had vanished. She was alone in the darkened cabin, and her nervousness quickly turned to fear. Where was everyone?

"Cole?" she exclaimed, suddenly panicking. She switched on her overhead light. His seat was empty and even the attendant was gone. Where the hell were they? Unbuckling her seat belt, she stood, just as the plane took another violent nosedive, driving her back into the seat. "Cole!" she screamed. Her plea was met with silence.

Lindsay struggled up and out of her seat traversing the distance to the cockpit. The turbulence swung her from side to side, bouncing her off the curved walls of the Falcon. She grabbed the handle of the cockpit door, steadying herself as the jet shook underneath her feet. Pounding on the door, she called out Cole's name again. The door suddenly swung open, knocking her to the ground. The attendant emerged, followed by Cole. The look on his face sent a cold shiver down Lindsay's spine. Something was obviously wrong. Cole looked down, startled to see her sitting on her butt facing them. He reached out his hand and lifted her effortlessly up to her feet, as if she were a child.

"What's wrong, Cole?"

Cole grimaced. "We've got a little problem. It's Frank. I—I think he's suffered a heart attack or something. According to Bill, Frank cried out in pain just before collapsing in his seat. He seems to still have a pulse, but it's weak and irregular. Bill's going to have to land this baby on his own. And as you can see, the weather isn't being very cooperative."

"Oh God! Is Bill capable—I mean, he's just an assistant or a copilot, isn't he?"

"He doesn't have the flight hours or experience Frank has, but he's an able pilot. I used to fly myself, but it's been quite a few years and I no longer have a current license. We're afraid to move Frank and I have no place to sit, anyway. Unless you have a better idea, it's Bill or nothing."

"Can I see Frank? Maybe I can help. I've had some amount of medical training."

"Be my guest. Hey, Rodney, please let Lindsay through." Rodney pushed past the couple, clearing the cramped area and allowing Lindsay to enter.

The jet lurched hard to the left as Bill struggled to correct their flight path. They seemed to be going in circles. Through the forward windshield, Lindsay spotted faint lights flickering in the distance be-low. *Why aren't we landing?* she wondered as she leaned over Frank, who was slouched forward in his seat. She felt for a pulse. Just as Cole said, it was weak and irregular, but at least he was still alive.

"Has anyone got some aspirin? Preferably low-dose."

"Yes, we have some in the medical cabinet, but I think they're full-strength," Rodney replied.

"That's fine. Get two, crush them up, and put them in a little water. And hurry!" Lindsay was all business now, her fear replaced by concern for Frank. If it wasn't for her, he wouldn't have been here in the first place. He'd be home enjoying whatever he did on his day off. "Shit!" She cursed at herself. "Come on, Frank, don't die on me now."

Rodney returned with the aspirin, dissolving them in a couple of ounces of water. Lindsay turned to the attendant. "Please hold his head back and keep his mouth open. We've got to force-feed this into him."

The cockpit was totally cramped, but slowly they forced the liq-uid down his throat. Frank coughed involuntarily, trying to spit it up. Lindsay clamped his mouth shut and massaged his throat until she was satisfied the drug was in his stomach. Lindsay then placed a hand over Frank's heart, whispering something inaudible.

"Frank, can you hear me? If so, just nod." Frank nodded weak-ly, gasping for breath. "Now, listen to me, this is important. I need you to keep coughing. Cough and then take a deep breath, then cough again. Keep doing that for as long as you can. Understand?" Frank nodded again and emitted a faint cough, followed by a rasping breath. His second cough was louder and more forceful.

Lindsay turned to Rodney. "We need to get him out of this cramped space and into a more comfortable sitting position. Give him a minute or two to ensure he's capable of continuing the cough-ing regimen, then we'll move him to one of the passenger seats in the outside cabin. Under no circumstances can he be allowed to lie down, though."

"Bill, are you in contact with ground control?" When Bill nodded, Lindsay continued. "Let them know we have a pilot who has suffered a severe heart attack. They need to have an ambulance with paramedics ready who know how to deal with this sort of trauma, waiting on the runway when we land. Speaking of landing, when the hell are we going to be touching down?"

"They've got us on hold. We've been circling the airport for fifteen minutes. They're having problems and we're in line behind a half-dozen other flights."

"That's not acceptable, damn it! They need to give us priority, if they don't want Frank's death on their hands. He doesn't have much time." Lindsay turned to the open door. "Cole, get your butt in here. Use your influence or a bribe, whatever it takes to get us on the ground pronto."

Rodney looked at Lindsay in shock at the way she was addressing his boss, but he remained mute. He moved away as Cole entered.

"Hand me Frank's headset. I'll see what I can do," Cole said. Less than two minutes later, the deal was done. They had been moved to the head of the pack, for a small fee of twenty thousand American dollars, all to be delivered in small bills.

"What should we do about Frank?" Cole asked.

"Leave him where he is. We'll be on the ground in a few minutes and as long as he continues coughing, we just may make it. It would probably cause more harm at this point to move him now," Lindsay said.

Bill maneuvered the Falcon into position and started their final descent. He did a credible job of landing the aircraft under extremely difficult conditions. When they touched down safely at San Salvador Airport and began to slow, Lindsay slapped him on the back.

"Way to go, Bill! That was awesome! Wait until Frank hears

about that landing. He may be looking for another job."

Bill laughed nervously, and Lindsay could literally see the stress drain out of his body. His palms were wet and his shirt was drenched in sweat. But he had done it—performed under fire.

Outside, red lights were flashing in the pouring rain. The ambulance was surrounded by airport security. Lindsay addressed the entire crew still on the plane, resting her hand on Frank's shoulder.

"Cole, can you please ask the paramedics to come onboard? They should be the ones to move him."

Cole disappeared in the blink of an eye, immediately returning with two men and a stretcher. Cole and Rodney took seats at the table in the main cabin, while Lindsay filled the paramedics in on what she thought had happened, along with the administration of the aspirin and the coughing regimen she had overseen. Frank was carefully unbuckled and fitted with an oxygen mask, before being strapped to the stretcher and carried out of the plane. Lindsay followed close behind. By the time they reached the ambulance, Frank appeared to be more alert.

Cole exited the stairs onto the tarmac, noticing that Lindsay was holding Frank's hand and speaking softly to him. She kissed him on the forehead before Rodney followed him into the ambulance and the rear doors were sealed. She watched as the ambulance disappeared into the gloom. Drenched from head to foot, Lindsay rejoined her comrades under the wing of the Falcon, while they waited for a limo to pick them up.

"Lindsay, thank you. You probably saved Frank's life," Cole said and turned to Bill. "We couldn't have done this without you, either, Bill. You have my sincere thanks, as well as a nice bonus for your efforts. I'll make sure Frank knows about your heroic landing." He turned back toward Lindsay, handing her the miniature umbrella from his drink. "Perhaps the legend is true after all…or maybe Frank had a guardian angel, but somehow we made it." There wasn't the slightest hint of sarcasm in his voice this time.

The limo pulled up and a driver stepped out holding three full-sized umbrellas. Lindsay entered the side door, but Cole lingered behind. The driver and Bill headed back up into the plane to retrieve the luggage, then returning to place it in the limo's trunk. Bill returned to the jet to steer it over to a nearby hangar.

"Aren't you coming, Cole?" Lindsay said through the rolled-down window.

"There's a little business I need to take care of first, and there'll be reports to fill out. You know, the usual red tape. I'll catch up with you later. Please ask the driver to return for me after you're settled in." Cole walked away without another word.

Lindsay watched out the car window until he disappeared inside the main building, as rain pounded against the car door. Twilight had fallen, and she suddenly felt a spike of mind-numbing coldness fill her insides. She motioned for the driver to leave. She turned her gaze out of the rear window, watching as the specks of diffused light surrounding the airport faded into obscurity. Then the fear returned.

15

It was nearly nine o'clock in the evening when Cole found Lindsay sitting on a veranda, outside the restaurant at the Bay Marina Resort. The term *resort* was probably an overstatement, but this was San Salvador after all. Compared to the resorts Cole had frequented, this was barely more than a collection of ramshackle buildings, but it did offer a spectacular view of the Bay. She was sitting alone facing the ocean, nursing a tall, tropical drink. There was a plate of half-eaten fish lying on the wooden table beside her. She turned as Cole approached. She had a pair of miniature umbrellas tucked behind each ear and one in her hand, spinning back and forth to the rhythm of a Jimmy Buffett song coming from nearby speakers. Her eyes were slightly glazed. Wearing a black-and-white-striped tank top and white Capri pants, she looked like a local, blending right in, hair pulled back in braids. She appeared different somehow.

It suddenly occurred to Cole that she seemed to take on an altered look depending on her surroundings. In his mind's eye, he recalled the different places they had been together during the past week, and in each scene, he could visualize her differently. Could it be that she adapted to her environment naturally, like a chameleon? That didn't seem remotely possible. He tossed the ridiculous notion aside and took a seat next to her.

"Been sitting here long?" Cole said.

"Awhile," Lindsay said.

"I see you've been enjoying the local cuisine," Cole said.

"Sort of. The tuna was overcooked, but the drinks are good."

Cole looked over at the leftover fish; it looked more like sushi to him, with the edges only slightly charred. Overcooked?

"You seem to have become the poster child for miniature umbrellas." Cole pointed toward her ears.

"Speaking of umbrellas…" Lindsay paused. "Have you heard the legend about why they are placed only on tropical drinks?" Lindsay said half-mockingly.

"I don't believe I have. Why don't you tell me about it?" Cole said, sounding amused.

"It all started way back, when two fraternity brothers from some Ivy League school visited Puerto Rico and noticed a little cantina in a back alley that was selling them. The cantina was conveniently located right in front of a brothel. The tops of the umbrellas were hand-painted with the flags of the different countries in the South Atlantic. They were really quite beautiful, works of art. Each one different from the other. One of the guys, the arrogant one, noticed that the bartender would place one of the flag umbrellas on top of each drink she sold to her patrons, as they were negotiating the price for their prostitute. On the inside of the umbrella, the girl's name was handwritten and a condom was attached, and the flag would be exchanged inside the brothel for the girl." Lindsay paused again, gazing into Cole's eyes accusatorily, then she continued with her story.

"He—the arrogant one—got this great idea to mass-produce the umbrellas in Asia with the image of the American flag on top and have them shipped over here. He began to offer them to restaurants and bars in the area. Since anything American sold well down here, his business grew and grew until he had finally amassed a fortune. Eventually, he cut his fraternity brother out of the business so he could keep all the profits for himself. In the process, he put the small

Puerto Rican factory, where the original flags were hand-produced, out of business. Many people lost their jobs. And to this day, the custom has remained." Lindsay hesitated again, squinting her eyes.

"The moral of the story is that if you buy a drink in the tropics with an American flag umbrella on it, you're going to get screwed!" Lindsay slammed down her glass and broke out laughing. Cole sat dumbfounded, unable to respond.

"So, how is Frank doing?" Lindsay asked, her tone turning serious, as if she had not even told her story.

Cole was too stunned to respond. All he could do was stare at her, wondering how she had come up with that parable, and whether or not it was Cole that she was speaking about. Of course, it was. Cole Hollingsworth— arrogant, rich, and without conscience. Lindsay and Cole were such opposites. Cole cleared his throat, trying to compose himself.

"Frank is in critical condition, but he's holding his own. Bill and Rodney are taking turns staying with him. They've rented hotel rooms near the hospital. If he's strong enough, the doctors will be doing an angioplasty on him in the morning to see what sort of blockage he has. Depending on the results, they may do bypass surgery or they may send him home for further tests. We'll have to wait until tomorrow."

"Did you actually see Frank, or did you just get a report from your staff—or better yet, an e-mail?"

Now it was Cole's turn to feel wounded. Did Lindsay really think that little of him?

"I spent a couple of hours at the hospital with Frank and his doctor. I told them not to spare any expense to help him get better. I—"

"Of course, you did! Money is the answer to everything, isn't it, Cole? You have your staff to watch over him while you hang out here. Isn't it about time for a Scotch?" No sooner had she uttered these words than the waiter appeared with a menu.

"Good evening, Señor. May I bring you a drink?"

Cole scowled, glanced at Lindsay, and ordered a double Scotch, just to spite her. He picked up the menu and pretended to consider the offerings—anything to get his mind off of Lindsay's comments.

"You might want to consider ordering the spiced chicken sandwich with the *jerk* sauce. That should go well with your Scotch!" Lindsay stood, wavering a little as she passed Cole. "We leave at seven in the morning. Pleasant dreams."

Cole watched as Lindsay walked toward her bungalow down by the beach. Her image seemed to fade into the ocean, like she was a retreating wave, until all he could see was the empty shoreline and the shimmering waters beyond. He pulled out his iPhone and sent an e-mail to Bill and Rodney, ordered another drink and dinner in a container to go, then headed to his own bungalow, wondering what the morning would bring.

Cole tossed and turned throughout the night, eventually drifting off, only to be abruptly awakened by a series of nightmarish dreams. In each scene he saw his mother reaching out to him, just before she plummeted beneath the ocean's crashing waves. And in every scene, there was Lindsay, too, standing nearby, watching and judging him. Images of shuttered factories and people on the street begging for food tortured him through the long night. He woke at 6:30 a.m., irritable and exhausted. Light streamed in through his half-closed blinds. His throat felt unusually parched, although he had not had that much to drink last night. He opened the small refrigerator nearby, popped open a beer, and chugged it.

He left a note he had written Lindsay the night before on her front doorstep and then hurried to catch a cab in front of the marina. Their expedition could wait one more day; he was off to see Frank at the hospital. Lindsay would just have to understand.

Lindsay opened the door to her bungalow, stretching cramped muscles, and noticed the envelope lying on the steps below her. This was odd. It must be from Cole, since who else knew she was staying here? She opened it. The handwritten letter was short and to the point.

Lindsay,

I can't join you this morning, you'll just have to go it alone today. I'm headed to the hospital to make sure Frank is taken care of properly. As soon as I know anything, I'll call. I'm sorry about last night. By the way, you were right, the jerk sauce went well with the Scotch.

Cole

Lindsay's first impulse was to scream Cole's name out loud, as if it had become her favorite new curse word. Then she smiled, albeit ruefully. He was attempting to apologize for being such an ass, but he was also looking after Frank. That alone meant something. A day by herself would be good. She was stressed, and some time alone spent walking the beach and swimming in the warm waters sounded soothing. One day couldn't make that much difference in the long run. She changed into a swimsuit and a cover-up, grabbed a book, her sunglasses, and her phone, and headed off to the far end of the cove, which lay mostly deserted.

It was sometime in the midafternoon when her phone rang, waking her from a semiconscious state. She was lying on a towel, bathing in the sunlight, listening to the waves lapping against the shoreline. The ringtone on her phone shattered her trancelike state. She checked the number on the screen. Cole. Finally—some news about Frank.

"Yes, Cole, how's he doing?"

"Better. He did well during the night. The doctor told me your quick action probably saved his life. There is a fair amount of blockage in three of his arteries. However, Frank was in top physical shape, which helps. They feel it would be best to fly him back to the States to get the best medical treatment possible. They suggest he undergo the bypass surgery as soon as possible after he gets home, though. I'm arranging for another experienced pilot to assist Bill and Rodney. I've also hired a cardiac nurse to travel with him…."

"Are the doctors sure he can fly so soon? I mean, it's been less than twenty-four hours, right?"

"Yes, they're confident, otherwise I wouldn't allow him to leave. They are refueling my jet right now and will be leaving within an hour. You have time to see him before he leaves…if you'd like."

Lindsay hesitated for a moment, indecisive. "No, that's alright. Please give him my best and tell him I'll check in on him when we get, um, home."

"Okay, I'll do that. I've gotta go."

"When will you be back?"

"A couple more hours, that is, if there aren't any holdups at the airport. How about dinner tonight? It's about time you explained your agenda to me, don't you think?"

Lindsay hesitated for a moment. "Dinner, it is. I'll meet you at the restaurant at seven thirty. Good luck." Lindsay hung up, unwilling to answer his question fully.

16

With Frank and the crew successfully on their way back to the States, Cole was finally alone. Rather than returning directly to the resort, he walked the streets of Cockburn Town, observing the locals, occasionally stepping into one of the long alleyways in search of Lindsay's cantina. He didn't expect to find the one that sold the miniature American flag umbrellas, or the brothel, but somehow, he hoped her story would be true. Her legend seemed far more human than the one he had fabricated. Human, if only for its weaknesses. The more he thought about her story, the more he saw a microcosm of life. Lonely men looking for love in a glass and a whorehouse. Women in subservient roles. The rich taking advantage of the poor, shutting down local businesses in order to profit from outsourcing jobs and products from third- world countries, exploiting cheaper labor. And in the center, the American flag was emblematic of it all. Were Americans really so arrogant that they actually believed they could be the policemen to the entire world, forcing their form of democracy on foreign people deeply embedded in their own cultures? Like missionaries spreading religion—the American religion, an embodiment of capitalism wrapped up in a promise of freedom. Cole was guilty of all those things. This newfound clarity was shattering.

Without realizing it, he had wandered down a long, narrow

alleyway and quickly became disoriented. The cobbled street grew narrower, shadows lurking everywhere as the stucco walls of the close-quartered buildings rose high above, blocking out the sun. Suddenly he was staring at the Cantina de la Noche, as if it had just materialized before his very eyes. The cantina was remarkably like the one he had envisioned in Lindsay's tale. At the front was an open bar, with a bamboo covering and doorways on either side leading into a darkened interior. Tall stools lined the three-sided wooden bar. There was a scattering of customers, sipping drinks. All men. Behind the bar were two handsome teenage boys, who appeared to be helpers, mixing drinks. Dressed in colorful outfits of black Gaucho pants, Gaucho dance boots, and white shirts underneath bright red and black ponchos, each one sporting a different colored Campero hat, they looked like they belonged more in Argentina than in San Salvador. And in the middle, stood the grand dame, a striking woman despite her age.

Long silver hair flowed from her crimson-colored *Entrerriano* hat. She was dressed in all black, her top studded with silver buttons. Her thin waist was made even thinner by a tight-fitting *Rastra*, a thick black leather belt covered with old silver coins come from a bygone era. Her high cheekbones, slender nose, and silky- smooth complexion spoke of royalty, but Cole instantly knew she had not descended from royal blood. She had earned her pedigree from the streets. She owned this establishment and everything that went with it—there was no denying that.

Cole stood and watched in silence as she conversed with a single customer. She used her hands in an eloquent manner, describing something that seemed to mesmerize her patron. The conversation apparently coming to an end, she placed a small, colorful umbrella in his drink. The man thanked her, stepped off of his bar stool, and made his way inside the establishment, closing the door behind him.

The woman moved over to her next customer, whispering

something in his ear. He smiled. She laughed fetchingly. She was a master, weaving intrigue into every gesture, every word. There was no wasted effort. She played effortlessly on the heartstrings of these lonely men, selling love in a glass.

Lindsay had been right. She had described this very scene last night. But how could it possibly be true? Cole flashed back to their dinner at Breeder's Steakhouse, when she had announced that she'd earned her college tuition by pole-dancing. Had she worked here? Had she known about this place all along, describing it with such conviction that Cole was unwittingly forced to search it out? Cole could hardly believe his eyes. He approached the bar, taking a seat. It wasn't long before the older woman settled herself in front of him.

"Now, what would a fine gentleman like you be doing at Cantina de la Noche?" The woman's voice was unmistakably Argentinean. The knowing smile on her face spoke volumes. She had sized him up in under a minute, and he felt naked in her presence. Cole cleared his throat, brushing away one of the young men attempting to take his drink order.

"Now, don't be rude. Miguel is only trying to earn a living. Please order something. I promise you'll like it, and then we can talk."

Cole turned to the young man. "Gin and tonic with a squeeze of lime, thank you."

The young man filled a tall glass with ice cubes and went to work on the drink. It was pleasant for a change to see a bartender not spinning a bottle in one hand and looking in the back mirror admiring himself.

"Now, tell me, sir. What are you looking for? Perhaps I can find it for you," the woman said.

"I was wondering if the name Lindsay Featherstone was familiar to you. She's a striking redhead. Slender, athletic. And she's smart, very smart. She may have worked here five or six years ago."

"And what makes you think someone like that would be working here?"

"I think we both know what goes on inside that building. Don't worry, I'm not a cop. Just interested in finding Lindsay. I've tracked her to San Salvador, and that's where the trail ends."

The woman's expression remained neutral, but Cole could have sworn he glimpsed a hint of recognition in her dark brown eyes, but it passed quickly.

"She may have been a dancer, or a bartender, or maybe something else. I'm sure you would remember her...if she had worked here," Cole said.

The bartender placed the drink in front of Cole. The woman reached under the bar, retrieving an object she cupped in her hand. A moment later, she placed a miniature umbrella atop Cole's glass. Cole's mouth dropped open. The umbrella depicted the American flag. He lifted it out of his glass and was startled to see that the slender pole it was attached to was painted metallic silver. Even more startling was the tiny half-naked figure of a mermaid, with part of a tailfin and one arm wrapped around the pole. The figure spun lazily around in a circle. Cole couldn't believe what he was seeing. How could this woman have produced such an object? He took a quick glance behind him, thinking he might find Lindsay standing there playing a joke on him. No Lindsay.

The woman then pulled out a rectangular pad of parchment-looking paper, scribbling a number between two gold-embossed lines: $150.00. Cole guessed this was the price of admission, like a ticket to an amusement park. She pushed the paper across the bar and leaned in close, her dark red lips pressed against Cole's ear.

"What you are searching for is not here, but you must see for yourself," the woman whispered, then kissed him softly on the cheek. "Seek her elsewhere."

Cole reached for his wallet and pulled out two one-hundred- dollar bills, placing them on the bar.

"Will you be requiring change?" she said nonchalantly.

Cole shook his head. "It's Miguel's tip. Perhaps he can put it toward school tuition. He would be better served doing something like that, don't you think?"

"Perhaps."

The transaction complete, the woman moved down to the far end of the bar, positioning herself in front of a heavy-set man, dressed in a black-and-white pinstriped suit with an open- collared, white silk shirt. His silver hair was thick and wavy and specked with hints of black. The stubble on his face suggested he hadn't shaved in a couple of days. His pudgy fingers were adorned with a collection of intricately carved sterling-silver rings, some containing gemstones. The bartender placed a short glass of crushed ice on the bar, filling it with dark amber liquid, which could only be spiced rum. Simultaneously, the woman put an umbrella with what looked like the Cuban flag in his drink, as though she already knew his desires. The flag was red, white, and blue, just like the American flag, but it contained only one star. The man handed her one of his rings. The deal was done.

Cole stepped off of his bar stool and headed inside, closing the door, just like the man before him had done.

17

Cole arrived inside the marina restaurant precisely at 7:30 p.m. Lindsay was already sitting at a table next to the open railing. The main dining room was a large circular space facing the Bay, with a bamboo-thatched roof and ceiling fans slowly turning, circulating the humid air. Cole took a seat facing Lindsay. She was dressed in a low-cut form-fitting dress. The ivory-colored fabric contained thin strands of gold thread weaved through it. The dress shimmered in the sea of candlelight lighting the space. Where could she have found such a gown? Had she been downtown during the afternoon after all? It would help make sense of what he'd experienced at the cantina. Her thick auburn hair hung loosely on her shoulders, and she had a tropical flower tucked behind one ear. The miniature umbrellas were conspicuously missing. In a word, she was *stunning*.

"You look very nice tonight. Celebrating a special occasion?" Cole said.

"No, nothing in particular. I just like being here. It feels like home to me."

Cole was dressed in a long-sleeved polo shirt with the sleeves partially rolled up and the top two buttons undone. The shirt hung over a pair of faded blue jeans and his feet were exposed through thick brown leather sandals. His favorite Ray-Ban aviator sunglasses were perched on top of his head. He couldn't have looked more like a tourist if he had slapped a large label on the back of his shirt embroidered with the words *Made in America.*

A waiter approached. A handsome, young local man in his early twenties, he offered the couple a pair of menus, while motioning to the busboy to bring them water.

"Good evening, may I offer you something to drink? Our specialty drinks are listed on the back of the menu." He stood patiently while Lindsay and Cole perused the back page.

"A Cerveza, please. Whatever you recommend. Preferably local," Lindsay replied.

Cole's eyes landed on something called a Head Cold—a combination of tropical fruit juices and five different types of rum.

"I'll have the Head Cold. It sounds interesting. And please, leave off the umbrella."

"Yes, sir. I'll be back momentarily with your drinks." True to his word, the waiter returned moments later with the Head Cold, a large frozen tumbler filled with ice, colorful fruit juice, and five shots of rum. A swizzle stick filled with chunks of fresh pineapple, mango, and lime adorned the drink. Thankfully, the umbrella had been left off.

The waiter handed Lindsay a chilled glass and a bottle of Old Harbor Kofresi Stout, brewed in Puerto Rico. He poured the beer into her glass. "I think you'll like this." He smiled and turned to Cole. "The Head Cold packs quite a wallop, so just fair warning. I'll be back in a few to take your dinner orders."

The pair raised their glasses in mock salute, each with different thoughts occupying their minds. Cole couldn't get the cantina out of his head. Lindsay struggled with how to tell Cole what was about to happen. There followed an awkward silence. Finally, Cole spoke.

"Lindsay, tell me what you know about a bar called Cantina de la Noche."

"So that's where you were all afternoon? I wondered where you'd gone after your jet took off. I might have known." Lindsay seemed irritated over such a simple question. "It didn't take you long to find *that* part of town."

"What…did I do something wrong? I just went sightseeing. I've never been to San Salvador before, so I thought I'd do a little exploring."

"So, did you find anything interesting on your little excursion?" Lindsay said, her voice laced with accusation.

"Actually, I did. I ran into an outside bar, down a deserted alleyway, called the Cantina de la Noche. It was remarkably like the one in the story you told me last night when you were describing your little theory on the American flag umbrellas in tropical drinks."

Lindsay took a long drink of her stout and then met Cole's gaze. "You're the one who came up with the umbrella legend in the first place, or don't you remember?" She paused. "Hasn't this whole thing about the miniature umbrellas gone too far? Enough is enough. The Cantina de la Noche is nothing more than a myth down here, although the legend somehow manages to endure. Its name literally means 'Tavern of the Night.' It's reported to be a place where every man's deepest desires are served. It doesn't exist, though, at least in the literal sense. Men use the name as a reference for when they visit one of the many brothels in the area. It's kind of like their secret dirty little joke. It's disgusting, really."

"What do you mean, it doesn't exist? I was just there today. I had a drink at the outside bar. I even met the owner. You must be confusing it with something else," Cole replied.

Lindsay rolled her eyes. "So, where exactly was this mythical cantina located?"

"Toward the center of town, in the middle of a narrow alleyway. I don't recall the street name. I just stumbled onto it. It was just there."

"And what did the owner look like, if I might ask?" Again, Lindsay's sarcasm was obvious.

"Well, she was interesting, I'll say that. *Intense* is maybe a better word. She appeared old, but her features were more like a young woman's. She was beautiful in a mysterious sort of way. She had long silver hair, dark brown eyes, and she was dressed in Gaucho- looking clothes. She had two young bartenders who looked to be in their mid-teens. Very handsome, dressed in the same garb."

Lindsay's eye widened. She suddenly looked shell-shocked. These people didn't exist, yet Cole had just given a perfect description of the mythical characters.

"Do you have any proof of this?" Lindsay said, her interest peaked.

"Only this." Cole pulled a tiny umbrella out of his shirt pocket and laid it on the table. Lindsay gingerly picked it up and examined it. She noticed the tiny mermaid figurine attached to the silver-colored pole, spinning slowly in circles. She couldn't hold back a gasp.

"It can't be," she whispered to herself. "You must have picked this up at one of those sleazy pawnshops down by the wharf. I'm telling you, Cole, the cantina is just a fable, it doesn't exist." Somehow the expression on her face said otherwise.

Cole recalled his visit inside. It was dark when he had entered. There were two long shadowy hallways. The one to the right led to a circular bar, surrounding a raised stage. In the middle stood a shimmering silver pole, the kind you would find in a strip club. But there was no one there. No customers, no bartender, no dancers, just the deserted stage. An icy breeze blew across the stage, carrying with it the faintest scent of salt. Then he remembered the owner's words outside. *What you are searching for is not here, but you must see it for yourself. Seek her elsewhere.* What exactly had she meant by that?

After a lengthy wait to see if someone would show up, Cole had finally headed back to the front doors to leave, and perhaps give the owner a piece of his mind. Two hundred dollars for nothing seemed a bit exorbitant, even for him. When he reached the door, there were no handles, just a tall, slender man dressed in an old- fashioned gray tuxedo standing to the side. The man had looked at Cole with deadened eyes. Cole felt like he was suddenly trying to go out through a one-way door. It reminded him of the eerie lyrics to the Eagle's *Hotel California*—something about running to a door to find a way back, and being met by a doorman who says you can check out, but you can never really leave?

The odd-looking man with the blank stare pointed back to the hallway from which Cole had just returned. "*It's that way,*" was all he said, and then he went silent as though melting back into the wall. Cole had basically run down the hallway eager to be gone from this place. He noticed the exit sign behind the curtain at the back of the stage. He pushed through it and suddenly found himself on a busy street, Nuevo Boulevard, crowded with cars and pedestrians. The bright sunlight momentarily blinded him. He glanced back, only to find blank walls of sun-bleached stucco with a scattering of windows high above. There were no doors. Cole was about to recount his experience to Lindsay when she spoke first.

"So, I guess you want to hear the rest of the legend?" Lindsay said unexpectedly.

"Do I have a choice?" Cole replied. Lindsay shrugged her shoulders.

"The owner, the woman you are referring to, was rumored to be a witch. Born of the incestuous affair between two first cousins of the royal bloodline of Spain, the family of Borbon, she was cast out of her own country, scorned, and declared a heretic. Fearing for her life, she snuck on to a freighter and headed for South America, ending up in Argentina. She eventually married and bore two sons, exactly one year apart. Those were the two teenage boys you supposedly saw. Her husband was killed shortly after in a civil war. In order to support her family, she turned to prostitution. Due to her stunning beauty, she had no problem attracting clients. Eventually, she became the sole owner of the leading brothel in Buenos Aires. Scandal followed with a prominent local politician, and she was forced to flee again, this time to the Bahamas. Her famous brothel was named Cantina de la Noche. The authorities burned it to the ground. It was also rumored that she personally negotiated the deals with her customers for the women who worked for her. After receiving payment, she would write each girl's name on one of those miniature umbrellas and stick them in the drinks. The men would exchange the umbrellas inside for their prostitutes. She supposedly asked each of her patrons what country they were from, and would give them the respective umbrellas with their national flag painted on them. It became kind of a tradition and was well-known for its originality. And that's the basis for the story I told you last night."

So, she was of Royal descent, Cole thought. "So, what's the connection to the bar I visited today in Cockburn? I don't understand."

"San Salvador was where she supposedly settled after leaving Buenos Aires. There were no laws here prohibiting prostitution, so she again set up shop, naming her new place Cantina de la Noche. Some years later, the Argentinean authorities caught up with her, and she, along with her two sons, were hanged to death. The legend states that she haunts the alleyways of Cockburn, and when people are searching for something vitally important, her cantina reappears in different locations and for a brief time is open for business. Local people swear the legend is true, but the police have never caught her or seen any proof of her existence. The legend remains a favorite part of the local lore."

Cole sat back in his chair, astonished. "It now kind of makes sense. It must be a group of local tavern owners who get together and set the whole thing up. There's no other explanation." As Lindsay was about to reply, the waiter returned.

"How are you two doing? Are you ready to order?"

"Not quite. Can you give us a few more minutes?" Cole said.

"Perhaps another round of drinks?" the waiter said, noticing

Cole's glass was empty.

"Sure. Lindsay, would you like another beer?" Lindsay placed her hand over her glass, shaking her head. "Just one then," Cole replied. The waiter returned with a second Head Cold.

"That still doesn't explain how you could have provided a perfect description of the woman, her sons, and the cantina, since you've never been here before or heard the story. It doesn't seem possible," Lindsay said, growing ever more suspicious of Cole's motives. And then it hit her. "You were having a drink at one of those seedy bars downtown and you heard the story, didn't you? Just be honest, Cole. There's no way you could have been at the cantina."

"Not true. I was there…or at the very least, I was at a place that was masquerading as the cantina. As I said, it was probably just a bunch of local tavern owners having fun reliving the myth. What's the harm in that?"

"It doesn't set a very good example for the families of this town. Celebrating prostitution and witchcraft probably aren't goals we should aspire to."

"Loosen up, Lindsay. Why are you so serious all the time? I'll tell you what. After we get through tomorrow doing whatever it is we're going to do, I'll take you downtown and show you the cantina. I'm sure I can find it again, and then you'll see it's all a bunch of nonsense and that will be the end of it. Now, drink up and enjoy yourself." Cole raised his glass to his mouth and finished about a quarter of it, while the waiter stood nearby in the shadows, listening with more and more interest as the story unfolded. He, too, was a believer and this was the first person he had encountered who had actually seen the cantina. He hoped to learn more.

Lindsay finished her beer and motioned for another one, more out of spite than anything. She didn't want Cole to think she didn't know how to have fun. The waiter returned with a fresh glass and bottle of stout.

"I think we're ready to order. I'll have the fresh abalone, barely cooked," Lindsay said.

"Excellent choice, miss. Our divers brought them in just a few hours ago. They taste like they were just taken from the ocean. Sir, what have you decided on?"

"I guess I'll have the grilled fish skewers and French fries. And another Head Cold. These things are growing on me."

"Cole, please be careful with those drinks. They're extremely potent. Remember, we have an early morning tomorrow," Lindsay cautioned.

"I'm not a lightweight like you. I'll be alright," Cole replied, beginning to slur his words. Lindsay knew not to push him too hard, and when Cole wasn't looking, she gave the waiter a reminder by slashing her throat with her hand, indicating that the next drink would be his last. The waiter winked back, acknowledging her intent.

"I wonder why these drinks are called Head Colds. It's an odd name for a drink, don't you think?" Cole said.

"They call them Head Colds because they freeze your brain and make you stupid," Lindsay rebutted.

The waiter returned ten minutes later with their order. The abalone was cooked perfectly, lightly sautéed in clarified butter with a hint of lemon and surrounded by a ring of steamed jasmine rice and grilled vegetables to add a touch of smokiness to the rich flesh of the shellfish. Cole's entrée was prepared with equal skill, although he seemed far more enamored with the Head Colds. The waiter brought Lindsay a glass of chardonnay at Cole's insistence. *"You can't have abalone without a good glass of wine,"* was what Cole had said. Apparently, that same logic didn't apply to his own seafood. They ate in silence.

The plates were cleared and dessert offered, but both refused. Cole pushed his empty glass toward the waiter. "I'll have one more, please…"

"I'm terribly sorry, sir, but the limit is three per customer. House rules, I'm afraid." Cole was about to object when he felt Lindsay's hand firmly on his wrist.

"No more, Cole. You'll thank me tomorrow. Here, you can finish my wine. I'm done." She slid the half-empty glass in his direction, which seemed to placate him for the time being. Alcohol was alcohol, after all, in one form or another.

The evening had been an interesting one, but they had yet to discuss the events planned for tomorrow. Lindsay had artfully avoided his questions, and once he had become inebriated, he no longer seemed to care. The restaurant crowd was beginning to thin out. It was getting late.

"Cole, how about a walk on the beach? The fresh salt air will do you good."

Cole looked over at Lindsay, his eyes glazed over. There was nothing quite so good as becoming intoxicated on fine rum.

"Okay, if you think you can keep up with me?" Cole stood, stumbling over his chair as he extricated himself from the table. Lindsay grabbed his hand and led him away as a nearby couple looked on.

"Please charge dinner to room 204 and add a forty-percent gratuity to the tab," Lindsay whispered to the waiter. He smiled, thanking her for the generous tip. The waiter then leaned over to Cole, offering to help show him around downtown Cockburn tomorrow if he needed a guide.

A few minutes later, the couple reached the beach near their bungalows. Cole turned to Lindsay.

"Have I ever told you how beautiful you are? I mean it, you're probably the most beautiful woman I know. You should have your own brothel. Give that ol' witch a run for her money." Cole laughed at his inept attempt at humor. Lindsay faked a laugh, too. Cole continued, "I'd be your first and only customer. We could stay down here forever." He wrapped his arms around her, drawing her close. He didn't know his own strength.

"Please, Cole, you're hurting me." She pushed him away.

"Not until I get a kiss." He moved in again.

"No, Cole, not this way. You're drunk!"

"I'm not drunk. I'm in love, can't you see that?" Cole said, his expression a combination of lust and desperation.

"You don't know what love is, Cole. That's your problem." Lindsay was shaking now.

"And I suppose you do? You know all about love?"

"No, not everything. But I know it isn't this. It's not about forcing someone to have sex."

"Hey, I'm not forcing you. We're consenting adults. You just need to consent, that's all." Cole smirked, as if his wit was all it would take to convince her to change her mind.

Lindsay pushed back hard at him, forcing Cole to the ground. He landed in the wet sand and looked up at Lindsay in surprise. She was glowering at him, hands on her hips.

"I think that's about enough for one night. I'm going inside. I suggest you do the same, unless you want to spend the night sleeping on the beach while the sand crabs pick out your eyeballs."

"Hey, that's not a nice thing to say." Cole struggled to get up but fell immediately back down on his butt. Lindsay took pity on him.

"Here, let me help you up."

Cole stood shakily, and Lindsay guided him over to his bungalow. "Where's your key? Your door's locked."

"It's in my pocket, I think." He clumsily inserted his hand into his pocket without a great deal of success. Lindsay sighed heavily. She tentatively placed her hand in his jeans pocket, withdrawing his room key.

"Are you trying to get fresh with me? I'm not that kind of guy, you know. You can't just have your way with me." He leaned forward, attempting to plant a kiss on Lindsay's mouth. She ducked just in time. She managed to open his door, pushing him inside.

"There, you're safe. I'll see you in the morning. Seven thirty, and don't be late. I'll leave a wakeup call for you. Good night, Cole."

"Good night, woman of my dreams. I'll leave my door unlocked in case you change your mind."

His words fell on deaf ears. Lindsay was already gone. She entered her own bungalow, securely locking the door behind her. Cole stumbled over to the minibar and withdrew a couple of 187-milliliter bottles of Scotch. He headed to his outside deck, which directly faced Lindsay's bungalow. He settled down in one of the two wicker chairs and poured himself a cocktail. It wasn't a Head Cold, but it would do.

Lindsay's room was closer to the water with a slightly higher elevation than Cole's. Her deck overhung a small rock ledge that dropped about eight feet to the water below. The deck seemed to flow directly into the ocean beyond, like one of those swimming pools located at the edge of a cliff and facing the ocean. Cole gazed at the lit windowpane of what was likely Lindsay's bedroom, wondering what she was doing.

The moon hung obliquely in the darkened sky beyond, appearing twice its normal size. They didn't have moons like this in Rhode Island. Tiny whitecaps atop gentle waves swept along with the tide, highlighted by the gigantic moon, shimmering in the darkness. Cole could smell the salt in the air. He had never wanted a woman this badly before. They were alone in this paradise, and she was refusing him. He poured another Scotch just as her room went dark.

"Damn!" he cursed. She *was* serious about going to sleep. He thought she was just playing hard to get. He had been through that game a hundred times before. Most women never wanted to give in so easily. What was he supposed to do, beg for it? Hell would freeze over before he'd do that. But then something happened he didn't expect.

In the stillness, he heard the faint sound of a sliding glass door opening. It was coming from Lindsay's room. A moment later, she stepped outside onto her deck. She appeared to be wrapped in a towel or a blanket, although his vision was severely blurred and it was difficult to make out what she was wearing in the flickering light. Aside from a scattering of tiki torches along the cove, only the moon provided a source of light.

Is she about to go swimming, or better yet, skinny-dipping? Cole wondered. He watched with anticipation as she walked to the edge of the deck. She looked around, apparently to ensure no one was watching. Cole had failed to turn on any lights, so his place remained dark. She let the towel slide down her body, piling on the wooden slats below. She was naked, but he could see no details clearly, due to the scant lighting. Her body was perfectly proportioned, an elusive silhouette against the shimmering water. Cole felt a slight stiffening beneath his boxers. God, she *was* the most beautiful woman he had ever met.

Unexpectedly, she raised her long, languid arms above her head, touching her hands together and forming a halo-like pose facing the ocean. Cole noticed her mouth appeared to be moving but he couldn't make out what she was saying. Her voice sounded high-pitched, birdlike. Was she singing to the ocean? And then she began to turn, like a delicate ballerina pirouetting in the moonlight. At first, they were determined, slow-moving circles, but slowly they gained in velocity. Her skin began to glow, emitting sparks of light like some ethereal fireworks display. The sparks of light coming from her body began to form shapes, turning into leaves or scales, he couldn't tell which. But she was changing, morphing into some alien form. Her singing became more intense, as though she were calling out to an unseen power in the water.

Cole watched in rapt fascination as the transformation took place. He noticed a slight movement out in the Bay. It first appeared like something moving toward the shore, a large fish, perhaps a small boat. It could have been anything, really. The sound of wind suddenly filled the air. The whitecaps rose and the wind howled more violently…and then it came into view—a wave growing in size at an alarming rate, gaining in speed as it raced toward the shoreline. It might have been a tidal wave or a tsunami, he couldn't tell in his drunken stupor, as he watched in horror at the churning ocean building in strength. The wave rushed forward, dark and ominous, blocking out the moon—its crest taking on the shape of some demonic sea creature. Lindsay was spinning faster and faster, emitting a blinding light, sparks flying everywhere. Cole yelled out for her to run, but his voice was drowned out by the howling wind. The next thing Cole saw was the tidal wave of water hit the land, engulfing Lindsay's bungalow until it was no longer visible.

"No!" Cole cried out and leapt up from his chair. He hit the beach running, stumbling over a rock and falling hard to the ground. He pushed himself up, fighting against the alcohol—the poison controlling his body. He felt like he was moving in slow motion. He stumbled again, pounding his fists against the wet sand. He looked over at Lindsay's room just as the towering wave of water receded, washing clean everything on the deck, including Lindsay. An instant later the sea was calm again, as if nothing had just happened. Lindsay's bungalow remained dark.

Fighting back the tears streaming down his face, Cole ran over to her front door, kicking it open. He called out her name, but was met with only silence. He frantically searched every inch of the three rooms but to no avail. Lindsay was gone, swallowed up by the ocean she loved. Cole hurried down to the shoreline, diving headfirst into the surf. The water was jet-black, the undertow remarkably strong. He struggled, holding his breath—fighting against the water overwhelming him. There was nothing he could do. He somehow instinctively knew this. If he went much farther, he would probably drown, too.

Drenched, defeated, and growing cold, he walked up the beach to his room. He reached for his phone, then abruptly put it down. What could he tell the authorities? They would never believe what he had seen. He would file a missing person's report in the morning; there was nothing he could do in the meantime that would make any difference.

He returned to his deck, staring blankly out to the sea, and proceeded to finish off the remaining bottles of liquor in the minibar. Slowly, he drifted off into oblivion.

18

A splitting headache woke Cole the following morning— that, along with an odd thumping on his skull. He was lying sprawled out on the sand like a beached whale. He opened his eyes to the full intensity of the sunrise. His shirt was covered with perspiration stains. His face, nostrils, and mouth were clumped with dried sand. Surf flies covered his body. A seagull perched on his shoulder was pecking at the flies in his hair. He felt a sharp pain in his right foot. A large sand crab had managed to cut through the thick leather of his sandal and was munching on his big toe. Blood was trickling onto the sand, staining it crimson.

Cole tried to sit up, but the effort was too painful. *I'm dead,* he thought. *And rightly so. The god of distilled spirits has finally taken me. I'm in hell and slowly being devoured by sea creatures.* He lay back down, resigned to his fate. It was better this way.

A sudden jolt of recollection shocked his body back to life. The image of Lindsay being dragged into the ocean filled his head with horror. She was gone, and he couldn't do anything about it. Or had it been a dream—a nightmare beyond description— caused by yet another drunken stupor? He'd experienced many such nightmares about his parents' death, why not Lindsay? Yet this nightmare seemed far too real. And then he heard a familiar voice coming from a distance. Someone was calling his name from another world. He brushed the seagull from his shoulder and kicked off the crab with a quick jerk of his foot. He heard the voice again, nearer this time. He looked over, spotting a figure standing above him, silhouetted in the bright sunlight.

"Cole, look at you. You're a mess! It's seven thirty and time to leave. Did you get in a fight or something?" Lindsay said, referring to the trickles of blood running down his forehead and off of his foot.

"Lindsay, you're alive! I can't believe it. How—" He stopped short of finishing his sentence at the look of disgust on her face.

"How could you do this? You knew how important this morning was." She glared at the empty bottles lying askew on the deck of his bungalow. "Head Colds weren't enough? You had to empty the entire minibar, too? I should just leave you here in your squalor and let the crabs have their way with you." The large sand crab sat only feet away, facing Cole and looking impatient. Lindsay growled at the crustacean, and it scurried back into the water.

"Here, give me your hand. You need to clean yourself up."

Cole reached out, and Lindsay grabbed his hand, lifting him up with amazing ease. Cole couldn't help but notice that something was different about her. Although he was startled by her strength, there was something else. She looked rejuvenated. Her skin emanated a soft glow, her eyes literally sparkled, and her thick auburn hair was even more luxuriant. The faint smell of salt lingered on her body, like an exotic tropical fragrance. What had happened to her? Cole suddenly felt ashamed of his own appearance.

She led Cole into his bungalow and positioned him to stand by the bed. She unbuttoned his shirt and stripped it off, tossing it out onto the deck. She sat him down and removed what was left of his sandals; apparently there had been more than one crab at work there. Both of the footwear was torn. She stood him up and then unzipped his jeans, yanking them down until the only thing left was his black-and-silver-striped boxers. *Who would wear something like that?*

Lindsay mused. She left the bedside and headed into the bathroom. Cole heard jets of water hitting the tiled shower walls. She returned a moment later and tossed a bath towel in his direction.

"I'll make you some coffee, and then I need to go out to the lobby to tell our driver we'll be late." She cast a disparaging look his way, then returned to the bathroom and filled the coffeemaker with the requisite ingredients. Cole ambled in with a towel wrapped around his waist. His long, muscular body and his six- pack abs didn't go completely unnoticed by Lindsay, although she did her best to ignore them. She placed the hot cup of black coffee on the sink, just as Cole dropped his towel and entered the shower. She lingered for a moment. It was tempting. *Snap out of it,* she admonished herself. *It would be a huge mistake.* Dismissing the image that had popped into her mind, she hurried outside and headed over to the bungalow containing the lobby.

Cole leaned up against the shower wall and let the steaming jets of water cascade off his back. He ached all over. He had never realized so many places on his body could hurt at one time. His head pounded and his throat felt like a furnace; his stomach was tied up in knots. As great a drunk experience as rum provided, the hangover was ten times worse. It would be a long day, he knew. He'd just have to find a way to get through it. He wasn't about to disappoint Lindsay again.

He turned off the twin spigots, reached for the towel, and quickly dried off. Next to the cup of coffee Lindsay had placed three aspirin. He swallowed them up and chugged the coffee in a couple of gulps. Aspirin had apparently saved Frank's life; maybe it would save his, too. Dressing as quickly as he could in a pair of shorts and a Harvard T-shirt, he stuffed his duffel bag with his swim trunks, a pair of athletic shoes, sunscreen, and a few other incidentals. He opened the minibar fridge and found only bottled water. He grabbed two bottles and headed outside. Before he reached the lobby, one bottle was empty, the other only half- full. Hydration was what he needed. He scanned the lobby, but Lindsay was nowhere in sight. He glanced over to the front desk.

"She's out front waiting for you, Mr. Hollingsworth," the attendant said, then turned his attention back to his computer. Cole didn't recognize the young man, but apparently, he knew who Cole was. Suddenly an image of what Lindsay's description of him might have been, flashed through his head. *He'll be the tall guy who looks like he's hung over. He'll be limping from a crab bite. He spent the night passed out on the beach. Just tell Mr. Hollingsworth I'll be outside waiting.*

The young man recognized him at once. Lindsay's description must have been accurate. Cole grimaced, making his way out to the street. Sure enough, Lindsay was outside, leaning up against a black Jeep Cherokee that had seen better days. She was reading what appeared to be a map and conversing with the driver. Cole approached. Lindsay gave him a quick once-over.

"Well, you look presentable, at least. You could have shaved, though. How are you feeling?"

"Better, thank you. Look, Lindsay, I'm really sorry about—"

"Don't apologize, Cole. You don't mean it, and I don't need to hear any more excuses. We're late and people are waiting for us. Please, just get into the Jeep."

Lindsay entered the front passenger's seat. Cole had been relegated to the back. Just one final reminder of who was in charge here.

"Cole, this is Burt, our driver. Burt, this is Cole Hollingsworth."

"Nice to make your acquaintance, Mr. Hollingsworth."

"Please call me Cole, and it's nice to meet you, too. I'm sorry we're late. It was all my fault."

"That's what Lindsay said, but don't worry about it. We'll be on our way shortly. Please buckle up. The ride tends to get a little bumpy."

Cole leaned back in his seat, sighing. That was all he needed, a rough ride while feeling the way he did. Burt seemed amiable enough. He was heavy-set, with white hair and a cigarette stuck behind each ear. His skin was leather- like; deeply tanned and wrinkled, as though he'd spent his entire life outside baking in the tropical sun.

Burt shoved the elongated gearshift into first and popped the clutch. The Jeep lurched forward out onto the main thoroughfare. Cole's stomach did likewise. He gagged, fighting hard not to retch on the spot. Lindsay watched Cole's pained expression reflected in the mirror on the windshield visor. *It serves him right*, she thought. She turned toward the backseat.

"I'm sorry this isn't a limo or your Maserati, with no Serena to talk to, but we need a four-wheel drive to get to where we're going," Lindsay said, a slight mocking tone in her voice.

"That's alright. At least the Jeep doesn't talk back," Cole replied, endeavoring to deflect her obvious sarcasm.

"You own a Maserati? I've always wanted to drive one," Burt said.

"No, you don't. Trust me, Burt. At least you don't want to drive mine."

Lindsay put her hand on Burt's shoulder. "Don't get him started, you'll regret it," she said. Burt nodded, but seemed disappointed.

After driving north on the Queen's Highway for approximately thirty minutes, Burt turned off onto a dirt road that appeared to lead up into the foothills, covered with thick brush and stunted trees. Cole had no idea where they were headed, but at the moment it was all he could do to avoid car sickness.

"I think it's time I gave you this, Cole." Lindsay handed him a slender glass container, filled with a peach-colored liquid that contained a head of foam, like a beer. Cole didn't think he could stomach any more alcohol and he held up his hand in protest.

"No thanks, Lindsay. I'd prefer water, if you've got any. I think I've had enough to drink, don't you?"

"This isn't beer, if that's what you're thinking. Think of it as a tonic for your present condition." She winked at Burt. "It will make you feel better, I promise."

Cole reluctantly took hold of the container, unscrewed the top, and took a sniff. He immediately retracted the foul-smelling concoction from his face. "What is this, contaminated sea water? It smells like sewer waste. You expect me to drink this?"

"If you want to get through the next few miles without making a mess in the backseat, I strongly urge you to grin and bear it. You need to trust me on this."

Cole glanced back down at the beverage, frowning. He lifted the container up to his lips, closed his eyes, and swallowed it. The putrid liquid burned going down, but when it reached his stomach, something wonderful happened. It felt like cool water on a parched throat, or ice on a feverish brow—an elixir that began spreading throughout his gut to every part of his body. He momentarily felt lightheaded, dazed. A rush of spine-tingling coldness engulfed his insides, and he no longer felt any pain. The poisonous aftermath of excessive alcohol had vanished. It was nothing short of a miracle. He stared at Lindsay in amazement. He sat up, his head cleared.

"What was that?" Cole exclaimed.

"Oh, just a little concoction I mixed up for you last night. I know your fondness for rum, but three Head Colds are the equivalent of fifteen full shots of alcohol, never mind the Scotch from the minibar. I knew you'd be hurting today. Rum is the favorite drink down here, but drinking too much of it for too long a time and it will drive you to insanity. I've seen it happen way too often."

"Well, whatever that was, thank you. We should bottle this stuff and sell it commercially. You'd make a fortune," Cole said.

"The tonic comes from a combination of ingredients accessible only in the ocean. It's available in limited quantities and only during certain times of the month. Sorry, Cole, but there'll be no empires built on this little secret."

Cole appeared disappointed, but remained mute. It was enough that it had healed what was probably the worst hangover of his life, at least that he could remember. Even his foot felt better. Damn crabs.

"So, where are we headed now?" Cole said, almost cheerfully, his attitude having taken a dramatic turn.

"We're headed to Redemption Bay. It's on the eastern side of the island, located in the southwest section of the Bermuda Triangle, with an unusually active tectonic shelf and large fields of methane hydrates," Lindsay replied. Cole looked at Lindsay sideways.

"What exactly are methane hydrates?" Cole asked.

"They're a form of natural gas, large bubbles released from deep under the ocean."

"And how are these relevant to my parents' disappearance?"

"You'll see. It's one of those phenomena that are difficult to describe. You need to experience it firsthand." The tone in Lindsay's voice implied that she didn't want to discuss it further in Burt's presence. He obviously wasn't a scientist, and he appeared to be the type that enjoyed local gossip—the type that would take payment from less-than-scrupulous reporters.

The road steepened and the terrain became littered with potholes as they traveled eastward. The Jeep bumped its way up the slope, brushing against low-hanging branches and thick vines. The sky had nearly disappeared. They were in the heart of a small section of jungle now. Although Cole felt remarkably better, he still wasn't enjoying the ride.

"Isn't there a better access road to the Bay?" Cole complained.

"The only other way to get to where we are going is by boat or seaplane. But I don't know a local pilot who'd fly you there," Burt said. "There aren't a lot of skippers who would risk their boats, either. I'm afraid I'm it. Sorry." Burt smiled apologetically into the rearview mirror.

"It's only a few more miles and we'll be there," Lindsay added.

In short order, they reached the apex of the mountain cropping. The entire island of San Salvador was really the peak of a mountain rising some fifteen thousand feet up from the ocean floor. The forested area cleared, revealing an expanse of endless blue sky. Cole caught his first glimpse of the eastern shoreline of San Salvador. The view was breathtaking. The shimmering, aquamarine waters of the Atlantic Ocean sparkled two thousand feet below. Although over 90 percent of San Salvador was at sea level or slightly above, this one section of the island had changed dramatically over the years, carved away by the ocean and tectonic erosion, pushing the landmass upward. This phenomenon was one of the primary reasons that the Gerace Research Centre was located here: to study the evolving geology of this section of the island, until it became too dangerous, too unstable, to explore further. A switchback road loomed ominously below them, snaking its way down the side of the jagged cliffs.

"Don't tell me we're going to attempt to travel down that road, if you can even call it that," Cole said with a heightened sense of alarm.

"Don't worry, Cole. Burt's made this trip many times. Right, Burt?"

Burt nodded, but the expression on his face didn't leave Cole with much confidence. He suddenly wondered how much Lindsay had paid this guy to drive them here. Whatever the amount, it probably wasn't enough.

Burt shifted into four-wheel-drive mode and inched the Jeep downward. The vehicle clung to the side of the cliff like a mountain goat. The road appeared to be the same width as the car. Loose rock and gravel crunched under the Jeep's tires. A sudden lurch and the SUV would be cast out over the edge, bouncing off the side of the crag until it smashed onto the rocky shoreline below. Cole shuddered. Maybe Serena wasn't so bad after all.

Cole couldn't bear it any longer. He sat back, closed his eyes, and returned to the ghoulish dream of the previous night. What had really happened to Lindsay? They hadn't had a chance to discuss it yet. Had it been a dream, or had it been real? And why was she so intent on bringing him here? With Frank's heart attack and Cole's bout of drunkenness providing such distractions, Cole still didn't understand what she expected them to find. A shipwreck? What was waiting below at Redemption Bay?

Suddenly Burt pressed down hard on the brakes, locking up the wheels. The Jeep slid forward, careening to the left. Cole felt a sudden jolt as the vehicle hit the side of the cliff and then came to a sudden, jarring halt.

"What was that?" Cole exclaimed, peering out over the edge of the precipice.

"It was just a jaguar moving across the road. They like to hunt along the cliffs. There are many forms of wildlife that make their home here. Jaguars are an endangered species in the Bahamas and I didn't want to kill one. That's serious business around here. A huge fine, maybe even some jail time."

"Quick thinking, Burt," Cole said, at the same time wondering who the endangered species really was out here on these cliffs. He didn't think it was truly the nimble-footed cat. "I've never heard of big cats in the Bahamas," Cole said, after further consideration. "Isn't the area known for its swimming pigs and endangered iguanas?"

"You're right, but jaguars were secretly imported from South America by a wealthy family that originally owned a large section of Cockburn. They were released into the wild and grew in population before they were hunted. Now only a few remain, and that's why they're a protected species."

Cole had a hard time believing this story, too. It was probably something Burt made up to avert attention away from his questionable driving skills.

"Are we almost there?" Cole finally said. He had no desire to have it all end here—jaguars or not.

"Almost," Burt replied. "Just a little farther. I'll have you there safe and sound in no time."

"Yeah, right! Out of the proverbial frying pan and into the fire," Cole muttered under his breath.

"I heard that, Cole. Mind your manners, okay? Burt's doing us a huge favor," Lindsay instructed.

"And what is this *huge* favor costing *me*?" Cole snapped back, becoming increasingly fed up with the folly of it all. Lindsay didn't answer, further irritating him. It was past time for some answers. He decided it would soon be time to confront Lindsay—that is, if they ever reached the shoreline safely. Cole looked out the side window. A pack of vultures circled overhead. That couldn't be a good sign.

19

Finally, the treacherous road began to level out and widen at the same time. Cole opened the car window and was hit with a sudden gust of sea breeze, carrying with it the briny scent of salt, along with another strong odor he didn't immediately recognize.

"It's methane," Lindsay said, anticipating Cole's next question. "What you smell is methane gas being released from the ocean."

"I didn't realize it would be so offensive. It's rank," Cole complained.

"To the uneducated, I suppose…no slight intended. You'll get used to it, after a while."

The Jeep came to a halt. Burt exited the driver's seat and opened the rear hatch. He laid their belongings on the sand. "Unless there is anything else, this is where we part company. Good luck. I hope you find what you're looking for," Burt said.

Lindsay embraced Burt, thanking him. Cole extended his hand and the driver took it, but said nothing more. He turned, entered the Jeep, and maneuvered the vehicle back toward the road and the arduous return trek up the side of the mountain. Cole looked up, wondering how in the world they had managed to make it safely to the beach. Gazing around, Cole suddenly felt an uncomfortable sense of isolation overtake him. He was surrounded by the starkest of elements: jagged rock cliffs, the glistening white sand of the crescent-shaped beach, and the endless ocean of blue beyond. He might have thought he was on another planet, if it wasn't for the small, solitary structure standing at the northern end of the cove. A single-story shack rose from a pier, jutting out about fifty yards into the glistening water. A rubber inflatable was moored to its side. Cole assumed this was their destination.

"Over there?" Cole asked.

Lindsay nodded, continuing to gaze serenely out at the inimitable ocean—as if it were *her* ocean. She took a few deep breaths, stretching and raising her arms above her head. Cole hoped this wouldn't be a repeat of last night's calamity.

Lindsay turned abruptly and smiled, as though she had suddenly read his mind.

"Cole, don't trouble yourself so. All will be revealed in time." Lindsay picked up her backpack and headed down to the pier. Cole watched her for a time. She moved so gracefully, like a fish in water. She seemed to glide across the beach. He picked up his bag and followed in her wake, failing to notice that, unlike him, Lindsay left no footprints in the sand.

Reaching the pier, Cole found Lindsay engaged in conversation with a tall, angular-looking man in his mid-thirties. His windswept blond hair, bleached almost white, complimented a deep tan. His long, muscular torso reminded Cole of an Olympic swimmer. The boyish smile on his face suggested he could have just as easily been a surfer bum living on a beach somewhere in Southern California. But Cole knew better. He was explaining something in detail to Lindsay, and she was nodding in agreement. He could only be a fellow scientist. Cole approached.

"Hello there," Cole greeted the stranger, extending his hand. The man smiled reticently, but he eventually shook Cole's hand.

"Cole, this is Doctor Andres Almquist. We worked together at MIT's Oceanography Institute, among other places. We have also conducted many deep-sea exploration and research endeavors at Gerace Research Centre up at Grahams Harbour, at the northern tip of San Salvador. Andres, this is the man I've been telling you about. Cole Hollingsworth. Hollingsworth Enterprises is one of Gerace's largest benefactors and has established a generous endowment to further our research. We owe his family a great deal."

Andres gazed at Cole suspiciously as though trying to figure him out.

"At last. By the way, Mr. Hollingsworth, thank you for your generous support of our research." Andres hesitated. "Your recent interest in oceanography wouldn't have anything to do with Lindsay, would it?" The manner in which he asked the question suggested there was a recent history between him and Lindsay, and that Cole was trespassing on his territory.

"Please call me Cole. My father was Mr. Hollingsworth. And by the way, it was my father who created the endowment, not me. He was a well-known philanthropist and a previous America's Cup skipper. He maintained a long love affair with the ocean and donated to many different organizations to further research and exploration. My interest concerns something else," Cole replied stiffly.

Lindsay saw the rancor in Cole's eyes at the suggestion that he might donate a great deal of money to buy her affections. Andres spotted it, too, and backed off a bit.

"Yes, of course. We were all terribly saddened by your parents' recent passing. It truly was a tragedy. It was quite the story around here. Are you aware that most people think their yacht sank in the general vicinity of Redemption Bay? I assume that's why you're here?"

Cole didn't know quite how to respond. He really didn't understand fully the reasons Lindsay had brought him here, but he didn't want to appear ignorant in this man's presence.

"Yes, why else would I be here? I'm hoping to find clues to put some amount of closure on their deaths. I was originally supposed to be traveling with them when their yacht was destroyed by the storm, but business interests wouldn't allow it." *Business interests* sounded a lot better than the endless partying he had actually been engaged in.

"Ah, yes, the life of the rich and famous. I understand all too well. There aren't many people who could command the private use of one of the Institute's most advanced bathyscaphes, along with one of its brightest researchers." He glanced over at Lindsay, whose face had suddenly turned crimson from Andres's rudeness. Cole felt his blood pressure rising, but he refused to let this Swedish scientist, or whoever the hell he was, get the better of him.

"I'm sure the idle lives of the rich seem quite superficial to you, Doctor, but the Institute wouldn't have that bathyscaphe you're so fond of without us. We each, in our own way, provide a service. It's much like a symbiotic relationship, where one can't exist without the other. In other words, we need each other. I'm sure you're capable of understanding that?"

Now it was Andres's turn to struggle with a comeback. Lindsay stood directly behind the doctor stifling a smile. Cole had shut the arrogant son of a bitch up with an artfully crafted détente. It was beautiful in its simplicity, and it was also spot-on. Cole was smarter than she had given him credit for. Perhaps the expensive Harvard education and debate team experience had paid off after all. Lindsay suddenly wondered why she had allowed her affair with Andres to go on so long. She was glad she had ended it. Affirmation was a great feeling.

"We should probably head out to the frigate. Ryan and Cassie are waiting. Lindsay, they don't know yet that you're heading the expedition. I thought it would be best if you told them yourself," Andres said. Lindsay nodded, but remained silent.

"Frigate!" Cole exclaimed. "How did you manage to round one of those up?" Cole's back had been facing the southern end of the cove, and he hadn't noticed the navy vessel anchored out at the far end of the Bay. He turned at once, spotting it.

"It's the USS Truett. It was decommissioned in the nineteen nineties, and eventually ended up at Gerace. All but one of the gun turrets was removed, and the lower deck and hull were renovated to house the submersibles that the Institute uses for its exploration," Andres said.

"Another generous donation by the US Navy, with its maintenance paid for by private donations," Lindsay added, with the slightest edge of sarcasm in her voice.

The threesome climbed down the metal ladder to the inflatable craft, stowing their things up front. Andres started up the outboard and steered it out of the cove and into the Bay beyond. The pristine water showcased a variety of colorful sea life down to a depth of about two hundred feet. Even though Cole had spent time in the tropics, he was still amazed by the clarity of the aquamarine waters. Back home, you couldn't see two feet below the surface.

As they sped toward the *Truett*, Cole wondered what Lindsay had up her sleeve and how a sailing vessel of this magnitude could be waiting for them. How many people did it take to man a ship this large? Even though this was one of the smaller classes of frigates, its size was still impressive; long and sleek, its gunmetal- gray color contrasted with the natural, bright organic colors of the Caribbean. A large green logo proclaiming the domain of *Gerace Oceanography*, painted on its hull.

Andres maneuvered the craft to the back of the ship, tying it off. There was a special loading platform extending off the ship's stern for easy access. Two metal hatches opened to stairwells, which led to the upper decks. A few minutes later, they were standing on the top deck looking back at the cove and the expanse of sandy beach. It looked much smaller from this perspective, the jagged cliffs beyond more benign. Cole hoped Burt had made it back safely.

Two figures appeared out of the main cabin, walking in their direction. One man, one woman, dressed in wetsuits, as though they had recently returned from a dive. As they approached, they abruptly stopped in their tracks, appearing stunned. Lindsay stepped forward. "Lindsay?" the man said breathlessly. "Is that really you? But I thought you had—" Lindsay raised a finger to her lips, silently instructing the man to hush up, and then extended her arms. The woman flung herself at her, too, as if she were a long-lost child come back from the grave. The man joined the embrace, and the threesome stood in silence holding each other for some time.

"Where have you been, Lindsay? We've heard so many rumors," the man said, clearly bewildered.

"Here and there. I needed some time alone after the incident. I did some traveling to"—she hesitated—"to get my head on straight. But I'm back now." Lindsay glanced at Cole to catch his reaction. Cole looked on with a puzzled expression, not quite getting the gist of the conversation.

"I hate to break up this little reunion, but we have work to do," Andres stated authoritatively, as though he was accustomed to being in command. Lindsay released herself from her friend's embrace.

"We'll talk later," Lindsay whispered to the pair. "Cassie, Ryan, this is Cole Hollingsworth. He's the reason we're here. Cole, this is Cassie Thomas and Ryan Walker, very good friends of mine and two of the most accomplished divers I've ever worked with. They've volunteered to help in our, um, exploration. In exchange for a little R-and-R onshore, of course." She smiled coyly at her friends.

Ryan continued to look awestruck, gazing at Lindsay in silence. Cassie looked far less stunned now, although her initial reaction had been quite emotional.

"It's great to meet you two, and thank you for helping out," Cole said, shaking their hands indecisively, not knowing exactly what he was thanking them for.

"Sure, we're happy to help out, especially for someone like you, Mr. Hollingsworth," Cassie said, her Australian accent obvious. Ryan rolled his eyes.

"Can we please get one thing straight? My name is Cole, okay? Everyone is being so formal." The pair nodded nervously, realizing the importance of what the Hollingsworth money meant to their research and at the same time wanting to show respect.

Lindsay grabbed Cole's hand. "Ready for a walkabout? It's pretty impressive," Lindsay said, impersonating her own version of Cassie's accent.

Cassie blushed, her smile wide and endearing. She was a beautiful woman in her own right, with thick brown hair streaked with gold, dark skin, a demur-like presence about her. Ryan looked just like one would envision a world-class diver to be. Deeply tanned, tousled hair, all muscle. Casual, yet possessing an air of confidence. Cole wondered if they were a couple.

Cole followed Lindsay into the main cabin to check out the navigation controls, before heading belowdecks to take a tour of the modified frigate. It appeared that money had not been an obstacle. Everything appeared to be first-rate. High-tech oceanography equipment and instruments lined the walls. The ship's radar capability seemed second to none. Depth finders, sonar devices, and just about anything else required for undersea exploration could be found below. In the center of the second deck a large rectangle had been cut out and lined with a metal railing. Below sat the *Harbinger II*, the flagship of the Institute's deep-sea submersibles. It was floating in its own pool of sea water, anchored to the sides with thick, metal cables.

Cole felt a sudden wave of claustrophobia wash over him. It wasn't that he was afraid of restricted spaces, but the impressive vessel below was intimidating—a close-quartered iron lung capable of taking them to the bottom of the deepest parts of the ocean, where only a few people had ever ventured before. Cole suddenly realized why Andres might have felt resentment over the special treatment he was receiving. This was no small excursion. This was a very big, very expensive undertaking. And all for what?

20

The group spent the remainder of the afternoon familiarizing Cole with the wide variety of equipment and its uses. Being familiar with boating himself, Cole caught on quickly, but he was nevertheless impressed with the capabilities of the *Truett*. Having spent his entire life around yachts and racing boats, the fact that he was now on a military-type war cruiser gave him an entirely new perspective. If only his parents could have been on a similar vessel, maybe it would have made a difference. His father could have afforded it, instead of the elegant but antiquated wooden yacht he was so fond of. But Cole couldn't afford to think like that now.

"Cole, would you like to take a closer look at the *Harbinger*?" Lindsay said.

He looked down at the submersible, suddenly realizing why he was here. He'd have to face it sometime; it might as well be now. It was obvious he would be taking a dive in it, even though Lindsay had yet to reveal exactly what her plans were. Cole nodded.

"Why don't you guys head up to the galley and see what's for dinner? I'll take Cole below and then I'll join you," Lindsay said.

The two divers headed back up to the top deck, while Lindsay led the way down the metal stairs. Lindsay spun the metal wheel on the top hatch and lifted it open. Cole heard a sudden *whooshing* sound, followed by a blast of air, like a vacuum-sealed compartment had just been opened. Lights flashed on, illuminating the interior space. Lindsay descended partway, looked back up at Cole as if she wanted to say something, then disappeared into the belly of the *Harbinger.*

Cole hesitated for a moment, realizing again that this appeared to be another point of no return. By going inside, he was agreeing to accept what awaited him there—what Lindsay had planned for him.

Cole slipped down into the cramped space, his large frame a hindrance. He continued to climb down through the float section of the submersible and into the crew cabin, technically called the pressure sphere. The interior made his fifty-million- dollar jet look like a child's toy. The clusters of scientific instruments, navigation controls, and auxiliary equipment filled the space, allowing barely enough room for the two- person crew. Previously hidden by the level of water surrounding the vessel, the front facing of the pressure sphere was a large, specially built Plexiglas observation window. Two smaller porthole-like windows were on both the port and starboard sides. Two seats, one behind the other, were positioned facing the observation window. What looked like oxygen tanks were attached to each wall. There was almost no room to maneuver around the interior space.

Cole wasn't sure what to think; all he could do was stare, imagining what it would be like to reach the bottom of the ocean's floor, if indeed that was where they were headed. He recalled Lindsay's vague description of the Mariana Trench and filmmaker James Cameron's historic descent into Challenger Deep, some thirty-five thousand feet under water.

"What do you think?" Lindsay said, as she continued to show him the interior of the cabin. "It's really something, isn't it?" She was talking about the *Harbinger* like it was a family member.

"Yeah, it's really something," Cole said awkwardly. He wasn't sure what else to say. "So…Lindsay, what's the plan? Where are we going? I can only assume with a deep-sea exploration vessel like this, you're taking me to the bottom of the ocean."

"More or less. Hey, I'm hungry and Cassie's a great cook. After dinner there'll be more time to talk." Lindsay headed up the stairway.

Cole lingered, even more conflicted than before. Why wouldn't Lindsay just be honest with him? What was she hiding? He continued to examine the interior of the vessel, attempting to envision the descent to the bottom.

When Cole returned to the top deck, there was a makeshift table arranged with four place settings. Cassie, Ryan, and Lindsay were already sipping bottles of beer. Andres was dressed in long khaki pants and a lime-colored linen shirt, staring out toward land. He obviously had other plans for the night.

"There you are," Andres said. "I'm headed back onshore. Just waiting to be picked up. I wanted to say good-bye."

"You won't be here tomorrow?" Cole said.

"No, my business is done for now. This is Lindsay's show. Good luck." Andres turned back toward the shoreline as though washing his hands of the whole thing. The sound of a sleek, go- fast boat grew louder as it approached, skimming across the Bay, a large plume of water following in its wake. Andres strolled over to the stern of the frigate and descended the steps to the platform below, without saying another word.

"Hey, guys, anyone hungry?" Ryan said, flashing a smile and handing Cole a beer.

"Starving!" Lindsay replied. "What are you treating us to tonight?"

"I thought we'd start with some octopus and sea urchin soup, followed by fresh sautéed marlin steaks," Cassie said, then took a little bow as if she had just been named chef of the year.

"Can't wait," Lindsay said and took a seat at the table.

Cole had never eaten octopus before—or sea urchin. Wasn't that a crustacean? His stomach suddenly turned queasy. Marlin sounded edible, though. He'd just have to make it through the soup course. A few more beers and he'd be fine.

"Dinner will be coming up soon." The two divers headed inside to finish preparing the food.

Cole stood for a moment, watching Lindsay with the sea breeze blowing her hair into her eyes. She looked so alive out here, like she drew strength from the ocean. The sun was beginning to dip behind the islands to the west. It really was a picture-perfect moment. And it would have been, if not for the uncertainty that loomed ever closer.

The divers returned with four bowls of steaming soup, if they could be called bowls. They were actually hollowed-out shells of the sea urchins themselves filled with chunks of octopus, shrimp, and clams, all floating in a savory broth infused with fresh herbs and a hint of garlic. A loaf of crusty bread accompanied the first course. Cole was stunned when he tasted the broth. He could have been at one of Newport's finest seafood restaurants—it was that good. Lindsay watched as Cole devoured the soup.

"I told you, Cole. These guys can cook anything. I tried to talk them into opening a restaurant a few years ago, but they declined. Said they could never stay put in one place that long."

"Kind of like you," Cole said, gazing pensively into Lindsay's gray eyes.

"Yeah, kind of like me," Lindsay replied wistfully.

"Ready for the next course?" Cassie said, noticing the underlying current of apprehension growing in Cole's demeanor.

"Do you need any help, Cassie?" Lindsay offered.

"Sure—thanks. Ryan, would you mind opening the wine?"

Ryan retrieved a bottle of chilled reserve chardonnay from the nearby wine bucket and proceeded to open it. He poured an ounce into Cole's wineglass and waited for him to taste it. Cole noticed the Napa Valley appellation on the label. *Is this a research vessel or a cruise ship?* Cole mused. They didn't seem to be lacking in the amenities.

"The wine is great, thanks. Grgich Hills Estate is one of my favorites. I'm surprised you have access to a limited vintage like this."

"We have our ways," Ryan said, grinning. "We do a little bartering on our trips. You'd be surprised what you can get in return for things like abalone, sea pearls—stuff like that."

Before Cole could question Ryan further on his questionable trading practices, the women returned with the next course. Again, plates had been replaced with a shell, but this time it was the aforementioned abalone. Cole wondered if the poor, unsuspecting sea snail was being served in one of Napa's numerous Michelin Star restaurants in exchange for the chardonnay. The perfectly seared blue marlin steak rested in a pool of lemon and butter foam, topped with a mélange of tropical fruit. It was almost too beautiful to eat. The crisp, slightly oaky wine was the perfect complement to the rich dish. Too soon the abalone plates were cleared, a second bottle of chardonnay was opened. A few minutes later, dessert was presented.

"Cassie made this especially for you, Cole," Lindsay said, unable to suppress a grin.

Cassie placed a large plate on the table, and Cole's mouth dropped open. Before him sat a pineapple upside-down rum cake, decorated with what looked like a miniature sand crab on one end and a seagull on the other, fashioned out of colorful frosting.

"Lindsay told us about your fondness for rum, so, well… we thought it was the least we could do to repay you for your generous support of our research."

"That was very thoughtful of you, Cassie," Cole said, eyeing Lindsay with a less-than-congenial expression. "I especially like your choice of decorations. I don't suppose Lindsay had anything to do with that!"

"No, of course not…" The threesome couldn't hold back their laughter any longer. "I'm sorry, Cole. Lindsay mentioned your little escapade last night, and we couldn't resist. I hope you'll forgive us," Cassie said between snorts of laughter.

Cole's face flushed with embarrassment, but there was little he could do. When it came right down to it, all his money, his power, his prestige, none of it meant shit out here. He was in their world now, not the corporate boardroom. This unsuspecting trio of sea-goers had suddenly stripped him naked of his pride, exposing him in a manner that he might have used to someone back home. After a long moment of contemplation, Cole looked up.

"I suppose I deserved that. But how…when could you have put this all together?" Cole said incredulously.

"While you were putting your things away in your cabin, Lindsay asked what we would be cooking for dinner. She told me about what happened last night and asked if I could come up with something creative to commemorate your first time here in San Salvador and she…" Cassie paused, "she helped me. It was either that or make a cake that resembled a prostitute from the Cantina de la Noche. Since I didn't have any miniature umbrellas, I chose the former. It had more of a nautical theme." The group broke out laughing again. However, Cole didn't join them.

"Come on, Cole, be a good sport," Lindsay said. "They're just having fun."

"That's what happens when you spend long periods of time at sea. You acquire a warped sense of humor," Ryan interjected. "It happens to everyone."

"At least I have that to look forward to," Cole groused.

Lindsay leaned over and gave him a kiss on the cheek. "Before you know it, you'll be just like us," she whispered in his ear. She smiled fetchingly at him, and slowly his embarrassment and anger drained away.

Cole might have remained angry with someone who had played a similar prank on him for days, if not weeks. He could dish it out, but he was not as good at taking it in return. But Lindsay, the schoolgirl he had taunted so unmercifully in the past, somehow possessed a mysterious power over him. He couldn't stay angry with her. In her eyes, he saw the reflection of the man he wanted to be, not the cad he had been all of his life.

Cole raised his glass in mock salute to his defeat, like a king suddenly dethroned, and began to laugh out loud at himself. "You know you've hit bottom when you've got a sand crab chewing on one end of your body and a seagull pecking your brains out on the other. I'm afraid my days with rum are over."

"Hear, hear!" Lindsay exclaimed and the trio raised their glasses, as well.

21

Evening stars filled the endless Caribbean sky, the moon a beacon of shimmering light turning the waves below to liquid silver. The night was quiet, so quiet. Cole began to feel as if he were slipping into a dream with Lindsay by his side, his two new friends snuggling together nearby on a deck cot. Ryan and Cassie rose in unison.

"We'll see you two in the morning. Pleasant dreams," Cassie said, and the pair walked hand in hand belowdecks, leaving Cole and Lindsay alone.

"Quite an evening," Cole said. "You're lucky to have such good friends."

"I know. They would literally give you the shirt off their backs if it would be of help. I've missed them."

"They seemed surprised to see you. Ryan, especially. By his initial reaction I got the impression he thought something bad had happened to you."

"They were just startled, that's all. They were made aware that you'd be here, but I think they assumed Andres would be in charge. I wouldn't worry about it."

"There's something you're not telling me, Lindsay. Don't you think it's about time to come clean and explain why we're really here?"

Lindsay looked over; her expression filled with an interminable sadness. "It's a long story, Cole. I'm not sure how to tell you…or that you'd even believe me if I did. Maybe it's better to let things just play out. It may be the only way you'll understand what really happened. All I can ask of you is for your trust." Lindsay went silent.

Cole considered her words, realizing at the same time that something was weighing heavily on her. A burden she was holding on to so tightly—a burden he was sure needed to be released. She seemed determined to tell him in her own time, though, and Cole had little choice but to trust her. Where else could he go? He decided to change the subject.

"Are there sand crabs on this beach?"

"What? What do crabs have to do with anything?" Lindsay said, her mind elsewhere and puzzled by the question.

"I thought it might be fun to sleep on the beach tonight. You know, be the only ones. We'd have it all to ourselves. It's a warm night, and I'm not drunk. I promise to control myself." Cole smiled, reaching over to stroke Lindsay's hand.

Lindsay's eyes widened at his touch. She gazed back at him with eyes like pools of moonlight. She instantly knew what Cole was asking of her. Perhaps a night of pleasure was what he needed before confronting the truth tomorrow. It was in her power to grant him his wish…and hers, too. Instinctively, though, she knew a connection like that might spell the difference between life and death when it came to a critical moment. Cole needed to maintain a clear head. Such a night would only confuse matters between them.

"Cole, this is a big ship, there's room for us all. The beach would be nice, but…" Lindsay's voice trailed off.

"But what? What are you afraid of?"

"I'm not afraid of you, if that's what you mean."

"Then what is it? Why won't you let me get close to you? You drop hints and then you turn and run away, retreat inside yourself. I don't understand."

"It's complicated—*I'm* complicated. In the long run you'd be better off without me."

"Don't you think I should be the one to decide that?" Cole hesitated, unsure of what to say next. "You make me a better man, Lindsay. When I'm with you, all the other useless crap I do just disappears. It's not important any longer."

Lindsay's heart sank. What woman wouldn't want to hear words like that, especially from someone like Cole? "Cole, let's just stay on deck tonight. Perhaps the beach awaits us another time. It's not going anywhere, you know."

She walked over to his chair and sat down on his lap. Wrapping an arm around his neck, she bit his ear playfully. She stroked the nape of his neck. Running her other hand down his cheek, she whispered something in his ear— an incantation in an unrecognizable language. His eyes drooped. His pulse slowed. Gradually Cole drifted off into a semiconscious state as the night grew darker.

Cole felt a sudden tugging on his arm and he was lifted up from his deck chair. Lindsay led him silently to the stern of the *Truett* and down the long flight of metal stairs. Cole found himself standing on the docking platform facing the water. Lindsay stepped into the inflatable boat, reaching out her hand for Cole to join her. He stepped down. Lindsay wrapped her arms around his neck, kissing him hungrily.

The next thing Cole knew, they were skimming along the water headed for the secluded beach. She had apparently changed her mind. Cole couldn't believe it. The raft ran up onto the sand, beaching itself. Lindsay hopped out, hesitated for a moment, then sprinted down the beach, occasionally looking back to ensure Cole was following.

She is going to make a game of this, Cole thought. So be it. He liked the hunt as much as anyone. It was like stalking a lioness, knowing that at any moment the predator could turn and attack, ripping him to shreds. He was helpless to resist—all that mattered was catching her. Gradually, he cut the distance between them. He heard her labored breathing as she struggled to maintain the lead. She veered sharply left, advancing up the slope of the beach toward the forested area. He had to catch her before she entered the tree line or lose her forever.

Pulling on his reserve energy, fueled by insatiable lust, he sprinted the last hundred feet, overtaking her just yards short of the trees. She ducked, barely able to avoid his grasp, and then veered back toward the water. Breathing hard, he turned and pursued, finally catching her near the water's edge. He grabbed her waist, taking her down like a fallen gazelle. They rolled over and over on the dampened sand and came to a halt, with Lindsay on top. Their chests heaved with the exertion of the chase, and they struggled to regain their breath. But this time, Lindsay didn't try to escape his grasp. Instead, she pressed her body down hard on his, kissing his mouth wantonly. He ripped off her blouse, exposing her perfect breasts. She tore at his shirt, slashing it with long, manicured nails, like the claws of a cat. He rolled her over and slid off her shorts, exploring every crevice of her luscious body with his mouth. She moaned in ecstasy.

Lindsay unzipped his shorts, frantically tugging them down his legs, then stroked his erect manhood. She guided him inside of her. They moved together like waves lapping the shoreline. Rhythmic, fluid, each thrust bringing with it a new wave of euphoria, until they were totally spent, collapsing on the sand, breathless. The warm, tropical water gently touched their feet before receding, shimmering and reflecting the moonlight. The air was still and silent.

They lay joined together in an ethereal embrace. Somewhere between the chase and the final rapture, morning had dawned, bringing with it a shuddering coldness. The weather had changed dramatically. Thunderclouds were forming on the eastern horizon, turning the dawn a deep, velvety scarlet.

Cole opened his eyes, shocked to find himself back on the ship, lying on a deck lounge, Lindsay by his side, her head resting on his chest with one arm wrapped around his waist, fast asleep.

"Lindsay, wake up! What are we doing back here?"

Lindsay opened her eyes sleepily. "What's wrong, Cole?"

"We were just on the beach. How did we get back here?"

"You must have been dreaming, Cole…and by the look of it, it was a very good dream." She pointed to a rather large erection bulging in his pants. He quickly tried to cover up but no blankets were available. His face reddened.

"It's okay, just a natural reaction from a healthy man. A little morning woody. Well, in your case, not so little." She grinned. "I can leave for a while so you can take care of that." She pointed again. "Or you can just think of something horrible and it will eventually go away." She said this with such laid-back indifference, Cole could hardly believe it, although her insinuation that he should masturbate riled him.

She rose from the deck lounge and faced the side of the ship, gazing out toward the water and running her hands through her long, tangled mane of hair. Cole looked away. That would only make him harder, watching her. He thought about the *Harbinger* and tried to envision himself on the ocean floor with water flooding in through a cracked porthole. The water was rising quickly to the top as he gasped for air, and it would only be a matter of minutes until he drowned. That seemed to do the trick.

Had this really been just another dream? No dream had felt like that before. He rose and straightened his shorts with the brush of his hand. He felt something coarse on his palm. He raised his hand, stunned to see that it contained grains of sand. He glanced over at Lindsay and noticed something odd. She was wearing a different top. He didn't recall her changing last night. He was about to confront her when she turned to face him. Her eyes had gone dark, her expression solemn.

"Are you ready, Cole?"

"Ready for what?" Cole replied, uncertain of her meaning.

"Ready for the dive. We can't put if off much longer."

Cole suddenly lost all interest in sex. The thought of descending to the bottom of the ocean scared the hell out of him, now that the time had come. He had no idea what to expect, only that it had something to do with his parents. Had Lindsay found their sunken yacht? The night of his birthday celebration she had told him it was not too late—that they could still save them somehow. But save them from what? As preposterous as that had sounded at the time, he didn't think she was the type to play games, at least not about something like this. But Lindsay had been so vague about it, and every time he had pressed her for clarification, she avoided answering his questions. He supposed some of those questions were about to be answered.

"I guess so. We might as well get this over with," Cole replied. Lindsay saw the fear in his eyes. But was his fear caused by the descent to the ocean floor or the truth that awaited him there?

"Cole, you should go below and have some breakfast. Eat lightly. Cassie's prepared a balanced combination of protein and carbohydrates. But no coffee this morning. And no alcohol under any conditions. I know you're nervous, it's only natural."

Cole frowned at her accusation that he needed a drink to find the courage to make the dive.

"After you've eaten, use the restroom and then find Ryan for your wetsuit. He'll fix you up with everything you'll need and explain the various characteristics of the suit. After that, we'll begin your orientation period."

"Anything else, Captain?" Cole remarked sarcastically. "By the way, what will you be doing all this time?"

"Preparing." With that, Lindsay hurried away, leaving Cole to contemplate the fate that awaited him. Cole stood for a moment, watching Lindsay disappear belowdecks and wondering how the hell he had gotten himself into this mess. Suddenly the burden of running his father's empire seemed almost mundane.

"Sleep well, Cole?" Cassie asked, as she handed him a plate of scrambled eggs, wheat toast, and steamed ham. "Water or milk?"

"Water, thank you. And to answer your question, no, I didn't sleep particularly well. What is it about the tropics? I have the strangest dreams down here."

"Oh, I don't think *strange* even begins to describe it." Cassie smiled and disappeared without further explanation. Cole shook his head and began to eat. Although the food was nicely prepared, it was about as bland as anything he had eaten in some time. *Did they run out of salt and pepper on deck?* Cole wondered. Dinner last night was incredible, but this? It would not be difficult to eat *lightly*, as Lindsay had put it.

Twenty minutes later, Cole was standing in a cramped cabin room filled with diving gear. Ryan was rummaging through a variety of items when Cole announced his arrival.

"Hey, Cole, did you sleep well last night?" Ryan had a smirk on his face, like he knew something that Cole didn't. *Why is everyone so concerned about how I slept*, Cole thought.

"Yes, I slept fine, thanks," Cole replied, not wanting to engage in any further cryptic conversations.

"If you say so," Ryan said, continuing to grin.

"Lindsay told me to come see you for my wetsuit…" Before Cole could finish his thought, Ryan turned away and continued his search through the myriad of gear hanging from all four walls, talking to himself.

"Is there something wrong, Ryan? What are you looking for?"

"Just for something that will work. Most of this gear hasn't been used in some time, and a lot of it looks like it needs repairing. I can't believe the Institute would let this stuff remain on deck. Safety has always been their top priority. I guess they're just slacking off. Budget cuts!" he muttered.

"You've got to be joking!" Cole exclaimed, horrified that equipment so vital to a diver's survival would go unmaintained.

"Hold on, I think I found something. It may be a bit small for you, but I think it will do. You don't mind being a little restricted, do you? Besides, the space inside the *Harbinger*'s pressure sphere is so cramped you really can't move around much anyway. You'll get used to it. After a while." Ryan yanked a wetsuit off of the wall, holding it at arm's length and scrutinizing it like it was somehow contagious.

"That'll be enough, Ryan!" a familiar voice sounded from behind the men. "You're scaring poor Cole to death." Cassie tapped Cole on the shoulder. "Don't pay any attention to him, he's just being a jerk!"

And then it dawned on Cole that he was being played again, made to feel the fool.

Ryan turned and broke out laughing. "Poor Cole? I rather doubt that," Ryan replied. "I apologize, Cole, just having a little fun with the rookie. If I'm ever in your boardroom in Providence, feel free to give me some shit in return, okay? After all, turnabout is fair play."

"That's Newport, actually, and I look forward to it," Cole said contemptuously.

"Now, now, gentlemen, let's play nice," Cassie said.

The thought suddenly occurred to Cole that this was all contrived. They were subtly stripping him of his pride—bringing him down to their level. The great and famous Cole Hollingsworth, heir to one of the largest fortunes in the United States, being made fun of, like some schoolkid on a new playground. His thoughts flashed to Lindsay. This was how he had treated her all through high school. God, what an asshole he had been. He now knew how it felt. Roiling with anger, he somehow managed to maintain his cool.

After an extended moment of awkwardness, Cassie broke the silence. "Cole, let's go next door and get you set up. This room is where we store the diving gear we find during our explorations. We bring it all back to the Institute and have it repaired and then donate it to various organizations. You'd be surprised at how much we find."

Ryan stifled a laugh and headed out the doorway. Cole cursed. Cassie led Cole to a spacious room that looked like a showroom at a scuba gear convention. The space sparkled like it had been recently scrubbed, everything appearing brand new and placed precisely in the right position and labeled appropriately. It was a diver's dream. State-of-the-art equipment that looked like it had hardly been used.

"I think this one will do," Cassie said. Ryan lifted the heavily padded latex suit off of the wall, a mixture of interwoven burgundy and dark gray material of exceptional quality. Circular tubes ran up and down its sides. Two metal rails protruded from the back. A combination rubber and metal neck seal and wrist cuffs created a watertight system. It seemed like something a Marvel comic book superhero might wear—a cross between a spacesuit and a wetsuit.

"Why don't you try it on? There's a changing room through that doorway," Cassie said, pointing to the far end of the cabin. Cole grabbed the suit from Ryan and headed toward the changing room.

"Sorry it's not an Armani, Cole, but this whole gig was fast-tracked and we didn't know your size. You understand…"

Cole's body stiffened. He was about to turn and give Ryan a piece of his mind when he heard Lindsay's voice in the background.

"You guys about ready? We're heading out to sea in thirty minutes and I want Cole to have ample time to acclimate to the *Harbinger*."

"Be right there," Cassie said, turning to Ryan. "Be nice, okay? Cole doesn't deserve your sarcasm," she whispered tersely.

"Are you sure about that?" Ryan replied as he strode past Cassie and out the door.

Ten minutes later, Cole joined his companions on the deck overlooking the famous bathyscaphe. It suddenly looked far more ominous. When he had first seen it, Cole was fascinated by the technology, along with everything else on display in the frigate. Now that he was about to embark on a journey deep into the ocean, Cole felt far less enamored by the *Harbinger*.

"It's a good fit," Lindsay said, admiring Cole encased in the wetsuit that fit his body like a glove. Tall, lean, yet muscular, Cole looked like an alien warrior standing there. Dark eyes, black hair, unshaven, he no longer resembled an East Coast businessman. Lindsay liked the way he looked now. The one-piece suit had heavily padded feet, long sleeves, and a stiff open collar.

"Hey, Aqua Man, looking good," Cassie said, flashing him the thumbs-up sign. That brought the hint of a smile to his face. Finally, a compliment.

"Thanks."

"Hey, stud, are you ready for the big dive?" Ryan said as he entered the deck area. His demeanor had changed noticeably, as had his expression. He seemed all business now. "You couldn't have a better guide than Dr. Featherstone. There's no one else I'd trust more."

Dr. Featherstone? At first it failed to register with Cole. Somewhere along the way he had forgotten that Lindsay was a renowned oceanographer and PHD Laureate. Not a bad accomplishment for the awkward teenager with the braces and Coke bottle–lens glasses. At least she had made something of herself, unlike him. Everything he had had been given to him. Everything she was, she had earned. He felt a strange sense of gratitude—gratitude that she was by his side for this terrifying undertaking, although he still did not understand what they were trying to achieve. He continued to stare at Lindsay furtively.

"What are you looking at, Cole? Are you alright?" Lindsay said.

Cole nodded but said nothing. Both Cassie and Ryan couldn't help but notice the intensity in their wordless gaze, like the world as they knew it was about to come to an end. Breaking the silence, the *Truett's* engines roared to life and the entire ship vibrated.

"Well, I guess it's time to join our crewmates," Cassie said, her Australian accent adding a sense of international intrigue to the situation. "We'll see you two before submersion."

The two divers left the area. The whole situation was feeling more and more surreal. It began to feel like it was spiraling out of control, and they hadn't even begun the descent. Cole's sense of helplessness grew with every passing minute. He preferred to be in control, at least when he wasn't drinking, and even then, he had some sense of what was happening to him. Lindsay crooked her head, continuing to stare at him, as if she were reading his thoughts--again.

"Are you ready to get started, Cole?" Lindsay's voice seemed to be coming from a distance, waking Cole from his meditative state.

"I suppose so. What do we do now?"

"We're headed southeast about thirty miles out. While we still have some time, I'd like you to get acclimated to the inside of the *Harbinger*. It takes a little getting used to. We'll strap you in and put your helmet on. Since the craft is partially submerged in seawater and all of the port viewing will be underwater, you'll get a sense of what it's like when we begin the dive. Follow me."

Lindsay led Cole down the narrow entrance tunnel through the float section, which measured nearly sixty feet long and twelve feet high. At first sight, the bathyscaphe seemed to Cole more like a small submarine, and its sheer size had relieved some of his anxiety. However, it now felt as restrictive as if he had just been buried alive in a metal coffin. The divers' cabin, or pressure sphere, seemed even smaller than it had on his first visit: two seats, a couple of Plexiglas viewing ports, and more instrumentation per square inch than anything he had seen before. Lindsay switched on the lights and the cabin's interior suddenly glowed eerily green. Cole's blood pressure spiked and he could feel his pulse quicken—and he hadn't even left the confines of the frigate's lower deck.

"Take your seat here," Lindsay said, pointing to the second

seat behind the main controls. Cole eased his large frame into the cramped space, as an unwelcome sense of claustrophobia washed over him. He wasn't really afraid of small spaces, but something about this seemed different. The fact that they would soon be over five miles underwater, weighed down by a crushing pressure of seventeen thousand pounds per square inch in total darkness, might have had something to do with it. Lindsay had previously explained some of this to him, but what really awaited at the bottom of the ocean was anybody's guess.

Lindsay reached around Cole, strapping him in. He noticed a pewter-gray oxygen helmet locked into the lower section of the seat in front of him. "Release the lock, Cole, take out the helmet, and put it on. It will lock into the metal ring on your collar. It's been specially fitted to your wetsuit to be airtight. Next, we'll hook up the oxygen-flow tubes to your suit. This is a safety measure should anything go wrong with the ventilation system inside the *Harbinger*. It's just precautionary, of course."

Cole locked the helmet into place, and the interior of the *Harbinger* seemed to suddenly restrict, like the walls were collapsing in around him—his line of vision reduced by about 40 percent. A second wave of panic hit him.

"Just breathe slowly, Cole. You'll get accustomed to it." Lindsay's voice was barely audible.

Cole forced himself to relax. Closing his eyes, he envisioned the two of them lying on a secluded beach surrounded by an expanse of blue sky and sun. He felt Lindsay's hand on his shoulder. How could she be so brave? He suddenly felt like a boy standing on top of the high diving board for the first time, surrounded by people yelling at him to jump. Fortunately, it would be Lindsay at the controls; otherwise he would have unstrapped himself and left this accursed craft, never looking back.

Lindsay knocked on his helmet, mouthing the words *"I'll be back in a few minutes and connect the intercom controls between our helmets."* Cole reached out to grab her hand, but she had already passed beyond his grasp.

For an excruciating period of minutes that felt like hours, Cole sat in silence, strapped into what seemed more like an electric chair than a seat in one of the world's top submersibles.

It had gone very quiet—and the stillness was unnerving. But as Lindsay had predicted, calm slowly set in, and Cole found himself able to breathe normally, his pulse slowing. He began looking around, out through the portholes. All he could see was the murky water and the vague metal insides of the submersion chamber, but it did provide a sense of being underwater. He tried to imagine what the world of deep-sea diving would look like. Surely it would be different than the brightly colored coral reefs he and his buddies had snorkeled in, chasing girls clad in skimpy bikinis. He didn't think he'd find any of those at twenty-seven thousand feet. A mermaid, perhaps? The thought of that made him smile. Maybe mermaids really did exist. Now *that* would make a great story for one of his publications. *Cole Hollingsworth encounters a real-life mermaid on a historical dive to the bottom of the Bermuda Triangle.* Yeah, right! Back to reality.

Lindsay returned ten minutes later accompanied by the divers, all looking particularly somber, as if they already knew what dangers lay below. Lindsay jumped into the water to the side of the *Harbinger*, pushing herself down to Cole's level. She gestured for him to unbuckle and return topside. Cole took little convincing and quickly extricated himself from the cabin. Lindsay stood next to Cassie and Ryan, as the seawater cascaded down her wetsuit. Her hair was tied up in a tight net. She had donned a deep-sea chronometer and was holding a clipboard filled with underwater charts. Her expression remained implacable as she spoke with the divers and reviewed last-minute details. She appeared as resolved as Cole had ever seen her.

Before Cole could question her, all three turned in his direction. Cassie was the first to speak.

"Cole, we will be in contact with both of you at all times. We have water-to-surface communication devices installed in the pressure sphere and also directly to your helmets, should you need to put them on. All atmospheric conditions within the bathyscaphe will be monitored from the communication center on this frigate. We also have video feeds directly into the cabin. The descent to the ocean floor is about three hours in duration. Any last-minute questions?"

Cole might have had a hundred questions, but he was consumed by only one thought. *Where the hell are we really going… and why?*

"No, but thanks for asking. All joking aside, you guys have been great." Cole smiled, trying his best to sound convincing, then added, "See you back up topside."

"You can count on it," Ryan said, without a hint of sarcasm in his voice this time. The divers watched silently as Cole and Lindsay disappeared into the *Harbinger*. When they were safely buckled in and ready, Lindsay pressed a button on what looked like the primary navigation center.

"We're ready. Cassie, please begin the undocking protocols." Lindsay continued to inspect a variety of monitors and check them off on a sheet of paper. Ryan turned a series of sturdy metal levers, while Cassie stared at a computer screen. A loud *swishing* sound followed as the bottom doors of the frigate's holding chamber swung open. The area immediately flooded with more seawater. A moment later the *Harbinger* vanished. Cassie and Ryan exchanged worried looks. There was no turning back now. Events that would irrevocably change the lives of a number of people had just been set in motion.

22

Submerged in liquid space, the *Harbinger* began its descent through the clear, aquamarine water. Cole stared out in amazement as the craft sank slowly into the depths. Colorful fish and other aquatic life filled the nearby space. A school of blue- striped snapper darted sideways, as the submersible crossed their path. They looked like trained dancers, moving in perfect unison and making the Radio City Music Hall Rockettes look like amateurs. Their bright blue and yellow scales shimmered like jewels, highlighted by the sun's rays penetrating the pristine water. A group of dolphins approached, cutting through the ocean like well-oiled machines, their snouts touching the clear portholes as if to say hello. Lindsay reached out her hand, touching the transparent shield in a sign of welcome. Something unspoken seemed to pass between them. The school shoaled closely for a time before abruptly departing. The dolphins were immediately replaced by a large, menacing-looking white shark, its jaws open revealing rows of razor-sharp teeth. *Had Lindsay warned the dolphins somehow?* Cole wondered. At this point it almost seemed believable.

The clarity of the water rapidly disappeared as the surrounding area grew darker. Outside the vessel, halogen searchlights sprang to life illuminating the space around them. It was time to say goodbye to the tranquil upper level of the ocean, where everything felt relatively safe.

"How are you doing, Cole?" Lindsay said.

"So far, so good. It's really quite beautiful underwater. How deep are we?"

"We're approaching five hundred feet. But there is equal beauty below, if not quite so idyllic. Nature is a magnificent thing, Cole. As the pressure increases the deeper we travel, the life forms change, adapting to their environment. Look around and see for yourself. It will help you pass the time."

A voice crackled through the interior speaker system. "How are you doing down there, guys?" The Australian accent was undeniable.

"We're fine, Cassie. How do things look from your perspective?" Lindsay replied.

"All systems are operating normally. You're right on schedule. No unexpected bleeps on the sonar screen. Cabin pressure is perfect. I wish we were down there with you."

"I'll be more than happy to trade places with you," Cole said, sounding nervous in spite of Cassie's attempt to make things sound routine, like they were merely out for a joyride.

"Cole, don't be silly. This dive is for you," Cassie said good-naturedly. The trepidation in her voice was well-disguised. "We'll check back at two thousand feet. In the meantime, enjoy the scenery."

Things went quiet as they continued to descend into the murky depths, the only sound the rhythmic spinning of the overhead props, like the purring of a giant cat. Although the float section had nearly nine tons of metal shot and air tanks that had been flooded with seawater to help make it sink, propellers had also been added to speed their descent and return. Props had been installed on both the top and sides, in an attempt to make the submersible more maneuverable. At full speed the craft could descend at four feet per second, its speed limited on purpose.

The colorful species of sea creatures had been replaced with thick, muscular fish with gaping jaws, peering at the craft as if it was trespassing. Ghostly jellyfish drifted by, turned into ethereal- looking creatures by the *Harbinger*'s powerful lights. If felt as if they were entering an alien world, where the standard rules no longer applied. This was Lindsay's world, viewed only by a select few. The ocean covered nearly 70 percent of the planet's surface and yet it was taken for granted by the vast majority of humans occupying it. Cole suddenly felt guilty. He had never given it much thought, this vast wilderness so essential to life. According to Lindsay and her fellow abiogenists, this was where human life had begun, in the great soup kitchen. *Is it even remotely possible?* Cole wondered.

Without warning, the *Harbinger* was rocked by what felt like a shock wave, startling Cole.

"What the hell was that!" Cole exclaimed, wondering if some chthonic sea monster had taken notice of their intrusion into its space.

"Just a methane bubble being released from one of the ocean's subterranean caverns. It has nowhere to go but up. Although I must say, that felt like a larger-than-average one. That's actually good news."

"Good news? What's good about it? It almost flipped us upside down," Cole replied in disbelief.

"It means we're in the right area. The shifting of tectonic shelves and methane releases are one of the reasons so many shipwrecks have occurred in this area, along with the storms, of course. A very large methane bubble, or a series of smaller ones, can displace a smaller ship and sink it."

"That's reassuring. I can't wait for the next big surprise," Cole said, trying not to think about where they were. He turned his thoughts to golf, imagining himself on the links at Gull's Point, enjoying a carefree day playing and drinking beer. What was he doing in this part of the world, heading for the bottom of the ocean? Glancing out the side-port viewing area, he felt like a mis- hit golf ball sinking into one of the lakes on the course, never to be seen again. A speck in an endless void of liquid. No matter how hard he endeavored to do so, he couldn't concentrate on anything but the descent. He wondered how many unanswered e-mails were in his in-box, and not even the image of the Swanson sisters could hold his attention. Frustrated, he decided it was time to challenge Lindsay on the events of the previous two nights. Maybe she could shed some light on that and at the same time, keep his thoughts away from their claustrophobic descent.

"Lindsay, can we talk, or do you need to concentrate on steering this thing?"

"Yes, I can talk. What's on your mind?"

"Can they hear us up top?"

Lindsay hit a switch. "Not now. What's up?"

"Our second night at the marina, you know, the night I had too much to drink—"

"I'd call that an understatement, but yes, I remember," Lindsay interjected.

"Not long after you entered your bungalow, I saw you standing on your deck facing the Bay. My vision may have been a little fuzzy, but what I saw was unbelievable. I don't think I'll ever forget it."

"Just what do you think you saw?" Lindsay said suspiciously.

"You started to spin in circles and were glowing or something. Maybe it was the deck lights, I don't know, but then this giant wave rose out of the water and raced straight toward you. The next thing I knew, you were gone—washed right off the deck. I ran over to try to save you. I dove into the waves and searched, but it was totally dark and impossible to swim. Somehow, I knew I wouldn't find you, so I came back to shore."

"Is that all? I mean, you're sure there wasn't something else, you know, like you emptying your minibar of every bottle of liquor left? Do you think that might have had something to do with your so-called *vision*? Or have you forgotten how I found you lying on the beach the following morning, unconscious and being eaten alive by sea creatures?"

"Okay, I admit I was pretty hammered, but still. I know what I saw."

"It was all a dream, Cole. The excessive amount of rum was like a poison in your system. You couldn't tell reality from fiction. You were a mess."

Well, that wasn't very productive, Cole thought. He changed the subject. "Then what about last night? When we were on the beach and I was chasing you. I wasn't anywhere close to being drunk. Are you going to tell me that didn't happen, either?" Cole said with a more confident air. At least his memory was more intact about that incident.

"Sorry, Cole, but that must have been a dream, too. We spent the night on the deck, sleeping. Perhaps it was the aftermath of the hangover that hadn't completely left your system, combined with exposure to an abnormal amount of methane gas. You remember the strong odor you experienced when we first arrived on the beach? It takes some getting used to." Lindsay had an answer for everything. And yet, her answers only left him more conflicted.

"Lindsay, when I woke up this morning my shorts were covered with sand and you had changed tops. How do you explain that?"

"I remember something else when I woke up. You had a little condition in those shorts of yours, or don't you remember that, either?" Cole blushed as Lindsay continued, "I didn't notice any sand. If there was any, it was probably residue from your night spent passed out on the beach. You were covered with it when I took you inside to clean up. It's probably mixed up in everything you carried in your backpack, too. As far as my top is concerned, I changed in the middle of the night. I was cold and so I put on a heavier covering, that's all."

Cole couldn't come up with an adequate response, but deep

inside he knew there was more to this than just another vivid dream. He sank back in his seat, sighing, resigned to the fact that Lindsay would never be totally honest with him.

"Anything else you'd like to discuss, Cole?" Lindsay said nonchalantly.

"No, I think that's sufficient."

Lindsay switched the communication system back on. "Cassie, Ryan, are you there?"

"Yeah, we lost you for a few minutes, but everything appears to be operating normally now. Are you guys okay?"

"We're fine. It was just Cole asking a lot of dumb questions again. I set him straight."

The sound of laughter coming from the intercom infuriated Cole. Why was he suddenly the butt of every joke around here again? He didn't like the feeling—a feeling that was foreign to him. He tuned out the rest of the conversation between the divers, intent on getting even. He'd had about enough of the bullshit. Who did these people think they were? Their jobs depended on people like him, and his father.

"Cole, how come you're so quiet?" Lindsay said after some time had elapsed.

"I don't have anything to say, that's why," Cole replied tersely.

"Are we feeling sorry for ourselves again? Is that it?"

"No, we're *not* feeling sorry for ourselves! You know, Lindsay, the more I'm around you, the more you remind me of Serena."

"Why, thank you, I'll take that as a complement," Lindsay said, recalling their brief ride in Cole's Maserati. "Can you hook us up with the artificial intelligence software firm that created her? I read about it in *People* magazine when they did the article about you buying the car. I think it was a Swiss company? I'd like to integrate it into the *Harbinger*. God knows, some of our guests are so obdurate."

Having heard the entire conversation, Cassie punched Ryan in the arm just as he was about to make a rude comment. "Shh," she said, but it was too late. Cole heard her admonishment over the intercom.

Suddenly flushed with anger, Cole couldn't contain himself. "Did you all hear our conversation? What are you guys, voyeurs? You get off on other people's embarrassment?"

"Sorry, Cole, really, we're sorry. It wasn't intentional," Cassie said, then added, "Lindsay must have left the intercom switched on."

"Gee thanks, Cassie, throw me under the bus while I'm down here and can't defend myself," Lindsay replied.

"You *mean* she left it live on purpose. She's as bad as you two. I don't know why I came on this fucking trip anyway. Wouldn't it be better if I just returned to Rhode Island and continued sending you checks? It's a lot more difficult to laugh at money!" Cole exclaimed. For a moment, he forgot about the descent into the ocean or even the reason he was here. He just wanted to lash out at someone. But the sound of a pin dropping could have been heard after Cole's rebuttal. Suddenly, things didn't seem quite so humorous. A long silence followed. The intercom crackled.

"Approaching twenty thousand feet. Changing to manual mode and slowing to two feet per second," Lindsay said, all business now.

"She's all yours, good luck," Cassie replied with equal solemnity.

"Twenty thousand feet? We're at *twenty thousand* feet?" Cole replied incredulously. "How did we get so deep so fast?"

"Nice work, Lindsay," Ryan said. "We knew you'd be apprehensive, Cole. Everybody would be who was in your situation. I don't know anyone who has ever dived this deep on their first attempt. We were just trying to take your mind off of it. Congratulations, you've just entered an elite company of people. Well done, Cole," Ryan added with obvious enthusiasm, finally showing some respect.

Cole didn't know whether to curse, to cry, or to laugh out loud. Flabbergasted, all he could muster was a weak "thank you." Lindsay switched off the intercom temporarily.

"Let me be the second person to congratulate you. Really well done, Cole. Most people are deep into panic mode at half this depth, even drivers that have been on previous descents, and they usually require medication to continue. I've found that anger is sometimes the best medicine. But I must warn you, the going from here on may be a little"—she hesitated—"tricky."

Cole immediately looked out of the porthole and was stunned to see dark shapes looming in the distance, barely visible at the end of the searchlight's reach. The vista reminded him of a mountain range or a deep canyon, he couldn't tell which.

"We're passing the southern edge of the Tongue of the Ocean Trench, where it drops off to the much-deeper Puerto Rico Trench. This is the deepest trench in the Atlantic. It's similar to the structure of the Grand Canyon, if you've ever been there. Deep fissures. However, while the Colorado River continues to shape the canyon and gradually deepen it, the trenches are re-formed by movement in the tectonic plate system, and they can shift at any time. It can be rather volatile down here. We'll proceed cautiously."

"What are we trying to find?" Cole said, his demeanor changing quickly to one of panic.

The time had come to start telling Cole the truth, Lindsay decided. Or at least as much that could be safely passed on—or that he might believe.

23

Lindsay guided the submersible deeper and deeper into the trench, while Cole looked on in astonishment. It really did seem like another world, so unlike anything he had experienced before. He had spent a lot of time on ships and on the ocean, but everything had appeared normal somehow, like it all fit naturally. Even the exotic coral reefs he had snorkeled and scuba-dived in were nothing to fear, just a colorful playground to explore. But now—now he was face-to-face with mysteries he could no more comprehend than the concept of being poor. Just the two of them were drifting here in an alien graveyard. Why the word *graveyard* had suddenly been conjured in his mind, he wasn't sure. Maybe it had something to do with the subdued images of sunken boats that came into view, littering the landscape, covered with thick algae, nebulous ghosts of the past. These vessels and their occupants were too deep to explore effectively, and far too expensive. The secrets they held would remain a mystery forever, their stories eternally imprisoned in a watery grave. The rhythmic drone of the *Harbinger*'s props only added to the eeriness of their surroundings, like somber chamber music of a funeral dirge.

"Okay, Lindsay, it's just you and me now. I'm asking again, what exactly are we searching for?" Cole's voice had taken on a renewed sense of determination. Lindsay switched off the intercom, taking a deep breath.

"We're looking for an opening of sorts. The portal to a vast subterranean cavern. Some have referred to it as the Bermuda Triangle wormhole…a portal to another dimension."

"Hold on!" Cole exclaimed. "You're not trying to tell me we're looking for an entrance to another world? I don't buy that."

"Not really another *world*, Cole, just an extension of our own." Lindsay hesitated. "Cole, I've seen it. It's imperative that you believe me—so much depends on it. It's time I told you more." She took another deep breath. "I was stationed at the Gerace Research Centre doing local research, when I heard the news about your parents' disappearance. Because your family is a major financial donor and a family friend, I asked the Institute's director if I could help with the search. They agreed and allowed me to take the *Harbinger I* underwater, since the local authorities weren't having any luck finding them. I spent over two weeks searching where the Coast Guard and those maritime investigators you hired couldn't—"

"Why didn't you just tell me this?" Cole interrupted. "You've kept this a secret all this time? Why?"

"I didn't think you'd believe me, I mean, that you'd believe what I discovered. What I had long suspected." Lindsay went silent.

"You discovered what, exactly?" Cole said suspiciously, while bracing himself for another of Lindsay's absurd allegations.

"I found it. Cole, I discovered the portal. It really exists!" Lindsay's voice was suddenly vibrant, as though shot through with a powerful current of electricity. "It took four more dives before I found a way to enter it. And when I did, what I discovered was breathtaking, unimaginable. I still struggle to explain it. I'm not sure adequate words exist in the human vocabulary to properly describe its magnificence." A long silence followed as Cole struggled to comprehend what Lindsay was attempting to tell him.

"You're talking in riddles, Lindsay. Just what exactly are you trying to tell me?"

"What I found, Cole…what I found…was the passageway to the afterlife," Lindsay replied, still overwhelmed by her discovery.

Cole was too stunned to respond. His head started to spin, and he suddenly became dizzy. Panic spiked to a new level, overcoming him. He wasn't sure whether the sensation was caused by Lindsay's revelation or the intense pressure of the ocean as they reached the twenty-four-thousand-foot depth. He struggled to regain his normal breathing, fearing he was being dragged to his death by a madwoman, intent on scaring him to death. And all for what? Was she going to hold him hostage until she got what she wanted? Was she capable of ejecting him out of the craft—to be instantly crushed? Wild, illogical thoughts flooded his mind. Nothing made sense. He couldn't think straight, as he struggled to calm himself to avoid passing out.

Time passed in silence as Lindsay allowed Cole to take it all in—to internalize his thoughts—realizing Cole was struggling to comprehend.

"What do you really want, Lindsay?" Cole's voice was shaky, his mind still gripped by the panic attack. His breath came in quick, labored gasps. "Money? You can have whatever you want, just get me back up to the surface. This is all a big farce."

"Cole, no, I'm trying to help you! Please believe me. I'm not my parents."

Lindsay's voice faded, like a whisper deep in a forest. Suddenly all Cole could see were white spots spinning in his line of vision— as he plummeted into unconsciousness.

Lindsay switched the intercom back on, shouting into the microphone. "Cassie, Cole's gone into a state of hyperbaric shock. Decrease the cabin pressure, pump in one hundred percent oxygen, and prepare for an emergency ascent. We're too deep in the trench for me to help him. Prepare a recompression chamber and have saline solution available. I think he's also badly dehydrated."

"We're on it!" Cassie's response was immediate. Lindsay guided the *Harbinger* up toward the surface as quickly as she could given the circumstances, engaging extended sonar range. Ascending too fast would only complicate Cole's condition. Complicating matters, there were too many jutting rocks and cliffs beyond the range of their lights. A jarring collision would sink them instantly. Like a monstrous spider rewinding its web of fine silk, the submersible rose silently in the murky depths, a glowing speck in a boundless void of darkness.

The bathyscaphe finally reached the open ocean above the trench safely, after a treacherous ascent through the cavern-like walls. Lindsay called out to Cassie again to put them on autopilot and she unbuckled herself from her seat. Cole's head was slumped over to one side, his face ashen. Perspiration dripped down his forehead, and his breathing was irregular. She quickly took his pulse from the vein on his neck.

"Cole, can you hear me?" she spoke softly. No response. She opened his closed eyelids and was met with a blank stare. "Cole!" she said, louder this time, while shaking his shoulders. He stirred for a moment, then went limp again. Lindsay reached under her seat to retrieve the diving helmet. She pressed it down over his head and hooked up the two lines of tubes to the portable oxygen tanks. Watching closely as the electronic monitor on the helmet's side flickered on, she waited until it stabilized. Making a minor adjustment to the oxygen flow, she held her breath until she could feel Cole's body relaxing and his pulse returning closer to normal.

She held his hand as they continued their ascent, reflecting on their earlier conversation. Had she told him too much? Had her explanation been too abrupt? How exactly was she supposed to tell someone like Cole Hollingsworth, someone so grounded in the physical world of business, that she had discovered the answer to the greatest mystery of all? She cursed at herself for causing him to go into shock and said a silent prayer that she might have a second chance. If she knew Cole, as soon as he was able, he'd call for a private helicopter and leave at the earliest opportunity, relieved to be gone from her. He'd head straight for the airport and be soaring skyward on his Dassault Falcon before anyone could say "*crazy woman.*" She couldn't blame him, really. Who in their right mind would believe her story? Sometimes even she doubted it had actually happened—considering that it might have all been just a dream. But the harsh reality of her present condition rendered that impossible. She desperately needed to convince Cole of the truth before it was too late.

Both Cassie and Ryan were standing by with an array of medical equipment as the metal cables lifted the *Harbinger* back into the belly of the frigate. The top hatch swung open and Lindsay emerged.

"He's still only semiconscious. Have a look while I change out of this wetsuit." The divers hurried down the narrow stairway to the pressure sphere. Cole was sitting upright now, looking around as though he didn't have a clue where he was. That was a good sign, at least.

"Cole?" Cassie said as she approached. "How are you feeling?"

Cole turned toward the sound of her voice, still wearing the bulky diving helmet.

"Here, let me help you out of that," Ryan said. He unlocked and lifted the device off of Cole's head and looked into his eyes. The sudden change in the intake of oxygen rendered Cole momentarily unsteady, but he recovered quickly. Cassie had a hold of his wrist monitoring his pulse while she unbuckled the top metal straps of his wetsuit. She placed a Littmann stethoscope against his chest. Cole's pupils were dilated, but he seemed to be coming around.

"Let's get you into the recompression chamber just to be safe," Cassie said. "We can better monitor your condition there. The divers' cabin maintains a fairly constant pressure, but I think your condition was most likely caused by too rapid a descent without stops along the way. That's a lack of planning on our part. We assumed certain things that we shouldn't have. The fact that you were most likely dehydrated was probably a contributing factor as well. I'm so sorry, Cole."

Cole waved his hand in the air, as if to fend off Cassie's concerns. "If dehydration was a cause, that was purely my own fault. It was the drinking." Cole shook his head in disgust at himself.

He went quietly to the recompression chamber. He was still feeling dizzy and nauseous, and he wanted some time alone to reconsider what Lindsay had told him, or what he thought he had heard her say. It still seemed mixed up in his head, having become convoluted as he had drifted into unconsciousness while underwater. And then suddenly he was on deck, as if Scotty had just beamed him up from a planet below. At this moment, it would not have surprised Cole to see Captain Kirk striding into the sickbay to check on him before conferring with Commander Spock on a more urgent matter. What could be more important than discovering the portal to the afterlife? He was caught up in a science-fiction nightmare with no idea what awaited him next, only that it would not be normal.

Having checked out, passing all tests and confirming he was not suffering from a more severe form of hyperbaric shock, Cole changed into shorts and a half-buttoned shirt, joining his companions on the top deck for a debriefing. At least that's what Lindsay had called it.

Lindsay was leaning on the railing, looking out on the shimmering waters of the Caribbean as the sun was beginning to dip behind the squat mountains to the west. Cassie and Ryan were sharing a cold beer with the other crewmembers. The scene appeared routine, but Cole sensed it was anything but. He suddenly wondered how much the crewmembers knew about the reason he was here. Were they just playing dumb, or did they truly understand? Were they simply humoring the famous Cole Hollingsworth, ensuring the continuing supply of funds for their research? Was he the only one who didn't fully comprehend the situation? Again, he felt like a pawn in an elaborate chess match—a scheme that could end in betrayal and a large amount of money changing hands. He glanced at the bow of the ship and the solitary gun turret pointing out to sea. Lindsay had told him the gun remained on the frigate as a show of force. Piracy was still rampant in this part of the world, and they could ill afford to be forcefully boarded and robbed. The equipment on the *Truett* was valued in the millions and would bring a nice bounty on the black market.

Cole approached Lindsay guardedly. Before he was near enough to be heard, however, she turned to face him. Her long hair blew slightly in the tropical breeze, her eyes glistening like pools of sparkling seawater, azure-like. Gone was the distinctly slate-gray color that normally met Cole's gaze. Barefoot and dressed in tight, seafoam-colored Capris and a matching top, she could have been a mermaid, or a sea goddess straight out of Greek mythology. She stood in silence, her gaze mesmerizing Cole. The air around her seemed to quiver, as if she was wrapped in a cocoon of iridescent light. She emanated an otherworldly power, like the promise of hope in a hopeless world. Cole broke the connection momentarily, looking back to where Cassie and Ryan were sitting, anxious to confirm they were also seeing what he saw. Instead he was stunned to see the deck completely empty, only ghosts remaining where the crewmembers had just been, their images evaporating on the spot. Confused, Cole still felt lightheaded from the dive and the decompression. *I'm just imagining things,* he muttered to himself. *Snap out of it!*

Cole turned back to Lindsay just as a bolt of lightning flashed brilliantly in the darkening sky. Lindsay's outstretched arms were a magnet, drawing Cole closer. He was powerless to resist. Before he realized what had happened, he was standing only inches away from her, Lindsay's breath warm on his skin. Her scent was musky, combined with a hint of intoxicating sweetness. She wrapped her long arms around his neck.

"Is this what you want, Cole?" Her voice was like music carried atop distant waves, a lilting melody filled with the mysteries of the inimitable sea. She had asked him the same question on the night of his birthday party.

Cole drew her closer. She melted into him like their bodies had suddenly gone liquid. Cole felt an irresistible heat slowly overwhelm him. His muscles tensed as the heat took control, like a disease infecting every fiber of his body. He was suddenly consumed with fire, the searing heat scorching his heart with desire he had never imagined possible. He screamed out as the fire burned deeper, unsure whether his cries of helplessness were caused by pain or ecstasy. Still Lindsay held firm, as her cocoon of light engulfed them both, their bodies entwined in a space devoid of time, in an endless climax. World without end.

Images of his parents began to materialize, blinding Cole with their intensity, held in stasis by an unrelenting electrical current. They appeared trapped between two dimensions, tormented— unable to move. Cole screamed out to them, but to no avail. They were blind to his pleadings. Cole screamed again as the inferno raged within him. And then, the sense of his own body vanished; only pure thought remained. Transcending the physical world, Cole morphed into another dimension, suspended somewhere between life and death. His body writhed in a mixture of pain and pleasure impossible to describe, until there was nothing left to feel. Hours—or perhaps days—later, totally spent, he felt devoured by a power so far beyond imagination that all that remained was oblivion. Yet Cole no longer cared.

24

Cole awoke in his cabin, dazed and drained of energy, as he struggled to rise up from his bed. Light streamed in from a nearby porthole, highlighting the dust motes floating in the air. Cole suddenly felt famished, unable to recall the last time he had eaten. Sitting directly opposite him, perched on the opposite bed, Lindsay stared at him with a curious expression, her slate-gray eyes having returned to normal and boring intently through his.

"I was beginning to wonder whether you were ever going to wake up, Cole. The dive must have really taken its toll on you. How are you feeling this morning?"

Cole ran his hands down his chest and over his legs, suddenly realizing he was naked. He quickly pulled the blanket over his body and took stock of himself. He wasn't sure just *how* he felt. On the one hand, he felt renewed, as if a burden had been lifted, and yet his body felt like it had just been through a battle. Something foreign pulsed through his veins. He felt oddly disconnected from his surroundings, like he had suddenly returned from a long trip to a distant place, but for the life of him, he couldn't remember where he had been.

Lindsay rose and walked toward him, stopping just short of touching distance. Then she took another step forward, placing her hand over his heart. Their gaze met, and time slipped into slow motion. In Lindsay's eyes, Cole glimpsed two worlds, side by side, in an endless expanse of blue, the roiling ocean meeting the sky at the horizon, in perfect harmony. He heard her silent calling, beckoning him to understand the truth. And then he realized just what had transpired. All along he had thought that Lindsay was carrying a burden too painful to share, but in reality, it was his burden that she shared. With the gentle stroke of her hand—in a compassionate glance—Lindsay had taken his pain away. The guilt was gone. He hadn't failed his parents after all. Was this what Lindsay had been trying to tell him all along? She smiled knowingly, then turned and walked silently out of his cabin.

Cole joined Lindsay, Cassie, and Ryan for breakfast. Pleasantries were exchanged as though nothing unusual had happened. Cole wasn't about to mention his dream. Yes, it must have been just another vivid dream. Sex with a mythical sea goddess, along with an encounter with his dead parents, wasn't remotely possible in the real world. However, the look in Lindsay's eyes sent a mixed message, as if to say it might not have been a dream. The sudden image of unbridled passion passed between them. A hint of a smile briefly appeared on her lips, but quickly vanished. A shot of heat raced up his spine, followed abruptly by fear that the experience might actually have been real. *That dirty little water nymph*, Cole thought. Could he have possibly been drugged? Duped into accepting an alternative reality. But for what reason?

Endeavoring to get the tempestuous images out of his mind, Cole leaned forward. "So, what's on the agenda today?"

"More deep-sea exploration. We weren't able to complete the last dive," Lindsay said without insinuation. Cole blushed anyway. His weakness had forced Lindsay to abort their mission. "Are you feeling up to it, Cole?"

"Yes…why wouldn't I be?" Cole replied, as though his manhood was being called into question. *The last dive?* Cole suddenly wondered. *Have there been more than one and I just can't remember?*

"Good, then let's get on with it. Get your wetsuit and we'll meet you below in twenty minutes. The *Truett* is moving south, closer to the deepest point of the Puerto Rican Trench. We'll launch from there." Lindsay rose and walked out of the room. Cassie did likewise, while Ryan remained to clear the plates and utensils. Noticing that Ryan was balancing all of the plates on one arm, Cole couldn't resist.

"You look like you've had practice at that. Don't forget to de-crumb the table, Ryan. There's nothing I detest more than a soiled tablecloth at a fine dining establishment like this."

"Yes, sir, Mister Hollingsworth. May I shine your shoes afterward?"

"Perfect. I like a man who can take orders." Cole disappeared out of the galley, smirking.

Everything was ready when Cole reached the submersible docking station. Lindsay was already inside. Cassie was glued to the computer screen, while Ryan was inspecting the cable system. Cole descended the narrow stairway through the float section down to the pressure sphere. Lindsay was already strapped in and fiddling with the controls.

"Do you need any assistance, Cole?" Lindsay said, without looking in his direction.

"No, I'm fine, thanks." Cole took a seat and buckled himself in securely. His diving helmet was secured under Lindsay's seat.

"We're ready, Cassie. All systems are operating normally. Begin submersion," Lindsay instructed. All attempts at small talk or comforting comments had vanished. Lindsay was as serious as Cole had ever seen her.

"Copy that. Good hunting," Cassie replied. Cole felt the jerk of the cable as it began to unwind. The bottom doors swung open, and the space quickly filled with seawater. The powerful clamps released, and the *Harbinger* drifted slowly out of the body of the frigate. The sensation felt less stressful than before. Cole knew what to expect now, at least on the way down. He couldn't remember their previous ascent, and he wondered what awaited them today. More improbable discoveries, no doubt.

The initial part of their descent was much like before, crystal-clear waters alive with colorful sea life. The dolphins that had appeared previously were replaced by giant sea turtles. The ocean teemed with life, alien-like beings traveling through liquid space. Occasionally an interested spectator would swim close, peering into one of the port viewing areas, curious as to who was intruding in their world. Cole was suddenly struck with the feeling that he and Lindsay were specimens in a giant fish tank, being observed. Were the fish discussing how strange the two of them looked? At three hundred feet, the water began to turn cloudy, but visibility was still possible. The outside halogen lights flashed on, illuminating the space around them. Lindsay hit a switch, and the cabin suddenly filled with music.

I like to dream yes, yes, right between my sound machine.
On a cloud of sound, I drift in the night.
Any place it goes is right.
Goes far, flies near, to the stars away from here.

Well, you don't know what we can find.
Why don't you tell your dreams to me?
Why don't you come with me, little girl
On a magic carpet ride?

You don't know what we can see
Before the thing could answer me
Well, someone came and took the lamp away.
I looked around, a lousy candle's all I found.
Well, you don't know what we can find.
Why don't you come with me, little girl
On a magic carpet ride?

Well, you don't know what we can see.
Why don't you tell your dreams to me?
Fantasy will set you free.
Close your eyes, girl.
Look inside, girl
Let the sound take you away.

Deeper and deeper they descended, serenaded by Steppenwolf, the iconic 1960s North American rock band named after Hermann Hesse's classic novel of the same name. The book, an international success, portrayed the life of a middle-aged man's spiritual dilemma, a profound crisis between his humanity and his animalistic instincts, causing him to be unable to see beyond his own self-made concept. Having read and studied the book in school, Cole was familiar with its self-deprecating themes. Why had Lindsay selected this particular song? Was it merely the analogy of their flight to the bottom of the ocean on an extraordinary vehicle, hence the reference to a *magic carpet*? Or was it more profound, an allusion to the deeper meanings of the novel? Caught up in a spiritual void? What was she trying to convey to him? This appeared to be more than a search for his dead parents.

The music continued, switching from song to song as they drifted downward. Lindsay's choice of music was unnerving, and yet, somehow foreshadowing what lay ahead, as if choreographed specifically for their trip. Cole glanced out the port viewing area and noticed the shadowy images of cliffs surrounding them. They were entering the trench. Lindsay took control of the navigation system, carefully guiding the *Harbinger* down into the treacherous canyon. The cabin went silent midway through "Born to Be Wild." Then the music was over; it was time to get serious. Cole felt his pulse quicken with anticipation. He would not allow another panic attack to overwhelm him. The Valium he had secretly taken before their departure would help to ensure that.

"Cassie, I'm taking us to the bottom of the trench. Please monitor our progress carefully. I've increased our sonar range and turned on the exterior 3D digital cameras. If you see anything—anything at all—let me know immediately. There's been a shift in the plates since my last visit here six months ago. I've overlaid the electronic mapping from that dive over my monitor, and it doesn't match what I'm recording now."

"Copy that. Be careful, Lindsay." There was more than a little concern in Cassie's voice. If this section of the trench had recently experienced seismic activity and was unstable, there was no telling what could happen now. Cassie switched on the Institute's onboard seismoscope and seismograph, the two main devices used for measuring earthquakes. For the time being, all appeared normal. She glanced over at Ryan with a concerned expression. He simply nodded in return, continuing to scrutinize his monitoring devices closely.

Lindsay guided the craft skillfully along the edges of the trench's narrowest points, watching intently. *What exactly is she looking for?* Cole wondered. Cole watched with fascination as Lindsay made adjustments to her instruments, and recorded notes in an open journal at the same time. The *Harbinger's* lights were on full power, shinning on the crags and fissures along the walls of the cavern. The brightness startled what little sea life was present at these depths. Red-colored shrimp floated by. Small hermit crabs scurried about, propelling themselves deeper into cracks to avoid the light. Large single-cell amphipods clung to the trench walls. Something resembling a jellyfish floated by, entering their field of light, then shooting away, rocket-like with a fluid flapping of its tentacles. The word *alien* didn't begin to describe the deepest parts of the ocean, devoid of sunlight, with hydrologic pressures nearing 17,000 PSI.

Cole lost track of all time. Indeed, time meant little in this world; it was as if it stood still. Maybe life really had begun down here. Perhaps Lindsay and her fellow abiogenists were right. This sense of timelessness struck Cole with a new awareness—billions of years passing unnoticed in the darkness. Suddenly, Hollingsworth Enterprises seemed insignificant—a grain of sand in an endless ocean. His pedigree meant nothing down here—his arrogance a sin against nature. Without Cole noticing it, the *Harbinger* had come to a halt, facing a smooth expanse of wall in the distance.

"Cole, look!" Lindsay's voice blazed with excitement. "Over there." She pointed.

Cole gazed out the clear Plexiglas to see what looked like an immense darkened mirror, for lack of a better description. It shimmered under the submersible's lights, reflecting a faint silhouette of their craft. Cole thought he saw movement, like the gentle rise and fall of a human chest during slumber. Cole stared out, awestruck, as Lindsay cautiously guided the *Harbinger* closer. The sphere-shaped object grew in size as they approached, until they were within fifty yards or so. Close up, it appeared like a diaphragm, pulsing slowly in and out, as if alive, radiating a mysterious luminescence. Appearing semitransparent, vague images seemed to be lurking on the other side.

"We've found it, Cole. The portal. Do you know what this means?" Lindsay said reverently.

Cole was too thunderstruck to respond. All he could do was gawk, as a new wave of anxiety washed over him. Whatever Valium was left in his system suddenly evaporated. His heart rate spiked. Size and space were distorted at these depths, but the size of the diaphragm-shaped anomaly must have been several hundred yards in diameter. It dwarfed the *Harbinger* as they sat motionless in the water facing it, a miniature speck of glowing light in a blackened sky devoid of stars.

Cole…Cole, is that you? a vaguely familiar voice whispered, as though coming from a dream. Lindsay had clearly not heard it— or spoken the words. She remained intently watching the portal. The voice was in his head. *Cole...* He heard it again. The obsidian-colored diaphragm shuddered, sending a sudden spike of fear up Cole's spine. What existed beyond this barrier? A mass graveyard? Ghostly souls floating in a void? Dante's inferno? His parents?

"Cassie, please triangulate our location. I'm recording it, as well. We need the exact latitude, longitude, and depth. We've found it!" Lindsay's instruction failed to rouse Cole as he gazed out at something unfathomable, something so much larger than himself that it defied description.

"We're coming back up," Lindsay spoke into the intercom. "Do you have our location?" Still her voice failed to register with Cole, nor did the music, as she switched on Elton John's "Rocket Man." The music played as Cole continued to stare at the abnormality on the trench wall, as it slowly faded into darkness, as if it had never existed.

And I think it's gonna be a long, long time,
'till touchdown brings me round to find,
I'm not the man they think I am at home.
And all this science I don't understand
It's just my job five days a week.
And I think it's gonna be a long, long time...

Bernie Taupin's poignant lyrics were somehow prophetic. Did anyone know the man Cole Hollingsworth really was? If Cole didn't know, how could anyone else? The ascent from the ocean floor seemed to take days, or no time at all. For Cole, time had become irrelevant. Had he actually heard his mothers' voice beckoning to him from beyond the grave? Had he been so close to the truth that it had scorched his very soul? The pain in his heart becoming immutable, as the guilt came flooding back. He should have been there to save them—not guzzling Scotch and chasing women who meant nothing to him. Tears rolled down his cheeks, unconstrained, as Lindsay looked on in silence. She would not take his pain away this time.

25

The upper hatch of the *Harbinger* sprang open. Cole emerged and climbed to the catwalk, passing by Cassie and Ryan without so much as an acknowledgment. His blank face spoke volumes. Lindsay followed, her forefinger pressed to her lips. The two divers exchanged concerned looks. No words were spoken as the group ascended the steps to the upper deck. They arrived to see Cole leaning against the railing, staring out to sea. Lindsay was the first to approach.

"Are you hungry, Cole? Would you like something to eat?" Lindsay inquired, rather than asking him how he was feeling. She already knew that answer.

He nodded without turning. Anything to be left alone for a while. Sensing his need for solitude, she rejoined Cassie. Together they headed into the galley to prepare dinner. Cole continued to stare out to sea, slouched over and clutching the railing for support, as though he couldn't stand on his own.

There was little conversation as they ate. Cassie and Ryan had prepared a fish stew consisting of chunks of white fish, Gulf prawns, clams, and mussels, all in a savory tomato broth with a hint of saffron. Dark, herb-flavored bread and cold beer accompanied the meal. Cole complimented the cooking, but said little else.

Cassie sensed Cole's pain, as well, and her heart went out to the billionaire. All his wealth could not comfort him now.

Lindsay had finally explained to Cassie and later to Ryan the reason they were here. At first neither Cassie nor Ryan had believed it to be possible. But then, they knew what tragedy had befallen Lindsay—and her very presence was undeniable. In the end, she had convinced them.

The plates and remaining food were cleared. Cassie and Ryan said good night, then conspicuously disappeared belowdecks, leaving Cole to face Lindsay alone. The first pinpricks of light appeared in the evening sky as the ocean darkened and the horizon took on a lavender hue. The silence between them grew oppressive. Cole's eyes had gone cold, his body rigid. It took all of his strength to hold back his rage. Rage for his personal failures. Rage at Lindsay for bringing him here to face it. The world suddenly seemed cruel, heartless.

"It's alright, Cole. It wasn't your fault," Lindsay said, her voice a beacon of calm in the tempest raging inside his skull. He turned toward her, the ice in his gaze as cold as anything she had seen from him.

"How dare you say that! You weren't there. You weren't with me. You know nothing about my parents…or me," Cole said, his voice filled with desperation. Lindsay said nothing. Cole needed to hit bottom first. Only then could the healing truly begin. Only then would he be prepared for the next dive. Long moments passed in silence.

"Cole, what are you afraid of finding?" Lindsay finally said, without the slightest hint of accusation.

"What do you think?" Cole replied spitefully. "Why would you ask me a question like that when you already know the answer?"

"I don't know the answer, Cole. I can lead you in the right direction, but you must pass over the threshold. Only then will you find the answers you seek."

"Why do you always speak in riddles? Just tell me the truth for once."

"What truth? Whose truth?" Lindsay hesitated. "Let me ask you one question. What do you believe in, Cole?"

Cole was about to answer, but he struggled to find the words. He found himself so taken aback by the question, he absolutely had no comeback. They stared at each other in silence. There was no judgment in Lindsay's eyes, only compassion. Cole suddenly felt hollow, like a man without a soul. He had no idea how to answer Lindsay's question. All he could do was stare blankly forward, having just been stripped of everything his life had been about—of everything he had thought was important.

"Do you believe in God, Cole?"

The question failed to register at first. Cole's initial reaction was to say, "*of course I do,*" but in his current state of vulnerability, he didn't have an answer for that, either. With two simple questions, Lindsay had rendered Cole defenseless—his lack of humanity exposed. Speechless, Cole's eyes welled with tears again.

Lindsay continued her deconstruction of the billionaire, like a federal prosecutor tearing away at the fabrications of a hostile witness.

"It's a simple question. Do you believe—"

"No!" Cole screamed. He couldn't bear to hear the question again. "Are you happy now?" Cole stood abruptly, moving away from Lindsay, as if to say, *I've had enough, you win.*

"Please don't leave, Cole," Lindsay said calmly. She reached out her hands, palms upturned in a gesture of reconciliation. It was over. Cole finally saw himself for who he was; broken, and yet a man now potentially capable of seeing the world through a fresh set of eyes. The only question that remained was, would he?

"Come sit me with me, Cole." Guided by something beyond his control, Cole returned to sit by Lindsay's side. Again, just as she had done this morning, Lindsay had somehow lightened his burden.

"What did we see down there?" Cole said. "I mean, what was it, really?"

"The great barrier. There's really no name for it, at least not that I know of. It separates one dimension from another. It's like a circle within a circle. Neither can exist without the other. And on the other side, well, that's where you'll find the truth." Lindsay stroked Cole's cheek. Her touch felt like an eagle's feather gliding over his skin, cool and warm at the same time.

"You're taking me through the portal tomorrow, aren't you?"

"Yes, Cole, it's time. You're ready."

"Will we..." Cole struggled to get the words to form. "Will we see my parents? Can we still save them, you know, like you told me we could the night of my birthday party?"

"*Save* is a word subject to many interpretations. It's rooted in the word *salvation*. And in a way, that's what this is all about..." Lindsay's voice trailed off, as though she had suddenly drifted into another world herself. Her expression was pensive. Cole felt her breath on his neck, felt her life force flowing through her fingers as she cupped his face in both hands.

"Life is a wondrous thing, Cole. Don't take it for granted." With those final few words, she kissed him softly on the mouth, rose, and walked away.

Dazed by her touch, Cole watched as she disappeared somewhere into the darkness. Cole sat for a long time gazing up at the velvet-colored sky, now filled with a million stars. He pondered what tomorrow would bring, oblivious to the world he had recently left behind. It no longer called to him.

26

Cole woke well-rested, and yet filled with intense anxiety. He had spent a dreamless night, cloaked in a cocoon of slowly drifting liquid, as if he were still in his mother's womb, protected for a time from the harsh realities of life.

A knock on his cabin door snapped Cole out of his musings. Lindsay entered, taking a seat on the opposite bunk. She was dressed in a different wetsuit today, looking more like the spacesuit worn by the Borg in *Star Trek*. Tubes were running up and down it; long, slender pockets were attached to both legs. Some sort of metal rack was attached to her upper back, different than before. The metal collar around her neck was hinged. The suit's material appeared far heavier and more rugged than the composition of the suits they had worn on their previous dives.

"What's up with the new gear?" Cole said apprehensively.

"Just a little added protection. Ryan's working on yours now. Let's head up to the tack room and get you fitted, then we'll catch some breakfast."

Cole wondered if she meant that literally, like they were going to reel in something from the ocean to eat. He preferred Cassie's cooking.

Ryan was waiting for Cole when he arrived. "Here, try this on for size. It should fit you." Ryan handed him a heavily padded wetsuit.

He seemed more subdued than his normally acerbic self.

He loved to banter, especially with someone like Cole. But today was somehow different. It was as if he understood that something momentous was about to take place, and he just didn't have the heart to give Cole any shit.

The suit fit like a glove. The heavy-duty neoprene material was deep indigo in color. The upper-body section was ribbed like Batman's costume, armor-like. *Will I be doing battle today?* Cole wondered.

"Thanks, Ryan," Cole said, unable to think of anything appropriate to say.

"You're welcome." Ryan did a quick inspection, admiring his work, then disappeared out the door.

Cole picked at his breakfast; his stomach tied in knots. Lindsay urged him to eat more, but the food stuck in his throat. The atmosphere in the dining area felt like compressed air in a giant wind tunnel, pushing them against a wall until they were finally crushed by a speeding test vehicle. Tension flowed like an electrical current. Even Cassie, the affable Australian beauty, moved with somber determination, as if this were the *Last Supper.* The image of Christ sitting at the table surrounded by his disciples was conjured in Cole's mind. *Will this be my final meal? Is there a betrayer among us? Who will be sacrificed this time?* Who, indeed? Lindsay's question last night about God still resonated in Cole's head, grinding away at Cole's fragile state. At the end of the day, would he be a believer? A voice inside told him that today would be life-changing. A miracle, a disaster—heaven or hell? What awaited him at the bottom of the ocean?

"Let's get on with it. I can't stand this any longer," Cole exclaimed, angst evident in his voice.

"Just leave everything here, I'll deal with it later," Cassie said.

The foursome lumbered out and down the steps to the lower levels of the frigate to the chamber containing the *Harbinger II.* Cole led the way, feeling more like he was headed to the gas chamber than a bathyscaphe. He wondered whether he would ever see this place again. Lindsay, Cassie, and Ryan followed silently in his wake. There was additional scuba gear waiting for them when they arrived. Twin oxygen tanks and a new, fortified diving helmet sat on a table next to the steps leading down to the submersible. The helmet looked like something out of a space odyssey, futuristic. Cole glanced at Ryan wordlessly.

"It's a prototype, but don't worry, Cole. The helmet was developed by the US Navy and Kirby Morgan, one of the top manufacturers in the world," Ryan said.

"It's been tested under the most extreme conditions," Cassie said reassuringly.

However, this did little to lift Cole's spirits. Why would he need such an advanced diving helmet inside the *Harbinger*? He'd sooner wear a Darth Vader helmet. Cole suddenly wished he had a lightsaber—anything to protect him from the demons lurking in the depths.

After a few last-minute instructions from the divers about the new gear, Lindsay suddenly hugged Ryan, then Cassie. The embrace between the women lasted longer than usual. The moisture in their eyes did not go unnoticed by Cole. Then Lindsay descended the steps from the catwalk and opened the hatch at the top of the submersible. Cole stood awkwardly by, unsure what to say. Ryan stepped forward, extending his hand.

"Good luck, buddy."

Since when have we become buddies? Cole thought. He shook Ryan's hand. The diver quickly retreated to the cable controls to ready himself for the submersion. Cole turned to Cassie. The look of trepidation on her face startled Cole. Her eyes were filled with tears. She grabbed Cole and hugged him with all of her strength.

"There's no one I trust more than Lindsay. I pray you find what you're looking for, Cole." She kissed him on the cheek and moved into position behind the computer screen, like a silent sentinel suddenly turned to stone.

Cole descended the steps, feeling like he was about to enter the first level of hell in Dante's inferno. There was no turning back now. He pulled the hatch shut over his head and turned the wheel tight until it locked in place. Surrounded by muted green darkness, he lowered himself into the belly of the beast.

Placing the diving helmet in the compartment below Lindsay's seat, he hung the replacement oxygen tanks in the slots on the right wall and took his seat. Cole felt the sudden drop as the clamps released the submersible out of the frigate's jaws, dropping it into the ocean below. A rush of bubbles clouded his vision out of the port viewing area. The props sprung to life, the floatation compartment above adjusting its ballast. The underwater world revealed itself, its crystal-blue waters alive with sea life. This subterranean world, so long a stranger, seemed more familiar now—and yet it held nothing but dread for Cole.

They slipped silently below the sparkling, pristine level of the ocean and began their descent into its murky depths, where the sea life changed as dramatically as the color of the water. Colorful species of fish were replaced by dark, grotesque-looking creatures with gaping mouths and thick, muscular bodies. Plankton drifted past, like sea wraiths gliding on a liquid breeze, highlighted by the *Harbinger*'s halogen lights. Cole was grateful for the time it took for the descent to the confines of the trench. Anything that would delay what awaited at the bottom suddenly felt like a welcome reprieve.

Lindsay remained unusually quiet, occasionally communicating with Cassie on their progress. Lindsay purposely slowed their descent speed to ensure that Cole would not have another episode of hyperbaric shock. Cole noticed the depthometer measuring nineteen thousand feet. They were getting close. Lindsay switched on the music, attempting to distract Cole as the cavernous walls of the

Puerto Rican Trench grew imminently closer. The music was different this time, soothing. The haunting melody and emotional lyrics of Sarah Brightman's "Only an Ocean Away," streamed through the speaker system.

I see a shadow every day and night.
I walk a hundred streets of neon lights,
Only when I'm crying.
Can you hear me crying.
So many times you always wanted more,
Chasing illusions that you're longing for.
Wish I wasn't crying.
Can you hear me crying?
There's an ocean between us.
You know where to find me.
You reach out and touch me.
I feel you in my own heart.
More than a lifetime.
Still goes on forever.
But it helps to remember
You're only an ocean away.
Was there a moment when I felt no pain.
I want to feel it in my life again.
Let it be over now.
Oh, Oh, over now.
'Cause I remember all the days and nights
We used to walk the streets of neon lights.
Oh I want you here with me.
Oh be here with me.
There's an ocean between us.
You know where to find me.
You reach out and touch me.

I feel you in my own heart.
More than a lifetime
Still goes on forever.
But it helps to remember
You're only an ocean away.
Only an ocean away...

The final notes of the song hung in the air like an epiphany. Having been lulled into a dreamlike state by the music, Cole suddenly saw the jagged walls of the trench coming into view, startling him. For a moment, he had forgotten where he was, but it all came flooding back. Lindsay maneuvered the craft to the predetermined location, guided by coordinates on the screen sent from the *Truett*. Too soon, at least for Cole, something dark shimmered in the distance, pulsating slowly like a giant aqualung. Lindsay slowed their approach as the nebulous image took on more of a solid form under the powerful outside lights piercing the darkness. The same sense of wonder—and of fear—gripped Cole all at once, as it had done the day before. Seeing it for a second time did not diminish the enormity of the encounter. Breathless, Cole gazed out of the pressure sphere. Lindsay seemed mesmerized as she, too, gazed at the ethereal singularity.

Are we staring at the face of God? What destiny awaits us on the other side? Cole suddenly felt numb. *How has it come to this?* They were positioned on the threshold to another dimension, or so Lindsay had confided. Cole had never felt so unprepared. *How will we pass through? And if we are successful, how will we return?* Cole pondered. Hadn't Lindsay told him that she had crossed over before? Yet here she was, safe. A sudden ray of hope gripped Cole. She was living proof that the portal could be traversed.

As if guided by an unspoken cue, Lindsay turned to Cole, her eyes filled with empathy.

"Let me know when you're ready to enter. In the meantime, do you have any questions?" Lindsay spoke so matter-of-factly, she might have been asking him to enter a doctor's office for a routine checkup.

Cole couldn't think of a question; his mind was clogged with so many he couldn't articulate a single one.

"I know," Lindsay said. "It's nearly impossible to comprehend. My reaction was much the same as yours when I first discovered the gateway. I didn't realize what it was I had found, but somehow, I knew it was unlike anything discovered before. Some things must be taken on faith. That was the only way I could summon the courage to attempt entering it."

Courage. The word reverberated inside Cole's head. This was one of the things he admired most about Lindsay. She was braver than any man he had ever met. Her intellect and beauty only added to her allure. As he sat silently summoning his own brand of courage, he thought about what reconnecting with Lindsay meant to him. And it hit him like a shock wave, as though he had suddenly been struck by lightning. He was in love with this woman. The feeling had been gnawing at him for some time—a feeling unfamiliar until now. He had never been in love before. Lust, yes, but never love. Why now? Why at this precise moment did this realization overcome him so abruptly? He cursed silently. Should he tell her? Should he confess his true feelings before plunging headlong into another world? It seemed so contrived. Like a trumped-up scene from *Romeo and Juliet.* She wouldn't believe him anyway. Not like this.

"What's on your mind, Cole? You seem lost in thought. Is there something you want to tell me?"

Had Lindsay just read his mind…again? Cole was convinced she possessed an uncanny ability to know what he was thinking. Was this what was referred to as *women's intuition?* The thought that a woman could actually read his mind terrified him.

"No, I was just thinking…thinking about what we'll find on the other side. No matter what you tell me, I just can't seem to get my head around it. But then, I never had much of an imagination," Cole replied, attempting to disguise what he was really feeling.

"I disagree with that," Lindsay rebuked. "I'd bet you have a very active imagination. Like what you're imagining right now. A truth for a truth?" she added.

This instantly conjured the same question she had asked him at Grinder's Beat, the coffeehouse where they had spent their first night together, talking. Cole smirked, recalling the conversation she had heard on his cell phone, while Art thought he was talking to Cole. His exploits with the Swanson sisters.

Lindsay suddenly laughed, too.

"Yeah, that was quite the revelation. I can just picture Art strutting around his bedroom, his chest all puffed out, crowing like a rooster." Lindsay laughed again.

"That's the perfect description of Art, the son of a bitch. He deserves…" Cole's voice trailed off, as the image of his friend filled his mind. Maybe he wasn't such a bad guy after all? Cole's opinion of him softened. Perhaps Art was just acting out like he thought Cole wanted him to. Art had always been in Cole's shadow, and likely his conquest of the twins was just to show Cole that he was his equal. *Some kind of friend I've been*, Cole thought.

For a fleeting moment, Cole had forgotten about the portal, until he heard the mysterious voices calling inside his head.

Cole, is that you?

"Did you hear that, Lindsay?"

"Hear what?"

"Those voices! Someone's calling my name."

"Sorry, Cole, but I didn't hear anything. It's probably just the extreme pressure your feeling," Lindsay said, but something in her voice was less than convincing.

Cole strained to hear the voices again—voices that seemed vaguely familiar. "It's time, isn't it?" Cole said, fear returning to his voice.

"Yes, I suppose it is. We need to get prepared. We'll hook up our oxygen tanks and helmets after we've passed through. You see those underwater flares over there?" Lindsay pointed to a small, clear plastic cabinet next to the tanks. "They'll slide into the pockets on the legs of your wetsuit. They may come in handy."

Cole appeared puzzled, but he followed Lindsay's instructions. When he returned to his seat, the thought suddenly occurred to him of just how they would enter. He didn't think they could just float right through. Yet certainly they couldn't leave the *Harbinger* and swim through; the massive pressure of the ocean above would crush them in a heartbeat, regardless of what sort of prototype suits and helmets they wore.

"So, how do we enter?" Cole said.

"I was wondering when you'd ask that question. It took me four dives before I finally figured it out. The membrane that separates the ocean water from the space beyond is indescribably powerful, capable of withstanding tremendous pressures. Yet it has a nebulous quality to it. While I was observing it on my third dive, I noticed that every now and then, one of the creatures that lives at this depth would try to swim through, only to be repelled by it. It was like they bounced right off its surface. No harm, no foul, just rejection. The theory of reverse polarity occurred to me—like magnets. Depending on their direction, magnets either attract or repel each other. Like north and south, they're opposites."

"You're telling me this gateway is really just a huge magnet?" Cole said, unconvinced.

"No, not exactly, but close, I think, at least in theory. It is the natural opposing force to everything that comes in contact with it on this side. So, I postulated that if I could reverse the polarity of the

Harbinger, then I might become attracted to it and be able to enter. And I was right!"

"How do you reverse the polarity of something like a submersible? It doesn't make sense."

"That's the trick, isn't it? It was a combination of two things, actually, and not that complicated. In fact, its simplicity was beautiful. I shocked the *Harbinger* with high-voltage electricity and reversed the props at the same time. Before I knew it, I was accelerating toward the wall and passed through without incident."

"How much electricity did you use?" Cole asked, concerned they would be instantly fried.

"A lot! But it's not really important to go into specifics right now. The science probably isn't something you would understand anyway."

"That's all great, Lindsay. But how did you avoid being electrocuted?"

"So, that's what you're worried about? You really *don't* know your science, do you?" Lindsay replied with a smirk, as though any schoolkid should have understood.

"Please just humor me. What was the secret?"

"Rubber. Our wetsuits are made of rubber, just like our shoes. We'll stand on thick rubber mats before I shock the *Harbinger* so that our bodies avoid absorbing the electrical current. I don't know if you noticed the two metal poles attached to either end of the floatation section, either, but they are basically lightning rods meant to direct the high-voltage current to specific sections of the craft."

"So that's why we're waiting to put on our helmets and tanks until after we've passed through?" Cole said.

"Precisely. We must avoid contact with all metal while I'm pouring two hundred seventy-five thousand volts of electricity through this baby."

"Two hundred seventy-five thousand volts? Is that all? Well, we shouldn't be worried, then, should we?" Cole said sarcastically. "I thought you were talking about *high* voltage, but not this… Lindsay, are you crazy!"

"That's approximately the same amount we used in some of our physics experiments. Don't worry, Cole, we'll be safe."

Cole rolled his eyes. If the electricity didn't fry them, they always had the other side of the portal to look forward to. It was merely another dimension, after all.

"What, no music to send us off? Something by the Electric Light Orchestra might be appropriate," Cole remarked.

"Why didn't I think of that?" Lindsay replied thoughtfully, as if she had just committed a major gaffe. "If you don't have any more questions, Cole, I see no further reason to delay. Take your position on the mat," she instructed, her tone becoming serious.

"Just one question, what's it like on the other side…"

Before Cole could even finish the question, Lindsay threw the switch. The *Harbinger* lit up like a Christmas tree on Times Square. Streaks of light flashed everywhere, the sound of revving props straining as they reversed course. Purple-colored electrical discharges crackled back and forth between the two lightning rods. Cole was momentarily blinded by the flash of brilliance. And then, miraculously, the *Harbinger* began to move forward, gradually at first, but rapidly gaining in velocity until it began rocketing through dark water heading for the center of the portal. Suddenly everything went dark, the submersible lost in a void of blackness so dense that Cole could no longer see his own hands as the interior went pitch-black. A deafening sucking sound filled the air, and all controls went dead as they passed from one dimension into another and then…then, there was only silence.

27

Cole experienced a disquieting sense of weightlessness, as if they were adrift in outer space. *Is this what astronauts felt like in zero gravity?* he wondered. The electrical charges had vanished, the muted green lighting of the divers' cabin having returned, but still everything surrounding them was cloaked in total darkness. Cole peered out of the porthole viewing area, straining to identify something, anything. To his shock, they no longer even seemed to be floating in water.

"Lindsay, where are we?" His words were no more than echoes, barely audible. The sound hovered, repeating itself like an out-of-sync, dissonant refrain. A moment later, something resembling Lindsay's voice echoed back.

"We're in the void. The space between our world and the next. Try to stay calm."

Slowly, the *Harbinger* drifted on a cushion of air, or maybe it was something else. It was impossible to tell. Cole focused on the navigation controls, hoping to see something there that made sense. The controls were spinning like a whirling dervish, out of control, unable to lock in on anything. The submersible's props had gone silent, too. Something external was controlling their movement, guiding them forward—but to where? With every passing moment, Cole's anxiety spiked ever higher. He glanced at his watch, as though the recording of time would ground him, but it had ceased working, too.

Cole had the strangest sensation that time had actually stopped—like it could no longer be measured. Perhaps they weren't moving after all, but they remained in stasis, frozen between one dimension and another. Alive and dead, simultaneously. Had they failed to survive the crossing? Were they passing into the afterlife? Yet Cole felt no immediate sense that life had been taken from him. If anything, his sense of dread was slowly being replaced with calm, as though the weight of the world had been lifted—his worries stripped away.

"Lindsay?"

No response.

"Lindsay?" he said again, louder.

Still no response. Cole moved toward the front and stopped dead in his tracks. He turned abruptly, scanning the interior of the cabin, but it was clearly empty. The calm he was feeling quickly morphed into fear. Where had she gone? The only other area large enough to conceal her body was the narrow stairwell up through the floatation section. He hadn't seen her pass by, but maybe in all the confusion she had slipped past, unnoticed. A quick check for her oxygen tanks confirmed his worst suspicions. They had vanished, too. He was alone. He cursed loudly. What the hell was he supposed to do now? She hadn't even given him any last- minute instructions—or warnings.

The surrounding space began to lighten. The *Harbinger* felt like it was moving again. Cole turned to face the front viewing port and his jaw dropped open. Before him an alien world revealed itself—there was no other description that made sense. The ocean water had been replaced with what looked like rain. White rain. Long, sinewy strands of substance that might have been the webs of monstrous spiders. The filaments were fragmented, though, shimmering with iridescent light and moving up and down like ethereal elevators. In between, darkness loomed. Ghostly shapes drifted in and out of the voids, visible one moment and in the next, vanishing into oblivion. Cole felt like he was trapped in a forest of living light—threads of quicksilver replacing what would normally have been trees. Up and down they undulated, like ropes being controlled by pulleys; the movement was spellbinding. The strangest sensation began to overtake him—the more he focused on the movement, the more it seemed like the patterns of light were a mesh of some type—as if they were holding one world attached to another, but not solid. Like a magical series of suspension bridges but without girders for support; wavering, coming in and out of focus. He couldn't begin to explain it, only wonder in stunned silence.

And then he spotted her. Lindsay appeared glassy-eyed, unfocused, her helmet on and the oxygen tanks attached to her back. She appeared suspended in a glutinous substance that possessed sufficient mass to support her body weight, yet she bobbed up and down as though controlled by a current created by the rise and fall of the glistening strands surrounding her. Her body seemed to enlarge and contract in sync with her breathing; it was like viewing someone through one of those distorted mirrors in a macabre funhouse. One of her arms moved limply in his direction, and she stared, blank-faced and milky-white.

Is she signaling me to join her? The thought repulsed him. The vista outside screamed of evil—dark and menacing. All Cole wanted was some sense of security, even if only a manmade submersible. At least it was something—something to protect him from the almost-certain devastation that awaited outside.

Cole continued gazing wordlessly in Lindsay's direction. Was this just an apparition—a devious attempt to draw him outside, only to cause his obliteration? Maybe he could figure out a way to navigate the *Harbinger* back out to the ocean depths, which suddenly seemed as nonthreatening as the swimming pool in his backyard. But that would mean leaving Lindsay behind. By the look of her, she was already dead. Who could survive in an atmosphere like this—prototype wetsuit or not?

But Lindsay gestured again, more resolutely this time. Her alluring smile returned; the blank, deadened eyes turned normal. Maybe she wasn't dead after all. Cole vacillated, suddenly ashamed by his fear. He couldn't just leave her here, could he? All he needed to do to escape was duplicate Lindsay's previous actions and turn this damn ship around. This hadn't been his choice. She had doggedly convinced him to come on this escapade under the guise of saving his parents, but his parents were clearly not here. The voices he'd heard in his head were most likely just his imagination. What had he expected to find? She had duped him into believing this preposterous tale, and he had fallen for it. Like father, like daughter. And all for more money to continue her self-serving interest in discovering the ocean's secrets. Little wonder that others had stopped funding her explorations. *More like exploitations*, Cole thought.

Still, Cole could not abandon her. Hadn't he just come to the realization that he was in love with Lindsay? Obviously, he wasn't thinking clearly, the situation was quickly becoming more and more confusing. Agonizing over what to do, he finally made his decision. He would leave the safe confines of the *Harbinger*, grab hold of her, return them both to the submersible, and leave immediately. They could rehash her motives once they were safely aboard the frigate. He would accept her apology, and they would work out some sort of arrangement. He had seen enough. It was time to take control.

After hooking up his twin oxygen tanks, he attached the hoses to his diving helmet and climbed the metal rungs to the top hatch, determined to take action. So, what if Lindsay had discovered some extraordinary deep-sea cavern? She could report it in the world's scientific journals and become famous. He would validate it. Then she would no longer be reliant on people like Cole for financial assistance.

The hatch swished open, and Cole pushed himself out into the void. He was immediately gripped by a sensation so overwhelming it literally took his breath away. His body was awash in blinding light—filled with a rush of something resembling … resembling immortality for lack of a better term, like he had just been reborn as a superior being. Awestruck with a sense of renewed power, and yet filled with tranquility and pure joy, he felt untainted emotion all at once. Lindsay glided toward him until she was merely inches away, her smile shining as brightly as the rising sun. In that moment he felt love like he'd never felt before, consumed by her presence. Nothing else mattered. Then the microphone in his helmet buzzed.

"I told you, Cole. Can I cook or what!" Cole gazed into her eyes— eyes that scorched him to the depths of his soul. "This is where all life began on earth and where we return after death. It's neither heaven nor Hell. Dante's *Inferno* is only a fable, a poem written by a heartsick man who had lost everything dear to him. They took away Beatrice, the love of his life, and Florence, the city that meant everything to him. Hell is just the bitter musings of those who have lost hope, or those who have fostered their own agendas over humanity. Heaven is the imagined manifestation of superfluous reward for human suffering. But there is only one true Creator. The Architect of the Universe. The Divine Source of all Creation." Lindsay said then paused reverently.

"Can you feel it, Cole? Can you feel the power that fills this space? It's the sum total of all knowledge that has come before us. It sustains our planet and makes everything possible. The earth is a living organism, and it reclaims its own in the end, absorbing each of us into its very fabric. Dust to dust, world without end." Lindsay's sense of wonder was palpable.

And suddenly Cole believed, too, unquestionably. There *was* life after death, just not exactly like the sermons preached on Sunday mornings--only conflicted attempts at explaining the unexplainable.

Cole grabbed Lindsay's arms, suddenly feeling the uncontrollable urge to laugh out loud. To laugh at the absurdity of it all. For the first time in his life, he felt totally free—liberated from all inhibitions, without guilt. He wanted desperately to feel this way forever.

"Cole, we don't have much time. We are surrounded by methane, hydrogen, and ammonia, all the building blocks that created life on earth. Our wetsuits will only provide limited protection, until the acidity of the atmosphere eats right through them."

This bit of sobering news brought Cole quickly back to reality. He glanced at Lindsay's body and saw that what she said was true. Her wetsuit was already beginning to deteriorate, slowly being eaten away by the gelatinous substance surrounding them.

Cole, are you here? the mysterious voice in his head implored. Cole froze. The voice had returned, only louder now and more insistent.

"Mother, is it really you?" Cole glanced frantically around, searching for a sign that he wasn't going mad—conjuring a voice that didn't exist, a voice he wanted to hear more than anything else.

Lindsay grabbed Cole's shoulders and turned him in the opposite direction. Indistinct images in the distance began to form, ethereal outlines of what looked like life forms, but altered somehow. Nebulous figures expanded and contracted, shimmering, but partially obstructed by the rain-like filaments moving up and down like curtains of light.

Cole, the voice sounded again. *You've come at last…*

"Yes, Mother, it's me. I'm here." Cole moved forward tentatively, as though guided through the viscous liquid by the power of his mind. There was no need to swim or even paddle forward; his body followed his own will. For an instant, he thought he saw the outline of his mother's face forming. A second later it vanished, replaced by a ghostlike image of something deformed—a body without the protective cocoon of skin to hold it in place. A globule of pure energy.

"Nooo…" Cole screamed, terrified he would lose the connection with his mother.

A sudden vibration ripped through the void like a massive tremor. Gigantic methane bubbles filled the cavern, rising from below. In the distance, Cole heard a deafening crushing sound, as though mountains were collapsing all around them. He turned to Lindsay and instantly saw the panic on her face. And then he heard her voice through his helmet.

"Cole, the tectonic plates are shifting. We have to get out of here—*now!*" The terror in her voice stunned him momentarily. He turned back around in a vain effort to reconnect with his mother, but all was mayhem. The glutinous substance churned and roiled angrily. He felt a strong grip on his arm, and before he could react, Lindsay was pulling him back to the *Harbinger*. They reached the craft, only to find it oscillating—being tossed and turned like a toy boat in a raging current of water. There was no way they could reenter it. Amid the panic, Cole felt a sudden heat licking at his body. He glanced down. His wetsuit had become paper-thin. He could vaguely see his own skin through the translucent veneer that remained, protecting him from certain incineration.

Lindsay flung herself forward, grasping a thick metal tube extending from the lower section of the divers' cabin. Her body thrashed as she fought to control the pitching submersible by the sheer strength of her will. But there was something more; a light was emanating from her body, as though she were emitting some incredible source of electrical energy. Gradually, the craft steadied itself, enough for Cole to open the top hatch. Cole squeezed himself inside, retrieved a metal safety cable, and tossed it outside. It sank toward the bottom of the *Harbinger* and Lindsay grabbed it with one hand, while still clutching the metal tube with the other. Cole reeled her up and inside, quickly sealing off the upper airlock, as the liquid was sucked back outside. With the *Harbinger* still being tossed violently about, Lindsay buckled herself into her seat and fired up the props. She shouted out for Cole to remove the tanks and his helmet and to stand on the thick rubber mat. She set the controls and a moment later joined him. She kissed him quickly on the lips, as if for luck, then threw the switch that would send 275,000 volts of deadly electricity pulsing through the hull. Just as before, the *Harbinger* lit up like a massive fireworks explosion and began to move rapidly back from where they had come. The tiny craft sped like a bullet toward the portal, crashing through to the darkened void beyond, until nothing remained but a quickly fading memory, growing more indistinct with each passing moment.

28

"Send him in at once, Barbara," Bill Gaines exclaimed through his desk phone intercom. Art entered apprehensively. He had been summoned by the CEO of Hollingsworth Enterprises for an update on Cole's whereabouts. No one at the office had heard from him in days. E-mails had gone unanswered, voice mails unreturned. Something was seriously wrong, and Bill was going to get to the bottom of it. If Cole's mysterious disappearance wasn't enough, the package Gaines had received two days ago had sent the CEO over the edge. Jacob Featherstone had Fed-Ex'd a package supposedly containing a prototype of the smart glasses whose production in which they had just invested fifty million dollars.

Excited that they would finally have something concrete in their hands, Bill had summoned the entire board of directors to witness the unveiling of the product meant to fast-track them into the digital future. When all of the directors were seated, Bill opened the package as the boardroom went collectively silent in rapt anticipation. The glasses had been wrapped in a velvet bag tied off by a cord. A blank greeting card was attached with a string. Bill unfolded the card and read the handwritten inscription out loud.

Cole,

From the bottom of my heart, thank you for the $50,000,000. Please don't take this too hard. In the long run, this will make you a better businessman, I promise.

Fondly,
Jacob Featherstone

Confused expressions spread around the room. Gaines hesitated for a moment, wondering what the cryptic message meant. The answer was supplied as soon as he opened the bag and pulled out a set of black plastic glasses attached to a plastic nose and mustache—the kind comedians used to wear in vaudeville shows. However, not a single person was laughing at this practical joke, as the realization of how they had been swindled swept through the boardroom like wildfire.

"Art, as you are one of Cole's best friends and his attorney, I assume you know where he is. It's imperative I speak with him immediately." There wasn't a hint in the CEO's voice that anything short of the correct answer would be tolerated.

Art fidgeted in his chair. He suddenly felt like one of the hostile witnesses he was accustomed to grilling on the witness stand.

"Well, sir, I believe Cole took a short vacation with Lindsay Featherstone, before returning to the office to assume his new duties as president. I spoke with him briefly at his birthday party at Gull's Point, but I never saw him after that. I—"

"Lindsay Featherstone! Are you telling me that Cole is right now off with Jacob Featherstone's daughter?" Bill's face suddenly turned crimson, his jugular vein protruding.

"I believe so, sir, but what's that got to do with anything—"

"Here, Art, have a look at this." The CEO shoved the pair of plastic glasses across his desk. "I assume you are fully aware of the venture we entered into with Featherstone to develop the Internet-connected glasses. Do you have any idea how much money we invested?" Gaines was literally shaking now.

"I believe the number was fifty million?" Art replied cautiously, beginning to understand.

"That's the number, Art. Now, tell me, do you think this set of glasses is worth fifty million dollars?"

The tension in the room hung like a metal curtain as the two men eyed each other. Art had no comeback. There was nothing he could say, short of lying, that would placate the man. *Poor Cole*, he thought. *What the hell has Cole gotten himself into?*

"Now Art, let's try the question one more time. Where is Cole Hollingsworth?" Gaines said accusatorily, as if Art was an accomplice in the whole scheme.

"I—I think he may have gone to the Caribbean. I heard that Frank Martin, his personal pilot, suffered a heart attack during the flight and returned two days later for bypass surgery. You might try contacting him. That's really all I can tell you, sir. I haven't heard from Cole since the party. He hasn't returned my messages, either." Art went silent, hoping he had supplied sufficient information. He didn't want to rat on his closest friend, yet he understood the enormity of the situation. This was serious shit. The firm was out fifty million, and Cole was vacationing in the tropics with the daughter of the man who was behind the scam. The media would have a fucking field day with this. Even Hollingsworth Enterprise's solid grip on the publishing industry couldn't cover up this one.

"If there is nothing else, Mr. Gaines, I'm due in court shortly," Art finally said, desperately wanting to leave the offices so he could try to contact Cole.

Gaines nodded and turned in his chair, staring out the window as if Art was no longer present. Art practically ran out of the office and down the stairwell, agonizing over how he could contact

Cole with this news. If he could get to him before Gaines did, at least Cole could prepare some sort of defensive strategy. God, what a mess. Pulling out his cell phone, Art punched in the number of Cole's executive assistant, Grace Foster. Maybe she knew how to get in touch with his friend.

Grace answered immediately, obviously recognizing Art's number and realizing the severity of the situation. The bad news was all over the company.

"Yes, Art, what can I do for you?" Grace said, dispensing with all pleasantries.

"Hi, Grace, I'm sorry to bother you, but I really need to contact Cole. It's vitally important." The angst in Art's voice was unmistakable.

"I don't know exactly where he is, Art, I'm sorry. If I did, I'd tell you. I can give you Frank's cell number if that would help. I know he flew the Falcon to an airport in the Bahamas." She rattled off the number.

"Thanks, Grace, you're a lifesaver. I owe you big-time. If Cole should contact you by chance, please ask him to call me right away." The line went dead. Art then dialed Frank's number, waiting impatiently while the phone rang. Frank answered on the fifth ring.

"Frank, it's Art Barkley, Cole's attorney. Can you tell—"

"Can I call you right back, Art? I've got Bill Gaines on hold."

"Shit!" Art exclaimed, then quickly apologized. "I just need a moment. I need to know where Cole is. I can't stress how important this is."

"I don't know exactly where he is now, as I was just explaining to Mr. Gaines. We flew him into San Salvador Airport and he was staying in Cockburn the last I heard. I think he had reservations at the Bay Marina Resort. That's all I can tell you."

"That's enough, Frank, thanks. By the way, how are you feeling?"

"Much better, thanks to Lindsay Featherstone, I'm told. Art, I've got to get back to Mr. Gaines."

Art then dialed International information and got the number to the Bay Marina Resort. He was talking with the front desk within minutes.

"This is Art Barkley, Cole Hollingsworth's attorney. I'm calling from Rhode Island in the United States. I have a serious problem, and I need to speak with Mr. Hollingsworth immediately. He should be registered there."

"Can you hold for a moment, Mr. Barkley, while I check?" The young man spoke with a heavy South American accent.

Art tapped his foot impatiently on the asphalt. *"Come on, come on, what's so damn tough about locating a registered guest?"* Art muttered to himself. Finally, the man's voice came back on the line.

"I'm sorry, Mr. Barkley, but he checked out five days ago."

"Did he leave a forwarding address?"

"Not that I could find. He left with a Ms. Featherstone and I overheard something about the Gerace Research Centre up at Grahams Harbour. They may have been heading there. Is there anything else I can do for you, Mr. Barkley?"

"No…thank you." Art hung up, wondering what the hell Cole would be doing at Gerace, a renowned oceanography research center. How was this connected? If anything, Cole should by lying on a beach, drinking rum, and putting the moves on Lindsay. And then it hit him. The Hollingsworth Endowment Fund was a large contributor to the Gerace Centre. Art quickly dialed Cole's office again.

Hi, Grace, it's Art again. Hey, I think I may have a lead on Cole. He was last seen in San Salvador, and he may be on his way to the Gerace Research Centre, a beneficiary of the Hollingsworth Endowment Fund. Can you get me the contact information for the Institute's director down there?"

"Hold on a sec, Art. I'll e-mail it to you in a moment. Keep me posted, okay?"

"You got it—and thanks."

As Art waited for the e-mail to arrive, he wondered whether Gaines had thought this through and come to this conclusion, as well. The man was as shrewd as they came. He could only assume he was in possession of the same information. It was now a desperate race against time, only Art didn't have nearly the resources at his command that the CEO had. The only advantage Art held was a fierce determination to help his friend.

29

The *Harbinger* burst through the portal's diaphragm like an escape pod jettisoned from a spaceship. The craft slowed as it re-entered the murky waters of the Puerto Rican Trench, over five miles below the ocean's surface. The submersible drifted silently, while Lindsay and Cole regained their bearings. They had made it somehow, against staggering odds. Both of their wetsuits were threadbare. How they had escaped serious injury was anybody's guess. But they were alive. The trench's waters were filled with debris—the currents still churning—as rising methane bubbles rendered the *Harbinger* unstable. Still, Lindsay managed to keep them on track. She navigated the craft back toward the portal to view any possible damage, but to her utter shock it no longer existed, replaced instead by a jagged wall of cliffs, barely visible under the halogen lights. Cole thought he heard her curse, but it was in a language he didn't understand.

"What's wrong?" Cole said, concerned.

"Look for yourself." She pointed in the direction from which they had just come. Cole squinted, trying to focus on what Lindsay was attempting to show him.

"It's gone, Cole. The gateway is gone!"

"How could that be possible? What happened?" Cole said in astonishment.

"The shifting of the ocean floor must have changed the landscape.

It happened before on my last dive when I was searching for your parents' yacht. We've lost it, Cole." Lindsay sounded defeated, filled with sadness—or was it disgust? However, her setback didn't come close to matching Cole's anguish as the realization sunk in.

With the disappearance of the gateway, so, too, disappeared any hope of reconnecting with his parents. Had all of this been for naught? He had come so close. Cole closed his eyes, retreating inward into a state of deep despair. All along he had believed their voyage would be fruitless, indeed, he thought it had bordered on the brink of lunacy. And yet Lindsay had made good on her promise and brought him through the most incredible journey one could ever imagine, only to be cruelly ripped away from their final destination just at the point of discovery.

Lindsay sensed Cole's agony, but she remained silent as they made their ascent slowly up the walls of the trench and into the open waters above. Steam hissed out from jagged fissures, and gaseous methane bubbles continued to ooze upward, released from the bowels of the earth. They weren't out of danger yet, and Lindsay remained cognizant of this fact, scrutinizing the navigation controls intently. Once they had put sufficient distance between themselves and the trench, Lindsay finally switched on the intercom.

"Cassie, Ryan, can you hear me? This is Lindsay. Come in, please." Lindsay's query was answered with static, the turbulence surrounding them making communication nearly impossible. She tried again, but no luck. They were still on their own, drifting upward without any means of communication with the surface. If they made it safely to the top, would the frigate still be there? Had the tectonic shift moved them somewhere else in the Atlantic? Could it even have caused a tsunami? These questions and more raced through Lindsay's head as Cole sat transfixed, staring out into the dark waters as though searching for something only he could see.

Something in the distance caught Lindsay's attention. It moved swiftly, with a herky-jerky motion, propelling itself forward in powerful spurts. At first, she thought it might be another submersible searching for them. The Institute had at least two on the ready at all times for emergencies like this. Had Cassie contacted them? The seismic activity must have registered in the high zone, and every detection device in the southern hemisphere would have recorded it. As the object moved closer, however, Lindsay realized the object was not manmade. Long, menacing- looking tentacles moved in unison as it sped directly toward them.

"Oh God!" Lindsay exclaimed as the abomination neared, a cross between a giant jellyfish and a monstrous octopus. Electrical charges pulsed with vibrant color within its gelatinous body. It was at least five times the size of the *Harbinger*. It could only have been released from some dark, desolate cave as the subterranean landscape had been shattered, releasing the chthonic sea monster from its prison. And it looked mad as hell.

"Cole!" she screamed. "Buckle up! Get ready for impact—"These were the last words Cole heard as the *Harbinger* was suddenly rocked, gripped by a tangle of muscular tentacles, drawn inward toward gaping jaws. All Cole could see were jagged rows of teeth and electrical discharges—before everything went black.

30

Art waited impatiently as the international operator connected him to the Gerace Research Centre's information desk.

"Hello, this is Carmen with the Gerace Research Centre. How may I be of assistance?"

"Hello, my name is Art Barkley. I'm calling from the United States. I'm Cole Hollingsworth's attorney. I assume you're familiar with the Hollingsworth Endowment Fund? Something very important has come up. Can you please connect me with Dr. Voteli?"

"Please hold. I'll try his office." The line went silent. Art anxiously thumped his desk with the fingers of his right hand. The phone rang. Good news, he had gotten through.

"Hello, you have reached the voice mail for Dr. Voteli, director of Gerace Research Centre. Sorry to have missed your call. Please leave a short message and a return phone number, and I will call you back as soon as possible." The message was repeated in Spanish.

"Damn it!" Art cursed into his cell phone. "Goddamn voice mail. Doesn't anybody answer their phones anymore?" He left a message meant to convey the urgency of the situation to the Institute's Director, then hung up. He dialed Grace immediately to check on Bill Gaines's progress.

"Hi, Grace, any news on Gaines?"

"I couldn't find out much, but he left the office and is supposedly headed to the airport. He's flying to San Salvador, Art. I'm sorry."

"It's not your fault. Thanks for the update." Art dialed his own personal assistant. "Anne, can you please call me a cab. I need to—" Another call suddenly came through. He checked the number as he held the phone away from his ear. "I'll call you back, Anne. I need to take another call.

"This is Art Barkley."

"Mr. Barkley, this is Dr. Voteli of the Gerace Research Centre returning your call. How may I be of assistance?"

"Thanks for calling back. I urgently need to contact Cole Hollingsworth. I was told by a staff member at the Bay Marina Resort where he was staying that he may be headed to the Institute. Have you seen him? He was most likely with Lindsay Featherstone."

"I'm sorry, Mr. Barkley, but I never saw Mr. Hollingsworth, at least not while I was here. I am aware that Lindsay has been in the area, however, and is accompanying him out to sea. They are on a special expedition on behalf of Hollingsworth Enterprises, along with other members of the Gerace staff. They are traveling on the Institute's frigate, the USS *Truett*, and carrying the *Harbinger II*, one of our submersibles."

"Submersible? Did you say *submersible*?"

"Yes, the *Harbinger* is our most advanced bathyscaphe used for deep-sea exploration."

Why in the world would Cole need a deep-sea submersible? Art wondered. It didn't take long for the dots to connect. Cole's parents…

"Dr. Voteli, do you know where they went, specifically?"

"I believe they intended to explore the Puerto Rican Trench, the deepest location in the Atlantic Ocean. It's over five miles in depth, and, I might add, quite difficult to navigate."

"Where exactly is that located?" Art replied, suddenly horrified.

"Approximately one hundred fifty miles south of San Salvador."

"Is it possible to contact them by cell phone? I can't stress how important this is."

"I can give you the number that should connect you to the main bridge of the *Truett*. I doubt any cell phone your client is carrying will work in the area. I suggest you contact Cassie Thomas or Ryan Walker. I'll e-mail you their contact information. They may be able to get word to Mr. Hollingsworth."

"Thank you, Dr. Voteli, you've been very helpful. Just one more question. Is there any way I can personally reach the *Truett* myself?"

"About the only way would be by private helicopter. You might find someone who would take you by boat, although most boaters avoid the area. You know, the legends and all."

"What legends?" Art replied suspiciously.

"Why, about the Bermuda Triangle, of course. I realize that most countries downplay its existence, but the local people have a completely different opinion on the matter. To them, it is very real."

"*Holy shit!*" Art exclaimed under his breath, then quickly apologized for the unnecessary use of the expletive.

"Will there be anything else, Mr. Barkley?"

"Do you have any contacts for a helicopter service in the area?"

"Please give me your e-mail address and I'll have someone forward that information to you, as well." With that final instructive, the director hung up, leaving Art to contemplate Cole's descent into madness.

31

Lindsay reversed the props and slammed down the lever, sending 275,000 volts of pure electricity through the *Harbinger* once more. The craft crackled like lightning in a torrential thunderstorm. The sea monster writhed in pain, absorbing the energy, the water around it vaporizing into putrid steam as its transparent flesh seared with fire. Slowly the creature recoiled, releasing the *Harbinger* from its steel-like grip. Lindsay wasted no time and shot out of reach, rising up through layers of shadowy water at top speed while the sea demon drifted away in a state of electrified shock. She knew she hadn't killed it, but at least she had given them some precious time. It might think twice about attacking any time soon. She tried contacting the *Truett* again, but without success.

"Nice work, Lindsay," Cole said.

"Thanks, that was close," Lindsay replied.

"Any idea how much longer until we reach the surface?" Cole said.

Lindsay checked the depth finder. If it was still functioning properly, they had about two miles to ascend before reaching the surface, but what awaited them there was still a mystery.

The remainder of their ascent was spent in silence. The surrounding ocean was still in turmoil from the shifting plates. Lindsay was on the lookout for other obstacles that might interfere with their reaching the surface safely. Cole still had many questions, but this was not the place or the time to ask them. He needed space to think. Lindsay needed time to reformulate a plan…and to prepare herself for the questions she knew would be forthcoming. They could have used some music to help pass the time, but she didn't think any of her previous selections would be appropriate. And so they drifted upward in a world of liquid space—a world still so foreign to Cole.

All these years the ocean had mostly been just a playground to Cole; he had paid no attention whatsoever to the life that existed below, only to the occasional game fishing excursions on which he had taken customers. The ocean's surface had been a mirror reflecting life on land, but he no longer considered it that way. He felt like Alice, who had just stepped through the *Looking Glass*, viewing a new world inside-out. There really was a rabbit hole, and it existed at the bottom of the ocean floor. Had Lewis Carroll known the truth all along when he wrote his classic novels? Others must surely have known about the portal, too, but they must have been sworn to secrecy, the realization so profound it became a burden. So, the knowledge had been shared surreptitiously through the ages through a story here, a poem there, a song—anything to relieve the bearer from the burden of such an intolerable weight.

Gradually, the deep indigo surrounding them turned to lavender, and then to aquamarine as sunlight pierced the upper layers of water. The change had little effect on Cole. He had become lost again inside his own mind, a prisoner to a nightmare that refused to release him. His skin was pale, his eyes blank. Lindsay had to literally shake Cole to bring him back to reality, when they finally reached the surface and she realized they were alone, bobbing in the waves with no frigate in sight.

The sky was a dirty gray, the water an angry green—their craft a tiny speck in an endless ocean that stretched in every direction to distant horizons, beyond which could only lie more disappointment.

Lindsay cracked open the upper hatch, climbing out and standing on the top of the floatation section, attempting to gain her bearings. In her left hand she clenched a compass; in her right, a flare gun. Cole emerged through the hatch and stood beside her, surveying the waterscape. There was nothing but ocean, only the two of them left against the world. It was unnervingly quiet, except for the waves splashing against the submersible's hull, rocking the *Harbinger* back and forth like a toy boat in a vast and unpredictable lake. Lindsay turned to face Cole.

"I'm sorry—so sorry, Cole. I never expected anything like that to happen so quickly. I—"

"You don't need to apologize, Lindsay. It wasn't your fault. You don't control the ocean floor," Cole said, his eyes dark, searching.

What do you say to someone who had been so close to discovering a truth that defied description? Words seemed meaningless now. Perhaps it was better just to remain silent, to allow Cole's brain to process this newfound information in a manner that would not drive him insane. Lindsay fired the flare gun high into the air, its light appearing like the fiery tail of a comet, arcing across the sky and hanging there unsuspended.

And then they waited.

The flare had long since died out by the time they heard the sound of powerful rotors whirring mechanically in the distance. A dark speck approached from the west, growing larger. They had been found—but by whom? Was their rescue imminent? Cole suddenly wondered whether there was anything truly left of him to rescue. Was this the end? Would he simply pack up and head back to Rhode Island, with the memory of yet another failure in his mind? He supposed it truly was time to leave.

The Lynx helicopter hovered above them, the strong downdraft from the main rotors making the surrounding water choppy, spraying the couple with seawater. A thin rope snaked down from the main cabin, attached to a harness. Lindsay offered it to Cole first, he supposed because most of this equipment was financed by people and companies like his. He refused, but she wouldn't take no for an answer, and Cole lacked the fortitude to argue with her. It was like calling someone *sir*, a signal of superiority, a recognition of power, that he would go before her. The closeness—the bond that he had shared with her—was disappearing as rapidly as the image of Lindsay standing alone atop the *Harbinger* while the chopper sped him back to the *Truett*. She would be responsible for protecting the *Harbinger* until they returned for her. It was too valuable to the research center to lose. But what value did they place on Lindsay's life? He could not bear to look down at her, growing smaller and smaller until she disappeared into the waves completely. He sat alone in the back of the helicopter cabin, his head resting in his hands.

Cole had no idea how much time had elapsed when the helicopter finally touched down on the heliport pad toward the stern of the frigate. Cassie and Ryan were standing below waiting anxiously for their return. Cole was helped out of the chopper and he made his way down the metal ladder to the upper deck, where he was immediately embraced by Cassie. Even Ryan seemed distressed, wrapping his arm around Cole's shoulders.

"Where's Lindsay?" Cassie asked apprehensively, as though her sudden absence spelled disaster.

"They left her behind with the *Harbinger*. She's guarding it, if you can believe that!" Cole replied bitterly.

"You mean, she's all alone out there?" Ryan's voice was accusatory, but because of who Cole was, he was clearly trying to hold his temper in check.

Having overheard the conversation, the helicopter pilot shouted down, "We're leaving now to go get her. We'll lead her back to the *Truett*."

"You're not going without me!" Ryan shouted back and practically flew up the stairs to the helicopter. He entered the chopper, as the long, flat blades rotated slowly. A roar of engines, combined with a sudden rush of wind, and the aircraft lifted away, a dark silhouette against the ashen sky.

"Come inside, Cole. Let's get you cleaned up. I'm sure Lindsay will be back soon." However, the look on Cassie's face suggested apprehension. Cole followed dutifully behind the diver, wondering what her look had meant. Did she know something he didn't?

An hour later, dressed in dry clothes, Cole stood alone at the edge of the helipad, watching the sky for any sign of the aircraft's return. Something *was* wrong. It shouldn't be taking this long. He pulled a set of binoculars from the railing and scanned the horizon. It felt as empty as his heart.

"Goddammit, Lindsay! Where are you?" Cole muttered.

The sky was beginning to turn dark as the afternoon faded to twilight, and still no Lindsay. Cassie joined him on the platform, sliding her arm inside of his.

"She'll be back, Cole. Lindsay is the most resourceful person I know. She'll find her way back to you. Be patient. Something must have happened and she probably just took precautionary measures, that's all. They'll find her."

Cole said nothing. His eyes burned as he gazed out to sea. He should never have let them leave her out there alone, submersible or not. Worst-case scenario, he could have bought the Institute another one. The *Harbinger* was replaceable. Lindsay was not. If she didn't return soon, someone would answer for this, and it wasn't going to be pretty. The pair stood in silence, watching... waiting.

A pinprick of light in the distance caught Cole's attention. Cassie spotted it, too. They pressed hard against the railing, straining to see what it was. Could it be the first evening star, poking through the gloom, or was it the light from a helicopter? It was moving, drawing nearer. That could only mean one thing. A horrible thought suddenly occurred to Cole. There were no lights below it on the surface of the water. Where was the *Harbinger*? Was Lindsay onboard the chopper, or had it become too dark to continue searching? Something in his gut told him it was the latter.

The aircraft hovered above, buffeting them with a strong downdraft from the powerful rotors. Lit up like a spacecraft, it lowered itself onto the platform. There was no submersible attached. Had they been forced to abandon it? This class of chopper could easily have transported the submersible by air. The aircraft was equipped with a heavy-duty lifting crane and reinforced metal cables. Cole's heart sank. Ryan was the first to disembark, followed by the pilot and copilot. The look that passed between Cassie and Ryan said it all. Lindsay was not onboard. Cole stepped forward.

"What the hell is going on? When you picked me up, everything was fine. The *Harbinger* was in good shape, the ocean was relatively calm. It should have been a no-brainer to bring them back!" Cole exclaimed, incensed.

"A lot can happen out there in a very short time," explained the pilot. "When we returned to the exact coordinates, the submersible was nowhere in sight. We searched the entire area within a fifty-mile radius. The only thing we found was a whaling boat heading south. We tracked it down, but the captain hadn't seen anything. He promised to contact us if they located the *Harbinger*. But it doesn't look likely. They were sailing in the opposite direction…"

"Great! So, what do we do now?" Cole asked, staring the pilot down as if he was about to rip his head off.

"It's too dark to continue, and we were running out of fuel. We'll be out at first light tomorrow." He turned to Cassie. "Please continue trying to contact her via the ship-to-ship communications."

"This is unacceptable. There must be something else we can do. I'm not leaving her out there all night alone!" Cole insisted.

"Cole, there isn't anything else to be done. Lindsay can survive the night in the *Harbinger*…" Ryan's voice trailed off. *That is, if it's still afloat or even in one piece,* he thought.

The image of the giant jellyfish—or whatever the hell it was that had attacked them—flashed in Cole's mind. Had it tracked the submersible all the way to the surface? Or had something else happened? Cole pondered the situation for a moment.

"We can at least sail the *Truett* in the direction where we last saw her. If she's still in the area, she might see us—she might even send up another flare," Cole offered. Cassie nodded her head. Ryan headed into the main cabin to inform the crew of the change in course.

The pilots turned in early, right after dinner was finished. Cole, Cassie, and Ryan lingered on deck, making small talk. There wasn't much to say, really. Cole wasn't about to discuss what he and Lindsay had found at the bottom of the trench. Cassie didn't dare ask him, either. That subject was off-limits for now. When Lindsay returned— *if* she returned—they could broach the subject then. Ryan was the first to rise from his chair.

"It's getting late and we'll be up before dawn. Good night," Ryan said, then moved silently to his sleeping quarters. Normally Cassie would have accompanied him, but tonight was different. She thought Cole might need to talk, and he would probably be more comfortable talking with her. Cassie gazed compassionately at Cole, waiting for his questions.

"Is there anything you want to talk about, Cole?" she finally said.

For a moment it appeared Cole was about to say something, but instead he hesitated, withdrawing. He smiled ruefully, suggesting it was time for Cassie to depart, too. She caught his drift, rose, then kissed him softly on the cheek.

"She'll be back." With that, Cassie was gone, leaving Cole sitting alone in the darkness, sparsely lit by the deck lights. The sound of the waves and the drone of the ship's Westinghouse turbine engines were Cole's only companion now—their rhythmic patterns eventually lulling him to sleep. He succumbed to the exhaustion even though he struggled to stay awake in the slim hope that Lindsay would somehow show up.

A gentle shove against his shoulder roused him out of a deep sleep. Hours still separated dawn from darkness. It took a moment for Cole's gaze to come into focus. His eyes immediately widened, and something guttural made its way out of his mouth.

"Lindsay, is that really you?" Her image standing over him silhouetted against the light of the pale moon appeared ethereal, like an angel hovering between two worlds—between darkness and light. It could only be a dream. No person could appear so perfect.

Lindsay wrapped her arms around Cole protectively, quelling his pain. He felt as though he was being cradled in feathered wings, soft, comforting. And for the remainder of the night, she held him in a cocoon of tranquility, until a sliver of light appeared on the eastern horizon. Then she vanished like an apparition.

Ryan emerged from belowdecks, followed by the two pilots. Cassie was not with them. Cole opened his eyes groggily, as the commotion surrounding him became louder.

"Cole, do you want to accompany us?" Ryan said. "We'll be leaving in fifteen minutes, so please get ready quickly if you want to go."

Cole rose and glanced over the railing at their surroundings. The morning was a glorious one, the haze and clouds of the previous day having been swept away by the tropical breeze, revealing an ocean of sparkling blue and a sky pale with golden light.

"I'll be back in a few minutes. Wait for me—I'm coming with you," Cole said. The pilots climbed aboard and prepared for liftoff.

"Hey, where do you guys think you're going?" A familiar voice sounded in the distance, stopping Cole and Ryan in their tracks. Both men turned in unison. The expressions on their faces must have been identical as both Cassie and Lindsay broke out in laughter.

"Lindsay!" Ryan exclaimed, dumbfounded. Cole didn't hesitate, and rushed over to grab her up in his arms.

"When—how? I don't believe it!" Cole said, hugging her tightly against his body like he would never let her go again. Cassie winked in his direction, as if to say, *I told you so.*

"Why didn't you wake me?" Cole said; a hint of annoyance in his voice.

"I tried, but you were so deep in sleep you couldn't keep your eyes open. I sat with you for a while before going below to find Cassie."

Cole lowered Lindsay back to her feet, releasing her, while recalling the mysterious dream he'd had about an angel coming to him in the night. No, it couldn't have been true, and yet there was something in Lindsay's expression that suggested it might have been real. Cole shuddered at the thought.

"How did you find us?" Ryan said. "You had totally disappeared when we came searching for you yesterday. What happened?"

"It's a long story, so I'll try to make it short. After the helicopter left with Cole, I spotted a ship on the horizon. It appeared to be headed south, until the crew noticed the *Harbinger* sitting alone and unprotected in the middle of the ocean. It abruptly turned west and headed in my direction. It took me a while to discover who it was. A band of sea pirates, perhaps drug dealers, I really couldn't tell. All I knew was that they wanted us, or at least, they wanted the *Harbinger*, and I wasn't about to let them have it. It would have brought them a fortune in bounty—and I would definitely have been expendable."

"So, what did you do?" Cole interjected.

"The only thing I could. I jumped back inside and took her underwater. They followed the best they could. They must have had some fairly sophisticated sonar gear, because they were tracking me pretty closely. I was running out of usable oxygen before long, but fortunately it was getting dark. I dove much deeper and then reversed course, apparently beyond their sonar capability. Eventually I detected a much larger vessel approaching. Thank God you guys had decided to navigate the *Truett* closer to me. I guess they eventually gave up. I took a chance and rose to the surface, to find that their running lights had disappeared. It only took a few more minutes to get to you. I moored the *Harbinger* to the rear platform and came up on deck. That's when I discovered you sleeping in that chair."

"Is the *Harbinger* still safe? I mean, couldn't they have followed you and taken it later?" Cole asked.

"It's safe, I just checked on it. I doubt they would have tried that. Not against a ship this size with a five-foot, fifty-four-caliber gun plainly in sight. No, they had their chance and they blew it. I'm sure they're headed off on some other exploit. They never stay in one location very long."

The pilots seemed impressed with Lindsay's escape. The head pilot approached.

"Well done, Dr. Featherstone. Is there anything more we can do for you before we leave? Does anyone need to return to Gerace?"

Lindsay glanced quickly at Cole to see his reaction, then turned back to the pilot, satisfied that Cole wasn't going anywhere. "No, but thank you so much for your vigilance in trying to find me. Please tell Dr. Voteli that everything's okay. We'll be in contact with him later," Lindsay replied.

"As you wish. Good luck." The pilots reentered the helicopter and within minutes had lifted off, speeding north like some prehistoric marine bird gliding over the water.

Cole stared at Lindsay in amazement. She gazed back at him with one of those curious, half-amused expressions, as though attempting to read his mind again. Realizing he had almost lost her, he was bursting with the need to tell her something important, but he constrained himself in front of the others.

"Cole, I need to get a few hours of sleep. Would you come with me? I have something I want to discuss with you."

Cassie and Ryan looked on as the twosome disappeared, once

again exchanging concerned looks. Cole followed Lindsay into her cabin, where she lay down on the bed, leaning back against the side of the interior wall and patting the mattress beside her, beckoning Cole to join her. He slid down alongside her body, facing her. Her eyes sparkled, her mouth wet. It was all he could do to refrain from kissing her. She wrapped her arms around his neck, drawing him closer.

"Don't blame yourself. It wasn't your fault," she whispered. "I told the pilots to take you first. As an employee of the research center I am responsible for the *Harbinger*. I was the one who had to stay. You understand, don't you?"

Cole's blood pressure spiked. He actually didn't understand. How could anyone have left her behind unprotected? He should have been the one to stay. His face flushed with anger, with embarrassment. Although she had returned safely, he hadn't forgotten his promise to hold someone accountable for the misstep. But he also didn't want to upset her, so he did his best to remain calm.

"Now, Cole, promise me you won't come down on anybody." Her lips formed into a pout as if she knew what he was thinking. "Everybody was simply doing the best they could. It's not worth making a scene over. Besides, you're above those sorts of things now, aren't you?" She smiled seductively.

How could he say no to her? Lying there, alone in her arms in the middle of nowhere, he was exactly where he wanted to be.

"Okay, if you insist. But if anything else like this happens, there'll be hell to pay."

"Big, bad Cole Hollingsworth." She laughed fetchingly. "The defender of the weak and powerless. If you want to take it out on someone, take it out on me." She leaned forward, kissing him softly on the lips. A sudden surge of heat filled his body.

"Now, about that sleep? You can stay with me if you want to." She looked dreamily into his eyes. He suddenly felt drowsy, too. A moment later they were fast asleep in each other's arms. His questions would just have to wait.

Hours passed. The sun rose higher in the southern sky. Life moved slower in this part of the hemisphere. The pressures of urban life, the running of a major corporation, all seemed as far away and indistinct as the distant horizon. Cole lingered in Lindsay's arms, his worldly cares fading away like the light of day as dusk settled in. And still they had not moved. Neither Cassie nor Ryan bothered to disturb them. It wouldn't be much longer now, and Cole needed whatever peace he could cling to before the truth was finally revealed. Lindsay was again preparing him… preparing him for the shock of his life.

<h1 style="text-align:center">32</h1>

The sun had nearly set when the angry whir of mechanical rotors invaded the stillness. Another helicopter was back, but it was different this time. A black, stealth-like bird dropped from the sky like a giant predator wasp attacking its victim. It landed unannounced on the helipad. The rotors continued to spin as two men with briefcases clambered out the side doors. They were dressed in suits, and there was little doubt as to who they were. Businessmen. CEO Bill Gaines and the corporate attorney scaled down the metal ladder and arrived on the deck. Ryan was the first to greet them.

"Excuse me, but who are you, and what are you doing on our ship?" the diver asked.

"Who we are is not as important as why we're here," Gaines replied, his voice a bastion of authority. "Is Cole Hollingsworth onboard?" This was not really a question, but rather more of an accusation.

"Yes, he's here. Is he expecting you?" Ryan said, stepping forward, ready for a confrontation. No suits were going to intimidate him.

"This is Mr. Gaines, CEO of Hollingsworth Enterprises." The attorney spoke as if Gaines needn't announce himself to this deckhand. "I'm Jack Saunders, Hollingsworth Enterprise's corporate attorney, and it is extremely important that we speak to Cole at once." The two men glared at Ryan. Cassie appeared on deck, walking toward the three men.

"Ryan, what's this all about? And who are these men?" Cassie said as she approached.

"The CEO of Hollingsworth and his lackey attorney friend," Ryan replied, his body tensing.

"Cole's asleep. Is it really necessary to disturb him this very minute?" Cassie asked.

"And who might you be, ma'am?" the attorney said condescendingly.

"I'm Cassie Thomas, team leader for this expedition. You're on my ship now, and I would appreciate being spoken to in a civil manner."

"This may be your expedition, but we were instrumental in paying for this ship and just about everything on it. You might want to reconsider your attitude and go wake up Cole," Gaines said, taking a step forward. "Or I'll do it for you."

Cassie considered the man for a moment. "That won't be necessary. I'll be back shortly."

"Saunders, follow her below deck. I don't want Cole to get any advance warning of our arrival or be given an opportunity to disappear," Gaines instructed his attorney.

If it would have been any other person but the CEO of the research center's largest benefactor, Ryan would have decked him on the spot for his mistreatment of Cassie. Gaines turned toward the diver.

"Don't you have something better to do than stand there and stare at me? My conversation with Cole will take place in private," Gaines said.

"You're right. I have plenty of things better to do than watch your action. Where do you get off acting so superior to everybody else? No wonder Cole needed to get away from you guys." Ryan walked off, clenching his teeth. *The arrogant son of a bitch*, he thought.

Cole dressed quickly at the announcement of the CEO's arrival. Lindsay remained below, at least for the moment. Five minutes later,

Cole and Cassie arrived on deck, followed closely by Saunders.

"Bill, what on earth brings you all the way out here? Something wrong up at the shop?" Cole said good-naturedly in an attempt to defuse the obvious tension onboard, or to ascertain the real reason the CEO had appeared unannounced.

"Something *wrong*? Have you lost your mind, or has the tropical sun fried your brain?" Gaines replied disdainfully. The two men stared at each other as the sudden realization of why the CEO of his father's company had traveled all this way took hold. It had to be something really bad. The Internet glasses—it couldn't be anything else.

"I received a package while you've been away," Gaines began. "Actually, it was addressed to you, but since you decided to take a vacation at one of the most critical times in the company's recent history, I took the liberty of opening it myself. And do you have any idea what the package contained?"

Lindsay emerged from belowdecks and walked slowly in the direction of the men. From the corner of his eye, Cole spotted her and swung his arm behind his back with his palm facing her, signaling for her to stay back. She stopped in her tracks, immediately feeling the tension between the two men. Cassie took a step back, too, thinking this was about to get ugly. Cole pressed forward, placing more distance between he and Gaines and the women.

"I assume you received a prototype set of glasses that Jacob Featherstone promised to send to me. Was something wrong with the model?" Cole said apprehensively.

"Something *wrong*! You tell me." Gaines opened his briefcase, retrieving something resembling a pair of glasses, and handed it to Cole. Cole fondled the pair of plastic prank glasses in his hands.

"Surely you're jesting. It must have just been a joke. Jacob likes to kid around. You know how he is."

Lindsay grimaced. Cassie looked confused. Ryan watched from a distance.

"That was my immediate reaction also—until I read the note he had addressed to you." Gaines handed Cole Jacob's handwritten note. Cole read it in silence.

Cole,

From the bottom of my heart, thank you for the $50,000,000. Please don't take this too hard. In the long run, this will make you a better businessman, I promise.

Fondly,
Jacob Featherstone

The letter dropped silently from Cole's hand, caught by a sudden breeze. It fluttered over in Lindsay's direction, landing at her feet. She scooped it up and read it, then closed her eyes. *What has my father done, adding insult to injury? As if it wasn't bad enough that he has stolen from Cole, now he is openly mocking him.* Suddenly ashamed beyond humiliation, her gaze caught Cole's, who had turned back to look at her, his expression merciless. There was no need for words. The deception was immeasurable, absolute. Lindsay felt her breath leave her body.

Cole turned back to Gaines. "So, what are our options, Bill? Has Jacob been located?"

"Not yet. We have our best men on it, but it appears he and his two associates have left the country and stashed our money in untraceable bank accounts. Who knows, they may be nearby in the Bahamas or the Caymans, enjoying themselves and laughing all the way to the proverbial bank! Wouldn't that just be fucking ironic?" Gaines said, his voice rising to a mild roar. "How could you have been so stupid, Cole? How could you have sold the board on a concept without having foolproof evidence of the product and the production schedules? We took you on your word, and just like your father, we believed you, relied on your integrity as a family member.

And now we're out *fifty million dollars* and we'll soon be the laughing stock of the tech world!"

Cole's chest tightened; his head felt about to explode. This was *entirely* his fault. There was no one else to blame, unless Jacob Featherstone and his con-artist friends could be blamed for their brilliance. No, he was responsible for this debacle. Featherstone had played him like a violin—a priceless Stradivarius—and not even one of those would bring back fifty million. Had Lindsay's allure also been part of the master plan? The plan to get him away so that Jacob would have sufficient time to transfer the funds and make good on his escape, while the board of directors waited patiently for the fateful package to arrive? And all under the guise of finding his dead parents clairvoyantly. What a scam! He suddenly felt nauseated, fighting with all of his strength not to retch on the spot.

"Bill, I don't know what to say. I don't…" But the words wouldn't come. After a long moment of indecision in which Cole had never before felt so exposed, he met the CEO's eyes. "Is there anything I can do to make this right? I'll personally repay the debt, if it's the last thing I do, I swear it."

Gaines said nothing. Instead he stared at the young man, as though anticipating what this confession—what this moment of opportunity—truly meant. How he could use this to his own personal advantage?

"Cole, I suggest you return immediately to Newport. The board will want a full accounting of all that transpired since Featherstone first contacted you. As a major stockholder, you will still be able to be a part of the company, at least in ownership, but the board will recommend that you be terminated as acting president of Hollingsworth Enterprises. From there, we'll just have to wait and see what the fallout will be and how we can cut our losses. The humiliation of this scam alone will send a terrible message to our shareholders. The loss of their confidence in us could send our stock value plummeting."

Gaines hesitated. "By the way, Featherstone's daughter will need to make a report, as well. I suggest she comes voluntarily, if you don't want her deposed." Gaines nodded toward Lindsay, failing even to have the courtesy to call her by her name.

There was not a hint of compassion in the CEO's voice, no recognition that Cole hadn't done any of this intentionally. No mercy. His words were as surgical of a strike as if Navy Seals had just boarded the *Truett* to capture a global terrorist. Cole had been demeaned to nothing more than a lame duck, someone with wealth, yes, but without power. No say over what his own family-controlled business would do. He was suddenly adrift in a corporate sea of sharks, not unlike the actual ocean he found himself on now.

"I'll make the necessary arrangements. Is there anything else, Mr. Gaines?" Cole said, his voice ice-cold.

"No, I think that will do—for now. May we offer you a lift back to San Salvador?" Gaines's tone seemed to suggest he was extending an olive branch to a beaten man.

"That's alright, Mr. Gaines, I'll find my own transportation. I need to clean up some loose ends before I leave here. I'll see you back in the office in a few days."

"Make sure not to delay. The board will not look favorably on you extending your little vacation," Gaines replied sternly, a final parting shot before he and the attorney climbed back up the steps and entered the aircraft. A few minutes later, they were disappearing into the darkening sky, as the final remnants of sunlight dipped behind the islands to the west.

No one moved. No one uttered a word. It was like a moment frozen in time. Cole stood alone on the deck, again a broken man. Not only had he recently lost his parents to death, he had just lost his company in a foolish decision of his own. He turned and walked past Lindsay, failing to touch her outstretched hands, his gaze as hard as steel.

33

After gathering his things, Cole remained in his cabin. He planned to leave in the morning as early as possible. There was no need to prolong the inevitable. He would say his good-byes then. He would question Lindsay, arrange for a separate time for her to appear at the company headquarters, but he couldn't face any of them now. He needed time to decompress, to compose himself, and to let it all sink in. He was afraid of what he might do if he acted now. Were Cassie and Ryan in on all of it, too? Had Lindsay convinced them to aid her in this deception? In return for what?

As he reflected on the events of the past few days, it seemed more dreamlike than real. Maybe he had been drugged? It seemed entirely possible. All kinds of drugs were available in this part of the world. Perhaps Cassie had laced his food with something powerful and then Lindsay had taken him underwater into the trenches below and played with his mind. Had tricked him into believing they had discovered an underworld portal where spirits returned after death. What a fool he had been! But then, she had learned from a master deceiver—her very own father. Their last trip had ended in failure; the portal had suddenly disappeared. How convenient. Nothing but lies. Corporate espionage took on many faces. The more creative, the more lucrative the results.

He would return to face the music at company headquarters, and pay his dues—or whatever the board demanded of him—then take his wealth and build something else. Maybe Jacob's letter had been prophetic. This *would* make him a better businessman. At least he better understood the rules of engagement now.

Cole closed his eyes and sat back on his bed. He knew he wouldn't find sleep any time soon. He and Lindsay had slept most of the day away. The demons inside his head would allow him little rest in the coming days. Thankfully, in the early hours of morning he drifted off, the stress getting the better of him and relieving him temporarily from his misery…from his humiliation. It wasn't bad enough that people like Ryan and that Swedish scientist, Andres, already despised him for his over-the-top wealth and playboy lifestyle; now they could point to his incompetence, as well. What a mockery he had made of himself.

The dreams came hard and fast, torturing his restless sleep. Spirit voices spoke, admonishing him for his stupidity. He woke in a cold sweat, bolting upright in the darkness, his sheets wet with his own perspiration. To his utter disbelief, Lindsay was across from him on the opposite bed, sitting cross-legged and staring back at him. Her eyes radiated a soft glow, like distant beacons of light on the cold, dark horizon.

"What the hell are you doing in here?" Cole exclaimed. "Haven't you had enough of this charade? You want to witness my final nightmares before I leave, too? You want to know your victory is complete? How dare you sit there in judgment of me!"

Lindsay said nothing, continuing her penetrating gaze into his eyes, as though looking into his very soul. Her silence was unbearable.

"Say something, damn it!" Cole was standing now, naked except for a pair of boxer shorts. Lindsay rose and approached him in silence. For a moment she stood only inches away. He could feel her breath on his neck. He smelled the distinct aroma of salt water on her body. She was glowing. He had seen her in this condition before, when she had returned from the ocean, renewed. Lindsay wrapped her arms around Cole's upper body, and warmth flooded through him. He started to push her away, but he was unable to escape her grasp.

"Relax, Cole. I know how upset you are," she whispered. "Do not allow your anger to consume you. It will destroy you in the end. Let me be your guide. Allow me to take you one more time, and all will be revealed. Trust me, and you will see a world unlike any other. It *will* set you free. Our work here is not yet done."

Just as Cole was about to object, Lindsay faded away, like snow melting on a hot spring day. Her image evaporated just as the darkness was replaced by sunlight streaming in through the nearby porthole. Day had come without Cole even noticing it. He stood half-naked in the sunlight, wondering what had just happened. Another one of his vivid dreams? What was she trying to tell him this time?

Cole lingered, gazing silently at his packed duffel bag nearby. For a moment he considered Lindsay's final words. *"Trust me, and you will experience a world unlike any other."* How could he possibly trust her now? Everything had been a lie, a deception designed to distract him long enough to allow her father to escape. And it had apparently worked to perfection. The unexpected arrival of Bill Gaines had confirmed that. The pair of prank glasses stared back at him from the table next to his bunk, mocking him. He couldn't even remember bringing them back to the room with him. Yet there they sat, a harsh reminder of his naïveté. He pounded his fist down hard, smashing the plastic glasses into pieces. Dressing quickly, he picked up his bag and strode determinedly out of his cabin and up the stairs to the upper deck. He'd had enough. It was time to leave and face his persecution. The sooner he got through that, the sooner he could move on with his life.

When he reached topside, he did a double take. A new helicopter was waiting on the helipad with the Institute's logo emblazoned on its side. Two pilots were standing outside awaiting instructions. Cassie and Ryan stood below the platform as if at attention. Obviously, someone had called them here, anticipating Cole's decision to leave. *Lindsay…where is Lindsay?* Cole wondered as he scanned the deck. She was conspicuously missing. It was probably best this way, though. Another confrontation would only get ugly. He sighed and approached the stairs to the helipad. Cassie stopped him at the base of the steps.

"Cole, don't leave this way. It's not what you think. Lindsay is not like her father."

"Do you really expect me to believe that? Seriously? I know you guys are close friends, but enough is enough. The charade is over. They won. But believe me, Cassie, or whatever your real name is, it will never happen to me again." He pushed past her, only to be confronted by Ryan, who was blocking the stairway.

"Listen, Cole, Cassie is telling you the truth. Lindsay would never have done this to you. You owe it to her to at least say good- bye, to let her explain…"

Cole dropped his bag and grabbed Ryan's shirt collar with both hands, shoving him up against the railing.

"I've had just about enough of your bullshit, surfer boy! Now, get the fuck out of my way." Cole threw him aside, and Ryan stumbled to the deck, but was immediately back up on his feet.

"Don't even think about it, asshole, if you know what's good for you," Cole exclaimed. There was something in his voice, in his demeanor, not previously apparent. Ryan knew he wasn't joking and so he backed down.

Cole grabbed the railing, hoisting himself up the metal steps toward the aircraft. Cassie's voice calling to him stopped him halfway up.

"Cole, Lindsay's waiting for you in the *Harbinger*. She contacted the Institute and requested the helicopter for you. But she hoped you might reconsider. She's sick over this. She couldn't face you, but she wanted to at least give you a choice. Trust her, Cole. Trust her one more time…please?" The sincerity in Cassie's voice was undeniable.

Hadn't he just heard those same words spoken by Lindsay in a dream?

"You owe it to her," Ryan said, his voice uncharacteristically emotional. "Especially after what she did for you…" His voice suddenly trailed off as if he had just said too much, revealing something he shouldn't have. There was passion in his voice, as though he was hiding a bitter truth. His sense of regret was unmistakable.

"If you leave now, Cole, you'll never know the truth. Run back to your precious company and live out your life in ignorance. But when you're old and lonely and the only thing you have to keep you company is your money and a whore, the truth will haunt you to your grave," Cassie said, unabashedly. There existed no deception in her voice. Her honesty unnerved Cole. These people whom he barely knew were fighting with everything they had to keep him here. But why? What did they know that he didn't?

"At least go down and see her one more time, and then… then you can leave if you still want to. She won't try to stop you." Cassie's voice had an edge of finality to it.

Cole stood, his back facing the divers, staring up at the helicopter like it was his last, best chance at freedom. If he turned back, he might never escape their clutches, destined to be used again and again for his wealth. But if he entered the aircraft right now, he faced another nemesis, the soon-to-become-embroiling legal battles and inside maneuverings. He wasn't sure which choice was worse. As he continued to stand alone, waging an internal war over what decision to make, his parents' images flooded into his head. What would they want him to do? His father would most likely demand that he return and fight for the company. But his mother would urge him to stay—reminding him that love was the higher power. *You may only get one shot at it, so don't be a fool and miss it,* his mother had often told him.

Cole gestured to one of the pilots to place his bag beside the helicopter. He whispered something to one of the men, who nodded. It seemed he had made his decision. Cassie's shoulders slumped. Ryan turned away in disgust. But when Cole turned back and descended the stairs, the two divers stood speechless as he made his way past them and disappeared belowdecks. They watched in silence as he vanished, their expressions hopeful. The chopper's engines fired up and the large rotor began to rotate. Ryan considered telling the pilots to stay put, and he was about to shout out the order, when he felt Cassie's hand on his shoulder.

"There's no need, Ryan. Cole won't be coming back here. Let them go." How she knew this was beyond Ryan's comprehension.

Women's intuition? Perhaps. A moment later, the pilots lifted off, heading back to the research center empty-handed.

Cole found Lindsay sitting cross-legged on top of the submersible, her head lowered in what looked to be a state of meditation. He watched for a moment, studying her. She was outfitted in another prototype wetsuit; her long, thick hair falling freely to her shoulders. Sitting next to her was the glimmering prototype diving helmet, reflecting the overhead lights. Its ebony color glistened like obsidian, the glasslike mineral that was created in lava flows, reminding Cole of a volcano. She looked like a warrior ready for battle, taking in her last few peaceful breaths before embarking to the combat zone.

Before Cole could say a word, she looked up at him, her expression so convoluted, Cole was taken aback. What was she thinking that could render her so impossible to read? Her eyes were filled with compassion, yet her face was steel-like, as if it had been chiseled from solid rock. Cole felt the power of her gaze shoot right through him, like a sudden jolt of electricity. She rose up, her movements as fluid as quicksilver. For a brief moment, she appeared to become liquid herself, before quickly morphing back into solid form. Cole blinked, rubbing his eyes as though they had gone temporarily out of focus. For a long moment they gazed at each other, speechless.

"Just one question, Cole. Will you trust me?"

Cole hesitated. He hadn't been prepared for this question to be the first thing out of her mouth. It caught him off guard. *Trust?* In a single word, Lindsay had cut to the heart of the matter. Her father had used the same word in his brief, defamatory letter, promising that his actions would make Cole a better businessman. Now his daughter, who obviously had known about the scam, was using the same word. *Trust her for what?* he wondered. *To take me to the bottom of the ocean and play games with my head again?* Chances are, they would never find the portal again, even if it really did exist, which he was beginning to doubt more and more. What did she want to show him? Certainly, they would not find his parents. Maybe all she wanted was for him to see the wreckage of their yacht, so that he would finally believe and could move on with his life. She knew what his parents' disappearance had been doing to him and what still remained unresolved in his heart. This discovery would be the final piece of the puzzle. This, at least, made sense.

"I will trust you, Lindsay. This one last time."

Lindsay nodded and pointed to the far end of the chamber, where Cole's diving gear hung on the wall.

"I'll be in the divers' cabin. See you in a few minutes." Lindsay walked purposely to the top hatch and descended into the belly of the submersible, while Cole stood for a moment wondering whether he had made the right decision. He could have been headed back on the helicopter to the Bay Marina Resort and the outdoor bar for some liquid refreshment and his pick of scantily clad women—but now he was about to be stuffed into the cramped quarters of the *Harbinger*, heading over five miles down to the ocean floor. The decision really shouldn't have been that difficult. But he had promised he would trust her, even though something about this dive seemed far more ominous, although he couldn't say why. Maybe it was the look in Lindsay's eyes, or the dream he'd just had. Or maybe it was something else, a feeling or a premonition that was eating away at him. Something inside him had to know what this was all about. If he turned and walked away, he'd never know. Cassie's final words resonated in his head and had been the deciding factor. *If you never know, the truth will haunt you to your grave…* Her words seemed almost prophetic.

34

Fifteen minutes later, Cole was sitting inside the *Harbinger*, attired in the prototype diving gear. He looked more like an astronaut than a diver, tubes running the length of his body, the underwater flares filling the oval-shaped pockets running down his legs. The newest neoprene wetsuit was tight, foamed with nitrogen gas and added spandex for less compression at greater depths. These were replacement suits. The ones they had worn on their last dive had been destroyed. This neoprene was unusually thick, measuring fifteen millimeters, almost twice the thickness of other deep-sea diving suits. The suit was restrictive and nonflexible, but it provided excellent buoyancy and insulation properties—all things Cole considered necessary for the type of exploration Lindsay engaged in.

Lindsay spoke into the intercom, letting Cassie and Ryan know they were prepared to descend. It was time to get on with it.

"Are you ready, Cole?" Lindsay said matter-of-factly.

"Ready as I'll ever be, I suppose."

"Open the lower hatches," Lindsay instructed. Water immediately flooded the chamber, air bubbles rising all around them. This first sensation still sent a shiver up Cole's spine, as he visualized being dropped into the water below. The heavy metal cables jerked. A moment later they were released from the safety of the frigate's umbilical cord, drifting unaided into the shimmering depths of the

Atlantic. Cole was more familiar with the various forms of under-sea life now, yet they continued to intrigue him—everything about the various species so unlike humans. Yet Lindsay was claiming that life itself had begun in the depths of the ocean. The land and the sea seemed more like two disparate worlds, foreign and somehow at odds, and yet one could not exist without the other. It was as if some greater power had fused the two together like magnets, each one clinging to the other in an incontrovertible balance of nature.

The brilliant, aquamarine water soon gave way to the murky darkness below, where sunlight disappeared. The shapes of the sea life changed just as dramatically. With each layer they descended, life changed with it, adapting to the more extreme pressures. During his first dives, Cole had thought these deep-sea creatures were gro-tesque, but as he became more familiar with the dives, he saw a beauty in them, too. Their environments had shaped them, evolving them for protection, so that they, too, could live and reproduce. Who was he to pass judgment?

The first half of the dive passed in relative silence, as both he and Lindsay acclimated themselves. The tension between them was still evident—the pain of Jacob Featherstone's betrayal as raw as a festering wound. The silence was becoming unbearable to Cole, yet Lindsay remained composed, bathed in a cocoon of tranquility.

"So, aren't you going to say anything, or are you going to keep me guessing?" Cole said out of sheer frustration.

"What do you want me to say, Cole? You're angry with me. You blame me for what my father did to you and your company. I'd prob-ably feel the same way if I were in your shoes. However, I'm not. I can only try to understand what you're thinking and respect your feelings." Lindsay's response only served to infuriate Cole further.

"Stop being so goddamn polite and just be honest with me, okay?" Cole replied, angrily.

"I am being honest with you. I always have been. I—I just couldn't tell you everything in the beginning. You wouldn't have believed me, and then you wouldn't be here now."

"Okay, okay, I get it. That's past history. Now, please tell me what to expect— what we're going to find so we can avoid any huge surprises. Is that too much to ask?"

"No, it's not too much to ask, but I may not be able to give you the type of answer you're looking for. So much depends on you..." Lindsay's voice trailed off.

"Depends on me? How can you say that when I don't even know what I'm supposed to do?" Cole replied indignantly.

"Oh, but you will...you will. If you allow yourself to be open to the possibilities." Just as Cole was about to come back with a retort of his own, Cassie's voice sounded mechanically through the intercom.

"How are you guys doing done there? Everything okay?"

"Yes, all systems are operating normally, including Cole's anxiety about not being in control," Lindsay replied, a hint of sarcasm registering in her voice.

"Good luck," Cassie replied.

"No, don't tell me we're going to go through this again," Cole said.

"Don't worry, Cole. We won't put you through *that* again," Lindsay said jokingly. Somehow Cole didn't believe her. He quickly changed the subject.

"I assume we're attempting to find the portal again and you have some idea where it's located?"

"Your assumption is correct," Lindsay replied, as though conversing with a fellow scientist.

"I'm still not sure I believe you, you know, about the spirit world that exists beyond its barriers, or whatever you call it, but I want to know more about it," Cole said insistently. He wasn't about to let Lindsay off the hook so easily.

"Well, what exactly do you want to know?" Lindsay replied, as if she were the expert on all things spiritual.

Cole was struck by her nonchalant response, like she'd been expecting this question all along. He struggled with exactly what question to ask next, anxious as to what her reply might be.

"When we first entered the void, there didn't seem to be any pressure, like the bottom of the ocean would usually have. I couldn't believe we could just go outside of the *Harbinger* like that."

"That's because it's not the ocean. There's no water beyond the great barrier. It's separated from the physical world by a dimensional rift of sorts. Time operates differently inside. Actually, there seems to be no passage of time on the other side. It's a dimension in stasis."

Cole was stunned by the certainty of Lindsay's response. How could she possibly know all of this? This sort of insight could only be accessed by someone who had spent a certain amount of time there, who had crossed over. But that was impossible. Lindsay couldn't be— Cole pushed the thought from his head. She was here, wasn't she? In the flesh?

"How large is it? I mean, exactly where does it exist, what space does it occupy?" Cole asked, struggling with how to express his concerns. He wasn't sure he could even ask the right questions to unveil this mystery.

"The barrier beyond encircles the entire planet. It acts like a layer beneath a layer, a sphere within a sphere. It coexists with other layers beyond the earth's crust, yet it is on a different physical plane. Think of it as a multi-universe, rather than the singular universe you are more familiar with. It forms the foundation of all things." Lindsay paused, realizing Cole was becoming even more confused by her explanation.

"Then why hasn't it been discovered before, by offshore drilling or something? If it's that large, there must be more entrance points, or portals," Cole said.

This was the question Lindsay had hoped Cole would not ask. There *were* other access points, but she could not tell him without revealing a much darker secret. She considered the question for a moment.

"There is another method of entering, but I—I don't think we can find it, so we'll just have to rely on the gateway at the bottom of this trench. I'm confident we'll find it again. It emits a strange electrical charge that doesn't register normally on our sensors. I've come to recognize it as a slight blip on the screen, so to speak."

"You're talking in riddles again, Lindsay. I don't understand what you're trying to tell me. What really exists on the other side? It looked like white rain, or long, elastic spiderwebs to me before, drifting up and down in a type of void. Yet it was buoyant enough for us to float in it. And I swear I heard voices in my head."

"Hold your thought—we're about to enter the trench. I need to concentrate. Here, how about a little music?"

David Bowie's voice sounded through the onboard speakers. *Why him?* Cole wondered. And why this particular song? *Anything else would have been better.* The opening lines to "Space Oddity" sent a chill up Cole's spine.

> *Ground control to major Tom*
> *Ground control to major Tom*
> *Take your protein pills and put your helmet on*
> *Ground control to major Tom*
> *Commencing countdown, engines on*
> *Check ignition and may god's love be with you*
> *This is ground control to major Tom, you've really made the grade*
> *And the papers want to know whose shirts you wear*
> *Now it's time to leave the capsule if you dare.*
> *This is major Tom to ground control, I'm stepping through the door*
> *And I'm floating in a most peculiar way*

And the stars look very different today
Here am I sitting in a tin can far above the world
Planet Earth is blue and there's nothing I can do
Though I'm past one hundred thousand miles, I'm feeling very still
And I think my spaceship knows which way to go
Tell my wife I love her very much, she knows.
Ground control to major Tom, your circuit's dead, there's something
wrong
Can you hear me, major Tom?
Can you hear me, major Tom?
Can you hear me, major Tom?
Can you…
Here am I sitting in my tin can far above the Moon
Planet Earth is blue and there's nothing I can do

The final line of the song echoed in Cole's head like a prophecy whispered in a trance. The jagged, dark walls of the Puerto Rican Trench loomed in the distance, their nebulous shapes bringing Cole back to present reality. Breathless, Cole stared out of their own version of Major Tom's tin can. They had entered the danger zone—the eye of the storm—where Cole's reckoning awaited, only he had no idea of the consequences that would soon confront him.

Like a minuscule light in a distant galaxy, the *Harbinger* descended into a pit of blackness so dark there appeared no hope of salvation, only oblivion. The extreme pressure bore down on them like the weight of the planet. The silence was deafening.

The outside surface of the submersible pinged with a sound like it was about to crack. Cole suddenly wondered if it needed maintenance. How many dives could the submersible take before it required inspection? That thought only added to Cole's angst. Had they come this far, only to face mechanical failure—the *Harbinger* on the threshold of breaking apart as the ocean's hyperbaric pressure crushed everything into finite bits of matter, spreading their remains across the ocean floor like grains of sand? Their lives seemed so inconsequential down here—like subatomic particles racing through a supercollider toward their own annihilation.

"Cole, take your position on the rubber mat. We've arrived." Lindsay's voice sounded like a whisper in a dream, far-off and numinous. Without Cole realizing it, Lindsay had guided them right to the gateway, the portal to another dimension. He gazed out the side porthole in the submersible's dim light at the immense diaphragm, pulsating with iridescent light against the wall of cliffs. Cole's breath caught in his throat. With all Lindsay had told him— with all he had seen so far—he was still completely unprepared for this, lost in his own delusions. Lindsay threw the switch, and the *Harbinger* came to life with 275,000 volts of electricity coursing through its hull, lighting it up with crackling, purple fire. With an angry groan, the props reversed course, jettisoning the craft forward like a cannon shot.

35

"I think you two should come top deck ASAP. You're not going to believe it, but another chopper is approaching," a crewmember on the bridge barked through the intercom. Ryan shot Cassie a disparaging look, as if to say, *"What now?"* Was Gaines back with more demands, or was it the Institute checking on the condition of the *Harbinger?* Whenever anything of mechanical significance went wrong with the craft, Gerace engineers were automatically sent an electronic message through the onboard auto-diagnostic system.

Cassie quickly scanned her computer screen for anything that might look abnormal. All systems had gone blank. The blip on the radar that was the *Harbinger* had disappeared, like it had suddenly vanished into thin air. Cassie gasped. The descent had taken far less time than normal for the Harbinger to go off grid.

"Something's wrong, Ryan. I can't find Lindsay. Please go up top and see who's coming and I'll join you later."

Ryan hurried up the stairs to confront their next visitor, wondering what the hell was going on now. He arrived just as the helicopter landed on the platform. It appeared small by comparison to the previous aircraft, and it also looked beaten up, as if it had not been properly maintained. Its faded yellow and black paint reminded Ryan of a yellow jacket, stripes running along the insect's body. At the controls, a black man with long dreadlocks sat somberly, accompanied by another man whose skin was plastered with tattoos. One of his eyes was covered with a black patch, and a long, silver earring dangled from his left earlobe. Neither man was smiling or looked the least bit congenial. The one-eyed man grasped a military-grade A-16 automatic rifle. There looked to be a short missile launcher attached to the bottom of the chopper, but it appeared empty. They glared at Ryan as though they would rather shoot him than talk to him.

Following an uneasy couple of moments in which no one spoke, a man finally emerged from the backseat, neatly attired and looking the complete opposite of his comrades. He was obviously an American: white-skinned, wearing khaki pants and a Tommy Bahama shirt. He carried an expensive-looking briefcase and a duffel bag. He turned to thank the pilots. They nodded and wasted no time in lifting off, as though they were escaping a crime scene. The man stood for a moment on the platform, surveying his surroundings. Sunglasses hid his eyes, as he steadied himself against the railing, his skin pale. Ryan had seen the look many times before. Seasickness. Cassie arrived on deck as the man gingerly climbed down the metal stairs and approached the couple.

"Hello, I'm Art Barkley, Cole Hollingsworth's personal attorney. Am I in the right place?" Art extended his hand toward Ryan. Ryan hesitated, refusing to shake hands.

"Not another attorney!" Ryan snarled. "That's all we need." He raised his hands in frustration. Cassie approached.

"Mr. Barkley, I'm Cassie Thomas, and this is my partner, Ryan Walker. You are in the right place, but Cole is not currently onboard—" Before she could complete her sentence, Art interrupted.

"Shit! I can't believe I missed him. You have no idea how much trouble I've gone through to get here. My pilots, if you could call them that, held me for ransom once we were airborne and threatened to throw me out of the helicopter if I didn't come up with another ten grand, which, by the way, I didn't have on me. I gave the bastards two thousand and my Rolex watch, in addition to the fifteen thousand I paid them originally. Quite a racket you've got going down here." Art paused, his face glowing crimson. "It's vitally important that I speak with Cole as soon as possible. Can you tell me how I can get in contact with him?"

"You sound just like the other suits who were here yesterday," Ryan said in disgust.

"Someone was here yesterday looking for Cole, too?" Art replied.

"Yeah, you might say that. The CEO of Hollingsworth and his attorney showed up and…" Ryan's voice trailed off, as he quickly decided not to reveal the nature of Cole's humiliation.

"Bill Gaines was here…and Jack Saunders?" Art paused. "Then I'm too late. Damn it!" Art dropped his gear, putting his hands on his hips and cursing again. The two divers gazed at Art, not knowing exactly what to think of him. Was he friend or foe? He was an attorney; that was at least one strike against him. But why had he traveled all this way and spent so much money to find Cole? It appeared he had even hired some sea pirates or drug smugglers to fly him here. It must have been important.

"So, where is Cole? How do I get in touch with him?" Art asked again.

"He's at the bottom of the ocean in a bathyscaphe, with Lindsay Featherstone. I don't think your corporate cell phone is gonna work here. You could always call the Institute and have them bring over their other submersible and you can chase after him," Ryan said sarcastically.

"Yeah, right! And I'm fucking Santa Claus. I'm here to deliver your Christmas presents early. I told you this was important, now please tell me where my client is," Art replied. "I don't want to have to ask again."

Ryan took a step forward, fed up with Art's attitude. Cassie approached.

"Hold on everybody," she said. "Let's all just calm down. Mr. Barkley, what is so important that you need to tell Cole?" Cassie met Art's gaze. "And, by the way, Ryan is telling you the truth. Cole is at the bottom of the ocean with Lindsay. We've been monitoring their progress."

Art's mouth dropped open as if to object, then closed it just as abruptly. The look in Cassie's eyes convinced him she was being honest.

"What the hell would Cole be doing at the bottom of the ocean?" Art exclaimed incredulously.

"You'll just have to ask him that when he returns. Until then let's all try to get along. Are you hungry?" Cassie said, attempting to be the peacekeeper.

"Well, now that you mention it, I could use something to eat. But please don't go to any trouble. Whatever's handy?" Art's voice had taken on a more conciliatory tone.

"Come inside the galley and we'll fix you up with something. In the meantime, Ryan, will you please stow Mr. Barkley's things in one of the cabins below?" Cassie eyed her partner with a, *please just comply* expression. Reluctantly, Ryan grabbed Art's gear and trudged belowdecks, although his inclination was to throw the stuff overboard.

Art insisted on preparing his own meal. He made a sandwich, piled some fresh fruit onto a plate, and grabbed a beer out of the cooler. He took a seat at a nearby table and began to eat. Cassie sat down opposite him, but refrained from speaking at first. She cradled a cup of herbal tea between her hands, considering the man and exactly what to share with him. If Art was Cole's personal attorney, he was probably a friend, too. But could she trust him? Art finished his food, took a long draught of beer, wiped his mouth with a napkin, and focused his attention back on Cassie.

"I don't understand any of this. I thought Cole was just down here for some R-and-R with Lindsay before returning to assume his new duties as president of Hollingsworth Enterprises. And then all hell breaks loose after Bill Gaines discovered that the deal they made with Lindsay's father was nothing but an elaborate and very expensive con." Art took another swig of beer. Ryan returned and stood in the background listening.

"Jacob Featherstone and his phony investment pals stuck Cole for fifty million bucks and now they are nowhere to be found. The special Internet-connected smart glasses they'd invested in didn't exist. And when Gaines opened the package that supposedly contained the latest prototype and found a pair of plastic prank glasses, he just about had a coronary. He went ballistic. That's why I'm here. I was trying to warn Cole so he could be prepared when Gaines contacted him, you know, to see if he could salvage anything and save his career. The fact that he's out here vacationing with Featherstone's daughter looks horrible." Art shook his head in disgust. "But apparently Gaines beat me here."

"Unfortunately, he did. We witnessed the whole thing. It was pretty humiliating for Cole. He was just as stunned at the deception as the rest of you. Just so you know, Lindsay was not part of the scheme, at least as far as she knew, although she may have been a pawn in the overall scheme. She didn't know her father was going to secure that kind of money from Cole's company and then disappear. It nearly killed her when she found out the truth—which was at the same time Cole did."

"Well, at least that's something. Cole's in a lot of trouble. Not that he's going to the poorhouse or anything, but his presidency will most likely be terminated, unless he can figure something out fast. That's what I hoped to help him with, but…" Art looked away as if terribly ashamed he had let his friend down.

"You and Cole are good friends?" Cassie said.

"Yeah, I would say we're good friends, considering the nature of our relationship. I'm his attorney, so there is a professional side to it that I can't betray, but I've always admired Cole, even when he was doing things that weren't necessarily worthy of admiration. But haven't we all done those kinds of things at one time or another?"

Cassie smiled ruefully. "Amen to that!" she replied, her gaze turning toward Ryan.

"Hey, keep me out of this!" Ryan said, as though Cassie was accusing him of some kind of wrongdoing. Satisfied that Art wasn't here to make Cole's life even more miserable, he finally joined the pair at the table. He stuck out his hand toward Art.

"Why don't we try starting over?"

Art reached out, and the tension between the two men dissipated into thin air. It appeared they were on the same side after all.

"By the looks of those pilots, I'm guessing you had a very interesting trip trying to reach us," Ryan said.

"That's an understatement, to say the least. I think those guys were drug smugglers, but they were the only ones who would fly me out here. I had contacted Gerace to track down Cole, and they gave me the name of a helicopter service they thought I might use to get me here. I contacted them and arranged to meet them at the Bay Marina Resort, where Cole and Lindsay had been staying. They showed up, and I paid them with American dollars in cash— which they had requested. I went to my room to grab my things, and when I returned, the helicopter was gone—along with my money. When I called their phone number, I got a recording that it was temporarily out of service. I had to wire for more money after I got a tip from a guy hanging out in the bar for the guys who flew me here. They wanted a small fortune, but I really didn't have an option. That's what delayed me, otherwise I might have arrived here first."

"We'll make a note to advise the front office of Gerace to exclude that service from their referrals from now on. Sounds like Cole wasn't the only one who got scammed in all of this. Excuse me for saying this, but Americans are basically a target for this kind of thing. Easy money, they say. It happens a lot down here," Ryan offered apologetically.

Art didn't particularly like being called a "clueless American," but he had little comeback at this point. He was just glad the pilot and his dubious comrade weren't holding him hostage for an additional payday. The thought made him shudder. Art turned to Cassie, his expression growing serious.

"So, back to my original question, why is Cole at the bottom of the ocean? Isn't that dangerous, even for experienced deep-sea divers? Surely Lindsay isn't commanding the submersible."

"Actually, she is. She is a very experienced diver, and one of the brightest oceanographers at the Institute. She was in the area when Cole's parents disappeared at sea. She took the *Harbinger I*, the Institute's most advanced submersible, and searched for weeks, before"—Cassie paused—"before the search was called off."

Something in her voice disturbed Art. Was it a hint of sadness? A secret? A hidden truth? Art couldn't quite put his finger on it, but it was undeniable. He was, after all, very adept at reading people when they were being less than completely honest.

"What is it you're not telling me, Cassie?" Art pressed. Cassie remained silent. She wouldn't confide everything. It would all just have to play out; however, the look in her eyes failed to hide an inimitable sorrow. The pain obviously ran deep. Art backed off.

"How long until they return?" Art said, letting Cassie off the hook—at least for now.

"I'm not sure. The *Harbinger* can remain underwater for long periods of time. We'll just have to wait and see," Cassie replied, then rose and walked outside, becoming emotional and unable to continue their conversation.

"She's just worried about them. She and Lindsay are very close and this part of the ocean can be treacherous. You do know where we are, don't you?" Ryan said, almost mockingly.

"We're in the Caribbean, if I'm not mistaken."

"Yes, that's correct, but we're also in the area historically known as the Bermuda Triangle. Not that I believe in all that nonsense, but strange things do tend to happen down here." With that final piece of information, Ryan rose, too, and walked away, leaving Art to sit alone and ponder what the hell had just taken place.

36

Lindsay and Cole drifted in the void, like they were in a black hole in space. *The space between life and death,* Cole thought. None of the craft's instruments were operating normally; most had gone dark. The submersible seemed to be guided by an invisible force. The darkness was unnerving; not even the powerful searchlights of the *Harbinger* could penetrate the blackness surrounding them. Cole was vaguely aware of this space, having passed through it before, but at the time he had been pretty much out of it. The familiarity caused only anxiety for him as he waited nervously for their exit. It seemed to take much longer this time, but that was most likely caused by Cole's heightened sense of apprehension. There was something different about this dive, though; perhaps it was the inevitability that something extraordinary was about to happen. Lindsay had alluded to it, even though she hadn't explained exactly what they would encounter. Something in her demeanor suggested finality, and the feeling terrified Cole. It continued to eat away at him as they drifted silently along.

Without warning, the *Harbinger* suddenly blasted forward with incredible speed, bursting through the final barrier. Cole hadn't recalled their previous entry into the alternate dimension being so violent. Cole watched breathlessly through the side porthole as they entered another world. The *Harbinger* slowed and came to rest in the middle of something so foreign, it defied description. Long, sinewy white wisps moved up and down like strands of glistening silk, like shimmering streams of rain against a deep ebony backdrop. The rhythmic motion of the streams was hypnotic, somehow easing Cole's angst, yet the uncertainty of their arrival would not completely release him from his fear.

Why is Lindsay being so quiet, so calm? Cole wondered. She seemed unfazed by their entrance into this world beyond the world, like she felt almost comfortable down here. Still, she remained silent, while Cole studied his surroundings with a new sense of overwhelming foreboding. What was it that Lindsay wanted to show him? What discoveries awaited? These questions and more filled his head, when he suddenly heard the voice again.

Cole? Cole, is that you? He heard the voice much more clearly this time—the voice of his mother calling to him. It didn't seem possible. His mother and father were dead.

Cole, you've come at last. You've come to save us.

Cole abruptly stood, emotion ripping through his heart like wildfire.

"Damn it, Lindsay, what's happening to me?" He took a step forward to grab Lindsay by the shoulder and shake the truth out of her, if nothing else. The voice inside his head was driving him insane. Lindsay had disappeared like a ghost. He was again alone in the *Harbinger*. Hadn't this happened before? It was all so convoluted in his mind that it had become difficult to tell fact from fiction. Cole couldn't recall accurately what had transpired on their first voyage here. He felt as if his memory had been wiped. He had found Lindsay outside later, beckoning him to join her in the liquefied air, so buoyant they had been able to float right through it. Then everything had gone topsy-turvy, and yet, they had somehow managed to escape with their lives.

"Don't be afraid," a second voice whispered inside his head. *"Come join me."*

It was Lindsay's voice this time. Then he spotted her, drifting outside the submersible, like an out-of-focus image in a camera lens—her outstretched hands welcoming him. Cole locked his diving helmet onto the metal latches of his wetsuit and strapped on the two portable oxygen tanks to his back. He entered the floatation section, unlocking the hatch and taking a deep breath. The time had come for him to face whatever Lindsay wanted him to face. There was no turning back now. Another point of no return? Cole braced himself and forced his way outside the safety of the *Harbinger*.

He was immediately filled with a sense of euphoria unlike anything he had experienced before. This sensation was also vaguely familiar—a peacefulness so sublime it went beyond description. The image of his last encounter with it came flooding back. With the power of thought alone, he propelled himself toward Lindsay. They were only feet apart now. Lindsay's hand touched Cole's. Their gentle embrace sent a spike of elation through every nerve of his body. For a moment, he felt more connected to another human being than he had believed possible. Lindsay's eyes radiated a light so pure it was almost blinding. Yet Cole could not look away. The intense feeling of love overwhelmed him again. At this time and place nothing else mattered. Lindsay completed him. He wasn't sure if this was a dream or if it was real. It didn't matter. His only desire was to remain in this state forever. His former life seemed to fade away, like the remnants of summer giving way to autumn. A changing of the seasons, of life redefined, as all the leaves turned scarlet, signaling the inexorable march toward winter. *Winter?* And then it hit him. Autumn was that incorporeal state between life and death, nature's beginning cycle of renewal. Was it death he was experiencing—the mystifying, bittersweet passing to another place. He finally began to understand. Confused and at the same time repulsed, he stared at Lindsay with a heightened sense of alarm, and then he noticed a transformation taking place behind her.

Something was forming, a nebulous image coming together as though attracted by a circle of invisible magnets. Lindsay smiled and moved away, while Cole watched thunderstruck. He suddenly felt a wave of dysphasia overwhelm him, paralyzing his very movement, his thoughts—as though his brain had suddenly been rendered useless. Through the special polymer of the oxygen helmet's facing, he glimpsed the formation of his parents from the strands of iridescent mesh. They weren't actual flesh and bone—more ethereal than solid form—but they were undeniably his parents. Larger than life, they loomed before him, gesticulating like distorted reflections underwater. Their images lit up the dark void like a cluster of stars pulsating with a brilliant life force. His mother smiled like only a mother could, as if gazing at her son for the first time after bringing him into the world. His father hovered, a stern expression on his face, like only an overbearing father could portray. They wanted something from Cole—but what? Why had they appeared out of nowhere? Before Cole could gather himself sufficiently to speak, the voice inside his head sounded again.

It wasn't your fault, son. Do not feel guilt. There was nothing you could have done.

"I could have been with you, Mother. I might have saved you," Cole replied, emotion building in his voice.

How could you have saved us? Spread your arms and wished away the seventy-foot waves? Squelched a torrential rainstorm? No, Cole, no one could have saved our lives.

"I was too preoccupied with my own stupidity. Drinking, chasing women, avoiding responsibility, and all the while ignoring you. Perhaps if I'd just been there…" Cole couldn't get the right words to form.

Now you have a second chance to make it up to us, Cole. This time a masculine voice replaced the lilting tone of his mother. *Go back to Newport and run the company. Take it into the future. It's yours now,* his father said.

"No, it's not, Father. They're taking it away from me. I made a terrible mistake. I don't deserve to run Hollingsworth Enterprises. Only you were capable of that," Cole stammered, his shame clearly evident. "Bill Gaines will be at the helm now."

If you're referring to that little escapade Jacob Featherstone pulled on you, forget it. We all make mistakes. You have already learned a valuable lesson from it, if I'm not mistaken. Fifty million may seem like a lot of money to you right now, but it is a pittance in the larger scheme of things, as long as you take the lesson learned to heart. Do not hang your head, son. Had that deal been legitimate, it would have made you the all-star of the tech world. Now, go out and find something else. Your star is just beginning to shine.

Cole couldn't believe what he was hearing. This wasn't the father he knew. In life his dad would have chastised Cole to no end for his blunder. But now…now he was forgiving him. Even encouraging him to continue on?

"I can't believe you're saying this. I just can't walk back into the boardroom and demand to be in charge."

You can and you will. You now own fifty-one percent of the stock, both preferred and common, and no matter how much stock Gaines buys, he can't obtain control. It won't happen. You're my son and the sole heir, don't ever forget that. Challenge Gaines. The others will do what you say if you're forceful enough.

The image of his father seemed to grow darker, losing some of its previous luster. This was the father he knew—challenging him, pushing him to do more. The momentary forgiveness was vanishing. It was back to business as usual. All the years of confrontation came rushing back.

"I'll do my best," Cole stuttered, although he was still unsure how he could. Hesitating, he decided it was best just to be honest. He might never have this chance again. "I'm not sure I want that life any longer. Things have changed, Dad. I've changed. I—"

Nonsense, you're still my son. You possess more potential than you know. I see your future and it's as bright as the rising sun. Step up to the plate and be a man. I promise you, you will not be disappointed.

Cole wanted to scream, but he refrained from chastising his father. "I'll try..." Cole acquiesced.

Of course you will, son. But remember always that love is the higher power. Don't turn your back on it. You can have both.

His mother's voice was soothing, relieving some of his stress, yet Cole still did not fully understand what was transpiring. What did it all mean? He turned to Lindsay, his eyes filled with questions.

"Your parents are moving on, as do all who pass over. They remain in limbo until their deepest need is answered. For them, it was to reconnect with you. To take away your guilt. To ensure that you could move on with your life unfettered. Release them, Cole." Lindsay's voice reverberated inside his head, but this time it was not transmitted through the communication system in their helmets. She was speaking telepathically. Her thoughts were his thoughts.

"But you told me we could somehow save them. That's why I agreed to come here, to do this. Now it may have cost me the company. And all for what?"

"Didn't you hear what your father was saying? You haven't lost the company. It is yours to do with it what you want. Your options are unlimited. Your star really is just beginning to shine. There is so much for you to do, to accomplish. You're not your father, Cole. You don't have to follow the old model. Make a difference. This is your life now. Don't ever forget that." Lindsay hesitated, and at the same time, a look of concern crossed her face. She continued.

"You have saved them, Cole. Look, they're beginning to fade, to cross over. Tell them you love them before it's too late. That's all they need to hear..." Lindsay's voice trailed off.

Cole watched in horror as the images of his parents began to unwind, growing fragile right before his eyes. He was caught in a moment of frantic indecision, with so much more he wanted to know, to say, to understand. He wasn't ready to let them go. Too many things remained unresolved.

"No, don't leave me!" Cole screamed, but their images continued growing fainter.

Lindsay's words repeated in his head. "Tell them you love them…"

"Mother—Father, I need to know…" Cole hesitated. There was no time left; they were almost gone. "I love you both with all my heart, remember that always. I *am* your son," he shouted out.

Just before the faces of his parents vanished, they sparkled brightly for an instant, glowing with a brilliant, incandescent light, as if they understood.

It was done.

37

Cole floated silently in the void, surrounded by threads of glistening, silk-like rain, pulsating with something resembling electricity, as though they powered the planet with its life force. Lindsay had said this dimension was the foundation for all things. How was it even possible that he was here? What powers did Lindsay possess that could have transported him to this place? It had to be a dream. It couldn't be real. Turning to face her, Cole suddenly felt an intense heat surge through his body. His wetsuit had thinned considerably during the encounter with his parents' apparitions, eaten away by the acidity of the liquid that supported their weight. Lindsay's suit appeared to be in the same condition, becoming threadbare to the point of exposure. It was past time to return to the *Harbinger* and hope they could make it back through the gateway safely.

Cole started to move toward the submersible when a shock wave rippled through the void, thrusting him in circles, end over end. From the corner of his eye, he glimpsed the *Harbinger* rocking wildly about like a defenseless boat moored to a dock amid a torrential storm. Wave after wave of shocks followed closely together. Cole had no idea which way was up or down. The *Harbinger* continued to spiral out of control, growing smaller in the darkness as it was swept away. Before he knew it, Lindsay was by his side grasping his arm.

"It's happening again, Cole!" Lindsay screamed. "The tectonic plates are shifting, the gateway is closing."

"How could that be possible? Didn't this just happen the other day?" Cole said.

"It's totally unpredictable. The portal must move if for no other reason than its own protection. It's been breached. It senses we're here, and it's fighting to reject an infection, like an antibiotic." The urgency in Lindsay's voice was unmistakable. "There is little time, Cole. You must act now if you want to survive!"

Act now? What in the hell was he supposed to do? They had lost contact with the *Harbinger*. God only knew where it had gone. What was Lindsay talking about?

"What am I supposed to do?" Cole exclaimed, as terror welled inside. A wave of nauseating panic spread through him. It would only be a matter of minutes before their wetsuits would be useless. They would be burned alive or crushed by the ocean's unrelenting pressure if they couldn't find the *Harbinger* in the next few minutes.

"It's too late for the *Harbinger*. Set fire to the rain," Lindsay shouted. "Do it now!" She pointed a hand upward. Cole looked up only to see the portal above them collapsing in on itself, rapidly growing smaller in circumference.

"I don't understand!" Cole screamed back. "How do I set fire to the rain… What does that even mean?" Before Cole could complete his thought, Lindsay's wetsuit shredded, tearing away from her body, leaving only the neoprene undergarment exposed. "No!" Cole screamed again. He couldn't stand there and watch her incinerate before his very eyes. He moved protectively forward to shield her. She inched backward as though prepared to face her fate.

"Use your flares. Set fire to the rain, Cole. Cast them out into the void. Now!"

Cole was momentarily stunned, sure he had misunderstood her instructions.

"Do it before there is no escape. It's the only way you can save yourself," Lindsay implored. Cole looked up again as the circular gateway continued its collapse, constricting at an alarming rate.

"I'm not leaving without you. We'll find another way. The *Harbinger*..."

Time had run out for listening. Lindsay cut him off midsentence. "Do it now, Cole, there's no more time."

"I love you, Lindsay. I can't leave you! My life means nothing without you."

"You must live, Cole. There is so much left for you to do."

"No, Lindsay, don't make me do this..."

With catlike reflexes, Lindsay grabbed one of the supercharged underwater flares from Cole's wetsuit, yanking it out. She broke the flare in half and thrust it back into his hands. Sparks emitted from its ends.

"I love you, too. I'll find you again, I promise. Now, do it!"

Cole forced himself to act this time, although he had no idea where his newfound courage came from. With the portal's orifice only a few yards wide now, he struck the flares against one another and cast them into the void. Deep below, the glistening strands of mesh ignited in a crimson explosion, spreading an inferno upward in every direction. In the distance, Lindsay hovered as the miraculous transformation took place. Just as he had seen her on the beach at the Bay Marina resort, she began to glow and spin at the same time, emitting sparks of golden light. Spinning faster, 'round and round' until all that remained was a blur—a whirlwind of shimmering color in the darkness. Cole felt the updraft of the raging fire rapidly approaching.

Suddenly the cyclone of color that had once been Lindsay burst outward, like a steel cocoon had just ruptured under intense pressure. What remained took Cole's breath away. Lindsay, or the creature she had become, spread her wings—wings of molten silver, her body encased in scales that sparkled like precious diamonds. Her apparition shot forward, wrapping its protective wings around Cole and sheltering him from the firestorm raging around him.

From somewhere deep within the core of the earth, a mammoth shelf uprooted from the magma below. It caught Cole in its path, bursting through the portal with unimaginable power, ripping the void apart. It shot up into the ocean above, rising from the bottom of the trench, while Lindsay's protective cocoon prevented the water's crushing pressure from obliterating Cole's body. With blinding speed, they rose together, displacing millions of gallons of seawater. Somewhere during the ascent, Cole fell into unconsciousness, overcome by the sheer force of movement and the superheated water forming around him. Like a mythical demon from hell, the mountainous structure burst angrily out of the ocean's surface, hissing steam and liquid fire as it rose high into the sky above. The deafening sound sent shock waves everywhere; waves rose and fell with ponderous energy sending tsunamis in all directions. Hundred-foot waves raced across the water's surface as though propelled by an invisible force. And still the mountain climbed, casting ominous shadows over the glistening water. The world had grown dark—the midday sun vanishing in a blanket of smoke and ash.

More than fifty miles away, the seismograph on the *Truett* went berserk, as the instrument's finely tuned measuring system drew lines off the chart. The automated alarm system on the frigate blared, alerting the crew to impending danger. Cassie sprang from her bed, racing to the top deck. Ryan and Art followed close behind. They were met topside by a hot wind. The ocean had turned dark, the sky a menacing mix of purple and black, the air smelling of Sulphur. And then they saw it—a wave approaching at an alarming speed, towering above the horizon and heading directly toward them. There was no escaping it. They barely had time to react. Cassie raced onto the bridge screaming out orders to the crewmembers standing in disbelief and gawking out the windows.

"Lock the hatches and turn us directly into its path—and full speed ahead. It's our only chance!" Cassie shouted above the din of the howling wind. The crew complied without further questions and turned the frigate eastward with full throttle. The giant wave raced toward them growing in size as it approached. The final words heard on deck sounded from a distance, "*Get below and may God save us!*"

Then all hell broke loose as the *Truett* crashed headlong into the raging tidal wave and vanished.

38

Cole lay unconscious in a shallow pool of water at the base of the newly formed island, the clear polymer facing of his diving helmet ripped out. The helmet was still loosely attached to what was left of his wetsuit. The twin oxygen tanks had been ripped from the metal strapping on his back. Steam issued from cracks and fissures all around him, while thick lines of crimson-colored lava flowed down the mountain's sides from a peak rising miles above. Smoke and ash billowed out from the jagged upper rim of the volcano, disappearing into the stratosphere, a menacing plume of toxic debris reaching to the heavens. Long, twisted strands of seaweed and a plethora of scorched sea life lay strewn on the hot rock that formed the foundation of the island. Nothing seemed alive, the barren surface standing solitary against a broken sky. The water surrounding the landfill had calmed somewhat, although a putrid steam still rose from beneath its surface, smelling strongly of sulfur and methane. Even the tropical birds kept their distance. The foreboding landscape cast an ominous shadow across the normally sparkling tropical waters. The ocean had turned dingy; sunlight was shrouded in a cloak of toxic ash. The air remained searing hot as though it were on fire, too, adding to the intense humidity.

The afternoon network TV programs around the globe continued to broadcast graphic scenes of destruction from the outer islands of the Bahamas, remote areas of the Puerto Rican coastline, and parts of Southern Florida and Louisiana. It was too early to know what the extent of the damage was, and yet no deaths had been reported. Africa and Western Europe braced for the tsunami racing toward their shores. The scientific community was abuzz over the phenomenon. The earth's atmosphere was too full of debris and smoke for accurate satellite photos yet, but from what little descriptions were coming in from random sources, the discovery was going to be a monumental one. Scientific institutes were frantically making plans to visit the area as soon as possible. Shock waves continued to register on seismic monitors over half of the planet's surface. Most of the immediate emergency efforts were focused on assisting in what would ultimately be a catastrophic loss of life, caused by the sudden appearance of the tidal waves.

Any attempt at Gerace to contact the *Truett* had proved fruitless. There was little hope it could have survived the holocaust at sea. It, along with the costly *Harbinger*, were most likely lying at the bottom of the Atlantic, another tragedy caused by the power of the shifting tectonic plates. Search-and-rescue teams were hastily being assembled, but by the looks on everyone's faces, it was purely academic. No one expected to find survivors. And then there was the matter of Cole Hollingsworth, the billionaire benefactor to the Institute's ongoing research. Could it be possible that the entire Hollingsworth family had been lost in the same location in less than eight months?

The press would have a field day when the world was informed of the catastrophe. They would want to know why Cole, an unauthorized and untrained diver, had been using the Institute's deep-sea submersible for his own private agenda, accompanied by their top oceanographer, who also happened to be the daughter of the man who had just swindled fifty million dollars from Hollingsworth Enterprises. Nothing good could come from this. All that Vincenzo Voteli, director of the Gerace Research Centre, could hope for was some amount of damage control. He had personally approved the expedition, although it had been left off of the official record, a serious violation by a nonprofit organization that was held to a high level of scrutiny and full disclosure of its activities. It would be best if he was the one to announce it. At least it would appear that the Institute wasn't attempting to hide anything, just an administrative blunder. Someone would be fired for it, but it wouldn't be him. He would make it up to whomever that person was on the side. The most immediate need was to keep the Institute's reputation intact. He gathered a small group of trusted advisers and set about preparing the press release. Timing was everything. The research center was about to become a global topic, and Vincenzo had no desire to be the scapegoat for the hundred-million-dollar loss of the naval frigate and one of the world's most advanced bathyscaphes. They had barely survived the loss of *Harbinger I* only six months ago.

Badly shaken but still alive, the seven-person crew of the *Truett* emerged on the top deck to survey the damage. All communications were down, and they hadn't seen a single sailing vessel since the tidal wave had nearly cost them the frigate. Somehow, miraculously, the ship had made it through, as though protected by a higher power, as if God himself had reached down and pulled them out of the ocean's depths, returning the ship to the surface in one piece. Most everything attached to the top deck had been damaged or torn off by the tempest that ravaged the area. Even the front gun turret was missing, its heavy metal supports ripped from their foundation. The stairs and railing to the helipad were twisted and mostly gone. The helipad itself had vanished. *At least no more attorneys will be allowed onboard,* Ryan thought, although this did little to comfort him. The damage was significant, and yet they were still afloat, drifting without power in the middle of the South Atlantic, no land in sight. As they continued scanning their surroundings, attempting to obtain their bearings, Ryan spotted a plume of what looked like smoke rising like a shaft on the edge of the distant horizon, disappearing into the darkened sky above.

"Cassie, look at that. What do you make of it?"

Cassie squinted at the distant object, unable to identify its source. She asked a crewmember to return belowdecks and find a set of binoculars. Cassie turned to the ship's engineer.

"Any idea how long until we regain power?"

"We were just headed below to check out the condition of the engines. Everything is waterlogged and a few cabins are completely flooded. We'll get you an assessment as soon as we can."

"Thank you." Cassie turned to face Ryan, and their eyes met in a wordless gaze. Each one knew exactly what the other was thinking. Lindsay…Cole. They could not possibly have survived this disaster. There must have been a massive shift in the tectonic plates to cause such a violent tsunami. The *Harbinger* was no match for such power. Of course, there would be a search, especially with someone as famous as Cole Hollingsworth involved. The Institute would come under considerable scrutiny for this private excursion. No doubt Cassie and Ryan would be harshly dealt with, but that was not the immediate problem. The challenge was to restore power to the *Truett* and get in touch with Gerace and Dr. Voteli—and to discover what had actually happened to cause the tidal wave.

The crewmember returned with the binoculars, handing them over to Cassie. Military-grade, the binoculars had an extended range. When Cassie focused in on the distant object they had spotted, her breath caught in her throat. Totally unprepared for what loomed on the eastern horizon, she gasped. She passed the binoculars to Ryan in stunned silence. The expression on Cassie's face gave Ryan cause for concern. He focused the lenses and did a double take. It was almost too much to fathom. Before them stood a massive volcano spewing ash high into the sky, where there had only been ocean before. This was not some minor amount of debris that sometimes formed on the water's surface, thrust upward from movement in the shallower parts of the ocean floor. This was a major new landmass. How long had it been since something of this magnitude had been created? A hundred thousand years? A million years? They were staring at something so inconceivable it literally took their breath away. It wouldn't be long until the world's scientists, media, and other interested parties would descend on this place in a global feeding frenzy. And they would be smack-dab at the center of the controversy if they didn't do something fast. They weren't even sure how much time had elapsed since the wave had hit them. It seemed that time itself had stopped, holding them momentarily in its grip. It might have been minutes or hours—it might have been days.

"We've got to get this ship moving or there'll be hell to pay!" Cassie hollered to anyone close enough to hear her voice. Thankfully, she heard the rumblings of the ship's engines sound. They had done it. The *Truett* began to move slowly through the water. Cassie gave the remaining crew their directions and they headed toward the new landmass. They had to see it firsthand, before they made good on their escape. As they approached, the air around them became increasingly hot and arid, filled with debris. Their throats burned, but they had no choice but to face the elements. Soon the molten lava dripping down the volcano's sides became visible. Thick steam issued from large fissures. Daylight turned to twilight as the ash blocked out the rays of early afternoon sunlight. Soot covered everything. The stench of methane and sulfur filled the air, making the atmosphere almost non-breathable.

"Ryan, can you please go below and retrieve whatever oxygen masks and helmets we have left?"

Ryan disappeared in a flash. Just then a deafening explosion resonated, as a mammoth ball of fire shot straight up into the sky, a fiery, gaseous orb of magma escaping from the earth's core. The island shook with the sheer power of the explosion. A new wave of ash spewed out, spiraling for miles in every direction. It looked like the end of the world, or maybe more like one of those sci-fi movies predicting the end of the world—as if the earth's crust had just cracked open.

The heat was unbearable. Still the frigate moved forward. They had to know what had happened to their friends. Not that they expected anything but bad news, but at least they could report some kind of information to the Institute. A sudden jolt rocked the *Truett*. The ship's hull had collided with something hard. Was it part of the new island hidden beneath the murky waters—or something else? Cassie ordered the crew to shut down the forward motion and reverse the engines. The frigate came to a stop, engulfed in steam rising from the water below, shrouding their view.

"I don't think we can continue, not without risking serious damage to the hull," Cassie said.

"Let's take the powerboat from here. I'll get it ready and meet you on the docking platform below," Ryan said. He pushed the collection of oxygen masks and helmets to the crewmembers, piled on top of a metal cart, and grabbed two for himself and Cassie. He disappeared belowdecks again, while Cassie conveyed last-minute instructions to her crewmates.

Cassie then joined Ryan on the platform at the *Truett*'s aft. The sleek ocean powerboat was equipped with twin 8.2-liter MerCrusier V-8s, built to navigate choppy waters and strong currents. Cassie jumped in as Ryan fired up the engines. The pair donned gasmasks and departed the frigate cautiously. It was nearly impossible to see more than a few feet under the surface, as the pollution from the volcanic eruptions clouded the normally pristine waters of the Caribbean. Direct contact with a jutting rock below could rip the bottom of the hull out and sink the craft in seconds. Ryan guided the boat with precision, using the sonar equipment mounted on the instrument panel as a guide, ever watchful that at any time another eruption might take place, enveloping the divers in a lethal layer of burning ash.

As they approached the island, the volcano seemed to grow in size, towering miles above, dwarfing everything in sight. The mountain looked extraordinarily out of place, like it belonged in *Jurassic Park* or a deserted special effects lot in a Hollywood blockbuster movie. But in this case, it was real, unless this was all just a communal cosmic dream.

Ryan shut down the dual throttles and brought the craft to a halt, fifty yards or so out from the shoreline jutting above the water's surface. Where the barren rock touched the ocean, a layer of steam spiraled upward, partially blanketing what lay beyond. The diver jumped over the side and into the water, hitting solid ground only a few feet below, thankful for the thick neoprene wetsuit he was wearing. Even with the added protection, Ryan immediately felt the heat penetrate the buoyant material, stinging his entire body.

"Throw me some rope, Cassie, I'll tow us in." Cassie obliged and Ryan began pulling the boat the remaining distance to shore, disappearing momentarily behind the wall of steam. Cassie passed through the haze as Ryan was securing the rope to a nearby boulder. What met her gaze sent a shudder up her spine. A barren shoreline of obsidian-colored rock, hissing steam like it was its life breath, spread in every direction. Ribbons of brilliant fire flowed down the mountain like colossal volcanic tears, born of the earth's pain. Dead fish and seaweed lay everywhere, filling tide pools with an acrid odor. The base of the island spread for miles in all directions, and at its center the malevolent volcano towered like a prehistoric monument to a primordial world, as if the very formation of the planet were taking place before their eyes. It didn't seem possible. Two people witnessing an historic natural wonder for the first time. Why them? Why now? Life suddenly seemed surreal and yet so very precious for its fragility. The pair continued to stand in silence, thunderstruck.

Words could not describe what they were witnessing.

So mesmerized by the spectacle, they failed to hear the voice calling to them from a distance, dreamlike. Just a voice in their heads—echoes of a lost friend. Although the voice sounded familiar, neither of them responded until it sounded again. Startled, the pair turned.

"It's about damn time you found me. I was giving up hope until I heard the boat's engines off the leeward side of this accursed island."

Ryan's mouth gaped. Stunned, Cassie dropped to her knees as if she had just seen an apparition appear out of thin air. Striding in their direction, his wetsuit tattered and scorched, Cole Hollingsworth approached, as if his limo drivers had just shown up to take him home. The cracked prototype diving helmet dangled in one hand, while something resembling a driftwood cane supported his other arm as he limped his way forward.

"Nice of you two to show up," Cole said, the sarcasm in his voice still evident. Neither of the divers could muster a reply; all they could do was gawk in Cole's direction as though his sudden appearance was more astonishing than the newly formed island.

"Well, isn't anyone going to say something?" Cole said, a half-cocked smile pasted on his face.

Cassie rose from her prone position and wrapped her arms around Cole, bursting into tears. Ryan shook his head in disbelief. Only someone like Cole could have made an appearance like this, as nonchalant as if some society magazine photographer had just snapped his picture outside a trendy nightclub.

Cole sighed heavily, anticipating the next question—a question the divers were too afraid to ask. They already knew the answer, but the words would not come. Even the slightest delay in knowing the truth might prolong her life, if only for a few more minutes.

"She didn't make it. Lindsay's gone," Cole said, sparing them the agony of uttering the words themselves. He gripped Cassie more tightly, attempting to quell her pain, as the Australian beauty shook with unbridled emotion. The expression on Ryan's face mirrored what they were each feeling. They had just lost someone incredible. And yet, in Cole's mind, Lindsay had somehow been reborn in the imposing mountain towering above them. Her final actions had ignited it all. Together they had *set fire to the rain*, ripping an indomitable life force from the core of the earth and thrusting it violently to the ocean's surface, saving Cole's life. Lindsay had summoned a supernatural power beyond description, and in the process, she'd rearranged the natural world around them. Beyond that, Cole's parents were at peace, yet so many questions remained. What greater sacrifice could a person make?

A sudden rumbling underground brought everyone back to reality. The island shook violently, tremors spreading like waves around them.

"This island is highly unstable," Cassie said, quickly adding, "Let's get the hell out of here!"

It didn't take further convincing on Ryan's part, although Cole seemed reluctant to leave, as though there was something he wanted to hold on to, that leaving this place would take from him. He acquiesced and followed the divers to the powerboat. Within minutes they were waterborne and racing away from the island—and not a minute too soon. More fire and brimstone burst into the sky. A massive fissure formed only yards from where they had just been standing. A rush of putrid steam roared upward from the gaping hole left behind.

Cole braced himself at the rear of the craft by holding on to metal railings lining the stern, watching. Smoke and ash continued to discharge from the belly of the mountain, further darkening the sky above. Cole stared at the spectacle, unable to avert his gaze. Somewhere deep inside the core of this natural wonder, the spirit of Lindsay Featherstone existed. She had told him he had much goodness inside, that his time to leave this earth had not yet come. There was still too much for him to accomplish in life. And finally, she had told him she would find him again—that they were only an ocean apart. Tears welled in Cole's eyes as he relived everything this woman had done for him. His heart broke for the love he would never share with her. And now…now he was left alone to discover the answers to the purpose of his life. What was it that Lindsay wanted from him? Could she still be his spirit guide? These questions and more occupied his thoughts as they skimmed atop the waves on their way back to the *Truett*.

Cassie looked back, not at the volcano, but rather at Cole, and she was overcome with emotion again. One of the wealthiest, most eligible bachelors in the world stood slump-shouldered, clinging to the railing and gazing at the barren island as though he had left his very soul there.

Perhaps he had.

39

The two divers helped Cole onboard and up the steep incline of steps to the medical cabin on the second deck. His burns, bruises, and assortment of other injuries needed attending to. A change of clothes, a soak in a cool mineral bath, and plenty of electrolytes would help facilitate his recovery. But what treatment would mend his heart?

Modesty was a thing of the past, with everything they'd been through. Cassie sat beside the metal bathtub and washed Cole's back. His body looked more like it was covered with leather rather than supple skin, as though he had fallen asleep in a tanning booth. His tousled hair was singed at the ends. Blisters were beginning to form on his neck and arms. Yet he sat in the water silent and without complaint, his eyes closed like he was gradually drifting into another world. It was time to tell him the truth about Lindsay. A truth that only Cassie knew. Even Ryan, her lover, wasn't fully aware of the secret the two women shared. Not that Cassie didn't want to tell him, but Lindsay had made her promise—a promise she could only share with Cole when the time was right. Cassie supposed the right time had come. Ryan had been told that Lindsay nearly drowned after losing the *Harbinger I* while searching for Cole's missing parents. That Lindsay had been in a coma for months, had experienced irreparable brain damage and was not expected to live.

"Cole?" She paused. "I—I have something to tell you. It's about Lindsay." Cassie hesitated again, steeling herself for what she was about to confide to this relative stranger, who felt more and more like the brother she'd never had. For all of his failings, it was nearly impossible to avoid falling under his spell. His cavalier, cocky behavior could not quite conceal the passionate heart inside. Nor could the expensive clothes and over-the-top sports cars he wore like masks, camouflaging the man behind the reputation.

At the sound of Lindsay's name, Cole's body jerked; like he had just awoken from a deep sleep. He cocked his head toward the diver, yet remained silent.

"Lindsay loved you, Cole. She's loved you all of her life, from the moment she first met you as a young girl. She saw something in you that changed her forever. She left after high school because she couldn't face you any longer, couldn't hide the longing whenever she was near you. Her only thought was to reinvent herself and somehow become an equal before she came back into your life.

"When your parents were reported missing and the search for them was unsuccessful, she convinced Dr. Voteli, the director of Gerace Research Centre, to let her take the *Harbinger I* out to search for their yacht. If she couldn't save them, she could at least give you the truth, so that you could mourn them and then move on…" Cassie's voice cracked midsentence. It was the next part that would be the toughest to explain.

"The truth…the truth is that she drowned while attempting to find them, but what she discovered in the process at the bottom of the Puerto Rican Trench was beyond belief. This single discovery validated her life's work on the theory of abiogenesis. Not only did she find the birthplace of life on this planet, she discovered the afterlife, too. Of course, I didn't believe her at first. It was only after she took me there and I saw it, just like you did, that I believed. It took her four dives to discover the portal and two more going inside to find your parents. I accompanied her on one of those dives when she passed through the gateway. And what I saw changed my life forever. I still can't adequately describe it. On her seventh solo dive, the gateway collapsed and she became stuck between dimensions. Eventually, the methane and other toxic substances ate away at the submersible and Lindsay perished." Cassie turned away, tears streaming down her cheeks.

Cole sat halfway submerged in the water, speechless. Even with all he had experienced with Lindsay, he had not suspected this. But somehow it made sense now. Had she actually come back from the grave for him? How could that even be possible?

"Is that why Gerace needed a new submersible? We donated some of the money to fund that a couple of months ago, after we heard that something had happened. I never knew…" He looked over at Cassie, who was wiping the tears from her face. Cassie nodded, but remained silent, unable to find the words to express her sorrow.

"I'm so terribly sorry, Cole, but she swore me to secrecy. She appeared to me in a dream first, I think to somehow prepare me for her return. When I saw her again, I was sport-diving off the coast of San Salvador, and she appeared like an angel or something. I can't adequately describe it. She was glowing and emitting light. At first, I thought my oxygen had run out and I was beginning to hallucinate, but then we rose to the surface together and spent the remainder of the day on a secluded beach talking."

Cole recalled similar images he had witnessed at the Bay Marina Resort and on the *Truett*. Cassie continued.

"Lindsay believed that if she told you the truth, you'd never agree to come here. Above all else, she wanted you to find peace with your parents' passing. Peace, so you could move on and become the man she knew you could be. She made the ultimate sacrifice for you, and even after her death, she found a way to return. To return for you."

The enormity of Cassie's final statement left Cole in a daze. All these years and he'd never known how Lindsay felt about him. And just when he was falling in love for the first time—with her—it was too late. Lindsay had already passed on to the other side. How could he not have known? All the signs had been there. She had managed to convince him it was all in his dreams, most of them fueled by excessive consumption of alcohol. All Cole could do now was shake his head in awe as the pain gripped him, paralyzing his body.

"Cassie, I need to be alone for a while."

"Of course. I'll be in the next cabin if you need anything… anything at all. Just call for me."

Cassie left the room feeling as broken as she knew Cole was feeling. She just hoped the pain would not be so devastating that he would do something to harm himself. She lay down on her bunk alone, as mentally and physically exhausted as she'd ever been, wondering whether her life as a diver was over. The ocean no longer held the allure for her it always had. Perhaps she would return to Australia to be among family and old friends, to find time to heal herself. She closed her eyes and gradually drifted into a deep sleep, surrounded by black ocean and trenches, desperately searching for Lindsay.

Twilight was approaching by the time Cassie woke. She hurried to check on Cole. He was gone, although water remained in his bathtub. She rushed to the top deck, there spotting Cole and Art talking to Ryan at the ship's stern. They were dressed in street clothes. A duffel bag lay at Art's feet. It was obvious they were preparing to leave. Cassie looked past the men and glimpsed a shoreline in the distance. As she approached, she noticed lights reflecting off the surface of the water below. A seaplane had landed nearby, its large pontoons keeping it afloat. It had clearly been sent for Cole. The craft did not belong to the Institute; she would have recognized it. Someone else had arrived to shuttle Cole and his attorney to safety, before the media could get ahold of them.

Reality suddenly came crashing down on Cassie like a collapsing brick wall. It was all about to explode, to unravel, as the media and scientific community would soon be descending on the scene and into their personal lives. The concept of privacy was fading as quickly as the setting sun to the west. Their lives, their secrets, were all about to be exposed to the world. Even the Australian Outback could not shield her from the avalanche of reporters and photographers. They would track her down like a rabid dog, until they extracted the truth—a truth she could not possibly explain to them. She would not betray Lindsay, or Cole, even if it meant losing her reputation.

"Weren't you even going to say good-bye?" Cassie said as she sashayed up to Cole's side, pretending to smile like everything was okay.

"Of course, I was going to say good-bye. I was just finishing up with Ryan, and then I was coming down to see you. I wanted you to get as much sleep as possible. I know what you are about to face. If there is anything Art and I can do for the two of you, to help you through this mess, please call me. I know a damn good lawyer," Cole replied, slapping Art on the shoulder. Art handed both Cassie and Ryan his business card.

"Really, anything. I mean that. You saved Cole's life. We are forever in your debt," Art said. An awkward silence followed. The time had finally come to part ways. Cassie wondered whether she would ever see Cole again. They lived in worlds so different from one another it seemed unlikely their paths would ever cross. She slid her hand through Ryan's folded arms and tried her upmost not to break down on the spot. Cole reached over, extending his arms around the pair, and embraced them for a long moment.

"I'll never forget you guys, and I'll never forget what you did for me. And for Lindsay." Cole hesitated. "Cassie, can I have a moment?" Cassie nodded and the pair walked away to find some privacy.

"What is it you want to say, Cole?" Cassie asked.

"It's about Lindsay. What am I supposed to say when I get back to Newport? And what about you and Ryan? We can't just ignore her being here."

"No, of course not. You're right. Only a few people actually know, but Andres Almquist, that Swedish scientist you met when you first arrived at Redemption Bay, knows, and he's got a big mouth. Anything for publicity. He'll soon find out what happened, or at least some of it, and he won't hesitate to horn in on the media frenzy. If I know him, he'll probably be one of the first to step on the island and take some amount of credit for its discovery."

"Then I say, let him have it. The publicity will probably take his mind off of the details. Let him revel in the discovery. What does it matter, really?" Cole paused reflectively. "I hate to say this, but maybe this would be the appropriate time to announce her—I mean, Lindsay's *death*." Cole could barely get the words out. "The fact that the *Harbinger* has been lost will come out soon, won't it?" Cole added. Cassie nodded. "There's bound to be questions about that. It's not every day a world-class submersible goes missing."

"We could say that Lindsay left prematurely since you couldn't find the remains of your parents' yacht. Remember when the sea pirates chased Lindsay while she was guarding the *Harbinger*? What if we say it was stolen? That wouldn't be outside the realm of possibility. Maybe then Gerace could even collect some insurance money for its replacement?" Cassie said surreptitiously.

"Spoken like a true business person. Cassie, you've changed," Cole replied, grinning.

"Hey, I learned from the best. Besides, that way Hollingsworth won't get stuck financing another one. Your company has already done way too much in that regard."

"Sea pirates, it is. I like the sound of that. That will give people something to think about—and it'll give the media more to speculate about and take their focus off of Lindsay."

"Agreed. I think even Lindsay would like that one. I'll tell Ryan and the crew. I'll also inform Dr. Voteli. I'm sure he's looking for any explanation he can use to get out of this mess."

"God, I miss her, Cassie," Cole said, suddenly emotional. "She was a true hero. I've never known anyone like her."

"She was all of that, and more," Cassie said wistfully.

Cole and Cassie returned, and they exchanged one last group hug, which had an odd sense of finality to it. With that Cole released the divers and turned. Cole and Art disappeared belowdecks, heading to the docking platform at the aft of the ship, while Cassie and Ryan stood in silence wondering what the future would bring. A few moments later the sound of props revving up filled the air. The seaplane veered west and disappeared directly into what was left of the setting sun, vanishing, until only memories of the incredible expedition remained. Cassie closed her eyes and snuggled up to Ryan as darkness descended. But on this night no stars shone brightly; the sky was awash with smoke and ash belching up from the earth's core.

40

The seaplane landed in the bay to the north of Gerace Research Centre. While the area was well-lit from powerful lights onshore, the flight had been risky in the dark, navigating through unknown layers of ash and debris. However, the risk was worth it if Cole could avoid the deluge of media that would be taking place the following day. A large rubber inflatable waited nearby to transport Cole and Art to the privacy of the Institute. Local hotels were already filling up, not only on San Salvador, but on neighboring islands. Camera equipment and scientific gear were being unloaded from planes and boats. Every seafaring vessel available had been booked and more were coming. The media coverage of a major tsunami was always big news, but now that word had slipped out about a new island and a major volcano forming in the South Atlantic, the coverage would be over the top. The scientific importance alone would keep researchers busy for years. How often did they get a chance to study something of this magnitude? Dr. Voteli was waiting for the pair when they arrived at the front entrance to the administrative offices.

"Mr. Hollingsworth, Mr. Barkley, it is so good to see you. You can't imagine the relief when we heard you were safe." There was a nervous edge to the director's voice. "I trust your flight was an, uh, uneventful one?"

"Yes, Dr. Voteli, everything went fine, thank you. I just hope the damage to the *Truett* can be fixed without too much expense or downtime. We'll be contributing to its repair costs," Cole said, as though it was expected.

"That is most kind of you, sir. The frigate was scheduled for maintenance anyway, so it will be out of commission for a while. We'll be sending it to a remote shipyard for repairs, if you get my drift."

The farther away, the better, Cole thought. Anything to divert attention away from the Institute.

"Gentlemen, if you're hungry, my staff has prepared dinner for you. Two rooms have been made ready for you to sleep tonight. I've arranged for a limo to take you to the airport early in the morning. I'm sure you'll want to head home at your earliest convenience."

"Thank you, Dr. Voteli. We appreciate you making all of the arrangements. We are eager to get home," Cole replied.

"Felipe will take your things to your quarters. If you'll follow me to the dining room?" The threesome strode in silence down a long stone corridor, arriving at an elegantly appointed room with a polished mahogany bar and several tables spread about. Beyond a set of double doors, an ornate dining table and chairs were located. The area looked like something one might see in a luxury European hotel. Dark mahogany walls lined the two rooms, exquisite Oriental rugs decorated the wood-paneled floors. A bartender and two servers stood at attention, dressed in starched white uniforms waiting to take their orders.

"May I offer you a cocktail or a glass of wine?" Dr. Voteli offered. "We also carry a nice selection of locally crafted beers."

"A beer sounds great," Art said.

"Scotch on the rocks," Cole said without hesitation. He hadn't had one in a while, but he suddenly found himself in need of something stronger. Lindsay had almost weaned him off of the booze— almost. But now she was gone. Cole refused to allow the immutable grief of her condition to overwhelm him. Anything he could do to hold it at bay. Yet deep inside he knew it would return to haunt him. Scotch might be the only thing to ease the pain that was coming.

The evening passed uneventfully. The food was well-prepared, the alcohol better. The conversation was polite, yet it seemed sadly wanting. After a brief description of the newly formed island, Dr. Voteli seemed more intent on sidestepping the real issues, as if he didn't want to know the truth. Here sat the head of a prestigious oceanographic institute, and he didn't seem to have the slightest interest in one of the most important geological events in modern history? Something was wrong, but Cole was too distraught to care, and the Scotch was beginning to numb him to his surroundings. Art kept mostly quiet, mimicking Cole's behavior. There would be time later to review their strategy. For now, they just needed to escape San Salvador unnoticed and get through the next few days.

After a polite, but strained good night, Cole and Art headed to their rooms. They needed sleep. The four-thirty wakeup call would come before they knew it, and they didn't want to miss the opportunity to slip away.

True to form, the wakeup call the following morning did little to soothe Cole's headache or his parched throat. He should have been used to the feeling, but something about sobriety in Lindsay's presence had buoyed his spirits. He found he liked waking up in the morning feeling good, even though he had not known what the day would bring. It was amazing how fast the old routine could sneak its way back in, and the familiar aftereffects of alcohol seemed oddly like a long-lost friend.

Art and the Director were waiting for him near the dining area with Styrofoam cups of hot coffee and boxed breakfasts of fresh fruit and banana bread muffins. Obviously, they would not be lingering long. Dr. Voteli accompanied the two men to a covered carport at the opposite end of the Institute, where a nondescript white Lincoln

Town Car was waiting in the dimly lit space. The driver looked to be a woman, demure and small, but her black uniform, sunglasses, and chauffeur's hat covered most of her features. Why she felt the need to wear sunglasses in the dark was anyone's guess. Her auburn-colored hair was tied up and tucked inside her hat. There was something familiar about her, but Cole couldn't pinpoint it, and he immediately dismissed it from his mind. Cole turned to the director and shook his hand, promising to stay in touch.

The limo was soon on the road, heading southwest along the Queen's Highway. The glass partition that separated the driver's seat from the rear passenger seats was closed. At least they had some privacy. A few bottles of assorted liquor lined one side of the limo doors. Cole considered for a moment adding something to his coffee, but then thought better of it. The road was bumpy, and in some places, pocked with holes. His stomach was already queasy; he didn't need to add fuel to the fire. He could have used a bit of that special hangover relief tonic Lindsay had whipped up for him after his battle with the rum laced *Head Colds* back at the Bay Marina Resort. Cole sat back, sighing heavily, as recent images flashed through his head. Lindsay covered in shimmering scales and wrapping her silver- tinged wings around him protectively. The mysterious portal to another dimension. His parents' images underwater. And finally, Cassie's confession of Lindsay's drowning and reanimation. They all seemed like illusions now, slowly slipping from his memory like a dream. Had it actually been real?

Art remained mostly silent, showing an unusual amount of restraint on his part. He sensed something rather heavy was weighing on his friend and that in time, it would come out. But for now, Cole just needed a friend who would not judge or interrogate him. The lawyer in Art wanted desperately to know the truth. He sensed it was something monumental, and yet he couldn't imagine what it could be. And where was Lindsay, anyway? Had she gone her own separate way to avoid the media, too? Was her absence what was bothering Cole? Just what had they been searching for so deep under the ocean? Unable to get the troubling thoughts out of his mind, Art decided to change the subject and tell Cole what he had planned when they arrived back in the States. Maybe it would take his friend's mind off of his troubled thoughts. A little something to cheer him up—or to piss him off—he didn't know which. Anything was worth a try. He wasn't accustomed to seeing his friend so moody.

"Hey, bro, I've got some news for you. Don't get mad until I finish my story, okay?" Art said tentatively. Cole nodded his head, but still seemed a million miles away.

"It concerns the Swanson sisters…" Art trailed off, waiting to see if there would be any reaction. Nothing. Cole remained leaning back against the seat cushion with his eyes closed. "They're both Ralph Lauren models now. After all the commotion when they disembarked your yacht half-naked, the photos went viral. Leave it to them, they parlayed that little fiasco into a contract as the first twin models in the history of Lauren fashion. Lauren has a big budget for nautical-looking outfits, and they fit the image perfectly."

The brief narrative brought a hint of a smile to Cole's face, as if he was imagining the twins posing for a photo shoot scantily clad, the center of attention. Topless twins disembarking from his yacht. Sounded more like *Playboy* than Polo. Cole opened his eyes briefly.

"So, how does this affect me?" He eyed Art quizzically.

"Well…I've got a little surprise for you." Art hesitated, grimacing. "They flew down on your Falcon to meet us…"

"They what?" Cole exclaimed, suddenly coming back to life.

"For promotional purposes only. No funny stuff, I promise. They're anticipating that Green Airport will be jammed with media when we land, and they wanted to exit with you. It's the perfect photo op to start their new careers. The marketing VP at Lauren has promised to treat this with sensitivity and will run anything they intend to do promotionally past you and me first."

"That's just great, Art. I can't fucking believe you would pull a stunt like this!" Cole sounded disgusted. Just as he was about to start in on Art again, he heard muffled laughter coming from the driver's seat. Why would the chauffeur think this was so funny, even if she had overheard their conversation? Did she have the intercom switched on? He flashed back to the incident on the *Harbinger* when Lindsay had pulled the very same stunt.

"Cole—buddy, I needed to get back on their good side. Just this one last favor and we're done. I swear on our friendship." Art smiled sheepishly.

Cole didn't have the heart to further chastise him. After all, Art had been the only person to come after him in an effort to help. That counted for a lot.

"Okay, this one last time and then it's over, understood?"

"Understood," Art replied, half-heartedly.

The Lincoln veered left into the entrance to San Salvador Airport, and the driver guided the limo over to the area where the private jets were held. Cole spotted his Dassault Falcon 7X immediately, easily identifiable with its brilliant white paint and trademark red-and-gray striping. The luxury jet shimmered in the early morning light, reminding him of Lindsay momentarily. Was there no escaping her image? The Falcon was fueled up and ready for takeoff, resting near the airstrip.

The limo slowed and came to a halt twenty yards away. Cole and Art stepped out of the Lincoln, while the chauffeur carried their bags over to the jet. At the sight of their arrival, Sidney and Shelby Swanson emerged from the cockpit and bounded down the steps, all curls and smiles, decked out in something resembling nautical whites, but with a good deal less fabric than normal. Small blue, white, and gold captain's hats clung to their heads at an angle. They saluted in unison, as though they had been practicing for weeks, then marched toward Cole and Art. Cole had to admit, they were a stunning pair. The chauffeur checked them out, too, and Cole swore she shook her head and laughed again, but otherwise remained silent.

Shelby couldn't contain herself, flinging her arms around Cole.

"Thank God you're safe. We were all so worried," Shelby said tearfully. Cole wasn't sure whether she was happy he was still alive or if she was simply relieved that their photo op was still on.

"Thanks, Shelby. It was nice of you two to come all the way down here," Cole replied as sincerely as he could.

Art sighed with relief. Sidney slid her arm through Art's. They were all one big happy family again. The fact that in a matter of days their pictures would likely be appearing on the cover of every fashion magazine in the world didn't dampen their moods, either.

The chauffeur conferred with the pilot briefly, then turned and bowed to both Cole and Art. "Good luck, gentlemen, with whatever lies ahead." A moment later she was gliding away.

Cole watched as she walked toward the limo, mesmerized by her flowing movements. Unconsciously, he started to follow. Just before she entered the Lincoln, she removed her hat and pulled off her sunglasses. Her long, luxurious auburn hair fell to her shoulders, and she turned for an instant to face him, the glint of her slate-gray eyes stopping Cole in his tracks. She smiled. A moment later she was gone. The limo seemed to disappear, too, melting into the tarmac in rising waves of heat. Cole stood, breathless. Had he just seen Lindsay again? Had she ensured that he arrived safely to his jet, unhindered by the media frenzy?

"Time to go, buddy." Art's voice sounded from a distance. Confused, Cole turned and entered the Falcon, even more conflicted than before. A guardian angel? *His* guardian angel? So lost in thought, Cole didn't even realize when they went airborne. He sat alone at the back of the cabin, while Art entertained the Swanson sisters with a feeble attempt to inform them of what had recently taken place. Something about a new island and a massive volcano. Cole's journey to the bottom of the ocean in search of his parents' sunken yacht, none of which made much sense to the twins. They did their best to engage Art, smiling and shaking their long manes of golden hair this way and that. After all, they were about to become incredibly famous.

Cole continued to brood as the Falcon rocketed toward the East Coast of the United States. He'd have about five hours to consider what to say if, indeed, the media descended on Green Airport. Why would they even be there, though? The world's attention should be focused on the new island and the highly active volcano. Would anyone even know he had been on the island? How could they?

The sound of Art's laughing hit Cole like a sucker punch. Of course, Art must have leaked the news after they arrived at Gerace last night. That's why the twins were here in the first place. They had secretly arranged a hastily planned rendezvous, and the sisters had boarded the Falcon only minutes before its departure. They knew who would be waiting when they landed. In any other situation, Cole would have blasted Art for his selfishness, but what did it matter, really? Let them have their fame. Let Art have his pleasure. It was a small price to pay. Cole gazed out of the porthole as the sky cleared, turning a bright blue. The toxic ash had vanished, leaving behind an extraordinary series of events, one he thought he may never fully comprehend.

41

"We will be landing at Green Airport in fifteen minutes. Please prepare for landing," the pilot's voice sounded mechanically through the cabin speakers, jolting Cole from his semiconscious state. He'd been dreaming, trapped in a vacuum of total darkness at the bottom of the ocean, caught between two dimensions. It was quiet, so very quiet. Nothing existed except pure thought. He had been surrounded by the combined wisdom of the ages. Everything seemed clear: there were no mysteries in that space, only joy. Would he ever experience it again? Would he ever feel the euphoria that he and Lindsay had shared? In the transitory moments between sleep and wakefulness, Cole lingered in exquisite peace, until reality ripped it all away. He felt the all-too-familiar reaction to the descent as the Falcon fell from the sky. It was only a matter of moments now until they touched down. But this landing would be unlike any other. He suddenly knew the media would be there, like sharks circling just before the strike. His private life was about to become a living hell.

There was no escaping it, no place to run. His father had told him to face it like a man and take back the company on his own terms. His mother had said that love was the higher power. Lindsay told him that he had a vital purpose in life, but she had failed to explain just what that was. What was he supposed to do?

The jet lurched forward as the screeching tires made first contact with the asphalt. Powerful rear thrusters and brakes engaged simultaneously, as the Falcon's forward motion fought against the mechanical harnesses attempting to slow it. In the end, technology won and the craft came to a halt. Cole surreptitiously hoped that somehow the jet would keep going, breaking the bonds that held it and retaking flight to somewhere far away.

The pilot taxied to a stop near the private hangars and was immediately surrounded by a flood of human bodies. Cameramen moved like they were stationing weapons in position for an imminent attack. Photographers pointed telephoto lenses as if they were rifles. The time had come. Cole braced himself for the onslaught of questions, while thanking the pilots for a safe flight. Art, Shelby, and Sidney took positions directly behind Cole, looking anxious. The door swung open, and Cole descended the stairs, which suddenly felt more like a gangplank.

The initial reaction from the mass of people was applause, startling Cole. He hadn't expected this. It soon died away, though, as the twins made their debut. The scene reminded Art of the conquering hero returning, accompanied by his newly crowned queen, only this time there were two. Art loved every minute of it. He smiled, waving good-naturedly to the crowd. Most of the local reporters already knew who he was, but the host of national media were about to find out, too. This type of coverage couldn't hurt his law practice. He had gone out in search of his missing friend, one of the world's wealthiest men, and returned six days later, successful in his endeavor. Had he been responsible for saving Cole? Art had no intention of lying, but neither was there a need to be overly direct about what had happened, either.

As soon as Cole's foot hit the tarmac, he was surrounded by reporters, shoving their microphones in his face and asking him questions in rapid fire. It all became a blur, as though he was hearing a chorus of foreign languages coming at him from all angles. He had been exposed to press conferences before, but nothing quite like this. Even when his parents were reported missing, it hadn't stirred up this much commotion. Art stepped in between Cole and the surging crowd.

"Give the man some breathing room!" Art exclaimed. "He'll answer your questions one at a time." Art pointed to the woman from NBC Broadcasting, thinking the attractive reporter would make a good pairing for the evening news. And so, the questions began. One after the other, all aimed at discovering Cole's secret agenda. What had really happened in the tropics? What was his relationship with Lindsay Featherstone, the missing oceanographer? Was she somehow related to Jacob Featherstone, the man who had just stolen millions from Hollingsworth Enterprises? And what about this new volcano? Had Cole been in the area when it was formed? Had he witnessed the phenomenon?

With Art's occasional assistance, Cole patiently answered questions for nearly an hour, but in the end, he had not revealed much in the way of relevant information, frustrating the reporters to no end.

Nearby, the Swanson sisters kept the photographers busy. Reporters whose questions had been adroitly averted by Cole and his attorney, made their way to the models in the hopes of finding out a bit of juicier news, anything for a headline or an angle. Had they actually been on the excursion with Cole? What were their roles in all of this? They smiled and posed, and for the most part acted oblivious, stating that they were longtime family friends of Cole and Art, and were concerned for Cole's safety. Their silence on the subject only added to the speculation of what their part had been. Concerned friends? More likely providing comfort during the long, balmy nights. It really didn't matter what the reporters wrote, only that the sisters' pictures appeared in print, with the Polo logo emblazoned on every piece of clothing they wore.

"Ladies and gentlemen, that about wraps it up for now. Thank you for your questions. Cole needs some rest, and there are many people still waiting to see him at Hollingsworth headquarters. We'll have an official statement to you within twenty-four hours," Art said, leading Cole down the tarmac. They entered the company limo and were quickly shuttled away.

A second limo awaited the sisters, who appeared less eager to leave. The pair was still seeing stars from all of the flash photos. Even with cramped facial muscles from forcing smiles for over an hour, it had been worth it. Their new modeling careers were successfully launched, and in a major way. Tomorrow everyone would know who they were. They blew kisses to the remaining members of the crowd and reluctantly entered their black Town Car. The license plate was the last thing the crowd saw as the limo sped away: POLO X 2, as though one simply wasn't enough.

42

Cole entered Hollingsworth headquarters as employees lined the hallways to greet him. Art followed close behind. Applause broke out with each new grouping of employees he met. Everyone wanted to shake his hand or pat him on the back. The enthusiastic welcome startled Cole. He felt like he had just accomplished something miraculous, rather than allowing himself to be scammed out of fifty million dollars. Not a single person seemed to care. The Internet glasses appeared to be a thing of the past. Even Art was receiving congratulations from the employees. Cole was gracious as he made his way toward his offices. When he entered, Grace, his executive assistant, was waiting there anxiously, tears rolling down her cheeks. Two board members stood nearby, with mixed expressions on their faces. Cole couldn't read what they were thinking. Were they glad or disappointed that he had made it back safely? They remained subdued, but they offered their hands in greeting. The board member on the right took a step forward.

"Cole, we are so relieved you're back. When you've settled in, Bill Gaines would appreciate a word with you."

What a change in attitude from his last encounter with the chairman and his sidekick. He seemed to be asking rather than demanding.

"Of course, it shouldn't be long," Cole replied pleasantly. The two men abruptly left, leaving Grace, Cole, and Art to face each other. Cole let loose a well-deserved sigh. It didn't feel real being back here. It seemed like months had passed. It was a lifetime ago, and yet it had only been a little more than a week. Cole glanced at his desk. It was spotless. Not a single stack of papers was visible. The window shades were drawn. The space felt dead, as though no one was expected to return, or at least, no one who would be working in *this* office again.

Cole recalled the lecture Gaines had given him on the *Truett*. His presidency would be stripped. He would be a figurehead only—wealthy, yes, but powerless to guide his company. Something felt different now. Something had changed. But what?

"Grace, what's going on?" Cole said. Grace looked surprised. "The reporters at the airport, the response from our employees. I feel like I just saved the world or something. But for the life of me, I don't have a clue what's happening or why people are being so supportive."

"You mean you really don't know?" Grace replied. Cole shrugged his shoulders. "Maybe you should have a seat." Grace pointed to the leather chair behind Cole's desk. Cole sat. Art stood, remaining oddly silent, as though he was holding on to vital information only he possessed.

"I'm not sure where to begin exactly. It's been all over the news for the past twenty-four hours. They are calling you a hero. The billionaire who threw all caution to the wind in an effort to find out where and how his parents died. That you traveled to the bottom of the ocean, facing incredible danger in the deepest ocean trenches. That nothing would stop you until you discovered the truth. Most people in your position would be out enjoying their inheritance, but you risked it all for answers."

"What about the Internet glasses debacle? What are they saying about that?" Cole remarked.

"That you were taken advantage of by close family friends whom you were trying to help. They don't blame you, Cole…" Grace's voice trailed off. "Well, most people, that is. Mr. Gaines still seems pretty upset. But he'll get over it."

Cole glanced over at Art, who temporarily looked away.

"What do you think about all of this, Art?" Cole said suspiciously.

"I'm just as surprised as you are, bro!" There was something in Art's tone that was unsettling. He knew more than he was letting on. Art turned to Grace. "Continue, please."

"This is the most unbelievable part. When everyone thought you were gone, that your submersible had sunk, you showed up right there on the new island—alive. Not only that, but they found the remains of your parents' yacht beached on the island just a few miles from where you were discovered. The two divers who rescued you confirmed the story. They told reporters that the submersible hadn't sunk but had actually been stolen by sea pirates and that you had barely escaped with your life trying to defend it. Cole, you won't believe this. Everyone is calling it Hollingsworth Island, in honor of you and your parents. You are being credited with discovering the volcano. The first person to set foot on it. The Gerace Research Centre is backing the initiative with the Puerto Rican government, since the island resides just outside their territorial waters."

Cole's mouth dropped open in astonishment. He couldn't believe what he was hearing. Art's eyebrows rose, and he shrugged his shoulders, but otherwise looked nonplussed.

"One of the divers, Cassie Thomas, e-mailed pictures from her phone of you walking on the island toward their rescue boat and the photos have gone viral. You're holding some sort of diver's helmet in one hand and leaning on a driftwood cane, dressed in a shredded wetsuit. You've become the poster child for survival magazines everywhere." Grace hesitated. "You looked pretty hunky, if you ask me." She blushed.

Cole was thunderstruck. Unable to find the words to reply, he sat for a long moment as if he had just been told the world was coming to an end. The Headline Scoop, his parent's wooden yacht, discovered on the island? How could that have been possible? He looked over at Art again. The previously stoic attorney had the slightest hint of a smile on his face. Cole frowned. "You son of a bitch, this was all your doing," Cole said. Art raised his hands as if defending himself.

"Looks like you're out of the woods, ol' buddy," Art replied. "I think it's time for you to deal with Gaines. Give 'em hell!" Art reached over and hugged Cole, gave Grace a kiss on the mouth, then vanished out of the office without another word. Grace blushed again.

Cole entered Bill Gaines's office unsure of whom he would find this time, but determined to resolve their previous issues. Gaines was sitting in one of the two leather chairs in front of his desk, rather than in the imposing one directly behind it. He motioned for Cole to join him, in what appeared to be a conciliatory gesture, like they were now equals. Cole recognized the move. He had seen his father do this before, when he wanted to appear cooperative. Cole sat, but remained silent, waiting for the CEO to make the first move.

"Cole, I hope you know how relieved we all are to have you back home. You had us pretty worried," Gaines began. He had used the word *relieved*, not *happy*, and that spoke volumes. "About our last meeting. I think I came on a little strong. I was still very upset about Featherstone's scam. After all, the buck stops with me as far as our shareholders are concerned. I'm sure you can understand that?" Cole nodded. "Well, let's get back to the future. I'm not condoning your responsibility in the whole thing, but it appears investor confidence has returned based on, um, recent developments. Our stock is back on the rise. The public seems to think you were taken advantage of by a close family friend and are sympathetic. I don't know who it was, but someone effectively leaked the story and the press grabbed hold and ran with it. Leave it to them to see losing fifty million as a *feel-good* story. Goddamn media."

Cole smirked. It was that very same media that had made Bill Gaines a very wealthy man. But Cole supposed he didn't see it that way.

"So, let's cut to the chase, Bill. What exactly are you trying to tell me?" Cole replied, staring Gaines directly in the eye as if he would give no quarter.

"Well, now that you ask, I've been thinking about an alternative position for you, at least for a while. When you're ready, you'll be welcomed back as president of Hollingsworth Enterprises. You still need experience, but I'm confident you'll make the grade."

"You're confident, are you? That's nice to hear. Now, Bill, let me tell you how it's going to be." Cole edged forward in his chair while Gaines did a double take. "In case you've forgotten, I *am* the majority shareholder of this company, with fifty-one percent of the stock, and therefore I have the power to control the outcome of the board and its chairman. I have decided to keep you on as chairman, at least for the time being. Art Barkley will become president pro tem and will report directly to me. As far as your idea for me to take another position, I agree with that decision. My new title will be CEO. I'm going to be spending most of my time reevaluating the company's structure, what we are doing, and how. Where we should invest our resources. There will be changes coming, Bill. And finally, I will let you know when I will become president." Cole paused. "I'm sure you can understand that?"

Flabbergasted, Gaines was about to object, but he bit his lip at the last second. He was no idiot. Cole had figured it all out, and if Gaines wanted to survive at Hollingsworth Enterprises, he would need to capitulate. There would be other opportunities to reinstate his dominance later. The kid would probably screw up anyway. He would bide his time for now and wait for the opportune time to make his move.

"It seems you have grown up after all, Cole. I accept your terms." Gaines extended his hand. Cole shook it without a hint of emotion. He would never trust this man again.

Cole returned to his office as the head of the company. He could almost feel his father smiling. However, his father's mirth would be short-lived if he knew the plan Cole was about to embark on. Time would tell if the direction Cole was seeking would pay off. Redemption was still a long way off.

Grace was waiting in his office impatiently, eager to hear what had transpired between Cole and the Chairman. Cole's grin put her immediately at ease.

"You did it, didn't you?"

"Yeah, I guess I did. Mr. Gaines got a little of his own medicine back. Don't feel too excited yet, though. He's still the chairman of the board, but he's no longer CEO. That privilege has fallen on me. And, oh, by the way, Art will be acting president. He doesn't know that yet, but he'll come around."

Grace broke out laughing. "Good for you, Cole. It's about time Gaines got his comeuppance." His executive assistant's expression turned to one of concern, although it no longer centered on Gaines. "What really happened down there, Cole? No one seems to know. It's all speculation and gossip. It's hard to separate the facts from the hearsay."

Cole took a deep breath. He'd known this question was coming, and he didn't want to lie to Grace of all people. Not only was she a great employee, she had become one of his closest confidants. He gazed compassionately into his assistant's eyes.

"Grace, if I told you I doubt you would believe me. In fact, I really don't know if I believe it myself. You know that old adage, that truth is stranger than fiction? In this case, there may never have been a truer statement. Ask me another time, okay?" Cole paused pensively. "Perhaps I'll write a book about it someday."